P9-CCX-640

PRAISE FOR ROBERT HELLENGA AND
THE SIXTEEN PLEASURES

"Robert Hellenga's first novel goes well beyond the promise of the premise. Although the pleasure of reading this book can hardly compare with any of the sixteen, still, I'd put it high on the list of pleasures one can have alone." —*USA Today*

"A FASCINATING AND FREQUENTLY FUNNY BOOK."
—*The Washington Post*

"WITTY, SOPHISTICATED AND WISE . . . Graceful, assured prose, a wry but emphatic view of the human character and an authoritative command of fascinating background detail are among the distinguishing features of this deeply satisfying first novel." —*Publishers Weekly*

"*THE SIXTEEN PLEASURES* presents an exhilarating account of an American on the verge of a spiritual crisis who hears the call of the Old World. Hellenga gracefully weaves a wealth of technical and historical information into the drama; he also offers a host of wonderfully drawn minor players."
—*Philadelphia Inquirer*

"ABSOLUTELY COMPELLING . . . A wonderfully rich and absorbing story that seems far too assured to be a first novel."
—*Kirkus Reviews*

Please turn the page for more extraordinary praise . . .

"COLORFUL AND FREQUENTLY EROTIC, as mindful of human failings as of human heroism, and always deeply in love with Italy, both modern and ancient, *THE SIXTEEN PLEASURES* is an intriguing and highly original book."

—*Anniston Star*

"A TERRIFIC, SWIFT NOVEL about being in love with Italy, Italian art and Italians. If there's such a thing as an art thriller, this is it." —John Casey, author of *Spartina*

"There's a seventeenth pleasure—it's the enjoyment I received reading Robert Hellenga's absolutely delightful novel . . . a mesmerizing story."
—Warren Cassell, owner, Just Books, Greenwich, Connecticut

"A wonderful story told slyly and with cunning . . . rich with lore." —Richard Selzer, author of *Other Men's Daughters*

"ABSORBING . . . *THE SIXTEEN PLEASURES* is fascinating entertainment." —*Miami Herald*

The Sixteen Pleasures

Robert Hellenga

Delta
Trade Paperbacks

A Delta Book
Published by Dell Publishing
a division of
Bantam Doubleday Dell Publishing Group, Inc.
1540 Broadway
New York, New York 10036

The following chapters have been previously published in different form: Chapter 1, "Where I Want to Be" appeared in *Triquarterly* (Spring/Summer 1991); Chapter 2, "Pockets of Silence" appeared in the *Chicago Tribune* (January 29, 1989).

Excerpts from *The Divine Comedy* by Dante Alighieri, reprinted from The John Ciardi Translation of *The Divine Comedy*, Dante Alighieri, by permission of W.W. Norton & Company, Inc., Copyright © 1954, 1957, 1959, 1960, 1961, 1965, 1967, 1970 by John Ciardi; excerpts from *I Modi: The Sixteen Pleasures: An Erotic Album of the Italian Renaissance,* Tr. and ed. by Lynne Lawner, copyright © 1988 by Northwestern University Press by permission; portions of "The Road Not Taken" from *The Poetry of Robert Frost* edited by Edward Connery Lathem. Copyright 1944 by Robert Frost. Copyright 1916, © 1969 by Henry Holt and Company, Inc. Reprinted by permission of Henry Holt and Company Inc.

Copyright © 1989, 1991, 1994 by Robert R. Hellenga
All rights reserved. No part of this book may be reproduced or transmitted in any form or by any means, electronic or mechanical, including photocopying, recording, or by any information storage and retrieval system, without the written permission of the Publisher, except where permitted by law. For information address Soho Press Inc., New York, New York.

The trademark Delta® is registered in the U.S. Patent and Trademark Office and in other countries.

ISBN: 0-385-31469-8

Reprinted by arrangement with Soho Press Inc.

Manufactured in the United States of America
Published simultaneously in Canada

June 1995

30 29 28 27 26 25 24 23 22

BVG

To Virginia, Rachel, Heather and Caitrine

I would like to thank the National Endowment for the Arts for an Artists Fellowship that made it possible for me to spend six weeks in Florence as I was completing *The Sixteen Pleasures* as well as the Illinois Arts Council and Knox College for their continuing support of my writing career. I would also like to thank my editor, Laura Hruska, for the role she played in shaping the final version of this book.

Contents

The Sixteen
Pleasures

1

Where I Want to Be

I was twenty-nine years old when the Arno flooded its banks on Friday 4 November 1966. According to the Sunday *New York Times* the damage wasn't extensive, but by Monday it was clear that Florence was a disaster. Twenty feet of water in the cloisters of Santa Croce, the Cimabue crucifix ruined beyond hope of restoration, panels ripped from the Baptistry doors, the basement of the Biblioteca Nazionale completely underwater, hundreds of thousands of volumes waterlogged, the Archivio di Stato in total disarray. On Tuesday I decided to go to Italy, to offer my services as a humble book conservator, to help in any way I could, to save whatever could be saved, including myself.

The decision wasn't a popular one at home. Papa was having money troubles of his own and didn't want to pay for a ticket. And my boss at the Newberry Library didn't understand either. He already had *his* ticket, paid for by the library, and needed me to mind the store. There wasn't any point in *both* of us going, was there?

"Then why don't *I* go and *you* can mind the store?"

"Because, because, because . . ."

"Yes?"

Because it just didn't make sense. He couldn't see his way clear to granting me a leave of absence, not even a leave of absence without pay. He even suggested that the library might have to replace me, in which case . . .

But I decided to go anyway. I had enough money in my savings account for a ticket on Icelandic, and I figured I could live on the cheap once I got there. Besides, I wanted to break the mold in which my life was hardening, and I thought this might be a way to do it. Going to Florence was better than waiting around with nothing coming up.

My English teacher at Kenwood High used to say that we're like onions: you can peel off one layer after another and never get to a center, an inner core. You just run out of layers. But I think I'm like a peach or an apricot or a nectarine. There's a pit at the center. I can crack my teeth on it, or I can suck on it like a piece of candy; but it won't crumble, and it won't dissolve. The pit is an image of myself when I was nineteen. I'm in Sardegna, and I'm standing high up on a large rock—a cliff, actually—and I don't have any clothes on, and everyone is looking at me, telling me to come down, not to jump, it's too high.

It's my second time in Italy. I spent a year here with Mama when I was fifteen, and then I came back by myself, after finishing high school at home, to do the last year of the *liceo* with my former classmates. Now we're celebrating the end of our examinations—Silvia (who spent a year with us in Chicago), Claudia, Rossella, Giulio, Fabio, Alessandro. Names like flowers, or bells. And me, Margot Harrington. More friends are coming later. Silvia's parents (my host family) have a summer house just outside Terranova, but we're camping on the beach, five kilometers down the coast. The coast is safe, they say, though there are bandits in the *centro*. Wow!

It's my birthday—August first—and we've had a supper of bluefish and squid that we caught with a net. The squid taste like rubber bands, the heavy kind that I used to chew on in grade school and that boys sometimes used to snap our bottoms with in junior high. Life is sharp and snappy, too, full of promise, like the sting of those rubber bands: I've passed my examinations with distinction; I'm going to Harvard in the fall (well, to Radcliffe); I've got an Italian boyfriend named Fabio Fabbriani; and I've just been skinny-dipping in the stinging cold salt sea.

The others have put their clothes on now—I can see them below me, sitting around the remains of the fire in shorts and halter tops and shirts with the sleeves rolled up two turns, talking, glancing up nervously—but I want to savor the taste/thrill of my own nakedness a little longer, unembarrassed in the dwindling light. It's the scariest thing I've ever done, except coming to Italy in the first place.

Fabio sits with his back toward me while he smokes a cigarette, pretending to be angry because I won't come down, but when I close my eyes and will him to turn, he puts his cigarette out in the sand and turns. Just at that moment I jump, sucking in my breath for a scream but then holding it, in case I need it later, which I do. I hit the Tyrrhenian Sea feet first, generating little waves that will, in theory, soon be lapping the beaches along the entire western coast of Italy—Sicily and North Africa, too. The Tyrrhenian Sea responds by closing over me and it's pitch, not like the pool in Chicago where I learned to swim, but deep and dark and dangerous and deadly.

The air in my lungs—the scream and I saved for just such an occasion—carries me up to the surface, and I strike out for the cove, meeting Fabio before I'm halfway there, wondering if like me he's naked under the water and not knowing for sure till we're walking waist deep and he takes me by the shoulders and kisses me and I can feel something bobbing against my legs like a floating cork. We haven't made love yet, but it won't be long now. *O dio mio.* The waiting is so lovely. He squeezes my buns and I squeeze his, surprised, and then we splash in to the beach and put on our clothes.

What I didn't know at the time was that my mother had become seriously ill. Instead of spending the rest of the summer in Sardegna, I had to go back to Chicago, and then, after that, nothing happened. I mean none of the things I'd expected to happen happened. Instead of making love with Fabio Fabbriani on the verge of the Tyrrhenian Sea, I got laid on a vinyl sofa in the back room of SNCC headquarters on Forty-seventh Street. Instead of going to Harvard, I went to Edgar Lee Masters College, where Mama had taught art history for twenty years. Instead of going to graduate school I spent two years at the Institute for Paper Technology on Green Bay Avenue; instead of becoming a research chemist I apprenticed myself to a book conservator in Hyde Park and then took a position in the conservation department of the Newberry Library. Instead of getting married and having a daughter of my own, I lived at home and looked after Mama, who was dying of lung cancer. A year went by, two years, three years, four. Mama died; Papa lost most of his money. My sister Meg got married and moved away; my sister Molly went to California with her boyfriend and then to Ann Arbor. The sixties were churning around me, and I couldn't seem to get a footing. I tried to plunge in, to get wet, to catch hold, to find a place in one of the boats tossing and turning on the white-water rapids: the sit-ins, the rock concerts, the freedom rides, SNCC, CORE, SDS, the Civil Rights Act, the Great Society. I spent a lot of time holding hands and singing "We shall overcome," I spent a lot of time buying coffee and doughnuts and rolling joints, and I spent some time on my back, too, the *only* position for a woman in the Movement.

I'd had no sleep on the plane; my eyes were blurry so it was hard to read; and besides, the story I was reading was as depressing as the view from the window of the train—flat, gray, poor, dreary, actively ugly rather than passively uninteresting. And I kept thinking about Papa and his money troubles and his lawsuits, and about the embroidered seventeenth-century prayer books on my work table at the Newberry that needed to be disbound, washed, mended, and resewn before Christmas for an exhibit sponsored by the Caxton Club.

So I was under a certain amount of pressure. I was looking for a sign, the way some religious people look for signs, something to let them know they're on the right track. Or on the wrong track, in which case they can turn back. I didn't know what I was looking for, but I was trying to pay attention, to notice everything—the faces of the two American women sitting opposite me in the compartment, scribbling furiously in their notebooks; the Neapolitan accent of the Italian conductor; the depressing French farmhouses, gray boxes of stucco or cinder block, I couldn't make out which.

That's what I was doing—paying attention—when the train pulled into the station at Metz and I saw the Saint-Cyr cadet on the platform, bright as the Archangel Gabriel bringing the good news to the Virgin Mary.

I'd better explain. Papa did all the cooking in our family. He started when Mama went to Italy one summer when I was nine —it was right after the war—to look at the pictures, to see for herself what she'd only seen in the Harvard University Prints series and on old three-by-four-inch tinted slides that she used to project on the dining room wall; and when she came back he kept on doing it. My sisters and I did the dishes and Papa took care of everything else, day in and day out, and whether it was Italian or French or Chinese or Malaysian, it was always wonderful, it was always special. *Penne alla puttanesca,* an *arista* tied with sprigs of rosemary, paper-thin strips of beef marinated in hoisin sauce and Szechwan peppercorns, whole fresh salmon poached in white wine and finished with a mustard sauce, chicken thighs simmered in soy sauce and lime juice, curries so fiery that at their first bite unwary guests would clutch their throats and cry out for water, which didn't help a bit. Those were our favorites, the standards against which we measured other dishes; but our very favorite treat of all was the dessert Papa made on our birthdays, instead of cake, which was supposed to look like the hats worn by cadets at Saint-Cyr, the French military academy. We'd never been to Saint-Cyr, of course, but we would have recognized a cadet anywhere in the world, if he'd been wearing his hat.

That's why I was so startled when I looked out the window of the Luxembourg-Venise Express and saw my cadet standing there on the platform—the young man Papa had teased me about, the Prince Charming who had never materialized. He was holding a suitcase in one hand and shifting his weight back and forth from one foot to the other, as if he had to go to the bathroom, and his parents were talking at him so intensely that I thought for a minute he was going to miss the train. And his hat! I couldn't believe it was a real hat and not a frozen mousse of chocolate and egg whites and whipped cream with squiggly Italian meringues running up and down the sides for braids. That hat stirred something inside me, made me feel I was doing the right thing and that I ought to keep going, that things would work out. Just to make sure I closed my eyes and willed him into the compartment, just as I had once willed Fabio Fabbriani to turn and watch me plunge feet first into the sea. As I was willing him into the compartment I was willing the American women out of it—not making my cadet's appearance contingent on their departure, however, because I was pretty sure they weren't going to budge. I kept my face down in my book and waited, eyes closed lightly, listening to the noises in the corridor.

I was, I suppose, still operating, at least subconsciously, on a fairy-tale model of reality: I was Sleeping Beauty, or Snow White, waiting for some prince whose romantic kisses would awaken my full feelings, liberate my stormy senses, emancipate my drowsy and constrained imagination, take me back to that last Italian summer.

7

The train was already in motion when the door of the compartment finally opened. I kept my eyes closed another two seconds and then looked up at—not my Prince Charming but the Neapolitan conductor, an old man so frail I'd had to help him hoist the American women's mammoth suitcases onto the overhead luggage rack. These suitcases were to luggage what Burberrys are to rainwear—lots of extra pockets and straps and mysterious zippers concealed under flaps.

I asked him about the Saint-Cyr cadet.

"The next compartment," he said. "Not your type. Too young. You need an older man like me."

"You're already married."

He shrugged, putting his whole body into it, arms, hands, shoulders, head cocked, stomach pulled in.

"Better tell your friends"—we were speaking in Italian—"that the dining car will be taken off the train before we cross the border. You need to reserve a seat early."

I nodded.

"Unless," he went on, "they have those valises stuffed with American food. *Porcamattina.*" He glanced upward at the suitcases, tapped his cheekbone with an index finger and was gone.

I felt for these American women some of the mixed feelings that the traveler feels for the tourist. On the one hand you want to help, to show off your superior knowledge; on the other you don't want to get involved. I didn't want to get involved. They weren't my type. These were saltwater women—sailors, golfers, tennis players, clubwomen with suntans in November, large limbed, confident, conspicuous, firm, trim, sleek as walruses in their worsted wool suits. They reminded me of the Gold Coast women who used to show up around the edges of CORE demonstrations, with their checkbooks open, telling us how much they admired what we were doing, and how they wished they could help more. All fucked up ideologically, according to our leaders at SNCC: "They think their shit don't stink."

As far as they knew, I was a scruffy little Italian—I hadn't spoken a word of English in their presence, and I was reading an Italian novel—and it was too late to undeceive them. I had heard too much.

I knew, for example, that they'd met the previous summer at some kind of writing workshop at Johns Hopkins University and that they'd both jumped into the sack with their instructor, a novelist named Philip. I knew that Philip was bald but well hung ("like a shillelagh"). I knew that neither of them had done it dog fashion BP ("before Philip") and that they were traveling second class because Philip had told them they'd get more material that way for the stories they were going to write now that they were divorced.

Part of their agenda, I gathered, was to notice things, to pay attention. Maybe they were looking for signs, too, maybe not; in either case they seemed to be trying to impress the details of European railroad travel onto the pages of their marbled composition books by sheer physical force. Nothing escaped their notice, not even the signs, in French, German and Italian, warning passengers not to throw things out the window and not to pull the cord on the *signal d'alarme.* All the details went into their notebooks—the fine of not less than 5,000 FF, the prison term of not less than one year. And when one noticed something, the other did, too: the instructions on the window latch, the way the armrests worked, the captions on the faded views of Chartres Cathedral that hung on the walls of the compartment above the backs of the seats. (I was tempted to look at them myself, but I didn't want to give myself away or interrupt their game.)

I kept my nose in my book—Natalia Ginzburg's *Lessico famigliare.* It was a strenuous hour, and I was glad when, simultaneously, panting like dogs after a good run, they closed their notebooks and resumed their conversation.

Yolanda: Did you get the old man with the pipe?

Ruth: Got him.

Yolanda: The emergency stop?

Ruth: Got it.

Yolanda: The sheep?

Ruth: What sheep? I didn't see any sheep.

Yolanda: Hah! *(Licking her finger and scoring off an imaginary line in the air.)* There were six sheep in somebody's yard.

Ruth: Oh, shit. I wish Philip were here.

Yolanda: You can have Philip; I'll take the guy with the funny hat.

Ruth: What guy?

Yolanda: Back in Metz.

Ruth: Not fair.

Yolanda: How do you *really* feel about Philip? Do you think he just used us? I mean, who would have thought that first day—

Ruth: Do you suppose he screwed Alice, too? She's the one who really needed it. And how about Helga?

Yolanda: Helga, maybe. Alice, no. Too old. No talent.

Ruth: Do you suppose that's why he teaches those work-shops?

Yolanda: Do you suppose that's why we went?

(A silence.)

Ruth: I think I got a lot out of it. I mean besides a roll in the hay. I mean, I think I'm getting my head together, noticing a lot of stuff I never noticed before.

Yolanda: Like the emergency stop?

Ruth (nodding): Yeah. Maybe it's not important, but I'm learning to look at things. Really look. Like these pictures. Chartres Cathedral. Little stuff like that, or that guy with the funny hat. They all add up. It's like getting new glasses.

Yolanda: How about the announcement on the PA system? Did you get that?

Ruth (looking at her notebook): *Pardonnay* something or other, that's all I got. How about you?

Yolanda: I drew a blank. *(Looking out the window.)* I thought France was supposed to be beautiful?

Ruth (thumbing through her guidebook): We're in Alsace-Lorraine. Remember Alsace-Lorraine? I think it used to be part of Germany—lots of heavy industry and potash mining. Joan of Arc was born here.

Yolanda: Swell. How long does it last?

Ruth: Till we get to Switzerland, I guess.

Yolanda: It'll be dark by then. We won't be able to see the mountains.

The train, an express but not a "crack" express, had settled into a steady, comfortable rhythm that made me think of the books

I'd read as a child in which trains went clickety-clack, clickety-clack, down the track, down the track, clickety-clack. I shrugged my shoulders mentally and turned back to *Lessico famigliare.*

Ruth and Yolanda got out their notebooks and spent another hour writing—less strenuously this time—and then they read aloud what they had written, which I found more disturbing than listening to them talk about their sexual escapades with Philip. Disturbing not because it was embarrassing but because their stories brought me, against my will, into the quiet centers of their lives, to places where Philip had never been. And yet they didn't know I was there. I was totally invisible. So invisible that I hadn't even been noticed in their furious cataloging of authentic European details.

Ruth read first, staring down hard at her notes. Her father, she began, was an avid sailor. Sailing was his passion, and he knew the Chesapeake Bay like the back of his hand, from the Delaware Canal to Cape Charles; the Outer Banks too. But he was blind. Blind as a bat. He'd been blind since he was fifteen and had fallen off a horse, knocked his head, something like that. Anyway, he kept on riding, and he kept on sailing. He invented all kinds of nautical instruments for the blind—an audiocompass, a knot meter, a Loran-C with a verbal read-out. He always kept a man to look after his sailboats and to sail with him, to be his eyes; and sometimes he took one of his children, though not Ruth's mother, who was afraid of the water.

"We were beating upwind into the Port Arthur Narrows when we should have been heading home with the wind behind us. It was starting to rain, and there was too much of a chop. The shoal water was boiling, and we were slamming into the

12

waves, and Daddy made me strap on a life jacket, but he wouldn't wear one himself. He wouldn't believe we couldn't do it—he never believed there was anything he couldn't do—but we couldn't do it. We made two more passes, and then we had to pull off the wind to run back home. Coming about we got hit by a big sea, like a big hand slapping a fly, and we went right over. I came up under the sail, and when I got myself out I could see Daddy swimming the wrong way, away from the boat, out into the bay. I held onto the boat—I was afraid to go after him. He was a strong swimmer and I'd never have caught him anyway. I kept on screaming and screaming until I couldn't scream anymore—the wind had picked up, and I couldn't even hear myself—and then I closed my eyes and prayed. I prayed that Daddy would turn around. I promised God that if Daddy got back to the boat I'd never be naughty again blah-blah-blah. No more masturbating, no more sneaking the change out of the jewelry case on Daddy's dresser, no more sassing Mom, no more goofing off in school. You know how kids are when they pray."

"And?"

"And Daddy turned around and swam right back to the boat, and fifteen minutes later the Coast Guard picked us up, and the only thing Daddy said was, 'Don't tell your mother. Ever.' "

"Did you tell her?"

"I never told anyone before. Not one word."

"Did she ever find out?"

"I don't think so. Daddy paid the Coast Guard not to report it, and he paid somebody else to salvage the boat. He'd done something foolish, and he didn't want anyone to know about it."

Yolanda patted Ruth's thigh. "That's wonderful, Ruthy. Really."

"I've always thought I should have swum after him, even if I couldn't have caught him—he was a powerful swimmer—but I just let him go. I was too frightened. He had red hair and I could see the top of his head like a buoy that's lost its mooring, drifting farther and farther away, and then I couldn't see it at all till he was almost back at the boat. That's why I've never told anyone, that's why *I* didn't want anyone to know."

"And you've been a good girl ever since? No sassing your mom? No playing with yourself?" Yolanda leaned over and planted a sisterly kiss on her friend's cheek.

"No, no, nothing like that. You know me."

"Now it's your turn," Ruth said.

"It's so *tri*vial compared to yours. It's nothing. It doesn't *mat*ter."

"Yes it does, Yolo. You can't judge your own writing anyway. Philip said that over and over. You can't really see it yourself. That's why you need a reader, an audience. 'Every work of art needs a receiver.' "

It took a lot of persuading to get Yolanda to read what *she'd* written, but eventually Ruth prevailed. Yolanda opened her notebook, but she didn't look at it. She looked out the window and just talked.

"One day when I came home from school I opened the refrigerator to get a glass of milk and a rat jumped out."

"You've got to be kidding."

"My mother died, she just died. She was standing in the

14

doorway, all dressed up to go to the club. You should have seen her face. Here she is in this pink shantung suit, and this rat comes charging out of the refrigerator and runs across the floor into the butler's pantry."

"Oh my God," Ruth said.

"She stood there for about thirty seconds and then she closed the kitchen doors so it couldn't come back in and got on the phone. She told the exterminator that she was pregnant and that if he didn't come within half an hour she'd miscarry, and then when he did show up she made him go back out and pull his truck into the garage because she didn't want the neighbors to see it in the drive! Milton, my little brother, came down to see what was going on, and he kept shouting, 'A rat, a rat, there's a rat in the house!' And Mama couldn't shut him up, and she couldn't get us to go to the Hendersons, who lived up the Bay Road. She wanted us out of the way; but she didn't want us to tell Mrs. Henderson what was going on.

"The exterminator had a rat detector, kind of like those metal detectors you see people walking around with at the beach with a little box thing on a shoulder strap. We followed him all around the kitchen—the rat, he said, had probably come up through the wall and made a nest under the fridge and then eaten through the insulation. Kitchen, laundry room, back hall, butler's pantry, dining room. The thing started buzzing a little in the living room. 'It's behind the couch,' he said. 'Would you please leave the room and close those doors.'

"Mama protested. 'What are you going to do?'

" 'I'm going to kill it.'

" 'But how?'

" 'Please, Mrs. Kazen, I'm going to have to ask you to leave the room.'

" 'Yes, of course.'

"Between us we got Milton out of the room and closed the sliding doors. We heard the sound of furniture moving. Then a shot. Then another shot. I had goose bumps.

"Mama was sweating. It's the only time I've ever seen her really *sweat.*

"When the exterminator came out into the hallway, he had the rat in a kind of pouch. Milton wanted to see it, but Mama told him no.

" 'That'll be fifty dollars.'

" 'Fifty dollars? You can't be serious. That's highway robbery!'

" 'Look, lady, *you* called me. Hysterical. You're about to miscarry if we're not here in half an hour. Now you're telling me you don't want to pay fifty dollars, which is standard for an emergency like this? I got a business to run.'

" 'Really, I think you'd better talk to my husband.'

" 'You want me to show him the rat? Here, where you want me to put it, here on the dining room table? Or maybe back behind the couch? On the piano?'

"So Mama got the checkbook and paid him, and he took the rat away and was gone, and the next day we had a brand-new refrigerator."

There was a moment of silence, just slightly awkward, in which it wasn't clear whether the story had come to an end.

"That's it. The end. It's not very good," she began to protest, not giving Ruth a chance to respond. "It's dumb, really. I don't know what made me think of it. So there was a rat, and the man shot it. So what? It needs more theme, but I don't know what. I mean, where's the conflict?"

"I love it. Your mother's hysterical about the rat, and then she doesn't want to pay the bill. God, I know people just like that."

"So do I—my mother."

"Maybe you could do more with her worrying about the neighbors seeing the truck. A sociological angle. Did the neighbors find out?"

"Yeah, Milton told everybody. All his friends came over to see the bullet holes. One of them got plastered over, but the other one's still there, in the molding."

"Did anybody say anything?"

"Oh, yeah. They talked about it all right, but it wasn't any big deal. In fact, everybody had a rat story. Maybe *that's* the interesting thing. It didn't matter who it was, if Daddy told the rat story, pretty soon everybody was telling rat stories. Those old houses near the water, you can't help it."

"Kind of like everybody having secret fantasies, maybe."

"I tried to write about Philip, too. But every time I write about sex it comes out all wrong. You know, I never did it dog fashion with Teddy. We did a lot of things, but not that. But when you try to write about it, it just sounds stupid. It seems so meaningful when you're doing it, just physically, and all that mental stuff, too, breaking taboos, you know what I mean? But it's hard to write about. There's no good word for you know what. I mean, just plain *penis* sounds dumb. All those words sound dumb: prick, dick, dork, cock, schlong, wiener, whang. You can't tell the truth with them."

My invisibility had become too uncomfortable. I was op-

pressed by the weight of an intimacy I couldn't share, and by
the irony of the situation: two American women come to Europe in search of story material and what rises to the surface
when they put pen to paper? Mama and Papa, Papa swimming
blindly out toward open water, Mama bickering with the exterminator about the fee for killing a rat. I extracted my nylon bag
from the luggage rack—a little calf nestled between two big
bulky cows—and left the compartment without a word, turning to the left, which is how I found my Saint-Cyr cadet, *sans
chapeau,* on his way back from the toilet at the end of the car.
He turned abruptly and entered his compartment.

I tapped on the door of the compartment and opened it.
"Any room in here?" I said. *"Une place libre?"*

He shrugged his shoulders, though there was no one else in
the compartment, and no suitcases in sight except for his long-
ish brown duffel bag and my nylon one. He'd removed his
fabulous chocolate hat, which was on the seat beside him, along
with a smart attaché case he'd been using as a lap desk. He was
writing a letter.

"You have a very nice hat," I said in French, *"un chapeau
extraordinaire."*

I hadn't meant to embarrass him, but he blushed and covered
the letter he'd been writing with his hands, as if to keep me
from reading it.

"Vraiment," I continued, but then I got stuck. *"Vraiment,"* I
repeated, but I couldn't get any farther. "Truly, *vraiment, vraiment, un chapeau extraordinaire."*

Was *this* a sign, this language amnesia? Was my brain sending me a message, telling me to go home?

"Are you all right?" he asked in English.

"Yes, thank you. Whenever I try to speak French it comes out Italian, but I'll be all right now."

His hat was called a *casoar,* which is a kind of bird—a cassowary—that lives in New Guinea, and his name was Gautier, which I realized later is "Walter" in English—Walt; what a funny name for a Frenchman—and he was quite a nice young man, who was going to Mulhouse to visit his uncle before returning to Saint-Cyr-l'Ecole. He was quite amused when I finally explained about Papa's frozen dessert. He had never heard of such a thing, and I promised to send him the recipe. He thought his mother would like it. I still have his address and even his phone number in my little black address book, but I never sent him the recipe. I'm not sure why. Maybe it was because I'd tried to pin some hopes on him, to invest him with the power to tell me, by some word or gesture, either that I was doing the right thing and should persevere, or that I had made a terrible mistake and should turn back before it was too late, but I hadn't been able to do it. It wasn't his fault. It was just that the redheaded blind man kept churning his way through the dark waves of my imagination. What had *he* been thinking of? I wondered. And why had he turned back? That was the real mystery. And, like Yolanda and Ruth, I was thinking about my own papa and mama—Papa in his old age, alone, swimming blindly out into a darkness from which there would be no turning back. And Mama already there, Mama who once found a rat in the basement toilet. She put on rubber gloves, picked it up and wrapped it in foil and then in plastic so the dogs wouldn't smell it. Had it climbed into the toilet and fallen in, or had it come up through the pipes? Which was worse, imaginatively speaking? We'd talked about it a lot but never settled the question. You're right, I wanted to shout. Everybody has a rat story, just like secret fantasies. If things had worked out differently, I would have told you mine.

The second seating for dinner was announced, but Gautier was planning to eat with his uncle in Mulhouse, and I didn't feel like eating. I wasn't hungry. I offered him a Life Saver, which he accepted, and then I returned to my book and he to his letter. I managed to doze off for a while and was sleeping when my old friend the Italian conductor entered the compartment and offered to escort me back to my own seat.

I protested, but it was quite impossible, he said, for me to remain where I was. The couchette assignments could not be changed, and besides, the car I was in would be detached from the train at Mulhouse, along with the *vagone-ristorante,* the dining car. When I returned to my compartment Ruth and Yolanda were unhappy.

"You're an American, aren't you?"

It wasn't a question, it was an accusation. I'd heard it before in Europe, but usually as the prelude to a complaint about American foreign policy, not as an attack on my character.

"How did you find out?"

"The conductor told us. He speaks a little English."

The conductor had already made up the berths, two on one side and one on the other, so the three of us were standing in a row in the narrow space that remained—Ruth glaring at me over Yolanda's shoulder.

"You might have said something." Yolanda, who was doing the grilling, was hunching up her shoulders in righteous anger —I didn't blame her—breathing deeply and deliberately.

"I'm sorry," I said. "I wasn't planning to fool you, I just

. . . It's just that I was speaking Italian with the conductor when you came in, and then I guess I thought it would be easier to be alone. I didn't feel like talking."

They looked at each other in disbelief. A female, one of their own kind, who didn't feel like talking to them?

"But you listened to every word we said, didn't you? I'll bet you thought that was pretty cute."

"By that time it was too late. You know, there was a point right at the beginning where if I'd spoken up, it would have been all right, but once we were past that point . . . It was too late. I'd already heard too much."

"And you could have warned us that they were taking the dining car off the train. By the time we figured out that they were announcing dinner, it was too late. There's nothing to eat. Even those little carts that were coming by for a while have disappeared."

"I'm sorry," I said. "I have some Life Savers in my book bag. Would you like one?" But these women were not about to be appeased with Life Savers.

"Life Savers! Jesus."

What could I do but retreat, pull into my shell like a tortoise, climb into my berth with my clothes on and pull the blanket up over me. They kept on scolding and grousing for a while, but in a nondirectional sort of way, sending out complaints at random as I gradually faded from sight and as they struggled with their suitcases, taking turns because there wasn't room in the compartment to open both at once. They'd been expecting cozy Pullman accommodations, not these flat, drafty bunks with paper blankets and paper pillows. And they were hungry, really hungry. I was getting hungry too, but I tried not to let it bother me as I watched them undress.

Despite the unsatisfactory accommodations, they were not about to compromise their sleeping arrangements, not about to wrinkle their tailored suits by sleeping in them. They pulled down the shades and stripped right to the buff, teetering and tottering in the narrow space, bumping into the sides of the berths and into each other as the train swayed from side to side, showing themselves to me, from neck to knee, as freely as if I weren't there at all. I had resumed my invisibility.

Lying on my back, observing this display of bare leg and bare buttock, I was reminded of Meg and Molly, whose mysterious flesh I had often observed from the bottom bunk in the room I shared with Molly.

Ruth, like Molly, had bright red pubic hair and tufts of bright red hair under her arms, as if her body were bursting into flames. Yolanda bent over to remove her nylons and I inhaled, along with the gentle aroma of expensive perfumes, a powerful damp-dog smell. Someone was having her period.

I closed my eyes and breathed deeply. Something funny had happened. My initial animosity toward these women had turned into a kind of love; not erotic, I don't mean that, but the kind I felt for my sisters, whose memory caught me like a stitch in the side, and not inexplicably either. I'd taken—stolen —a ten-dollar bill from my mother's purse once, and since no one would confess to the crime we'd all three been sent to bed without supper. My sisters, though they had refused to tattle on me, had been hungry and ill tempered, not about to let me off the hook. Like Ruth and Yolanda, they'd wanted me to suffer for what I'd done. But not for long. They were never mad for long, and pretty soon we were fooling around just like we always did. Three travelers we'd been, starting out on a journey together, and then somehow we'd been separated, not by miles or kilometers but by husbands and lovers and children and Mama's death and Papa's money troubles. I tried to remember what I'd done with the ten-dollar bill. How had I spent it? Movies? Candy? Books? Toys? Had I spent it at all? Was it still hidden securely between the pages of some book? I couldn't remember, but I could remember Papa coming upstairs and saying that if we didn't settle down he'd have to spank us, and then he came up again and brought his guitar and sang "Pony Man" and "Bottle of Wine," our favorite songs. But we didn't get anything to eat till breakfast.

When the train arrived at what I took (correctly) to be Mulhouse, I decided to redeem myself by getting something for us to eat. If the dining car was going to be detached, I would have at least ten minutes, plenty of time to buy three *cestini*. I couldn't remember the French word, but I could remember quite distinctly one of the lessons in the French textbook we had used at the *liceo:* a young Italian, visiting France for the first time, leans out the window of the train and buys one of these little box lunches—a sliver of pâté wrapped in foil, a crusty roll, a demiliter of delicious *vin rouge,* and so on—from a friendly *campagnard* who instructs him on the geographical features of the region and on the nature of French food and wine and hopes that he will enjoy his visit.

I glanced out the window as I slipped on my loafers. No friendly *campagnards* in sight, but I was undeterred. I had found an opportunity to redeem myself, and I wasn't going to let it go by. Besides, I was hungry myself. *Starving.* I took it as a good sign.

"I'm going to get something to eat," I announced, popping out of the compartment before they had a chance to respond.

The platform was crowded with disembarking passengers, including my cadet. He gave me a friendly nod, but I had no time for him now. "Ten minutes?" I asked a uniformed man on the platform. He looked at his watch: *"Dix minutes? C'est ça."*

I went through the waiting room to the station restaurant. "I want to buy something to eat for the train," I said slowly in my best French. *"Quelque chose à manger pour le chemin de fer."*

The *garçon*-type at the stand-up bar in the station restaurant, which was nearly empty, looked alarmed, as if I had threatened him. I suppose now that I asked for something for the railroad to eat, but you'd think he could have figured it out, since we *were* in a restaurant. I was reminded of my first (and only) time in Paris, asking a taxi driver to take me to the Tour Eiffel, only to be met with a blank, uncomprehending stare.

"Speak slowly, please," said the man behind the bar. *"Lentement."*

It was funny. I could understand him, but he couldn't understand me. (You sometimes get telephone connections like that. You shout and shout and shout and the person on the other end says "Hello? Hello? Hello?")

"Cibo," I said in a loud voice. *"Un cestino"*—Italian words driving out French. I pointed at my mouth and at my stomach. *"Caisse,"* I said quite plainly. *"Poitrine, commode, boîte."* Still aiming at *cestino,* what I was saying was cashbox, breast, dresser, box. Box, that was it: *"boîte de picnic."*

24

"*Boîte de picnic?*" Once again his face assumed a pained expression.

A quick glance at my watch informed me that four and one-half minutes had elapsed since I'd disembarked from the train. I ran through the scene in the textbook once more, remembering as I did so that it had taken place in the station in Avignon, and that Petrarch had been born in Avignon, or else he'd gone to live there.

"Would you like something to eat?"

"*Sì, Sì.* I mean *Oui, oui. S'il vous plaît.*"

"Yes, of course, *mais oui.* Please take a seat." He gestured at a row of empty tables. "I'll bring you a menu. The poached chicken"—I think that's what he said—"is very good this evening."

"*Non importa!*" I shouted, once again in Italian. "It doesn't matter. Anything. *J'ai faim.*"

I could still hear him perfectly, but something was wrong at my end of the connection. Probably it simply didn't occur to a Frenchman that anyone would order a meal in this haphazard, thoughtless fashion. In any case I found it difficult to convey in words the sense of urgency that I felt, though my body must have indicated that I was in distress.

"Do you need to use the WC?" he asked.

"*Non, non, non. Le train parte tout de suite.*"

Another two minutes had elapsed.

"*Le train? Ahhh!* You would like *un panier-repas* to take with you on the train?" He jerked his head in the direction of the platform, where the train was making hooting noises and letting out loud bursts of hot air from the brakes.

"*Sì, sì, sì. Oui, oui, oui.*"

"Moment."

As he disappeared through a curtained door behind the bar I realized I had forgotten about Ruth and Yolanda. "Three!" I shouted. *"Siamo in tre. Trois personnes. Quelque chose pour trois personnes."* He glanced over his shoulder and nodded, holding up three fingers: *"Trois?"*

"Oui, oui, oui."

I decided I would give him three minutes. From where I was standing I could still see the last car of the train, which had backed into the station.

Two minutes passed. Three. By the time he returned I was almost-but-not-quite frantic. He presented me with a long, flat box tied with white butcher's string and a bill for one hundred francs, which I paid at the cashier.

I hadn't expected to eat for nothing, but one hundred francs was an astonishing sum, about twenty dollars for a couple of sandwiches. It was more money than I had, in fact, in francs, but I was able to cash a traveler's check without too much difficulty, though I had trouble signing my own name.

The train, having parted from the last three cars, was already in motion when I reached the platform. I hesitated a second or two to get my bearings, unable to believe in my heart of hearts that it would actually leave without me. In my head, of course, I knew that even in Italy trains didn't wait for late comers and that French trains might actually leave a little early, just for the pleasure of spoiling someone's trip. But in my heart I knew it wasn't right that I should be left behind when all I was trying to do was get something to eat for myself and those two American women—my sisters—who would think I got what I deserved and never know that I'd done it for them. It was simply too unjust, too unfair. Why hadn't the conductor made sure I was back on the train? I simply couldn't believe it, and then I was running along the long platform that stretched out into the night.

My legs almost buckled at first, but then I found them and they began to carry me faster and faster, speeding past benches and drinking fountains and, as I approached the far end of the platform, pushcarts piled high with boxes and bags and suitcases. In a film the scene would have been shot with a telephoto, cutting back and forth from me, Margot, the box of twenty-dollar sandwiches banging against my side, to the train itself; it would have peered into a lighted window, as I did, to see an old man's face pressed against the pane, or perhaps (in the film version) two lovers embracing. In the camera's foreshortened vision the train would chug and chug and chug without covering much ground and I would run and run and run without gaining on it. Actually I *was* gaining on the train. Overtaking it wasn't the problem; the problem was finding a place to get on, judging how far to lead—the way a hunter leads a bird or a bounding deer—the open platform on the last car of the train.

If the station platform had been longer—another twenty meters—I think I would have made it, but it wasn't and I didn't. Instead of catching the train, I took a leap in the dark at the end of the platform, landed on my feet, stumbled, tumbled on rough white rocks, and picked myself up (still holding the box of sandwiches). The train, carrying my luggage, my passport, my Icelandic ticket (open return), all my bookbinding tools, chugged indifferently down the track, displaying three red lights, like stars—fading red giants—the sign I'd been looking for, unambiguous. You could only read it one way.

I experienced a brief moment of relief and absolute calm in which I went over in my mind what I had to do, reminding myself that I had enough money for a hotel room and that my baggage—my nylon suitcase and my Harvard book bag— would certainly be returned the next day. This moment lasted about two seconds, and then I started to scream, to curse the train, first in English and then in Italian, in which I was quite proficient: *porcavaccamadonna, porcamadonnavacca,* and so on. Unfortunately—or perhaps fortunately—the only French swearword I knew was *sacrebleu,* which seemed pretty tame, but a sentence from my textbook suddenly popped into my head, an imperative: "Stop that man. He has stolen my umbrella!" and I began to yell at the receding red lights: *"Arrêtez cet homme. Il a volé mon parapluie! Arrêtez cet homme! Arrêtez ce train!"* Much to my surprise, the train stopped.

I didn't notice it right away. In fact I walked half the length of the long platform before giving a backward glance, and even then it wasn't immediately obvious that the three red lights were no longer receding. Sitting on a bench, trying to come to grips with the dramatic turn in my circumstances, wondering whether or not to call Papa and what he would say—would he be glad to have me back so soon, or would this disaster merely confirm his suspicion that I was not and never would be able to look after myself? should I ask him to call the Newberry Library, to tell them I was coming home? I looked once again in the direction of the departed train, and this time I noticed that the red lights were as bright if not brighter than ever, and soon they were brighter still. I was too astonished to get up from my bench. It didn't occur to me at the moment that the train might be backing up for any reason other than my own convenience. I was delighted—overjoyed, in fact—and I had to hug myself to keep from laughing hysterically.

By the time the train had backed into the station, the crowd of railroad employees who had gathered to greet it had been joined by half a dozen gendarmes in their handsome uniforms, and something told me to stay put, not to call attention to myself. The lights were on now in most of the compartments, and I caught a glimpse of Yolanda's face pressed briefly against one of the windows of what was now the last car. It was white as chalk in the artificial light of the carbon lamps. Then Ruth's, equally white. The gendarmes and the railroad men boarded the train. After a discreet interval I followed and immediately popped into one of the toilets. I was nervous and somewhat shaken, but pleased with myself.

When I emerged from the toilet I was told, roughly, by a *gendarme,* to return to my compartment *toute de suite.* I was also told (I think) that I shouldn't flush the toilet in the station.

"Okay," I said. "Okay." The *gendarme* let his fingertips brush against my bottom as I squeezed past him in the corridor. The French are so romantic. I brought my heel down on the toe of his shiny black boot.

The train was delayed for almost an hour and a half while the railroad people checked couplings and brakes and air hoses and the *gendarmes* interrogated the passengers. Someone had pulled the emergency-stop cord, a serious offense, not a prank. Com-

puters in three countries were rearranging timetables to accommodate the Luxembourg-Venise Express. Passengers, we were
admonished, might be forced to disembark and wait several
hours in the station. The *gendarmes* in general wanted to know
who had pulled the cord. And the *gendarme* in particular whose
fingers had tickled my rear end wanted to know who had
pulled the cord, and he thought my emergence from the WC
was a clue of some kind. There was something odd about it, but
he was no Sherlock Holmes and didn't know what to do with
it.

He questioned us in French, and I translated as best I could
for Yolanda and Ruth, who remained in their berths holding
their paper blankets up around their necks.

"Why on earth would we pull the emergency-stop cord?"

"*Pourquoi tireront-ils,*" I said, "*le signal d'alarme?*"

"*Non, non,*" he corrected me. "*Pourquoi est-ce qu'elles tireraient
le signal d'alarme?*"

That's what he wanted to know.

I glanced again at the warning, in three languages, but not
in English: *Défense d'actionner le signal d'alarme,* and at the penalty: 5,000 FF. No joke. A thousand dollars. And up to a year
in a French prison.

And why was I in the WC? he wanted to know, *after* the
train had stopped and the passengers had been told to remain
in their compartments?

"Because I had to pee," I shouted at him in a sudden burst of
fluency. "I had to *faire pipi.* Can't you understand that?"

We were all relieved when he left our compartment and went
on to the next, and even more relieved when, after a nerve-
numbing delay, the train once again pulled out of the station.

* * *

The truth is, I've never cared for the French, who, in my experience, have always been as rude and boorish as the Italians are charming and gracious. I even prefer Italian cooking. What it lacks in subtlety and polish it makes up for being true to the original ingredients, which are treated not as raw materials to be disciplined and totally transformed into something one would never have expected, but as, as, as . . . How should I put it? As themselves, I suppose, whose essential characteristics must be respected. And yet I have to admit that our hastily assembled *quelque chose à manger pour le chemin de fer* was a gastronomic joy, *un repas extraordinaire.* More than that, actually. Under the circumstances, it was a joy pure and simple.

We ate standing up, the food spread out before our faces on the top berth. The box of food had been tumbled around pretty thoroughly, and some olives had gotten pressed into the currant tart, but we soon had things sorted out. Tiny mottled olives, they were, that I've never eaten anywhere else. I stood between Ruth and Yolanda and we touched each other as we stretched out our arms for this or that, a sampling from the cold buffet: slivers of pâté, tiny boiled crayfish, a luscious pork-and-veal pie, marinated in red wine, that we ate, like everything else, with our fingers; smoked sausages and Gruyère cheese. We had to take down Yolanda's suitcase once again to get a corkscrew for the wine, which we drank out of the bottle, a delicious Riesling, somewhat shaken but still cool and presentable. There were small golden plums for dessert, along with the tart. I don't know when I've enjoyed a meal more.

We talked while we ate. I told them about Papa and the

Saint-Cyr *glacés* and how Mama had found a rat in the toilet and how my sisters and I had been punished and how I couldn't remember what I'd done with the ten-dollar bill I'd stolen from Mama's purse, and how I'd happened to go to Italy.

I had a pretty good idea by that time who had pulled the cord, but I didn't want to ask in case it wasn't true. But it *was* true, though they didn't tell me till we were halfway into the second bottle of wine. They had pulled it together, their hands interlaced over the wooden knob at the end of the cord.

"What if there was some way to figure out which compartment it was? Like in a dorm room, when you plug in an iron and blow the fuse, they can tell whose room it was."

"We had to take a chance. We couldn't just leave you. We could see you running, you know. You were going like the wind. We had to do something."

"Thank you," I said. "Maybe you can write a story about it. Two stories. I'll look for them in *Redbook*."

"Good idea. Our first European adventure."

It was midnight by my watch when we turned out the light and crawled back under our paper blankets, but I didn't have any idea what time it was when I woke up in the pitch-dark night. I didn't know if I'd slept half an hour or five hours. I listened for a moment to see if Yolanda or Ruth was awake, and then I climbed out of bed and pressed my face against the window to see what I could see. What invisible borders had we crossed in the night? Were we still in France? In Switzerland? Italy? If I looked up, was I looking at a high-peaked mountain? If I looked down, was I looking into a deep green-rimmed valley? If I looked straight ahead, was I looking at vineyards on terraced slopes? At high pastures sprinkled with old-world cows? I couldn't make out a thing in the rich darkness. But it didn't matter. It was a funny thing: I didn't know where I was, but I knew I was where I wanted to be.

2

Pockets of Silence

I didn't really know what I was going to do when the train pulled into the station in Florence, which it did at eight o'clock in the evening. I suppose I was only a phone call away from warmth, shelter, food, a glass of wine, but no one was expecting me. No one had asked me to come; and the many friends, bright images in the memory, who would doubtless have been glad to see me, had long ago ceased to write. For reasons I never fully understood, I had never answered their letters. And so I decided, although it was cold and raining, to stay in a *pensione,* at least for the first night.

According to a copy of *Il Paese Sera* that I'd picked up in Rome things had pretty much returned to normal, but in fact none of the *pensioni* around the station were open, and the taxi driver who picked me up as I was making my way back to the station from the unlit Via Fiume and drove off in the direction of the Fortezza da Basso launched into a tale of bitter recrimination against the government without bothering to ask where I wanted to go. Rome had announced *normalità,* he said, because the water had gone down! *"Normalità!* No public assistance, no bulldozers, no trucks, no food, no drinking water, no nothing. You call that *normalità?"* He tipped his head as far back as it would go and gestured aggressively with his right hand, fingertips pressed together, as if he were shoving something up something.

"Could you take me to a pensione, please?"

"Where?"

"Something near the center, if that's possible, but nothing fancy."

He turned and gave me an incredulous look without slowing down. He was steering with his left hand, moving the wheel back and forth as if he were trying to keep a small sailboat on a difficult course.

"Non c'è. There's nothing, Signorina. You have to go to Fiesole."

"How much will it cost?"

"Ten thousand lire."

I divided by sixteen hundred. About six dollars.

"Are the buses running?"

"Not tonight. Maybe tomorrow."

"There's nothing in town?"

"Niente. Nothing."

We had circled the Fortezza da Basso and were heading back to the station. It was raining harder now, not a downpour but steady. Was there going to be a second flood? Was it possible to have two floods so close together, or would it take more time for the water to build up in the lakes and rivers up in the surrounding hills, wherever the Arno comes from? I suddenly realized how little I knew about the hydrodynamics of the earth. But my immediate problem was to find a room for the night.

"Va bene," I said. "Fiesole."

We completed the circle and were soon heading north again. I sank back into the seat, exhausted. The man kept talking, one horror story after another: eleven people drowned in the underground passageway by the station; guard dogs trapped in basements; men trapped in stalled cars and drowned; the patients at the insane asylum had climbed out on the roof; twenty horses drowned at the Cascine park. His brother-in-law's furniture shop in Santa Croce completely destroyed. The *popolo minuto,* the little people, ruined. And still the government had done nothing.

Though there wasn't much traffic, we were going uncomfortably fast down a street I didn't recognize when suddenly the car lurched to the side. Cloppety-cloppety-cloppety. Cloppety-cloppety-cloppety. A flat tire. At first I thought the man was simply going to ignore it and keep going—it's a wonder he didn't ruin the rim—but at last he pulled over to the curb, put his head down on the steering wheel and started to cry softly to himself. His wife and son had gone to Siena, he said after a while, to stay with her mother, who had never liked him. No water in his apartment, no electricity, no heat and now it was going to flood again.

I was startled by a staticky voice out of nowhere. I couldn't tell what it was saying, but it roused the driver, who picked up a microphone and shouted into it that he had a *gomma a terra.* More static. More shouting.

"I'm sorry," I said. "Is there anything I can do?"

"Nothing. Make it stop raining."

"I don't think it can flood again, not for a while," I said helpfully. The rain drumming on the roof of the cab was so loud I had to shout.

He pulled on his hat and got out of cab. I could hear the sound of the trunk opening and feel the car vibrating slightly as he jacked it up.

My habit of looking for signs had not deserted me. The cadet, the receding lights of the train, the American women. And now a flat tire, a *gomma a terra.* The world seemed pregnant with meanings, all contradictory. I was thinking how nice it would have been if Ruth and Yolanda had been in the dark cab with me—then it would have been an adventure instead of a depressing nuisance—when I noticed a difference in the sound the rain was making, and a light at the window.

Which I rolled down to get a look. I was a little startled to see a man's face, barely six inches from my own, peering intently at me. He was holding in one hand one of the huge green umbrellas that you see in shops and at all the markets, holding it over the driver while he struggled with the spare tire. In the other he held a flashlight. He was a man in his fifties, clean shaven, and his face, beaming under a Borsalino, wore a slightly amused expression.

There was no wind, so the driver and the man were fairly well protected by the huge umbrella. He smiled and rolled his eyes upward in a meaningful way, as if to suggest that the management ought to be called to account. His presence was cheering, and I wanted to break into the circle of his charm, to place myself under his umbrella, so to speak, so I asked him if he knew where I could find an inexpensive pensione. It was the only thing I could think of.

"Mais non," he said, and began to speak rapidly in French. *". . . difficile . . . le centre . . . une deluge . . .* Fiesole . . . *rien à bon marché."* I believe he was saying what I knew already, that there was nothing in the center of town and I'd have to go to Fiesole, but I wouldn't find anything cheap.

How odd, I thought, to meet a Frenchman under such circumstances.

"She speaks Italian," I heard the driver say.

"Of course," the man said in Italian, addressing the driver on the pavement beneath him, "but I'm something of a linguist, and I detected a French accent."

"Stop that man," I said, reverting to my textbook French. *"Arrêtez cet homme. Il a volé mon parapluie."*

He started to laugh, and I started to laugh, too.

"You have a very fine umbrella," I said in Italian.

"Merci beaucoup," he said, and then added, in Italian, "But I see you are not French after all. Please excuse me."

He gave me an opportunity to reveal my true linguistic identity, which I declined to do, and then went on. "There's been a flood, seven meters of water in Santa Croce, you won't find a thing in the city, you'll have to go to Fiesole, and you won't find anything cheap, believe me."

"I know there's been a flood," I said.

"Then what are you doing here?"

"I thought I could be of use."

"Sì, sì. Un angelo di fango?"

A mud angel? I hadn't any idea what he was talking about.

"Of course," he continued, "you could stay with me. My *apartamento* is full of flood refugees from the lower floors, but one more wouldn't matter. No electricity, no running water, no heat"—a litany I heard many times in the next few days—"but dry."

"No no, I couldn't. I'd better go on to Fiesole."

"You speak firmly," he said, "like a woman who has made up her mind."

"You're very kind, but I think it would be better."

"*Magari.*"

Magari. One of those untranslatable words that sometimes rate a separate chapter in books on Italy.

I could feel the driver tightening the lugs, and soon we were ready to go. The mysterious stranger, as I thought of him, offered cigarettes. The mysterious stranger with a green umbrella. The driver accepted; I declined.

"*Arrivederla.*"

"*Piacere.*"

I rolled up the window and pulled my coat around me. The driver smoked his cigarette. "You're an *americana,* aren't you?"

"*Sì.*"

"I was thinking you were an *americana,* but you speak good Italian."

"*Grazie.*"

"*Prego.* You know what I think, if you'll excuse me?"

"Tell me."

"He was a nice man, *molto gentile.*" I leaned forward in the dark, to hear what he had to say. "But you did the right thing, saved yourself a lot of trouble." I leaned back.

Of course I'd done the right thing. I couldn't possibly have gone with him. But I appreciated the invitation, and in fact the whole incident left me with a good feeling, like a chance to warm myself at a cozy fire before turning in for the night.

* * *

The Pensione Medici was certainly not cheap, but it was more than comfortable—a double bed, an enormous wardrobe, private bath with bidet, and a view of the city. From my window, on what turned out to be a crisp, clear morning, I could look right down the Via Fiesolana, where Claudia's grandparents lived, right down at the gloomy Protestant Cemetery in the Piazza Donatello, final resting place of Elizabeth Barrett Browning and another poet named Clough, pronounced "Cluf." By eight o'clock I had packed my things, but I was reluctant to leave this lovely room, to exchange it for . . . ? The prospect of calling on friends whom I hadn't seen or heard from (mea culpa) for ten years was more daunting than I had anticipated. I imagined them now, married to people I didn't know, living in small apartments full of children and dogs. I put these visions aside for the moment and told myself not to worry. I had a return ticket. I could always go home, it was too soon to worry. But I suppose that was the problem: I *could* always go home. "Home is the place where when you have to go there, they have to take you in." Mama used to quote that line a lot. Somehow the idea tickled her. But there was something unsettling about it too.

I was surprised to find the breakfast room full of Americans. Declining an invitation to join a large noisy table, I sat at a small table by myself, where I could enjoy the view, and made a point of speaking Italian to the signorina who brought *caffelatte,* sweet butter, apricot preserves, and two slabs of day-old *pane toscano.* My instinctive aversion to American tourists was something I'd picked up from Mama, but as I listened to the conversations going on all around me I realized I was surrounded not by tourists but—even worse!—old Florence hands, old soldiers happy to be in harness again, exchanging observations about the flood, displaying their knowledge of the city and its history for the benefit of their admiring subordinates, graduate-student types, serious young men in their mid-twenties. Like me, they had come to Florence to offer their assistance. Like me, each had no doubt come for private reasons, too. Why was I so quick to judge?

I left my room key at the desk and walked out into a briskish sort of day, crisp and cold and sunny, like November in the Midwest. A limousine was waiting to whisk away some of the dignitaries; lesser persons were hurrying to catch the number 7 bus that was waiting in the piazza. I refused to hurry, and the bus left without me. I let it go, deciding as I did so to give myself up to the day, to give myself the day, one day without a plan, to follow my feet, as Papa used to say, to look at the political posters left over from the last election: Communist, Socialist, Christian Democrat; and the four-color circus posters, too, repeated in threes: elephants, polar bears on bicycles drinking glasses of milk, a young woman somersaulting through space, arms outstretched toward a pair of muscular hands coming down out of nowhere. In theory I was an existentialist, a creator of meaning and value, but in reality of course I was a seeker. I couldn't help trying to read the world like a book of signs: the cadet, the receding lights of the train, the American women, the beaming face of the man with the umbrella and now the circus posters. Who would catch me as *I* somersaulted through space?

I soon found myself heading not down toward Florence but up toward Monte Ceceri and Settignano, which like Fiesole is situated on one of the hills that rim the city. You're always heading somewhere, even if you're just following your feet without a plan. Mama and I had often taken this walk. Was I heading in this direction because I was thinking of Mama, or was I thinking of Mama because I was heading in this direction?

I stopped at a Casa del Popolo—one of the bars sponsored by the Communist party—for a cappuccino, as Mama and I had often done. It was two years later that she got sick, but the cancer that killed her must already have been at work when we were walking together, with every puff of the cigarettes she smoked. Powerful French cigarettes with no filters. She smoked in the bar, and she smoked as we walked, and I complained, but I liked the smell of the smoke in the open air, like the smell of leaves burning in the fall.

Mama had bought an enormously detailed military map so that we didn't have to stick to the roads. If you passed even the tiniest shed on the side of the path, you'd be able to find it on the map. We used to get a lot of pleasure from the map, joking that if it were much bigger it would be a full-scale map, a map as big as the country itself. You'd lay it over the country like a blanket of snow, and everything would match up, or not match, depending on how well the cartographers had done their work.

I didn't have a map with me now, but I was sure I'd remember the way somehow. You couldn't get too lost because the road was to your left and the city itself in the valley to your right, though in fact—now that I remember it—Mama and I managed to get lost every time we went out. We'd pore over our map as we went along, but then we'd get to talking, and pretty soon we'd be lost. But then we'd run into a road, or we'd come up to the edge of the valley and find the city at our feet: the Duomo, the Palazzo Vecchio, Santa Croce, Santa Maria Novella, the Uffizi, the Pitti Palace, the Badia, the Bargello, the green dome of the synagogue right across the street from our first apartment. This was Mama's city, her spiritual home, the place where it all began: Giotto, Michelangelo, Leonardo, the Medici . . . , the cradle of the Renaissance, the discovery of the world and of man.

But there was another city too, my city. My city was the Liceo Morgagni and the Paperback Book Exchange on the Via Fiesolana, and the bar behind the Mercato Centrale where you could get real American hamburgers, with everything on them, wrapped in waxed paper. When someone mentioned San Marco I didn't think of Fra Angelico but of the periodic student strikes that we voted on in school, each class voting separately. I never understood the issues, but I loved the camaraderie and the demonstrations, which took place in Piazza San Marco. My city was bus passes and the old cheese factory where we had our gym class once a week, and all the houses (apartments, actually) where I could ring the bell and someone would be glad to see me.

When I first came to Italy with Mama, in 1952 when I was fifteen, I was scared to death, but Mama, who was going to be in charge of a study-abroad program for American college students, was expecting heaven on earth. Which it was, in a way. But in retrospect. While we were living through it, it was

mixed. There were almost no study-abroad programs at the
time, so there was no one to turn to for advice. It was difficult
to find good housing for the students. The families with whom
they lived didn't want to report the money as income, which
created tax problems, and the police—the Questura—wanted
to know everything about the students, including how much
they were paying the families they were going to live with. The
students themselves were unhappy and disoriented. They were
allowed only two showers a week; the girls couldn't wash their
hair every day; their rooms were poorly lit; the weather was
unbearably hot; the teachers at Linguaviva, the language school
that had contracted to locate host families and to teach the
students some Italian, were strict and unsympathetic. And so
on. Moreover, the program itself had no legal status because it
didn't own any property.

And Mama and I had our own housing problems. Our apartment, across the street from the back of the synagogue, was
roomy but unsatisfactory. The arrangement of the rooms made
no sense: there was no place to sit down comfortably. From the
picture window you could see the green dome of the synagogue
but not much else. The people below us were always angry
because our bathtub leaked into their apartment; the toilet
clogged. And worst of all, it was brand new. I think Mama
would have put up with all these inconveniences if only we'd
been living in a medieval tower or a fifteenth-century palazzo,
but in a brand-new building they were intolerable.

I had my troubles too, which added to Mama's. There was an
American school, but Mama said it was too far out of town and
too expensive. She'd already given me three hundred dollars in
cash, as a bribe, to get me to agree to go to an Italian school—

it had seemed like a good idea at the time—and I'd already spent the money, so there was nothing I could do about it, even when the principal at the Liceo Classico Dante informed us that the school's experience with foreigners who knew no Italian had been so bad that he was unwilling to admit me, even though I had all my school records with me, from kindergarten through ninth grade, translated into Italian and stamped with a raised seal from the Italian Consulate in Chicago.

I was studying Italian at Linguaviva, but I didn't seem to be getting anywhere. The classes were large, and the other students (mostly German and Scandinavian girls in their twenties) were loud and aggressive. I went to classes for a month, but I still couldn't speak Italian and I didn't seem to have a friend in the world.

By the end of the summer we had become regulars at the American Church. Mama would never have admitted it, but we needed help. It was an Episcopal church, and there was lots of kneeling on leather-covered steps that folded out of the pew in front of you like the steps of a kitchen stepstool. Mama was not a religious woman, but I think she was actually praying, which was scary. I don't know if her prayers were answered or not, but things suddenly took a dramatic turn for the better, just as if someone had heard us and sent a fairy godmother to see what could be done. A fairy godfather, actually. A man with the euphonious name of Bruno Bruni, whom we met at the church itself at the coffee hour after the service. Signor Bruni was a godsend. He introduced Mama to the principal of the Liceo Scientifico Morgagni, a warm welcoming woman who said she would be very happy to have me in her school, that it would be difficult at first, but that her experience with foreigners who didn't know the language had been extremely encouraging. He placated the inquisitive Questura and helped us find a more satisfactory apartment, in Borgo Pinti, not far from the Duomo, one that was ancient on the outside and quite convenient and charming inside. I could look out my window in the morning and down on a little fruit market. I took dozens of pictures of it but never got it quite right.

Later on Signor Bruni helped Mama organize the obligatory student trips to Rome and Venice, and he helped me with my lessons. I didn't start to speak until Christmas, but I learned by heart the principal mountains, rivers, cities, etc., of each province, which I could rattle off in front of the class when I was being "interrogated"—often eliciting enthusiastic applause from my classmates. The terror of those *interrogazioni* was so great that though I can't remember isolated facts, once I get started I can still run through long stretches of that useful information.

By Christmas it had become clear that the year would be a success. We were coasting downhill, time was speeding up, the program was going well; I had lots of friends, and I could talk. I couldn't stop, in fact. Talk, talk, talk. Papa came for a surprise visit in the spring and went on the student trip to Venice with us, and Signor Bruni couldn't go at the last minute, and I got lost and took the vaporetto all the way out to the Lido, and Papa found me, and that night in a fancy restaurant on the Rialto Mama kept saying that some women at another table were giving her dirty looks. We never stopped kidding her about that, Papa and I. Why would anybody be giving her dirty looks? But she never backed down.

*   *   *

It wasn't till I returned to Florence two years later, to finish the last year of the liceo with my former classmates, that I discovered what must have been obvious all along to a more sophisticated eye, that Mama and Bruno Bruni had been lovers. It was a chance remark by one of the teachers at Linguaviva, whom I met on the street, that set me thinking: about Signor Bruni's presence when I came home from school, about telephone conversations in the night, about fresh flowers, and a man's glove on the landing, a new dress, a haircut. These were the pieces of the puzzle. I tried on various emotions, but none of them seemed to fit. I worked up a little anger, which I vented in a letter that I never sent, a little indignation, a little melancholy (the pleasing kind I associated with Chopin). . . . To tell the truth, I was just a little bit thrilled.

One of the things that used to turn up when Mama and I got lost on our walks was the beautiful little cemetery just before you get to Settignano. We'd come out of the woods, or up over a little rise, or around a curve on whatever path we happened to be following, and there it would be, and we'd know where we were. The little village would be just up ahead with another Communist bar, another Casa del Popolo, where we'd stop for something to drink before taking the bus down to the city.

When I reached the cemetery I paused for a while, hugging myself against the cold. The cemetery is a level plot, a stairstep cut out of the hillside just below the road. Many of the gravestones boast pictures of the deceased in waterproof plastic ovals that glitter like eyes in the sunlight. Many sport little lights that burn perpetually (as long as the family pays the electric bill every three months).

Shortly before she died Mama made a tape for us, several tapes. She had some things she wanted to say, big things, little things. It was kind of a mystery. What could she possibly have to say that she hadn't said, or couldn't say to our faces? After all, we weren't one of those families that couldn't talk to each other or express our emotions. If anything, we were at the other end of the spectrum.

"I just want to be able to say things as they occur to me. I don't want to have to call you. So many things come to me during the day, and at night, too, especially at night. So many happy memories—some unhappy ones too—but mostly happy. I want you to have a record of that. So many things to say to each one of you, and all of you."

So Papa set up a tape recorder by the bed. An amateur musician, he had lots of recording equipment and made quite a production out of it.

"Why don't you just get me one of those little cassette recorders?" Mama asked, but Papa had to do things in a big way. He set up his two-track tape recorder next to the bed, on the table where Mama kept her medication. He bought two new low-impedance microphones and tried out every possible permutation of microphone locations and settings on the tape recorder. It was his way of working off some of his frustration.

"Testing. One, two, three, four, testing. Now *you* do it."

But Mama didn't want to do it. "I feel like I'm onstage; on

the radio." One mike was on a boom that swung over the bed. "I want this to be private."

"Testing. One, two, three, four, testing."

And the tape recorder would repeat: "Testing. One, two, three, four, testing."

The finishing touch was a remote punch-in/out switch that Mama could keep on the bed beside her so she wouldn't have to twist around to start and stop the recorder. All she had to do was punch a button.

"I've always wanted one of these anyway," Papa said. "That's how professionals correct their mistakes. If you've got a sour note, you just play along with the tape, and when you get to the sour note, you punch in and then out and it records right over it."

Once Papa had everything in place Mama felt better. She had an object in her life, what remained of it. A mission. Something to be accomplished. Something that could not have been accomplished under any other circumstances: the recording of a happy and productive and sometimes turbulent life under the pressure of death. Death was a lens that would reveal things as they really were: what was important would assume its true importance; what was unimportant would recede into the shadows.

Mama kept the tapes right on the bed. She didn't want us to listen to them while she was still alive. But during the long summer afternoons we could hear the tape recorder clicking on and off. Sometimes, when I got up to go to the bathroom in the middle of the night, I'd hear the familiar click and put my ear to her door, but I couldn't make out what she was saying, only the faint murmur of her weakened voice.

She filled up half a dozen seven-inch tapes. Seven hours. And when she'd said what she had to say, she stopped talking. A week later she died, and ever since her death the house had seemed strangely silent, even when Papa was playing his guitar and we were all singing.

It was over three years before we worked up the courage to listen to the tapes, which had been stored on a shelf in the dining room closet next to the Waterford crystal that we never used anymore. When I say "courage" I don't mean that we were afraid of what we might hear. I mean we were afraid we wouldn't be able to bear it, especially during the holidays. But we'd had a wonderful Christmas, and we were feeling strong. Papa, who was an avocado merchant on Chicago's South Water Market, had let the business slide after Mama's death and was working for someone else now, but he was in pretty good spirits. After a two-year apprenticeship with a binder in Hyde Park I'd found a job in the conservation department at the Newberry. Molly had moved to Ann Arbor; Meg had married and was expecting, and her husband, Dan, was just perfect. Handsome, romantic, practical, talented. Papa had been teaching him to play the blues harp, and he'd learned so quickly that they'd made a tape together—Papa on the guitar, Dan on the harp, Meg and Molly singing the blues songs that had embarrassed us as children, and that still embarrassed me:

> Mr. Jelly Roll Baker
> let me be your slave
> when Gabriel blows his trumpet
> you know I'd rise from my grave
> for some of your jelly

some of your good jelly roll
you know it's doin' me good
way down deep in my soul.

It was New Year's Day. Meg and Dan were going to drive back to Milwaukee that afternoon. Molly would be at home with Papa and me for another couple of days before going back to Ann Arbor. It just seemed like the right time, and I don't think anyone was surprised when Meg brought one of the tapes into the living room, holding it tight against her big swelling belly.

Papa got up and without a word began to thread the tape; Meg poked a couple sticks of kindling under the smoldering logs in the fireplace and then sat down next to Dan at the piano and filled up the silence with a chorus of "Fum Fum Fum," Mama's favorite carol: *A venti-cinq de desembre, fum fum fum.* Molly and I were sitting at opposite ends of the couch, the bottoms of our bare feet pressed together.

Papa switched on the tape recorder and there was a moment of silence so intense that the dogs, snoozing in front of the fire, perked up their ears. (If Mama had been there she'd have made them lie on their own rug under the piano.) Papa hurried across the room and into his chair.

I suppose we each brought different questions to that moment, even Dan, who had never met Mama, but who'd heard enough about her, and maybe we *were* in fact a little apprehensive. What was going to emerge as truly important? What was going to recede into the shadows?

I don't know what the others were thinking, but I was wondering about Signor Bruni. I'd never talked Signor Bruni over with anyone, not even Meg or Molly, and I was still curious because I couldn't fit him into the picture I had of our family. Papa and Mama had had plenty of differences, which they never bothered to conceal from us, but on the whole our family life was shaped by the love they felt for each other and expressed, physically, all the time. Neither one could walk by the other without a little pat on the backside, and they were always taking naps when they couldn't possibly have been tired. So where did Bruno Bruni fit into the picture? Was he one of those things that was going to assume its true importance? Or was he going to recede into the shadows? I don't know why it seemed so important, but it did.

We waited and then waited some more. Papa got out of his chair and made some adjustments. Still no sound. He ran the tape forward for a few seconds and tried again. Still nothing. The big reels turned in silence. Papa ran the tape forward again. Nothing. He turned it over and tried the other side. Still nothing. Meg got up and brought the rest of the tapes from the dining room closet. They were all clearly labeled: August 5–10, 1960. August 10–14, 1960. August 15–19, 1960. And so on. Papa tried one after another, but there was no sound.

I'd never seen Papa—or any adult, for that matter—really lose control before. It didn't happen all at once, but you could hear it coming. He spent the rest of the day at the tape recorder, trying this and then that. If you've ever hooked up a sophisticated stereo system you'll know that in cases like this there's usually some button that needs to be pushed, or a knob that needs to be turned, or a patch cord that's plugged into the

wron[...] [...]ut Papa exhausted all the
possi[...] sitting in the kitchen, could hear
him [...] Occasionally there was a blast of
sound [...] [...]ric [...] r tape, or turned on the tuner, but
he couldn't coax any [...] out of Mama's tapes, and finally he
cracked. He didn't break anything, he just started screaming—
shouting, swearing as loud as he could. And then he started to
cry, really cry, huge rattling sobs, as he stumbled up the stairs.

Meg and Dan left for Milwaukee about three o'clock. Dan had
to go back to work the next morning. Molly and I emptied the
dishwasher and filled it again and washed the dishes that
wouldn't fit in the second load. We put the turkey carcass in
the stockpot and covered it with water and turned it on to
simmer. Molly scrubbed down the butcher's table with bleach,
the way Mama used to do, while I put the spices back in alpha-
betical order. And then we took all the jars and lids out of the
closet in the butler's pantry and matched them up. It was like
trying to match up socks; there were a lot of odd jars and a lot
of odd lids left over.

Finally, when there was nothing more to be done, we went
upstairs. I'd never been afraid to approach my father before,
even when he was angry. But I was afraid now, afraid of what
we'd find. We tiptoed through Mama's study and pushed open
the bedroom door. Papa was lying facedown on the bed. The
late-afternoon sun, caught by the beveled edges of small win-
dowpanes, covered the bed with tiny rainbows. Papa's pale hair
—once carrot red—was flecked with light.

Papa always slept on his stomach and I thought he might be

asleep, but when Molly tiptoed aro up at her.

"Papa? Are you all right?"

I could see him shake his head:

He kept the register closed, and t droom was very cold. Molly turned back the comforter and crawled in next to Papa. I did the same on the other side. There were still two comforters on the bed. I pulled the second one over me, and we lay like that while the sun went down, watching the little rainbows gradually grow together and then fade away completely.

About four or five times a year Ann Landers prints a letter from someone advising readers to tell their loved ones that they love them—before it's too late. Whenever I read one of those letters I think of Mama and her tapes. But the analogy is imperfect; the moral is not the same. Mama *was* trying to tell us.

But then what *is* the moral?

Check *all* your equipment? Well, of course. The problem, it turned out, was with the new remote punch-in/out switch, which had been activating the tape recorder without engaging the recording heads. Papa hadn't used it in the three years since Mama's death, so he'd never discovered that it hadn't been working properly. He sent the tapes to the Ampex Laboratory in Schenectady, New York, to have them analyzed on the off chance that a weak signal had gotten through, but there was nothing to be recovered. The tapes were virginal.

So, by all means, check all your equipment. Yes. But that's a moral for the head, not the heart. What can I say about the heart?

I suppose the real question is, why does it matter so intensely? What could Mama have said that would have altered the course of our lives?

I think about this question a lot—not all the time, but often enough—without coming any closer to an answer. All I know is that my life is filled with little pockets of silence. When I put a record on the turntable, for example, there's a little interval—between the time the needle touches down on the record and the time the music actually starts—during which my heart refuses to beat. All I know is that between the rings of the telephone, between the touch of a button and the sound of the radio coming on, between the dimming of the lights at the cinema and the start of the film, between the lightning and the thunder, between the shout and the echo, between the lifting of a baton and the opening bars of a symphony, between the dropping of a stone and the plunk that comes back from the bottom of a well, between the ringing of the doorbell and the barking of the dogs I sometimes catch myself, involuntarily, listening for the sound of my mother's voice, still waiting for the tape to begin.

3

The Road Not Taken

It's two miles from Settignano down to the Villa I Tatti, Bernard Berenson's old home, which now belongs to Harvard University. I'd been to I Tatti only once, for my Harvard interview ten years earlier, when I'd come back to Florence by myself to do the last year of the liceo. I was interviewed by a kindly wrinkled old professor whose name I have forgotten but whose interviewing technique made a permanent impression on me.

"Don't be self-conscious," he said after a few preliminary remarks about what a fine thing I'd done by coming to Italy. "Just imitate the sounds I make." And opening his mouth he made a series of nasal mooing sounds, sort of like French.

I imitated him as best I could, but I couldn't help being self-conscious: *ni:r, rylɑ̃, o:z, ɛ:r, fœ:j, wistiti, widi:r, uv, ɛ̃, vjeji:r, ksistr, vwa, koɑ̃, kommɣe.* From French we went on to Spanish and then Portuguese, proceeding in the same fashion. The professor would make a meaningless sound, and I would imitate him.

"You'll do well in modern languages," he said at last. "Have you studied Latin?"

"Yes," I said.

"Greek?"

I shook my head, and he shook his head, obviously disappointed.

"Do so," he said, apparently assuming that his authority was sufficient, without other means of persuasion, to compel me to take up the study of Greek.

He seemed to like me, however, even though I hadn't studied Greek, and he went out of his way to impress upon me the seriousness of the occasion. I Tatti was a very important place, he said, almost as important as Harvard itself. He was going to recommend me very highly and would be very disappointed to learn that I had been accepted—on the strength of his recommendation—and had then chosen to pursue my studies at some other institution.

I thanked him and went back to the Pariolis, my host family, bewildered but suitably impressed. "Harvard," the professor had said, "was looking for students who were devoted to things of the mind," and I began to think of myself as someone devoted to those things. All of a sudden I had a vocation, a higher calling. I began to think of myself as an intellectual. I started going to the museums and wrote the essay for my application on Botticelli's *Primavera.* I started out with all the tourists who passed by and gawked for a minute or two without even realizing that the painting was profoundly allegorical, that the Venus of antiquity had become the Venus Humanitas, the incarnation of Ficino's doctrine of love, that the metamorphosis of Flora was a symbolic reenactment of the neo-Platonic idea of intellectual contemplation, and so on. All this information was readily available in the guidebooks that were sold outside the museum, but it was new to me and wonderfully esoteric; and it was much easier to write about Ficino's doctrine of love than to describe my own responses to the painting, which, I'm sorry to say, didn't really amount to much.

When Mama called to say I'd been accepted—the whole thing had been her idea from the beginning—she was ecstatic, and I was, too. Everyone had heard of Harvard and would nod appreciatively when Signora Parioli mentioned that I was going there. And I began to notice the name in newspapers and magazines. So and so from Harvard had done this or that. It was impossible not to feel lucky and special and important. I resolved to go to concerts and to spend even more time in the museums and galleries, and I drew up a list of important books that I was going to read, starting with Plato's *Republic* and Aristotle's *Nichomachean Ethics* (I'd already read Homer in my Italian class) and ending with William James's *The Varieties of Religious Experience*.

When Mama became ill, of course, all this ceased to matter. There was some talk about trying to defer my admission for a year, but that never came to anything, and Mama herself seemed quite confident that I would receive a superior education at Edgar Lee Masters, where she continued to teach art history till she became too ill to go on, and where the classes were small and where I would be taught by real professors, not graduate assistants acting as section leaders.

As nearly as I can remember no one in our family ever mentioned Harvard again, except to say something derogatory about it, but when we were cleaning out Mama's things after her death I discovered, in the back of her closet, a stack of old *Harvard* magazines. Thirteen, a baker's dozen, a year's subscription plus an incentive copy. She must have subscribed right after I'd been accepted, and then she hadn't been able to bring herself to throw them out. I didn't untie the twine with which she had tied them up. I just carried them out to the garbage and dumped them. But it was a long time before I could shake the feeling that Harvard Yard, which I'd never visited, was a magical place, a charmed circle in which all the good things of life were concentrated, as in an alembic; and that there was another *me* out there, a ghostly double who'd made love to Fabio Fabbriani on the beach in Sardegna, who'd gone to Harvard, who'd apprenticed with Roger Eglantine in London, who'd been profiled in a Dewar's ad, and who'd gone on to become the first woman to head the conservation department at the Library of Congress—a me who mattered to the world.

Which of us doesn't have a similar ghostly double wandering around somewhere out there in the big wide world? A self from whom we parted company long ago, at some unlikely crossroads? But do we ever encounter these ghostly selves? Do our worlds ever intersect? I can't believe it. The one is too impermeable, the other too fine, too subtle.

And yet something like that happened to me as I walked down the long drive, between rows of poplars, to I Tatti. I imagined a young woman running down the lane to meet me as if she'd been waiting for me. Under a raincoat that sparkled as if it had been made out of fish scales she was wearing a lemon yellow silk suit with a low-cut shawl collar. I recognized her at once: my second self, my ghostly double. She kissed both my cheeks and put her hands on my shoulders, sizing me up. "Look at you," she said. "You look like a gypsy, like a tinker. Here, let me fix your hair." She snapped the rubber band that held my ponytail, fluffed my hair and tied it back with a scarf as yellow as her suit, took a pair of sunglasses out of her handbag and shoved the temples into my hair so that the frames rested on top of my head. She made me take off my windbreaker, held it by the sleeves, twirled it over once and threw it over my shoulders, tucking the sleeves together in the front, like tucking in a pair of socks. "There," she seemed to say. "That's better. Let's go in now, *we* can talk later."

I Tatti was much as I remembered it from my interview with the kindly wrinkled old professor. The rooms were small and dark with low ceilings, more like a nineteenth-century American farmhouse than an Italian villa, and there was a card catalog like the ones in a library. But the rooms were full of people talking in a very unlibrarylike way—men in shirtsleeves talking seriously, smoking seriously, laughing and joking seriously, too. The atmosphere was one of suppressed excitement, and I had the feeling that I'd intruded into a special place where I wasn't supposed to be—the bridge of a ship during a storm, the cockpit of a plane that's just lost an engine, the command headquarters during a battle, the base camp for an assault on Mount Everest. Or perhaps just a cocktail party to which I hadn't been invited. But Margeaux—my ghostly double—was right at home.

The only other woman in the room turned out to be Mrs. Steckley, the director's wife, who put a tray of sandwiches into my hands and asked me to pass it around and then bring it back to the kitchen, which I did.

I was on my third tray of sandwiches when Margeaux took the tray from me and handed it to one of the graduate-student types I'd seen in the breakfast room at the pensione and told *him* to pass it around and then take it to the kitchen, which he did.

Margeaux was so at the center of everything, so consulted about everything, so admired by everyone that there was no chance to be alone with her. But I found myself waiting around on the periphery wondering if I was going to be given an assignment. I had, I think, been hoping for a line to stand in, a line leading to a window at which volunteers could sign up for active duty, but there was no line, no window, nothing to do but wait around the edges and listen, as I sometimes found myself doing at cocktail parties. The conversation was mostly personal, which was reassuring if not edifying—who'd been able to come and who hadn't, who was staying at I Tatti itself, who was staying in Fiesole, who'd been left to fend for himself.

About mid-afternoon the door marked "Private" opened and Professor Steckley himself appeared and spoke for half an hour about the challenge of coordinating the American relief efforts with those of the Italian government. When he had finished he smiled, spoke briefly to me, and then disappeared again. I hadn't been forgotten. In fact I'd been given an important assignment: I was going to translate for Professor Eugene Chapin, from the Houghton Library at Harvard, who was arriving from Boston that evening. It wasn't exactly what I'd been expecting, but it wasn't too bad: I was a sailor on the ship, a member of the crew, a soldier in the army, part of the support team, one of the boys. At the very least I was an invited guest at the party.

I spent the rest of the afternoon wandering around the city, trying to imagine what it had been like during the flood itself. In places the water in the narrow streets had been thirty feet high, traveling at forty miles per hour. It was incomprehensible. Many of the streets had been cleared, but in the low-lying Santa Croce quarter it was still impossible to walk without boots. Bulldozers were plowing their way through the worst debris, and everywhere I went shopkeepers were shoveling mud out into the streets, where it was picked up by trucks that dumped the mud back into the Arno. I thought at the time that this was pretty stupid, because it would only make the riverbed shallower. (The practice was stopped a few days later.)

Temporary generators provided what electricity there was, which wasn't much, and drinking water had to be brought in by truck. None of the bars or restaurants were open in the *centro,* except at the station.

I was seeing what I had come to see, and I was going to be a part of what I wanted to be a part of—a government car would be picking us up at the pensione in the morning—but I couldn't help contrasting myself with Margeaux: beautiful, confident, successful. I couldn't imagine Margeaux wandering around the city looking for an inexpensive pensione because she couldn't afford the Pensione Medici in Fiesole. I couldn't imagine Margeaux worrying about what impression she'd make on some V.I.P. from the Houghton Library, and I couldn't imagine Margeaux squatting to pee behind some bushes in the Piazza d'Azeglio, which is what I had to do because there was no place else to go except the station, which was too far away.

I located a couple of hotels that had managed to remain open, but they were having a hard time providing for the few guests that remained, stranded, since the flood, and they were not inexpensive. The only alternative to the Pensione Medici was to join the mud angels, the hundreds of students from all over Europe who were flocking to Florence to be part of the scene. And a very important part they turned out to be. They were the ones who put on gas masks and went down into the poisonous atmosphere of the basement of the Biblioteca Nazionale to remove the books and archival material (and they were the ones who stayed on, long after the big shots at I Tatti had left, to carry the stinking mud, one bucket at a time, out of the cellars of the shops and apartments in the center). Sleeping quarters had been set up for them in boxcars behind the station, and food was provided by the government. They built fires on the walkways between the tracks, they slept and fornicated on blankets and bedrolls when they weren't playing their guitars and singing.

I found this picture, sketched for me by a waiter in the station cafeteria, mildly depressing. I won't say it didn't appeal to me, but to tell you the truth, twenty-nine is just a little too old for that sort of thing. Somewhere along the way I'd lost something. I'd crossed the border into another country. My visa had been canceled. I couldn't go back. I only hoped I'd gained something, too.

Professor Chapin was a recognizable academic type—ragg sweater, sleeves pushed up to his elbows, leather patches on the jacket slung over his shoulder like Jack Kennedy's. I hadn't spotted him the night before because I'd been expecting a kindly wrinkled old guy like the professor who'd interviewed me for my Harvard application, and he hadn't spotted me . . . Well, I don't know why he hadn't spotted me. In any case we didn't get paired up until a car arrived for us in the morning—we were waiting in front of the pensione—and the driver called our names.

Chapin knew a little Italian, but not enough to keep up with the driver, who spoke rapidly, and the car was soon filled with male energy as the two of them, ignoring each other, competed for my attention, one in English, one in Italian. By the time we reached Prato, our first stop, I was feeling light headed. You've got to remember that I'm the sort of girl who's always been praised for her good sense of humor.

Chapin was an acquisitions librarian, not a conservator, and I gathered that he'd pulled some strings to get to Florence. To be perfectly honest, his conservation skills turned out to be about as good as his Italian: not very. But he was one of those men who can't admit that there's a single thing he can't do, as I discovered when we reached our first destination, a furniture warehouse on the outskirts of town.

Chapin surprised me by leaping out of the car, introducing himself to the first person we encountered, and asking to be taken immediately to the *principale,* to whom he introduced himself at greater length: a visitor from Harvard University, a representative of the Committee to Rescue Italian Art . . . here by the invitation of the Italian government . . . to offer his services . . . and so on. This speech, which he had evidently memorized, tripped off his tongue so quickly that the *principale,* and everyone else present, assuming that he spoke

Italian fluently, began to speak rapidly about the business at hand. At this point I had to take over, though I'm not sure Professor Chapin ever quite understood this. He certainly made the best use of the little Italian at his command, and as we toured the premises he had a way of looking everything over and pronouncing it *buono,* or *bene,* as if he were bestowing his blessing.

As it turned out, the student volunteers were interleaving books with the Italian equivalent of Saran Wrap.

"Buono. Bene." Chapin nodded his approval.

But plastic, of course, won't allow moisture to evaporate. What was needed was paper towels, or even toilet paper, to absorb the moisture. All the books that had been interleaved with plastic wrap would have to be redone or they would soon be sprouting whiskers of mold. "It's a good thing I've got you along," Chapin said, "to look after the technical details."

Everywhere we went Professor Chapin made his little speech and offered his blessings and left the "technical details" to me. At Pistoia, for example, the wet books were being dusted with talcum powder to speed up the drying. But paper is porous. Once talc dries on a page it is impossible to remove without washing the paper in clean water and scrubbing it off with a stiff brush, which can damage the fibers. At Siena disbound books were being washed in hot water, which will destroy the sizing. At the monastery of the Certosa loose pages were being washed in an alum-water solution to disinfect them, but alum will create an acid condition in paper that will cause more problems in the future. In Arezzo student volunteers were pressing vellum leaves between plates of glass where they would certainly have begun to mold in a few days. I showed them how to stretch the vellum in order to dehydrate it and allow it to contract under controlled tension.

The students, fortunately, accepted my advice cheerfully.

After ten days of Chapin's *"Buono, bene"* I was fed up, and the enormity of the task was beginning to get me down. What was needed was a better heat supply to speed up the drying. Everywhere we'd been the heat had come from literally hundreds of space heaters of every shape and size, spread out on warehouse floors, in museum lobbies, in the basements of train stations, anywhere space could be found. When I mentioned this to Matteo, our driver, he thought for a moment and then, his face lighting up, suggested that we apply to the Agenzia Coltivazione Tabacchi in Perugia, where his brother worked. The tobacco leaves, he said, were dried in huge ovens, big as barns. We were on our way to Arezzo at the time, but the matter seemed so urgent that I didn't want to put it off even one day, or to go through official channels.

The Agenzia is located just north of town. Professor Chapin introduced himself and asked to be taken to the *principale,* to whom he made his little speech: he was a visitor from Harvard University, a representative of the Committee to Rescue Italian Art, etc. The *principale* turned out to be most helpful. The drying barns could be made available at once and could be used till the middle of December, when the next crop was ready to be cured. Everything would be at our disposal. It was the least he could do. He only wished that he had thought of it himself. He offered us cigarettes, which we accepted. I gave mine to Matteo, who had wanted me to tell the boss what a good worker his brother was.

We were shown around the drying barns by a factor to whom I gave very explicit instructions about temperature and relative humidity. When we returned two days later several truckloads of books had already been placed on the great drying racks that rose up almost fifty feet, like giant Christmas trees. Everything had been done according to my instructions, but many of the books had begun to smell like ammonia. I told the factor that this was probably caused by bacteria in the paper and recommended that the relative humidity be increased to 80 percent for the first four hours of the drying period and then lowered to 15 percent for the next four days; I also recommended lowering the temperature of the ovens to thirty-seven degrees Celsius when the humidity was lowered. When we returned four days later the ammonia smell was gone. I suspected that the sizing on the paper had reacted to something in the contaminated floodwater, but there was no time for a proper analysis. The treatment had worked; that was enough, more than enough. It was in fact a very gratifying moment, and we congratulated ourselves and drank a glass of grappa in the office of the *principale*. The factor and Matteo, too.

"*Buono. Bene.*" For once Professor Chapin—"Jed"—was right. It was good, very good, and we were in high spirits. On the way back to Florence Matteo taught us an Italian song that had been popular in the United States for a while, involving the sounds of various musical instruments: trumpet, flute, trombone, saxophone, whistle. Professor Chapin—Jed—put his hand on my leg, just above my knee, and asked if I'd be angry if he asked me to go to bed with him.

* * *

Does every woman's heart pound like mine when she's propositioned, even when she sees it coming, as I had? I'd seen it
coming for a couple of days, but I was taken by surprise anyway.

We were coming into Florence, past the Certosa, which we
had visited only the day before. Professor Chapin still had his
hand on my leg, not moving, paralyzed, like a stone. Was *his*
heart pounding, too? I could feel tears rising to my eyes, like
water rising in a cup. I closed my eyes, and when I closed them
I saw a map of the United States, all the states different colors,
pastels, and Illinois, my state, in light green, and I wondered if
it was green on all the maps or just on this one. I could almost
see our house on the map, Papa in the driveway in a new forest
green Cadillac, and me on the swing in the backyard, waiting
for him, swinging higher and higher while he unloads the
trunk of the car, pretending not to notice me, looking every
which way as he removes from the car a basket of tomatoes
from the market and a flat of avocados, and finally spearing me
with his gaze. I was thinking, No man will ever love me as
much as Papa does, and I was crying not because I was angry or
would be angry, but because I wasn't or wouldn't be.

Margeaux was waiting for us in the lobby of the pensione when
we got back to Fiesole. We left Jed standing in front of the
pensione, waiting for an answer, and went directly to my room.
Margeaux looked *très élégante* in a simple sheath dress that

pulled up over her knees when she sat down on the edge of the bed; I, of course, looked frazzled.

I told her, my ghostly double, the whole story from beginning to end. *She* made the comments I usually avoided making.

"He's not a bad person," I began, "but he doesn't know what he's doing."

She dismissed this observation with a wave of her hand. "He's all Harvard," she said. "Lowell House, double *summa* in history and poli sci, M.A. in history, Ph.D. in library science. He doesn't need to know what he's doing."

"Oh, come off it. He spent three years at the University of Minnesota after he got his degree, and the way he talks about it you'd think he'd been in prison."

"Old money," she said. "Family's filthy, lives in Ipswich. He felt lost so far from home base."

"I know all about it. I know his whole life story."

"You're frightened, aren't you." It was a statement, not a question.

"Why should I be frightened?"

"He's a man, he wants you."

"Nonsense. I'm a little upset, that's all, but I'm certainly not frightened."

"What are you going to tell him at dinner?"

"Tell him? I don't see why I should tell him anything."

"Once he's popped the question," she said, "you've got to say yes or no."

"Oh, that."

"Yes, that."

"Maybe I won't go down for dinner. I can't afford it anyway.

I thought I'd be able to stay till Christmas, but now I'll be lucky to make it to Thanksgiving."

"That's tomorrow."

"Thanksgiving's tomorrow? You're kidding!"

She looked at her watch. "Thursday, November twenty-fourth."

"Papa will be baking pies tonight," I said.

"Don't change the subject," she said, "and don't try to wriggle out of it. You don't want to do anything foolish."

The telephone rang and I answered it. It was Jed.

"You haven't answered my question," he said.

I covered the phone with my hand.

"Tell him you wouldn't be angry," Margeaux whispered. "You wouldn't, would you? I mean, you wouldn't be *an*gry, would you?"

"No," I said into the receiver, "I wouldn't be *an*gry."

"Good," he said. "Don't say anything more. I'll see you at dinner." He hung up.

"Well," said Margeaux when I put the receiver down, "that settles that."

"That doesn't settle anything," I said. "I said I wouldn't be *an*gry, that's all. I'm *not an*gry."

"But you're not pleased?"

"Certainly not."

"You've done this before, haven't you?"

"Of course."

"You don't act like it. You're as nervous as a racehorse. Come and sit down."

"I don't feel like sitting down." I opened the wardrobe to look for something to wear down to supper.

"Have you done it a lot?"

"Enough."

"Have you stopped counting yet?"

"Yes. I mean no."

"Yes you have stopped counting or no you haven't?"

"No."

"How many times?"

"Oh, a dozen or so."

"Exactly."

"Seven."

"Twenty-nine years old and you've only been laid seven times? That's not even once a year since you turned twenty-one."

"It's not quantity that counts."

"Did you come?"

"With a man?"

"Of course."

"No."

"By yourself?"

"Why are you trying to humiliate me?"

"I'm not trying to humiliate you, I'm trying to get you to face facts. Remember how Papa always used to say 'face facts'? Look at you, twenty-nine years old and still living at home with Papa. You've got a job that pays peanuts. No prospects; nothing coming up. And now you've got a nibble. So why not give it a whirl? Here," she went on, "give me that skirt. It's too bulky. Leave tweed skirts to the English." She started to go through my suitcase. "Look at these clothes! How could you *not* pack something more appropriate? You might have anticipated something like this." She tried the other side of the suitcase.

"Ah! Here's something." She held up a pair of red bikini panties. "You must have had something in mind when you packed
these. Right?"

"I don't know. I wasn't really thinking about it."

"Come off it. You might as well be honest with *me*. Do me a
favor and put these on."

I took off my jeans and underpants and put on the red panties. Margeaux removed my blouse and bra and looked me over.
"You've still got the beauty of youth," she said.

"The beauty of youth?"

"Tight skin, pleasant features, flat tummy, firm fanny, good
health. But you haven't got much time left. Now why don't
you take a nice hot bath. Pamper yourself. This is Italy."

I went down to dinner in my red panties, a pair of tight jeans,
and a man's shirt, one of Papa's. No bra. Dinner was served
family style: *penne* with a simple tomato sauce, pork chops,
green beans, mixed salad, fruit, red wine. The guests were
mostly American conservationists, experts of every sort—on oil
paintings, frescoes, furniture, old wood, marble—and everyone
talked shop. Jed and I were the only book people, though I
knew my boss from the Newberry was in town.

I was too agitated to enjoy the meal. I filled up on pasta and
gave my pork chop to Jed, who was very attentive. He was an
attractive man and talked easily, telling amusing stories about
famous acquisitions, and even more amusing ones about acquisitions that had gotten away, like the Boswell Papers. His boss
had actually seen the crates—tea chests—on the dock in Boston, on their way to Yale.

My apprehension was turning to excitement. I felt I'd never quite gotten the hang of sex. Certainly it had never been what I'd expected in those early days with Fabio in Sardegna. It had been, in fact, pretty rough and tumble. More rough than tumble. Young men in a hurry, young men with more important things on their minds: the revolution, closing down the University of Chicago, SNCC. They were intense, like little Fidel Castros. I was thinking, on the way up to the room, that this might be different. (Jed had assumed that not being angry was the same as yes, and I guess it was.)

One thing I hadn't counted on was Margeaux. *She* had turned the lights down low; *she*'d turned the bed down; and *she*'d left a vase of flowers and a split of spumante, iced, on the table next to the bed, and two glasses; and *she*'d opened the curtains to give us a view. The lights—the electricity was back on in many parts of the city—were romantic, and we looked at them as we drank the spumante, and then Jed put his arms around me and kissed me. It wasn't till we'd finished the preliminaries and gotten right down to business that I realized that *she* was still in the room, curled up in a chair in a dark corner. I waved at her, a kind of sideways swiping to tell her to get the hell out, but she just smiled and came up to the foot of the bed. "Lift your knees up." She mouthed the words silently. "Wiggle your bottom more." I did as she said, and she made a circle with her thumb and forefinger. Perfect. But it seemed to me that number eight wasn't much different from numbers one through seven. It seemed to me that Jed had taken off on a journey all by himself, and that no matter how much I wiggled my bottom, no matter how high I kicked my feet in the air, no matter how tight I squeezed, he was leaving me behind.

Still, it was nice to hold a man in my arms, and I was relieved, when it was over, that I'd gotten through it without
disgracing myself, and Jed seemed pretty pleased with himself.
At least he strutted up and down with the condom dangling
from his thing, a load of sperm to be flushed down the toilet
before he pulled on his underpants, which I noticed now for the
first time. They weren't just any old underpants, they were
boxer shorts with the Harvard emblem stamped all over them,
a little shield with an open book on it and the Harvard motto
written across the pages of the book: VERITAS. Truth. The
moment of truth had come and gone, but was I any the wiser?

"Well," said Margeaux after he'd gone. "That wasn't so bad,
was it?"

"No, it wasn't so bad. It was nice in a way, but I didn't
really feel anything."

"Don't worry about it. You showed him a good time. He'll
be eating out of your hand. He's taking you out for Thanksgiving dinner tomorrow. What more do you want?"

"When I was with Fabio I had intimations of something
different."

"You had 'intimations.' That's a nice word. Now go to sleep.
I'll see you in the morning."

The next day was Thanksgiving. In the morning there was a
meeting at the Uffizi at which Jed had to report on the various
book-treatment operations we had visited. In the afternoon we
were going to walk up to the Piazzale Michelangelo and have

Thanksgiving dinner together at a fancy restaurant someone had recommended. After dinner we were going to take the bus to Settignano, have a drink at the Casa del Popolo, and walk back to the pensione. Jed said that there was plenty of money around and that I shouldn't worry, he'd talk to Steckley. But then Professor Steckley invited Jed, along with all the other visiting American curators, to Thanksgiving dinner at I Tatti. What made me mad wasn't that Jed felt he had to go, it was that it never occurred to him that there was any reason not to go—that a date with me was no impediment. He gave me a wink and a squeeze. "See you tonight," he said, giving the "you" two syllables and leaning on "night." His broad back offered an inviting target for a woman with a gun, but unfortunately I didn't have one.

There's an Italian expression, not an expression, really, just a way of saying something, a useful phrase, probably universal: *Non vale la pena,* "It's not worth the trouble." But in Italian if you get the gender wrong and say *Non vale il pene,* you're in trouble. "It's not worth the penis" is what you're saying. During my first year at the Liceo Morgagni, when I was still struggling with the language, I used to throw that phrase around recklessly. "Better check with Signor Cipriani to see if the exam's going to be on Monday or Wednesday." *Non vale il pene.* "You want me to pick up some paper for you at the *cartoleria?*" *Non vale il pene.* I never quite understood the violent reactions I got, but it didn't matter. I was speaking Italian; I'd broken out of the prison of English. Finally Signor Cipriani, the English teacher, took me aside and set me straight, but by that time the phrase had become fixed in my head, or in my tongue, just like the fingering of a difficult passage on the piano. It wasn't easy to change. I always had to stop and think: Not *il pene* but *la pena*.

But you know, sometimes I think it doesn't make much difference, and sometimes I think my way is better. Every woman will know what I mean. It's an expression she ought to add to her vocabulary for occasions like this one: *Non vale il pene.*

> Two roads diverged in a yellow wood,
> And sorry I could not travel both
> And be one traveler, long I stood
> And looked down one as far as I could
> To where it bent in the undergrowth;
>
> Then took the other . . . ,
> . . . .

Where was Margeaux, my second self, the traveler who'd followed the road not taken? *She* was climbing into one of the limousines with Jed, bending over provocatively, waiting for him to pat her fanny. And suddenly I realized something I should have known all along:

> I shall be telling this with a sigh
> Somewhere ages and ages hence:
> Two roads diverged in a wood, and I—
> I took the one less traveled by,
> And that has made all the difference.

Mama always maintained that anyone who'd heard Frost read "The Road Not Taken," as she had, would know that the last line was ironic, a joke, but I'd never understood what she meant till now. There is no "road not taken," there's only this road. The road not taken is a fantasy. My mysterious double had never made love to Fabio Fabbriani on the beach in Sardegna; she'd never gone to Harvard; she'd never been near the Library of Congress; she'd never been profiled in a Dewar's ad: "Latest accomplishment: restoring the Book of Kells." She'd been right by my side all the time, filling my ear with might-have-beens and if-onlys, encouraging me to feel sorry for myself. And look where it had landed me. In bed with—I didn't want to think about it. A man who wore Harvard underpants.

So when I saw the limousine drive off down the Lungarno I was glad. Glad to be rid of her.

I say I was glad. But it was hard, too. She was my oldest friend, my closest companion. She knew me better than anyone else, better than I knew myself.

4

Un uomo mediterraneo

Standing on the steps of the Loggia dell'Orcagna, his back to
Benvenuto Cellini's *Perseus and Medusa,* Dottor Alessandro Postiglione surveys the piazza with a proprietorial air, as if the
workmen scrubbing the gray stones—caked with mud like the
hide of some immense pachyderm—were employees on his own
estate, as if the boy walking a German shepherd were his own
son or even himself, and the dog his own dog, his childhood
friend Ovid. "Sit! Stay! Heel!" the boy shouts, as if the dog
were hard of hearing. The dog jumps up and puts its muddy
paws on the boy's shoulders and licks the side of his face. The
dottore can almost feel the rough tongue on his own smooth
cheek.

Dottor Postiglione is one of those Italian men in their fifties
who only become more handsome as they lose their hair, and
for this reason, though he is aware that his vital powers are
slightly diminished—but only slightly—and though he visits a
barber in the Via Cavour once a week, he does not spend any
money on the hair tonics advertised in the back pages of *Domen-*

ica and *Panorama,* guaranteed to revitalize the scalp and the hair follicles.

Something of a rogue scholar, something of a ne'er-do-well artist, a good tavern companion, a corrupter of youth, a charming rascal (always late for appointments) who must be forgiven if he promises you the moon but delivers only a sliver of Parmesan cheese, he is a man sympathetic toward his own shortcomings, and toward the shortcomings of others. He is an older type: a lover of beauty and of nature, Mediterranean man, an endangered species. There is no place for him in the modern world. In the United States the type never existed; in England it has been deliberately exterminated; in France, where to live is to have your papers in order, it is almost extinct. In Spain? The Spanish are too serious. In Greece? Yes, and in Egypt. But the Greeks and Arabs are a perversion of the type, gross caricatures. Italy is the true home of *uomo mediterraneo,* but even in Italy the pace has become too swift. Even in Italy business demands punctuality. Go to Milan—you might as well be in Switzerland. Specimens like Dottor Postiglione live on, curious relics of an earlier age, like crocodiles or tourist attractions.

But this is to speak of the inner man. Externally the *dottore* is a perfectly ordinary citizen, as respectable as the man who stamped your visitor's permit at the Questura or the priest who blessed you when you sneezed in the Brancacci Chapel. Not *un medico,* not, as his wife—who now lives in Rome—liked to say, the sort of doctor who can do you any good, but a *dottore* of arts and letters and philosophy, a distinguished civil servant, the head restorer of works of fine art in the province of Tuscany.

* * *

79

At eleven o'clock in the morning it's already too late to go the Limonaia, which has been turned into a giant conservation center for flood-damaged paintings, and still too early, he thinks, to go to the Palazzo Davanzati, where temporary conservation headquarters have been set up. The coldness and grayness of the morning does not prevent Dottor Postiglione from enjoying the aftereffects of the unaccustomed physical exertion of the past three weeks. Muscles he hasn't used in years twitch minutely, as if a friendly dog or a cat were batting him with its tail.

At the meeting with the Americans and the British and the Germans in the directors' room of the Uffizi various reports had been given: this was being done, that was being done. These moneys had arrived, those had been spent. What was needed was more money. Everyone had been very animated. And now Professor Steckley is making his way through the small herd of Americans standing outside the door of the Uffizi, separating, like a skillful sheepdog, those who have been invited to Thanksgiving dinner at I Tatti from those who have not. A nod here, a handshake there, an averted glance. The sheep and the goats. Dottor Postiglione comes from the Abruzzi and knows enough about sheep to appreciate Steckley's skill, though he has himself declined an invitation.

The chosen are herded into waiting cars. Those who are left behind gather into small knots, stand talking, shoulders hunched, before going off in different directions. Only a few stragglers remain, one of whom is the girl he had spoken to two weeks earlier on the night of the flat tire, as he was returning from an assignation. He'd thought she was French, but now she turns out to be American.

He can't understand American men. How is it that this

woman has been left behind? What are these men thinking of? What do they have on their minds? Is it a failure of the imagination? An interesting possibility, actually. Take the clever chap who'd enlisted the assistance of the tobacco factory for the drying of books, and who must, therefore, have *some* imagination. She'd come in with him and had sat next to him at the table, translating for him when someone spoke in Italian, whispering in his ear, leaning over so confidentially that he (Dottor Postiglione) had been unable to catch her eye. He watches her start down toward the Arno and then double back toward the piazza, where the German shepherd has broken loose. The boy shouts angrily, but the dog pretends not to hear. The girl stops to watch. Dottor Postiglione watches her watching. She steps down, then back up again, watching intensely, as if she's looking for something that will help her make up her mind. A priest walks by, ducking and bobbing his head. He too stops to watch, still ducking and bobbing his head even when he's standing still.

"Vieni, vieni, vieni." Come here to me. The dog, dragging his leash, slides on the mud as he reverses directions. He tears all the way to the other end of the piazza and then tears back, stopping to lift a leg at the rusticated facade of the Palazzo del Ingresso, and to frighten a woman pushing a stroller, sniffing at her crotch, licking her baby's face. The boy runs after him, but the dog moves on easily, swinging his body like a tiger, looking back now and then but careful to avoid eye contact with the boy, who shouts and shouts, "Down, down, down! Down, Roi. Down, Roi!"

Suddenly the girl is shouting too: "Roi! Roi, Roi, Roi! Down, Roi! *Stai bravo!*" Startled by this new development, the dog stands and looks at her, then slowly lowers himself, first his back half and then his front, and waits while the boy comes up to him, grabs his collar, starts to scold, and then bends down and puts his arms around his neck and covers the long, narrow head with kisses. He picks up the muddy leash and, before departing, turns to the girl and blows her a kiss too.

Dottor Postiglione stands still while she walks by him. He can see that she is crying, not hard, but her eyes are watery. "Excuse me—" he says in English but before he can finish his sentence she jerks her whole body around, giving him a wide berth, as if he were one of those southern types who expose themselves to young women right on the street.

"Leave me alone," she snaps in clear, crisp Italian. "You're wasting your time." She enunciates each word, as if she were speaking to a foreigner—*Non mi scocciare!*—leaving him in the embarrassing position of having to ask to be forgiven. But what has he done?

She glances to the right and to the left, where a Roman soldier by Giambologna, attired in a sort of thong that exposes the buttocks entirely, hoists a struggling Sabine woman. The Sabine woman wears nothing at all.

A little sigh escapes him involuntarily. "Forgive me," he repeats, "for intruding. But perhaps you don't recognize me without my umbrella?"

She stops, turns, looks him over with gray-green eyes.

"You're the man with the umbrella. The mysterious stranger."

"*Ecce!*" He bows slightly. "*Arrêtez cet homme. Il a volé mon parapluie.*"

She doesn't smile. There is an invisible barrier between

them. But Dottor Postiglione, who is as familiar with these invisible barriers as a locksmith is with locks, smiles. Not a deceptive smile masking ulterior motives, but a genuine expression of his sense of well-being, his pleasure in the present moment.

"You have a way with dogs," he says, still in English, which he speaks with a slight British accent. "I was very impressed."

"Yes, I have a German shepherd," she replies in Italian. "He reminded me of my dog."

"A wonderful breed. We always had shepherds. My favorite was named Ovid, after the poet."

She says nothing, and he feels the need to explain. "Ovid— the poet, not the dog—was born in Sulmona. He was a Paligno, one of the mountain people, very independent. They're the ones who come down to the cities to play their bagpipes just before Christmas."

"Why are you telling me these things?" She continues to speak Italian.

"Because," he says in English, "Sulmona is my home, too. It's poor but very beautiful." His home is not, in fact, Sulmona but Montemuro. But it's close enough—why split hairs?—and besides, who's ever heard of Montemuro, which is a mountain village the size of a small neighborhood with one of most things and none of some things: one delicatessen, one dairy, one bakery, and so on. One bar. One restaurant. One *cartoleria,* now owned by his brother. If he had a picture, he would show her: the steep hillsides, the naked peaks above the timberline, the converted olive oil factory in which his parents still live with his sister, a widow, and her children, and a cat and tame pigeons and two dogs; the *cartoleria* with its reams of different papers, its mechanical pencils and ballpoint pens and drawing instruments and school supplies.

"I can't produce blue-blooded ancestors to impress you," he says, quoting Ovid. "My father's plain middle class."

Her silence is thoughtful rather than hostile, but like a driver who's gone off the road onto the shoulder, he gives the steering wheel a little jerk.

"And what do you call *your* dog?"

"*Si chiama Bruno.*"

"Bruno? An Italian German shepherd, how wonderful."

"*Sì*," she says. "*È molto intelligente.* He can open the fence gates, so we have to keep them locked. And he's learned to open the porch door *from the outside,* so he can come and go as he pleases. We have a husky, too, my father's dog."

It soon becomes clear that she is as determined to speak Italian as he is to speak English. More determined. He can feel not only the strength of her will, but its shape as well, like someone—an attractive someone—shoving past him in a crowded bus. If he resists her it is not to prevent her from getting past him but simply to feel her shoving.

"*Arrêtez cet homme,*" he repeats, giving the conversational wheel another little correction. "*Il a volé mon parapluie.*" And modulating through French to Italian, he surrenders graciously: "*Che cosa . . .* What on earth prompted you to say such thing? I haven't been able to get it out of my mind." There is in this surrender nothing humiliating. It's a distinctly pleasant moment, as if the sun were about to emerge from behind a cloud and illuminate the piazza, as it often does, even in winter, in Florence.

"It's a long story," she says, smiling.

The invisible barrier having been removed, he ventures the familiar form: *"Ti va un caffè?"*

"Perché no?"

Their first cup of coffee is strong and sweet, like a handshake or a promise.

She's very funny, he thinks, and full of surprises, and Dottor Postiglione is not a man easily surprised by young women: *"Arrêtez cet homme. Il a volé mon parapluie."* The phrase rises to his lips again, bringing a smile with it.

"It's a phrase from my French grammar," she explains. "It was the only thing I could think of when you spoke to me in French. I've found that it's very useful."

"How so?"

She tells him a story about a train, and some American women, and a wonderful dinner.

"Remarkable. I've never cared for the French myself, but they do eat well, there's no point in denying it."

There is a lull in the conversation, and the *dottore* orders two more coffees.

"So, you've come to Italia in our hour of need."

"Yes. I'm a book conservator. I thought I might be able to do something useful."

"And you've found satisfactory accommodations?"

"Not exactly. In fact I'll probably have to leave soon. The pensione I'm in is too expensive, and I have nowhere else to go. I have friends, but I don't know how to contact them. Besides, it's been a long time."

"Surely your colleagues will accommodate you. I Tatti has plenty of money."

She shrugs.

"What about that clever fellow you were translating for? Only an American would have thought of drying books in the tobacco barns. Surely he has some influence."

He can see from her reaction that something has passed between them.

She touches her cheekbone with the tip of her finger and pulls down gently, exposing the white of her eye: "He's not half as clever as he makes himself out to be. He doesn't know a thing about book conservation, to begin with, and the idea to use the tobacco barns was the driver's, not his. The driver ought to get the credit."

Dottor Postiglione adds sugar to his coffee and stirs. "That's something that ought to be rectified."

She shrugs her shoulders again: *"Non vale il pene."*

In any relationship there are decisive moments, often apparently inconsequential but which in reality determine the future, just as a rock or a fallen tree up in the mountains may determine the course of a stream. This is, in its way, such a moment. She blushes; not a gradual flushing of the face and neck, but a violent rush of pigment, as if someone had thrown a bucket of cinnabar red in her face, enough for a large canvas by Titian. Dottor Postiglione has witnessed many blushes, but none of this magnitude. He looks away, down at his coffee, out the window at a troop of schoolboys following a priest across the piazza. He can't help but smile at this little surprise, this *lapsus linguae* in one so proud of her Italian, a gaping hole in her linguistic armor. She has surprised him again, and for the first time in years he is at a loss for words, as if he were one of the schoolboys approaching the café.

"Giacomo," he calls to the waiter, *"due caffè, per favore."*

Giacomo, who has been listening, smiles as he fills the espresso holder. The entire bar is silent. An old man rattles a copy of *La Nazione,* which has been printed in Bologna since the flood. A young man holds six small cups on a tray, motionless, waiting for change.

"*Magari,* Signorina, it's a mistake anyone could make, believe me."

"It's not the first time," she says, pushing away the fresh cup of coffee that Giacomo has placed in front of her. "And probably won't be the last. But I can't drink any more coffee. Really, this is my third cup."

"I thought it might help."

"I know what you mean. It's something I used to say when I first came to Italy. It always had quite an effect on people."

"Yes," he says, "understandably. There's a famous story about an Englishman who once asked for marmalade with contraceptives."

Once the stream of conversation has been diverted to this dry bed, it begins to flow unimpeded.

She looks out the window at the troop of schoolboys. "Why do Italian men touch themselves so often?"

"Touch themselves?" Dottor Postiglione holds his cup at his lips. "What do you mean?"

"Touch themselves. You know."

"*Sciocchezza!* I don't know what you're talking about."

"You do too. Look at those schoolboys."

The schoolboys, all in uniform, are heading toward the bar, shepherded by the priest who is holding up his long cassock to keep it from dragging in the mud. Like tourists in the habit of touching their billfolds, the boys seem to make periodic checks of their male organs.

"Che bestialità!" Postiglione is discomfited.

"Even the priest. Look."

"He's just adjusting his cassock."

"That's what I mean. And you, too. I've noticed."

"Madonna! It's from sitting at a table with a beautiful woman. A man has to make certain adjustments, it's true. But tell me something. Where did you learn to talk like this?"

"From my mother."

"How interesting. Tell me about your mother."

"She loved everything Italian."

"Did she come to Italy?"

"Yes. She came by herself one summer, and we then spent a year here together when I was fifteen. She was the director of a program for American students."

"And that's how you learned Italian?"

"Yes. I went to the Liceo Morgagni, and then I came back to do the *ultimo anno* with my class."

"And your father? He didn't object? To your mother's coming, I mean."

"No. I don't think he was very happy about it, but he didn't object."

"What do you suppose your mother was looking for?"

"I've never been sure. Fatal charm, I suppose.

"Carisma fatale? How wonderful. Yes, I suppose Italy has always been a refuge for Anglo-Saxons. You come to taste the sweet life, to swim in the nude, to drink the wine, to live close to nature, to experiment. Everything is permitted. Love is no sin."

"Yes." She seems to be on the edge of saying more, but the troop of schoolboys bursts into the bar, calling for coffee and hot chocolate.

"Have you studied English?" Dottor Postiglione inquires of one of the boys. (All Italian schoolchildren study either English or French.)

"*Sì, sì.* 'An Italian friend is looking for a good restaurant where they prepare typical food.' "

Others join in with phrases from their schoolbooks: "At this restaurant they prepare good hamburgers and excellent beef-steaks." "At the white restaurant with the red door the prices are very reasonable."

"Boys, boys," the priest calls after them. "Don't bother the patrons with your nonsense."

"No trouble at all, Padre," says the *dottore*. "My friend is an *americana*. She's here to help with the books that have been damaged."

"In that case," says the priest, "we should give her a song, a typical American song. What do you say, boys? How about 'Home on the Range'?"

The boys crowd around the *americana* and after several false starts manage to get through the first verse and two choruses of "Home on the Range":

'ome, 'ome on the range
Where the deer and the antelope play
Where seldom is 'eard
A discouraging word
And the skies are not cloudy all day.

The *americana* applauds enthusiastically.

"Just like home?" Dottor Postiglione asks her.

"Just like home," she says.

I've never been superstitious, but my heart sank when Dottor Postiglione suggested that I look for a position at the Carmelite convent in the Piazza San Pier Maggiore, at the end of Borgo Pinti, not far from the apartment that Mama and I had lived in.

"The abbess is my cousin, and I happen to know that they will need help with their precious library. I can't imagine that they managed to remove the books in time."

Surely, I thought, the need for conservators in Florence was great enough that I wouldn't be reduced to living in a convent, something I could imagine only as a last resort. Look at the good work we'd accomplished already. The disasters averted at Prato and Pistoia, the thousands of books being dried in the tobacco barns in Perugia, and now in Arezzo too. And yet, although I was determined not to spend another day with Professor Eugene Chapin how could I go back to I Tatti and ask for another assignment? What would I say? How would I explain?

"But I'm not at all religious," I said. "I haven't been to church since . . . I can't remember. And then it was a Protestant church. Surely they wouldn't want someone like me around."

"Of course, of course. But my cousin is a remarkable woman, a woman with a late vocation. A woman with a gift for business, very successful in the world, lots of money. Very beautiful, too. I couldn't have been more surprised when she decided to become a nun. I think you would find it very interesting. I'll arrange everything, but it will take two or three days. Do you have enough money to last that long?"

Without waiting for an answer he took out a pair of glasses, put them on, and wrote something on the back of a business card, like a doctor writing out a prescription.

"Call me at this number in two days."

"But what would I wear?"

"What would you wear?" He laughed. "What does it matter? It's not a salon or a fashion show, or a fancy restaurant."

Translation: There aren't any men around.

"I mean, would I have to wear a habit? And a . . . , a . . . , a . . . , how do you say . . . ?" I was looking for the word for *wimple,* which I tried to describe with my hands.

"Un soggolo," he said, smiling to express his satisfaction.

I noticed that Dottor Postiglione himself was impeccably dressed. Nothing flashy, no pointy shoes that Italian men are so fond of, but everything handsome. A silk tie. Starched collar. Topcoat over his shoulder like a cape. Gold ring. Gold watch. All sparkling. He looked perfectly fresh and comfortable in the uncomfortable bar chair. He knew just how to sit in it.

"There are some remarkable frescoes, too, that are going to need attention. I've offered to look at them myself in the past, but of course no men are allowed."

"What are they?"

"No one really knows anything about them except that they were painted by a woman, Lucia de' Medici. Lucia practically bankrolled the convent in the seventeenth century. She was a remarkable woman too. But I don't know anyone except my cousin who has actually seen the frescoes, and she's not very communicative on the subject."

"Do you talk to her often?"

"Not often. Two or three times a year, since she's become the abbess. Before that, almost never. It's a contemplative order, you know. They don't have the sisters scurrying all over the city like the Franciscans. And they have no telephone. You have to write in advance and make arrangements, and then you speak through a grille. It can be quite disconcerting."

I was still searching for (and suggesting) possible alternatives when Dottor Postiglione asked Giacomo for the time, though he had a watch on his wrist, and rose to leave.

"Maybe I could find something in the Archivio di Stato."

"Signorina, you know I will do what I can to help you, but nothing is easy, and I may not be able to arrange it in any case, unless you wish to become an *angelo di fango* and sleep in a boxcar behind the railroad station. If you had money or if I had money"—he smiled—"or if you could stay with some of your friends . . . then it would be easy. But without money nothing is easy. *Coraggio.*"

"I'm sorry," I said. "I didn't mean to seem ungrateful." After all, he was under no obligation to help me. What bothered me, I think, was the feeling that once again I had ventured out into the world of men, the rough-and-tumble world of adult sexuality, only to fail, to be found wanting, inadequate. And now I was being sent away to a safe place where I wouldn't hurt myself or make a nuisance of myself.

Jed came to my room again that night, about nine o'clock. He'd been drinking and had a bottle of scotch with him but was still coherent. And horny. He sat down on the edge of the bed and pried his shoes off without untying them, and then he poured some scotch into a used water glass on the table next to the bed.

"You'll ruin your shoes that way," I said.

It wasn't too late to change my mind. Actually I hadn't even made up my mind, hadn't burned any bridges. In fact, the sound of music and laughter in the lounge had been tempting me to go downstairs, where there would be dancing and word games, at which I always did well. Nothing irrevocable had been done, I told myself, but I felt unclean, used, and the body sitting on the bed undressing itself seemed particularly repulsive, like a large, smelly sack of garbage that had somehow come alive.

He swallowed some scotch and handed the glass to me. "Have a real drink," he said.

What was I afraid of? Poverty? Chastity? Obedience? Not really. It was boredom that terrified me. There were too many blank spaces in my image of convent life. I couldn't fill them in. I was like the girls who used to come for a sleepover when I was a teenager and panicked when they learned we didn't have a TV. All of a sudden the evening stretched out before them like an uninhabited desert.

Not having a TV was Mama's idea. She was scornful of people who didn't have sufficient inner resources to get through an evening without a TV to distract them, to fill their heads with junk. But by inner resources she meant the ability to amuse oneself by reading a book or writing a letter, or playing the piano or the guitar, or making something, or drawing a picture or doing a puzzle. She didn't mean meditation or praying or saying the rosary, or whatever nuns do to fill up the day. And the night. It was simply beyond my comprehension. Dottor Postiglione had said it was a contemplative order. So much the worse. What did they contemplate? I had read, in my Italian class, Dante's *Paradiso,* and our teacher, Professor Martelli, had tried to bully us into liking it as much as we liked the *Inferno.* Eager to please, I'd done my best, and for a while it seemed to be working, but the effort was too great, and in the end I had to admit that like most readers with whom I've compared notes, I found it excruciatingly boring. Screamingly boring. You couldn't pay me to reread it.

That's what I was afraid of when I thought about the convent. That it would be like reading Dante's *Paradiso.*

But what about those few readers who weren't bored? Were they deceiving themselves, or did they really get something out of it that most of us just didn't catch on to? Like Rossella Moretti, who always read aloud with such feeling, and Giovanni Bicci, who memorized the entire section about the rose? There are always a few in every class. Are these the ones who go on to become monks and nuns? To pursue the spiritual life?

I had to remind myself that I was not being asked to *join* a convent but to spend a month there plying my own humble vocation.

"Keep your shirt on, Jed," I said, meaning the expression literally.

"What are you talking about?"

"I may enter a convent."

"You *what*?"

He raised himself up a little and slid his pants down to his knees. I could see the little Harvard shields on his boxer shorts. VERITAS. Somehow that tickled me, and I started to laugh.

"What's so funny?"

"Harvard underpants."

"You're sore, aren't you, because we didn't go to the Piazzale Michelangelo, and because we didn't take your little walk to Fiesole. What the hell was I supposed to do? Do you know who was at that dinner? Besides Steckley, who holds the purse strings? How could I say 'no'? Honestly, now. What was I supposed to say, 'Sorry, I can't come to Thanksgiving dinner at I Tatti because I've got a date'?"

"You're a Harvard man," I said. "You should have been able to think of something."

He patted the bed beside him. "Take it easy," he said. "We've got a good thing going. Let's not spoil it."

I was standing by the door. Not that I expected any trouble, but I didn't want any physical contact.

"I'm going downstairs for approximately fifteen minutes. When I come back I'll expect you to be gone."

"If that's the way you feel," he said, "as far as I'm concerned, you're fired. F-I-R-E-D. Is that what you want?"

"I'm not sure what I want."

"Try calling I Tatti tomorrow, see how far you get. I'll speak to your boss, too, what's-his-name? I've heard he's not too happy about your being here anyway."

I went down to the bar and drank a glass of *acqua minerale,* glad that the time for decisions was past. When I came back he was gone, but he'd left a note on the vanity table: "Please call my room. It's not too late."

I'd already unbuttoned my blouse and was reaching around

to unhook my bra when I saw it in the mirror. It was under the hairbrush. I undressed completely and took a good look at myself in the mirror. My body seemed to be in a transitional period that perhaps corresponded to the one in my spiritual—if that's the word for it—life. I still had the "beauty of youth," according to Margeaux. It's a phrase that used to puzzle me when I came across it in Victorian novels. Beauty is beauty, isn't it? Either a woman is beautiful or she isn't. But sometimes when you see a young woman with her mother you can see what the old novelists were talking about. You can see that what was beauty in the one will soon lose its charm, that it's heading in the wrong direction, so to speak. Or in some cases there is a quality that remains constant. And that's your true beauty. That's what Meg and Molly had. When they stood next to Mama you could see that they were going in the right direction, that their beauty would hold. But my beauty was of the first type; it was going in the wrong direction. What was left of it wouldn't hold on much longer. I'd never paid much attention to "beauty aids"—wrinkle creams, skin moisturizers, bust developers, all those things. I'd always been too high minded. But maybe I'd made a mistake. And maybe it wasn't too late, even now.

"Nah," I said to myself, crumpling up the note, *"Non vale il pene."*

5

What Nuns Talk About
at Night

The *Ordo Carmelitarum* traces its origins back to the days of the prophet Elijah, who, having retired for religious contemplation to Mount Carmel, was prompted by an angel to found a society of contemplatives for the worship of the one true God. His disciples included some of the lesser prophets (Jonah, Micah and Obadiah) and, later, Pythagoras *("il filosofo rinomato di Magna Graecia")*. Elijah's wife founded a similar society for women, which later included the Virgin Mary.

In 1154—to skip over roughly two thousand years—a Calabrian monk named Berthold, accompanied by a dozen or so like-minded men, took up where Elijah left off, though official recognition—by Pope Honorius III—was delayed till 1224, just about the time of the construction of the great monastic churches in Florence. In 1593 the order was split down the middle over the question of whether or not to wear shoes. Those who wished to return to the primitive austerity of the original rule, which had been somewhat relaxed earlier under

Pope Eugenius IV, became known as the *Carmeliti scalzi,* or Barefoot Carmelites.

The feet of the sister who came to lead me to my room, my cell, were concealed by the skirts of her dark habit, and she walked so softly, with such small nunny steps, that I couldn't tell if she was wearing shoes or not. Did she or didn't she? For some reason—maybe because those stone floors looked so cold and hard—I had to know, so at the very last minute I opened a door that was closing behind me.

"Scusi, suora," I called after her.

"Dimmi, cara." She stopped and turned to face me.

"Tell me something, would you?"

"Certamente."

"Are you wearing shoes?"

She gave me a surprised look and, coloring slightly, slowly extended a dainty foot. We both looked at it for a moment. I was relieved to see that it was firmly clad in a sensible black shoe.

"It's only till Christmas," I told myself, but in my cell I was reminded of a prison. There was no place to hide, not under the table, not under the rough woolen sheets on the small hard bed, not in the tiny wardrobe. A prie-dieu summoned me to my knees; a crucifix on the wall glared malevolently at my residual Protestant soul; the window, slanted upward, high above my head, revealed nothing but a rag of dirty gray sky, spattered with bird droppings. I stamped my shod foot just to hear a sound.

There was no place in my cell to hide the sack of *romanzi gialli*—detective novels—some in English, some in Italian, that I'd bought at the Paperback Exchange on the Via Fiesolana.

Hercule Poirot, Travis McGee, Lew Archer, Nero Wolfe. They'd have their work cut out for them this time, rescuing me from angst and ennui, especially the latter. I started an Agatha Christie in English and then switched to John D. MacDonald in Italian: *Il Canarino Giallo.* I wanted something a little more robust than Agatha Christie, but about ten pages into *The Yellow Canary* I remembered the ending—a particularly horrible torture scene that I didn't want to read again. For once Travis bites off more than he can chew and has to be saved by a deus ex machina, a mysterious Israeli secret agent who shoots the ex-Nazi just as she's about to get to work with her implements of torture. That was a little *too* robust.

Nero Wolfe was soon lowering his seventh of a ton into the only chair he was ever comfortable in, made by a Swedish cabinetmaker. I loved it, but I couldn't seem to concentrate, to evoke an imaginary environment intense enough to cancel the crucifix bearing down on me from the wall above my bed, or the prie-dieu coming at me from below. I needed a window. I let my mind wander, and soon it was peering out imaginary windows: at an ore boat on Lake Michigan from Meg's apartment in Milwaukee; at Papa's herb garden, which you could see through a little kitchen window that had once been an ice chute; at the old Victorian houses, big as barns, that I could see when I looked down Chambers Street from my own window over the porte cochere. If Meg were here, what would *she* do now? But Meg was married to Dan, a doctor, who, though he hadn't started practicing yet—he kept adding one specialty after another to his list of credentials—seemed to have plenty of money. Meg had two kids and was thinking of starting a business of her own. She wouldn't be here in the first place. And

Molly? There was never any telling what Molly might do. Right now she was living with an Indian mathematician in a run-down apartment in Ann Arbor. If you looked out her kitchen window you saw the Salvation Army.

I stacked the books in two piles on the table. Not only was there no place to hide the books, there was no place to hide, period. Maybe that was the idea. Maybe there was a peephole in the door too. I checked. There was, but someone had closed up the hole with wood putty. Good for her. And then I had an idea. Maybe I'd been using the wrong metaphor. Maybe my room wasn't a barren prison cell at all but a snug ship's cabin. Maybe I wasn't a prisoner but a passenger on a fabulous liner, bound for a new world at the ends of the earth.

Like most passengers, once I'd stowed my gear I was ready to go out on deck to see what I could see.

My door opened onto a corridor with doors on one side only, like the corridor of a European train. None of the doors had numbers, nor were they marked in any way that I could see. There was no sign of my fellow inmates, or perhaps I should say passengers. I wanted to escape, but I've never had a very good sense of direction and couldn't have pointed toward the street to save my soul. To the right or to the left? I turned to the right and discovered, after a couple of turns that confused me completely, a door somewhat larger than the rest that opened onto a square cloister, like a prison exercise yard, only smaller. It was full of mud and debris from the flood. Stone benches, too heavy for two strong men to lift, had been overturned by the force of the water. The waterline, like a dirty ring around a bathtub, was higher than the capitals of the columns that supported the small rounded arches of the arcade. Looking down from the loggia, I could picture small knots of nuns, gathered in groups, talking about whatever nuns talk about. I could even hear them singing, in the distance, too far away to make out the words.

There was not much to look at except the sky—no hills or towers rose high enough to be seen above the red-tiled roof— and the frescoes on the inner wall of the loggia. To tell you the truth, I've never cared much for frescoes. Give me your Dutch paintings with lots of interesting details on a tiny scale—tavern scenes with people drinking and playing cards and, inevitably, a little baby going to the bathroom in one corner, or Rembrandt's side of beef, full of drama and mystery; anything by Rembrandt, in fact. But frescoes are always so big. I mean, the figures in them are big. There's no exciting detail, and the colors are dull earth tones—browns and dull reds, sepia, umber, maybe a dash of ultramarine to set off the Virgin Mary's head, but no more than a dash. There's usually not enough going on, and if something is going on, it's generally bad. I looked anyway, the way a person will read *Good Housekeeping* or *Family Circle* in a doctor's waiting room, just because it's there and nothing else is.

According to my *Guide to Florence* the paintings were remarkable chiefly for the fact that they had been done by a woman, the niece of Grand Duke Cosimo III, who had entered the convent in 1714, at the age of thirty-nine, bringing with her a considerable dowry and an exaggerated sense of her own abilities. This was the Lucia that Dottor Postiglione had told me about.

I must say that the fact that they had been done by a woman did pique my curiosity, and I examined the paintings more closely than I might have otherwise. The fact that they had been done by a woman may also have colored my impressions. In any case, it seemed to me that the Virgin Mary was confronting the angel Gabriel with a certain uncharacteristic insouciance, her thumb marking the place in the book she has been reading so that she can find it again once she has sent him on his way. It's Gabriel, not the Virgin, who wears the traditional "Who me?" expression. In another panel the infant Christ is dwarfed by the powerful figures of his mother and grandmother, and in still another, the crucified Christ is the young consort who has been abandoned by his disciples but not by the three Marys, who stand menacingly at the foot of the cross.

I was trying to sort out my impressions of these strong women when I heard a noise behind me and turned to find myself face to face with a tall, wimpled figure.

"Hhhhhhuuuuhh." I'd been caught, a Peeping Tom in the act of peeping. "*O Madonna.* I'm sorry," I said, wishing I hadn't left my room and feeling the need to apologize for poking my nose into something that was none of my business. "I don't know what I'm doing here."

"That's perfectly normal. None of us knows for sure until it's revealed to us, and then it's generally something quite different from what we expected. But I'm sorry I startled you. I'm the *superiora;* the sisters call me Madre Badessa."

I thought maybe I was supposed to kneel down and kiss the ring on the extended hand. But I didn't. I took the hand and shook it. Madre Badessa—Mother Abbess—shook back.

"I will treat you," she said, "just as I would want my own daughter to be treated if she were wandering around the world so far away from home."

There was nothing ironic in her remark, nor in my gratitude, which I found difficult to put into words, for she reminded me of my own mother, though Mama, who had refused to see a priest on her deathbed, had always regarded the church with the gravest suspicions.

"I see you've discovered our secret," she said. "But come now, we'll talk about it later. Right now I must show you the library. There's a great deal of work to be done, and the sooner we start the better."

The library was small by some standards, large by others. I'd say about two thousand volumes, give or take a hundred. The Widener Library at Harvard, I recalled aloud, has more than eight million volumes.

The great library at Monte Cassino, Madre Badessa reminded me, contained fewer than five hundred books in the High Middle Ages. "Which was the greater center of learning?" she wanted to know. "Monte Cassino or the Widener Library?" She was very persistent, Madre Badessa. She wouldn't let me off the hook. An idle remark on my part had become the occasion for a lesson in history. Monte Cassino, founded in 528, destroyed by the Lombards in the sixth century, rebuilt, captured by the Saracens in the ninth century, destroyed by an earthquake in the fourteenth. The collection, formed and reformed, remained intact until it was bombed by the Americans in 1945, when the war was practically over, when all that had been necessary . . .

I apologized to Madre Badessa for . . .

"I didn't mean to lecture you," she said. "The point I wanted to make was simply that all learning, all knowledge of antiquity, was channeled through the monastic communities."

"What about convents?"

"Convents, too, of course, though the first important convent library was not established until 1142 at Montepulciano, and the idea that nuns might be scholars has never sat very well with the princes of the church. But it's time to get to work. Let me introduce you."

In addition to Sister Chiara, the librarian, my staff consisted of four other sisters who had been waiting in silence: Sisters Priscilla, Maria, Sofia and Angelica. I nodded to each one, resisting the impulse to stick out my hand.

The library was a long, narrow room, like the Laurentian Library, though much smaller, with the books arranged in tiers that divided the room into bays, like little chapels, opening off the main aisle. The books had already been removed from the top shelves, but those on the lower shelves, which had been under water, had swelled up so that it was impossible to get them out. They were under too much pressure.

I contemplated the problem for a minute or so without arriving at a solution. What we needed at that point, I thought, was a man. Sisters Chiara, Priscilla, Maria, Sofia and Angelica awaited my instructions, which made me nervous. I'm a book restorer, not a carpenter.

"I think that what we need at this point," I said, "is a man."

No one responded.

"I'm afraid we'll have to take an ax or something and smash out the ends of the presses so we can get the books out. Or maybe a saw. I don't see any other solution."

"I think," said Sister Maria, with what I took to be a gentle but ironic smile, "that that is a typical American solution, but perhaps we can remove the moldings and disassemble the bookcases in the order that they were built—I mean just reverse the order—before we move them upstairs, so we don't do any further damage to the wood. We wanted to hear your opinion before we proceeded."

"Very good," I said, tossing my head as if to say, Just what I was really thinking all along, that I'd only mentioned the ax as a joke.

Sister Angelica was already opening a man-size tool chest. She and Sister Maria, with the confidence of experienced carpenters, or cabinetmakers, started to work on the ornate moldings, first with tiny chisels, then with larger ones, then still larger ones, prying them loose gently—no mean trick since they'd been nailed in to stay with handmade charcoal-iron nails. Seventeenth-century nails, said Sister Angelica. Which is when the bookcases were built, to hold the library that Lucia de' Medici brought with her, as part of her "dowry" when she entered the convent. That much I remembered.

The bindings, mostly seventeenth- and eighteenth-century, though there were a number of books in the limp vellum of earlier ages, had been ruined but I doubted that the books themselves had been damaged too seriously. The fact that they swelled up and were under pressure kept the naphtha or fuel oil, which can do much more damage than water, from penetrating too deeply.

In most early libraries the books were simply placed on the shelves in order of acquisition, exceptions being made for very large or very small volumes. The catalog, if there was one, would indicate the vertical row, the shelf number (from top to bottom) and the number of the book on the shelf (from left to right). Thus the famous *Beowulf* manuscript, for example, is known as Cotton Vitellius A.xv, which means it was located in the library of Sir Robert Cotton under the bust of Roman Emperor Vitellius, on the top shelf, the fifteenth book (or bound manuscript) from the left. Lucia, Sister Chiara explained, had employed a much more sophisticated system, one that anticipated modern classification schemes. But Sister Chiara's explanation was interrupted by a small explosion as the board at the end of the bookcase, no longer held in place by the moldings, gave way with a great wrenching, under the tremendous pressure exerted by the waterlogged books, which spilled out of the shelves like a crowd pouring out of a stadium after a football game, or perhaps I should say a soccer game.

Sisters Maria and Angelica continued to work on the moldings. The rest of us carried the damaged books to the church, where there was room to spread them out. By noon six of the library's twenty-four tiers or bays had been disassembled, and we had all worked up a sweat in spite of the cold.

We worked in silence. Not absolute silence—not the *silenzio maggiore* of the night—but saying only what was necessary. At least the sisters said only what was necessary. My own impulse was to chatter, to fill the air with remarks about the weather and with stories about the book-drying operations in Prato and Pistoia, the tobacco barns in Perugia, the way Professor Chapin had taken the credit for thinking of using the tobacco barns, and so on. But as I became more comfortable working with the sisters, I began to talk less, and by the end of the day I had settled into a steady, comforting rhythm that reminded me of the produce market, as if we were unloading a carload of avocados instead of a library of old books. After a few days the silence seemed normal. If a sister spoke it was because she had something to say. What a difference it would make, I thought to myself, if congresses and parliaments operated on the same principle. Whenever I went out, as I did almost every afternoon, to scavenge for blotting paper and other supplies, I was shocked to step out of the silence of the convent into the noise of the piazza.

There was still no running water, and none of the stores had reopened yet, but everywhere men were digging out the mud, scraping the stones with their shovels, and noisy crowds of men, women, and children gathered around the water truck, and around the portable vegetable stand that opened up every afternoon. And every day at three o'clock a woman would sing two or three folk songs as she hung her laundry out the window of the medieval tower opposite the convent. I tried to time my comings and goings so that I could hear her, but even though she sang beautifully, it was always a pleasant relief to hear the heavy convent door close behind me, shutting out some of the confusion of the world along with its noise.

My days began with a knock on the door of my cell, to which, after a prolonged mental and physical struggle, I would answer, *"Deo gratias."* I didn't mean it, and I didn't actually *have* to say it, but according to Sister Gemma it's what one says at five o'clock in the morning to indicate to the knocker that one hasn't died in one's sleep. Sister Gemma had been assigned to look after me, to show me the ropes—an expression that doesn't exist in Italian—and to empty my chamber pot, for there was still no running water for toilets or baths. Nor was there any heat, since all the furnaces had been put out of commission by the flood.

The sisters greeted the day, before sunrise, in a handsome church designed by Giuliano da Sangallo in the thirteenth century: six small chapels open off either side of the nave, under beautiful arches in the clear Tuscan limestone called *pietra serena*. Were they as sleepy and cold as I? Did their knees hurt from kneeling on stone? Did they get tired of oatmeal for breakfast every morning? Did they regret the vows that bound them, perpetually, as surely as prison bars? That's the question that was always on my mind. What was the payoff? What did you get in exchange for the whole world? In exchange for family, friends, lovers, husbands, children? The more I got to know the black-habited figures, the more mysterious each became. Each had her own story, one that had led her to this point, to the little door cut out of the big door that separated the convent from the piazza.

Mornings I supervised my team of lay sisters (choir sisters had to spend a lot of time singing the divine office) at their work. The job of interleaving two thousand books with absorbent paper was time consuming and unpleasant. The vellum used for old books will last forever, but it's generally been sized with animal glue that gives off a powerful odor when wet—the mud angels who went down into the basement of the Biblioteca Nazionale had to wear gas masks—and forms a nasty scum that makes your fingers stick together. The books become bricklike and yet fragile at the same time. Each different strain of mold has its own characteristic visual and tactile properties that might test the resolve even of those accustomed to dressing the wounds of lepers. The sisters, who soon learned how to treat the books so that the spines wouldn't be torn apart as the paper absorbed water, were less squeamish and more patient than I, fortunately, though their work was not relieved, as mine was, by trips to town. More sisters had been enlisted, including Sister Gemma, my cicerone, who was about my age and who would be taking her perpetual vows in a few months. They knelt on the cold stone floor, like charwomen, as they patiently turned the pages of the books and inserted sheets of paper. They didn't keep shifting their weight and twisting this way and that, as I did, to try to find a more comfortable position. Personal comfort was not a high-priority item in Santa Caterina Nuova. I did the best I could, but I preferred to leave the work of interleaving to the nuns.

They were good workers, good carpenters, and soon two large thymol vapor chambers had been constructed to my specifications. A thymol chamber is really nothing more than a tightly closed box with a tray for thymol crystals and, in this case, supporting rods to hold the books. The heat from a light bulb at the bottom of the chamber activates the crystals, and the vapor inhibits mold, which is potentially far more dangerous than water.

The chambers were set up in one of the small chapels at the end of the church, near a door that opened onto the lower level of the cloister and provided some ventilation, since the vapors can be harmful. Each chamber held about thirty books, which would need to be subjected to the vapors for two days. I was anxious to get started but hadn't managed to locate any thymol crystals, which were in great demand.

Dottor Postiglione, whom I was reluctant to call at first, turned out to be very helpful in this matter. He was a man who knew how to *farsi arrangiare*—a phrase I'd always associated with Signor Bruni—a man who knew, that is, how to get things to arrange themselves in a satisfactory way. He put me in touch with a binder in Prato who had some old sewing frames and other old equipment for hand binding. He located a supply of absorbent paper, which was in very short supply; ditto for thymol crystals. He was a good-natured man, always pleased to be able to help; but he was also a man who enjoyed mystery and indirection, the sort of man who likes to suggest that the bottle of perfume he is giving a woman has been smuggled into the country when in fact it comes from the corner drugstore, or that the wine he orders in a restaurant is from a special cache kept specially for him when actually it's the second-cheapest on the wine list. So I never found out where the blotting paper came from, or the thymol, though I knew that the CRIA people were having trouble getting it.

In the evenings, during *ricreazione,* we sat in the *sala comune,* a room twice as long as it was wide. It was not particularly handsome, but it was comfortable, though chilly. Two Renaissance *cassoni*—large, heavy chests—sat at one end; at the other folding chairs were grouped around the fireplace. This is where everyone congregated, and where I had set up our makeshift conservation lab. We talked as we worked. Or worked as we talked, depending on how you look at it. It was during these evenings that I felt most at home in Santa Caterina Nuova. I felt as if I'd been admitted backstage after the daily performance and could sit and chat freely with the actresses and get a sense of what was really going on.

And a lot was going on. The Carmelites are a contemplative order, but Santa Caterina Nuova was a busy place. The nuns didn't just sit around contemplating, as I had imagined. There were extensive properties to be managed. These properties, like the library, had been part of the dowry of Lucia de' Medici. (The chapter, I soon realized, would never have survived the eighteenth century—a difficult time for all religious orders— had it not been for that dowry.) These lands produced honey, olive oil, and wine for the convent's own use and also for sale. Some of the properties, those in the plain of the Arno, had been flooded. Beehives had been destroyed, grapevines had been un- strung, the mats used in pressing the olives had disappeared, the press itself needed repair.

At first I was secretly amused at the keen interest the suppos- edly contemplative nuns took in these worldly matters but I soon learned to appreciate the precariousness of their position and their determination to keep their financial affairs in their own hands and not turn them over to the bishop of Florence, their technical superior, who had handled all the finances him- self before the election of the present mother superior, Madre Badessa, and who had diverted most of the income into the diocesan treasure chest despite the terms of Lucia's dowry, which specified that all revenues from the dowry belonged to the convent and were to be controlled by the abbess alone. The bishop was not pleased with this arrangement, and the more revenue the land brought in, the less he allotted to the convent from the diocesan budget; but the less money he gave the con- vent, the less control he had over it.

The church is, of course, a human institution, but these re- minders of its humanness—the power struggles, the concerns about money—were as shocking to me as the periodic scandals in the Vatican Bank, which is called, rather deceptively, the Institute for the Works of Religion. Madre Badessa, on the other hand, regarded these human problems as a matter of course. Illusions about bishops and power and money were for novices like me, and she was prepared to oppose the bishop every step of the way: over the finances, over the new habits (why should a few old men dictate how the nuns dressed themselves?), and especially over the fate of the library, which the bishop wanted to remove to San Marco. His position was that the monks at San Marco were much more experienced in the editing of old texts and that they could make more productive use of the books at Santa Caterina. Madre Badessa's position was that the crucial texts in the library at Santa Caterina dealt with matters that ought to be treated by women, since men had botched them so badly in the past. Sister Chiara had already published an important monograph on the role of women in the early church demonstrating that women had been full-fledged bishops with the power to administer the sacraments. (The application of the Greek words *diakonos* and *presbytera* to women as well as men can be explained away only by the most fantastical interpretations.) The bishop had tried to block the publication, but Madre Badessa had circumvented him by obtaining the church's *nihil obstat* through the intervention of a certain cardinal who, like Madre Badessa, was from the Abruzzi.

In short, something important was going on. I had expected peace and calm and (frankly) boredom, but I felt instead that I've stumbled into the backroom headquarters of a revolution. Was this Madre Badessa's "secret"?

* * *

By the first week of December most of the books had been disbound and interleaved with blotting paper. Several hundred of these had been treated with thymol to inhibit mold spores and were ready to be reassembled, so there was plenty to do. I'd been teaching some of the sisters to do simple case bindings, using equipment I'd begged and borrowed from the binder in Prato who'd supplied us with the sewing frames: bone folders, a backing hammer, band nippers, brad awls, several weights of thread, and some old-fashioned presses for nipping, holding, and ploughing. They were apt pupils. I myself had started work on the jewel of the library, the famous *Legenda Sanctissimae Caterinae,* set in ragged Gothic type—one of the first books printed in Florence. The eighteenth-century leather binding had been completely destroyed, but the paper itself had suffered little damage and did not need resizing.

It was a Thursday evening, the feast of Saint Bridget of Sweden, and we were each allowed a glass of *vinsanto* and two or three *biscotti,* which we dipped into the sweet wine. Sisters Bernardo and Annamaria had been modeling the new habits, which they had designed, and there was a certain amount of excitement in the air as they completed a final circuit of the room and swept into the circle by the fire. The nuns applauded as if they were at a fashion show. My sympathies were with them. The traditional habit is a cruel garment. The floor-length skirts make it difficult to walk; the wimple interferes with peripheral vision; the linen *serre-tête* chafes. The new postulants suffered terribly. Their *serre-têtes* were always greasy from the lotion they put on their necks. No one expected the bishop to approve without a struggle. But the nuns were prepared for a struggle. As I've already noted, something was in the air, something exciting that wasn't going to be stopped by bishops.

My apprentices looked up from their work as Sisters Bernardo and Annamaria, heads erect, trying not to smile, pivoted, their short (below the knee) skirts swishing, and made their way to the back of the long room, where Madre Badessa sat quietly on a horsehair sofa, reading. She, too, looked up, trying not to smile.

I turned my attention back to the *Legenda Sanctissimae Caterinae.* I lined up the cords with the markings on the spines, screwed up the frame, removed all but the first signature of the book from the bed of the frame, and prepared to demonstrate to Sister Gemma, who had joined our sewing circle, the kettle stitch that links the signatures together. In Italian, as Sister Agata had been pleased to inform me, it's called *una maglia legata,* something I hadn't known before.

I put down my needle and placed the second signature of the *Legenda* carefully on top of the first. "How did Caterina happen to become a nun?" I asked casually. I was familiar with the general outline of her life, but I wanted to hear what the others would say.

"When she was seven years old," said Sister Chiara, the librarian and an authority on Saint Catherine, who is the patron saint of nuns, "she was coming back from an errand and saw a vision of Jesus and the saints, all dressed in white, standing in a loggia in the sky."

A loggia in the sky, with people looking down at you. It was a curious image. I didn't know what to make of it. But to tell you the truth, it wasn't really Caterina Benincasa who interested me. It was Sister Chiara herself, and Sister Agata, who had almost finished sewing the last signature of the book in the makeshift sewing frame, which she insisted on holding on her lap, despite my protests, and Sisters Bernardo and Annamaria, who had modeled the new habits, and Madre Badessa too, sitting quietly in the shadows, and Sister Gemma, and Annapaola, a new postulant who had arrived shortly after I did and whose *serre-tête* was not pulled tight enough to prevent chunks of dark hair from poking out around her face.

Needles flashed in the firelight. (The fire, incidentally, was a necessity, not a luxury; none of the furnaces in the *quartiere* had yet been put back in working order.)

"Is it always like that?" I asked. "A vision? Is it all decided in a single moment? Like a man proposing to a woman? Or is it different for everyone?"

Had I been too bold? My heart was thumping, the way it had thumped when Professor Chapin propositioned me, but I plunged ahead recklessly into the silence that had fallen across the room. My apprentices had stopped their sewing, and the other sisters, gathered around the fire or around two electric heaters in the back of the room, had stopped their sewing, too, or had put down their books.

"How is it decided? How was it decided for *you*, Annapaola? Did *you* see a vision?" I felt guilty about singling out Annapaola, who was not accustomed to speaking, but her vocation was the most recent, the freshest. I wanted to know.

The silence was palpable, like the silence after a bell has stopped tolling, as each of the women in the room contemplated, for a moment, the circumstances of her own vocation.

I don't know why I was afraid. Maybe it was that I still

believed—in spite of my own experience in the convent—that at the heart of it there was nothing, a cipher, and that a woman who looked into her heart honestly would discover that she had made a bad bargain, had given up everything for nothing.

It was not Annapaola who spoke up but old Sister Agata, who had finished sewing the small prayer book I had given her and was ready to start on the headband, for which I had purchased several spools of beautiful silk thread. She was a southerner, she said, speaking directly to me, as if it were just the two of us in the room. A *calabrese,* the last of eight children, four of whom had died before she was born. She punctuated her remarks with a kind of cackling laugh. Her family lived in two rooms, she said. No water. No toilet. No heat. No food. When her father died her mother began to work at the hospital. She left every morning at five o'clock to chop the wood to heat the water in the big kettles in which she did the laundry for the whole hospital, and the neighbors wouldn't talk to her and the boys called her *puttana,* whore, because a decent woman isn't supposed to show her face in the street for three years after her husband's death. The sisters opened a school in the village. "They took me in. The food was good. It was warm, warmer than it is here! I knew a good thing! *Meglio star da papa che da zingaro!,"* she laughed. Better to live like a pope than a gypsy. She kept on cackling after she'd stopped talking, and then the bell rang for compline and the cackling stopped as suddenly as it had started. No one spoke another word. No one turned another page. No one took another stitch. Recreation was over, and I was reminded of the strict discipline that separated me from these women.

* * *

It was time for me to return to my detective novel, a Travis McGee (not *Il Canarino Giallo),* but I didn't want to break the circle, the ring of fellowship, or sistership, so I followed the nuns through the frescoed cloister and into the church, where I soon found myself alone in the impending darkness.

I don't think I've ever felt so utterly alone. The dis-ease I'd experienced when I was first shown into my little cell was nothing compared to what I felt now. I'd been telling myself all along that the true life of the convent was to be experienced in those cozy hours in the *sala comune,* which I could understand and participate in, and not in a mystery that I found as inexplicable and incomprehensible as the Latin of the antiphons and the psalms the choir intoned in a single clear voice. No music could have been more absolutely celestial—everything sensual had been refined from it—and yet I was strangely reminded of Papa's blues, of men standing in railroad stations, suitcases in their hands, waiting for trains to carry them back home or away from home, depending. The music had the same effect on me: it seemed to go where ordinary music can't go, so that I was overwhelmed with an intense longing, as painful as homesickness but wonderful at the same time.

I thought of Agata Agape and her strange vocation: no food, no heat, no water, no toilet. She had never ridden in an automobile, never watched a television program, never talked on a telephone, never loved a man. She had seen eight abbesses come and go, and as many bishops. Although she could neither read nor write, she was an excellent seamstress and without a doubt the star pupil of my little bookbinding class. She had a feel for the materials, could judge with her fingertips what thickness of thread to select for a particular book, a matter that depends on several variables: the thickness of the paper and the number and thickness of the signatures. She could round the back of a book without a single unnecessary stroke of the hammer. She could cut endpapers to size without measuring them. She had strong hands to screw up the nipping press, and sharp eyes, and a sharp tongue, too, for anyone who tried to usurp her comfortable chair next to the fire in the *sala comune.*

Had the daily and seasonal rhythms of the convent filled her life with meaning? Had it been enough?

On winter nights when I was little my sisters and I used to get out from under the covers and take off our pajamas and stand bare naked in front of the open window just to see how long we could stand it. That's what I did that night in Santa Caterina Nuova. I took off all my spiritual clothes and stood there bare naked, just to see how long I could stand it. I don't know how long I actually lasted. I kept waiting for something to happen, but nothing happened and nothing happened, and then on the way back to my room I turned a corner and suddenly felt that I was not alone. I'd been taken by surprise in a dark corridor, and my heart began to thump. Would it all be decided in a single moment, perhaps against my will? Did I have to *do* something or would it all be done for me? Or to me? I could already feel, rather than see, myself in the rough serge of the habit, could feel the *serre-tête* pulled tight around my face, cutting sharply into the soft skin under my chin. Had it been like this for the others? Or was it different for everyone? I still didn't know, and I never found out for sure.

6

What Sort of a Thing
Is a Man?

When I returned to the convent after one of my afternoon forays, lugging a small iron nipping press, this time from a local bindery, I realized immediately that something was terribly wrong. It was the only time, I think, that I actually found the silence maddening. I could get nothing out of Sister Gemma except that Madre Badessa had forbidden them to talk about it. About what?

At supper, which consisted of thin broth with pasta in it, two of the postulants—Annapaola and a girl I didn't know—spent the entire time lying facedown, arms outstretched, on the stone floor. The silence was deeper than usual, and when Madre Badessa tinkled her bell to indicate that conversation was permitted, no one had much to say.

It was not till evening that I was able to pry the story out of Sister Gemma. I had lured her into my cell with a promise of some Dutch chocolate that I'd bought at the station. Normally the sisters are not allowed into one another's cells, but Sister Gemma had permission to visit mine.

She was, as her name suggested, a gem of a woman. Tall, soft spoken, good humored, intelligent. "You should have been a teacher," I told her more than once. "You remind me of my fifth-grade teacher, Mrs. Insulman. Her classroom was always full of gerbils and snakes and model volcanoes and odd plants. Full of interesting surprises, like you." It was only to Sister Gemma that I could say such things.

"You must stop thinking that my life is wasted here," she reminded me. "*This* is my vocation, not teaching little children." But I think she was pleased nonetheless.

I rummaged around in my book bag for the bar of chocolate, which weighed a hefty hundred and fifty grams.

"So what happened?"

"It was nothing, really."

"Then tell me." I unwrapped the chocolate, broke it in half, and handed a piece to Gemma. Semisweet.

"Annapaola and Maria discovered a book of pictures."

"A book of pictures?"

"Obscene drawings."

"Ah, a pornographic magazine?" The newly reopened newspaper kiosk in the piazza was full of them, along with more refined books on the ideal of feminine beauty in the Renaissance, etc. My first thought was that Annapaola and Maria had stepped outside the convent on an errand or that some practical joker had stuffed a dirty magazine under the convent door.

"No, no, it was a book from the library."

"From the library?"

"Yes, they discovered it when they were interleaving the books."

Now here was something exciting indeed. Gemma licked the

chocolate slowly and thoughtfully, as if it were an ice-cream cone. I took a big bite out of mine. I've never been able to eat chocolate slowly.

"Did you see it?"

"Just a glimpse. There was a big commotion. I went to see what was happening. Sister Vincensina, the novice mistress, came at once and took it away from them."

"Well, they couldn't help finding it, could they?"

"The thing is, they found it yesterday, and Sister Maria kept it in her cell last night. They just pretended to find it today, but Sister Matilde saw them."

"Someone should call *Oggi* or *Novella 2000.*" (These were the Italian equivalents of *The National Enquirer.*)

"Really! That's why Madre Badessa forbade us to talk about it."

"Don't worry. I won't tell anyone."

"But I will have to tell Madre Badessa."

"That you've talked to me?"

"Yes."

"Why is that?"

"Because we have no secrets."

"What will happen to you?"

"Nothing much. Madre Badessa is very understanding."

"You won't have to lie facedown on the floor during supper? How barbarous!" (I was really annoyed with Madre Badessa.)

"How much did you see?" I asked.

"I didn't get a very good look, and I didn't know what I was looking at, but whatever it was looked like a kind of monster, like a giant squid with big tentacles reaching out at you and a beak and one dark eye."

"A giant squid?" I couldn't picture what she was describing, but I didn't want to press her.

How fragile the infrastructure. No matter how strong the walls, the fortress can always be betrayed from within. And what was the purpose of these walls? Nothing about monastic and conventual life excites more curiosity than the vow of celibacy. In theory the libido is redirected toward God. The nuns —and monks too, in fact—are "brides of Christ." They dress up in wedding dresses when they take their perpetual vows. But can the divine embrace ever match the warmth and passion of the human one? I suppose I was too steeped in Freudian assumptions to believe it. Not that my own experience had been characterized by any exceptional warmth and passion. (I was thinking of Jed Chapin.)

"Sister Gemma," I said. "Are you happy?"

"Yes," she said. "Very happy."

Of course, I thought, that's what she'd say even if she weren't happy. But she didn't *look* unhappy.

"Have you ever wished . . ." I was treading on thin ice, reluctant to go on, but my curiosity was too strong. "Have you ever wished," I repeated, "have you ever regretted, have you ever been sorry, that is, about not knowing a man?"

"Oh, yes," she said. "Very much, in a way. But you know, it's all so strange. I wouldn't know what to do. And I'm not sure it's that important. Madre Badessa has talked to us all."

I had finished my chocolate long ago but Sister Gemma still had most of hers. She broke off a piece and gave it to me. I accepted. I needed something in my hand, like a drink.

"When you say Madre Badessa has talked to you, whom do you mean?"

"Those of us who have come directly, when we were young, before we were . . . with men. There are many women here who have lived in the world, who have experienced everything, all the things you are thinking of. But when they come here they envy us our innocence, they would trade their experience for our innocence. It must seem strange to you. Does it?"

"Yes, in a way. But what about you, Gemma? Would you trade innocence for experience?"

"Do you know the story of Piccarda in the first part of the *Inferno*?"

"Sort of. I remember we read it in my Italian class."

"Yes, everyone should read it, it's so perfect."

"Piccarda was a nun, wasn't she? But she gets married?"

"Her brother Corso took her away from the convent and forced her to marry Rossellino della Tossa, a very important man in Florence. They lived right across the piazza, you know."

"And Piccarda winds up on the bottom rung of Heaven, isn't that it?"

"Yes, that's true. But there's something more important. That passage explains so much, that's why it's so beautiful: 'the essence of this blessed state of being / is to hold all our will within His will, / whereby our wills are one and all-agreeing.' To hold all our will within His will, that's what we try to do every day, and that will is our peace: *la sua voluntade è nostra pace.* 'It is that sea / to which all moves, all that Itself creates / and Nature bears through all Eternity.' "

Sister Gemma still had some of her piece of chocolate left. She broke it in two and gave me a piece.

"No, no, Gemma," I protested, even as I was holding out my hand. "I've already eaten most of it."

I took the piece of chocolate and popped it into my mouth. Gemma still had a one-inch piece left. Maybe that was the difference between us.

Madre Badessa's office, on the ground floor between the refectory and the cloister, was full of file folders that had been spread out to dry, on the floor, on the chairs, on the sills of the deep-set windows that opened onto the cloister, on top of the file cabinets in which they belonged, on the surface of the large desk behind which sat the woman whose first words to me had been an offer to treat me as she would want her own daughter to be treated. She was tall and handsome, and I could see the resemblance to her cousin: sharp gray eyes, high forehead, an easy smile like an embrace. I was never sure how to greet her. I felt like a country bumpkin in the presence of royalty. I felt that I ought to *do* something—kneel, curtsy, kiss her hand—but I didn't know what.

She didn't look up from the letter she was writing until she had either finished it or else found a suitable stopping place. There was a book on the edge of the desk, and I knew, without having to ask (which I wouldn't have), without being told (which I wasn't), that it was the book of pictures.

When she did look up I could see that she had been thinking very intently about something other than my visit. "Ah, yes," she said, putting down her fountain pen. "Sister Gemma tells me that you have been having some interesting conversations."

"Very interesting."

"And instructive too?"

"Very instructive, Madre Badessa. I've learned a great deal about convent life. And about life itself, too," I added.

"When you say 'life itself,'" she asked, smiling, "what exactly do you mean? Do you mean the world outside the convent, the world of business and politics, marriage and family life? Or do you have something else in mind?"

"Why," I said, taken by surprise, "life itself is, well, life itself is, just itself. It's having your father make a Saint-Cyr glacé for your birthday, it's jumping off a cliff into the ocean, it's going for a bike ride with your sisters, it's having your mother come up to your room and sit with you when you've been sick, or walking with you from Fiesole to Settignano."

"Yes," she said, "life is all those things." She paused, and I waited for her to go on to say that life was also something more, that there was a religious dimension to things, but she surprised me again.

"But what is your life right now?" she asked. "Right at this moment? What makes it more than a sequence of pleasant moments?"

I'd taken a course in modern philosophy at Edgar Lee Masters—Berkeley, Hume, Kant—but it had never given me a good handle on questions like this.

"I don't mean anything complicated," she explained, "like a definition of consciousness. I simply mean, what is the good in your own life now that is good just for its own sake, not because it's a means to some other end?"

What came to my mind immediately, without my summoning it, was an image of Jed Chapin pulling on his Harvard shorts: VERITAS. This was hardly an example of what the abbess was getting at, but a point of reference, like a travesty or a parody.

"Hard work," I said, playing it safe. "Working on the books in the library. We've made a lot of progress. It's my vocation."

"It's a good one. If I had a daughter I'd be pleased if she became a book conservator. To work with your hands as well as your head, and with your heart, too. I can imagine a conservator loving the objects of her work. It might be something for us to look into at Santa Caterina."

I was aware, as she was speaking, of the book on the edge of her desk. It didn't *look* like a book of obscene pictures!

"And you know something of the value of books?"

"Something," I said. "It would be impossible not to."

"The aim of convent life," she said, abruptly changing the subject, "is to form one's spiritual life not according to whim, or chance, or even personal inclination, but according to the will of God. Poverty. Chastity. Obedience. Those are the vows. Poverty, chastity, obedience." She gave each word its full weight: *povertà, castità, ubbidienza.* "Which do you think is hardest?"

"I'd think it would depend," I said, "on the individual. If you're young and beautiful, like Annapaola, chastity might be hardest."

"Yes," she said, nodding as if in agreement, though she was not in fact agreeing.

"Chastity can be a burden," she said. "Sometimes I think it would be better if we admitted only women with a late vocation, like myself, who have had some experience of the world, and of men. It would demystify the whole business, take away some of its power, its fascination. But virginity is precious, too.

Every society, except perhaps our own, has known how to value it. And lack of sexual intercourse won't make you go blind! But I'm sorry," she added, perhaps responding to my look of surprise. "I didn't mean to be facetious."

I was a little uncomfortable at the abbess's frankness, which was almost coarse. (I'm the sort of person who doesn't mention baldness in the presence of a bald man or the joy of sex to a spinster.)

"And poverty might be very hard on someone who was used to luxury, like Sister Gemma."

"Yes, but in the case of poverty you're giving up something that's good, at least potentially, for something better, at least in theory; you're adopting a mode of life that most thinking people, whatever their actual behavior, have always regarded as an honorable estate. The poverty of the convent is a systematic discipline that is good for one. The extreme poverty in the south, or in most of Asia, is another matter. That's a political scandal—not the kind of poverty that does you any good."

"That leaves obedience," I said.

She nodded. "Poverty and chastity are hard," she said, "but obedience is much harder."

Were we getting somewhere? Was she starting to tell me about herself?

"But whom do you have to obey?"

"We are all subject to the rule of the order, which dates back to 1433, though it's been relaxed somewhat. The church, you know, is somewhat like an army, with a commander-in-chief and generals and colonels and majors, et cetera, all the way down to sergeants and privates, first class, second class, and so on. Only much more complex. No one person can begin to sort it out. And the religious orders are like battalions or divisions and so on. But in fact convents tend to be more like webs or nets, much more democratic than an army. The novices have to obey the novice mistress, of course, and everybody has to obey me. But they can vote me out if they want to."

"Really?" I was genuinely surprised.

"Oh, yes, we've always been very democratic in some ways."

"And whom do you have to obey?"

"I have to obey the bishop of Florence."

"And you find it difficult?"

"*Molto difficile.* The bishop is opposed to everything we're trying to accomplish. It's a very difficult situation. Fortunately I have some influential friends."

I wasn't sure what she meant by 'trying to accomplish.' "What do you try to accomplish in a convent that a bishop would disapprove of?" I asked.

"Oh, heavens!" She laughed. "Bishops have always disapproved of convents. They're always meddling. They can't leave us alone and never have been able to. Certain reforms in the order, to begin with, that would allow us greater self-governance. With regard to the habit, for example, which is unsuited to our present needs. Why should a group of men prescribe our dress for us? And that's only a minor thing. We're hemmed in in every way. We can't celebrate the mass without a man. And what an old stick they send us.

"But the main thing is our work. There's a whole tradition of female spirituality and scholarship, too, that has been neglected for centuries. All the books have been written and edited by men. Or not written and not edited! Everything has been distorted, and doubly distorted, in the actions and in the record of the actions. Why were so many women driven to such extremes to defend their virginity? Why did they cling to it so desperately? Because the flesh is evil? No, it was so they could retain control over their bodies and their lives instead of handing them over to men. It was the only way. What were the alternatives? Marriage, years of childbirth, no right to own property. That's why their virginity was so precious. But who has told their story truly? No one. And it's all right here. Countless stories that no one found worth the telling. Lucia de' Medici had the foresight and the means to collect everything she could find, and her relatives thought she was crazy. She wrote a book herself and no one would print it; she painted pictures and was treated like a freak. If she hadn't been a Medici she would have been put in prison. She joined Santa Caterina so she could be free. And she frescoed the walls in the cloister. Where I first met you. You should spend more time there if you want to understand. And now that we're starting to tell those stories, the bishop is up in arms. He's threatened. It was only through the intervention of an old friend that Sister Chiara was able to receive the *nihil obstat* for her history of women in the early church. And now he wants to turn the whole library over to the monks at San Marco. *O Dio . . .*" She made the sign of the cross. "We have to be cunning as serpents, as well as innocent as doves.

"But take a look at this without opening it, and tell me what you see," she said. She handed me the book on her desk. (It had been interleaved with blotting paper to absorb moisture, but the embroidered binding, which had been damaged beyond repair, was damp and unpleasant to the touch.)

I handled the book carefully. The title wasn't legible but I could see that it was a prayer book—at least it looked like a prayer book—probably seventeenth century, in pretty bad shape. I said as much.

"What else can you tell me about it?"

"Embroidered book covers were popular items for the upper class from the fifteenth to the seventeenth century. Usually they were for private devotional books or service books. They were more popular in France, Germany and England than in Italy, though some examples survive. The earliest examples come from the thirteenth century, generally embroidered by cloistered nuns."

"Now open the book."

I did so, tentatively, as if it were a box holding a snake or some sort of nasty insect, but the title was a standard one—*Le preghiere cristiane preparate da Santa Giuliana d'Arezzo*—and the contents familiar: a selection from the Roman Missal—the Office of the Dead, the Penitential Psalms and Litany, the Hours of the Cross and the Holy Ghost, and so on—followed by the personal prayers of the saint. I was relieved. Something that I had thought was going to be complicated had turned out to be simple. It was a shame, though, that the binding had been destroyed. The binding had probably been more valuable than the book itself.

She took the book from me and let it fall open in her hands. "Look," she said; "you see, two books have been bound together."

She moved her chair so I could see better; I slid mine around so that we were sitting side by side. She opened the book flat on the desk. I could see the second title page: *I sonetti lussuriosi di Pietro Aretino.* I translated *lussuriosi* as "sensuous," to myself.

"The practice of binding two books together," I said, still speaking with the voice of authority, "was not altogether uncommon in the early Middle Ages but it would have been very unusual in the seventeenth century."

"Yes," she said. "But such strange *compagni* we have here."

She began to turn the pages.

"What sort of a thing is a man?" she asked at last, looking up at me.

"I haven't any idea," I said. I was feeling quite agitated.

"You should have by now."

I didn't say anything.

"A man," she went on, "is a nest of Chinese boxes. He's a rational philosopher—Plato's thinking reed. He's an aggressive warrior—an Achilles or an Odysseus. He's a *paterfamilias* and a domestic tyrant, a bundle of neuroses because in reality he's irrational and cowardly. And at the inner core he's a collection of images, a little picture gallery, as private as the pope's bathroom in the Vatican. Let me show you."

She continued to turn the pages one by one till she came to an illustration. "I believe this is what Sister Gemma was trying to describe," she said. "You can see the resemblance to a monster."

What I saw did indeed resemble some sort of monster, but I was blushing furiously and couldn't bring myself to look directly at it. I shook my head and sneezed as if I'd just looked into the sun on a bright day. I couldn't focus my eyes.

"You can see the arms and legs," the abbess went on, "like the tangled tentacles of a giant squid."

I did see it now, a man preparing to mount a woman from behind. They were drawn from behind so that both their heads

131

were concealed by their bodies. The man's anus stared at the viewer like a great dark eye, his member, cleverly foreshortened, hung down past his noselike scrotum like an elephant's trunk, or like a great hooked beak.

She turned to the next illustration: a woman on her back, legs in the air, a man lowering himself on top of her. I've looked at all sorts of pictures, of course—who hasn't in this day and age?—but I really couldn't look at these drawings in the presence of the abbess. I was too self-conscious.

"Well," said the abbess. "What do you think?"

"It's quite extraordinary."

"You've never seen anything like it?"

"Not exactly, though my sister took me to an adult bookstore once."

"An 'adult' bookstore?"

"A bookstore that sells pornography."

"How interesting, and you call this kind of store an 'adult' bookstore. This was in Chicago?"

Like most Italians she gave "Chicago" a *tch* sound at the beginning, like "Tchaikovsky."

"Yes. Men have to pay fifty cents to get in but women get in free. There are magazines on racks on the wall, and books on revolving stands like the ones in the front of the Paperback Exchange. It was pretty disgusting. I wanted to get out of there but Molly said I had to stay."

"Molly is your sister?"

"Yes. She'd do anything. 'You've got to know about this stuff,' she kept saying. It was as if she was shouting in the reading room of a library: 'Look at this, look at this.'

"The shop was arranged in sections, like a grocery store or a

boutique. There was something for everyone. I don't really remember what I saw on the covers of the magazines and books.
What I remember was the way the men all stood around trying
to make themselves invisible. No one looked at anyone else.
They kept their eyes down when they moved around. They
were furtive, that's what they were, *furtivi.* There were business-
men in respectable suits, a soldier with his service cap pulled
down over his forehead, a couple of kids who looked like college students. And nobody said anything. I think they were
afraid of us."

"The brotherhood of man, of men," she said. "You see what I
mean?" she said. "They'd rather look at pictures than at a real
woman."

"I hadn't thought of it that way."

"The pictures don't frighten them. They can't talk back."

I was relieved when she closed the book. It was like someone
shutting off a bright and annoying light.

"But you've never heard of Aretino?"

"The name rings a bell."

"He was a remarkable man. He wrote a biography of Saint
Catherine, actually, but he was better known for his satires. He
was called the 'scourge of princes,' and everyone was afraid of
him—even the popes—because he had such a vicious tongue.
He could ridicule anyone. Truth, of course, didn't matter a bit."

"Did he do those drawings?"

"No, he wrote the sonnets, and somebody else did the drawings. Giulio Romano, I think. The point is, the book caused
quite a scandal. There are lots of allusions to it—'Aretino's
postures,' the 'sixteen pleasures' that sort of thing—but the
pope was scandalized and ordered all copies of Aretino's book

destroyed. If a copy still existed, it could turn out to be valuable."

"How valuable?"

"I really haven't any idea. I thought *you* might know."

"It depends on so many things—the condition of the book, which is not very good. I mean the binding is ruined. The scarcity. You'd have to see what kind of a track record such things have at auction houses. Things like that."

"Perhaps you could look into it for me?"

"Certainly, but it will be difficult with the Biblioteca Nazionale closed. I'll have to find . . . I'm not quite sure. Auction records, I suppose. There must be something that tells."

"But you will try?"

"Yes, of course."

"I want you to start with Signor Giustiniani in the Piazza Goldoni." She wrote down the name and address on a small square of paper. "But you must be very careful."

"*Capito.*"

"And there's another thing."

"What's that?"

"The book can't stay here."

"Of course not."

"You'll have to take it with you. I think that Signor Giustiniani will—how shall I say?—realize its true worth, and I think you must show it to him and trust him. At least a little bit. But if you feel unsure, you should perhaps place it in a locker at the *stazione.* I'll leave it up to you. It would be awkward, you understand, for me to dispose of it myself."

"Yes, I understand."

"So I'm going to leave it in your hands."

"But I really don't know . . . I'll be leaving before Christmas."

"But you'll do what you can?"

"Of course, Madre Badessa."

"Do you remember the first time we met?"

"In the cloister?"

"And you said you didn't know what you were doing here?"

"Yes."

"Do you still feel the same way?"

"No, Madre Badessa."

"Good."

I rose to leave.

"Remember. Be very careful."

"Do you think it's really valuable?"

"Yes, in fact, I do. *Very.*"

"Could you give me an idea of what you have in mind?"

"I don't want to mention a particular figure," she said "because I may be wrong—but I think it's the only copy. I think all the copies were destroyed except this one. I may be wrong, but I think men will be willing to pay any amount of money for it, perhaps even enough to save our little library from the bishop."

7

Pray Without Ceasing

On the morning of November 4, the morning of the flood, Dottor Postiglione, alerted by one of the gallery's watchmen, left the door of his apartment wide open for his less fortunate neighbors who lived on the lower floors, and waded through oily water, already knee deep in Piazza Santa Croce, on his way to the Uffizi. The water was rising rapidly, and he could hear guard dogs, trapped in the basements of the warehouses along Borgo de' Greci, barking wildly. At the Uffizi he was soon joined by the director of the museum and her assistant, and by an official from the *Soprintendenza del opificio delle pietre dure*. The four of them, along with the watchman who had telephoned Dottor Postiglione, rushed to the Vasari Corridor, the enclosed passageway that connects the Uffizi with the Palazzo Pitti on the other side of the river, and that crosses the river on the tops of the goldsmiths' shops on the Ponte Vecchio. The corridor contains the finest collection of self-portraits ever assembled: Filippo Lippi, Raphael, Titian, Rubens, Rembrandt (two: one as a young man, one as an old), David, Corot, Ingres, Delacroix, and others. Dottor Postiglione's first thought had been of these self-portraits, for if the old bridge gave way, the corridor itself would be dragged down into the raging Arno.

They carried about twenty paintings to safety, but the floor was trembling so violently beneath them that Dottor Postiglione, fearing for their safety, ordered them to stop.

They made their way to the restoration rooms in the basement. One of these was already inaccessible, but in the other, the Vecchia Posta, a rescue effort had been mounted by members of the museum staff, who were sliding a huge framed canvas across the slippery tile floor when they arrived: Botticelli's *Incoronazione.* All in all some three hundred paintings were waiting to be cleaned and restored, including the famous Raphael *tondo* from the Alte Pinakothek in Munich, which Dottor Postiglione carried, by himself, up the stairs to the safety of the mezzanine.

At nine o'clock the *soprintendente* himself appeared, Signor Giorgio Focacci. He was shaken, white faced, unshaven, soaking wet, but when he learned that the portraits in the Corridoio Vasariano were still in danger, he marched off to save them. Dottor Postiglione and the others raced after him and tried to stop him, but the crisis had rejuvenated the old man, had given him the strength of youth, with which he fought off those who tried to prevent him from risking his life. "I'm an old man," he shouted. "I've lived my life. I have no family, no children. Let me go, I tell you!"

With this there was no arguing, but neither the *direttrice* nor her assistant nor Dottor Postiglione was willing to let the old man go by himself, so the four of them mounted the trembling stairs, trembling themselves, to finish the rescue effort that had been abandoned earlier. Soon they were over the Ponte Vecchio, which was being battered by automobiles and oil drums and whole trees that had been uprooted upstream. The debris below them was clogging the arches of the bridge, forcing the water to pass through the narrow openings over the central arch. They could hear the small shops below them exploding like bombs under the assault of the water.

Most of the portraits could be managed easily by two people. The *direttrice* and her assistant worked together, Dottor Postiglione with the *soprintendente,* the *dottore* marveling at the old man's strength and stamina as they hefted the two Rembrandt portraits at the same time.

It took them two hours to empty the corridor. On his last trip Dottor Postiglione, who was bringing up the rear, paused for a look out one of the curtained windows. What he saw beneath him, or thought he saw, was neither an inexplicable act of God nor a simple natural disaster, but the breakdown of civilization itself, the failure of civilization, that is, to act upon what it knows and has known for centuries. The danger of the weirs and the need for reservoirs had been recognized in the Middle Ages. During the Renaissance the divine Leonardo had drawn up plans for sluices to drain off floodwater. But instead of acting on this knowledge in order to alleviate the problem of flooding, men had chosen instead to aggravate the problem by covering the floodplains with concrete and by hacking down the forests that once acted as natural sponges to absorb excess rainfall. And then, to top it off, they continued to store their most precious documents in basements along the river and to refuse to move the conservation laboratories to safer ground at the Fortezza da Basso (one of the *dottore*'s pet projects). Dottor

Postiglione noticed a bloated cow floating toward him, on its side, heaving and kicking as if it were still alive. The cow, deflected by a log, spun around and slammed into one of the piers of the bridge. Dottor Postiglione thought he could distinguish the impact from a thousand other impacts by its peculiar dullness and stupidity.

When it stops raining, he said to himself, there will be a great noise in the newspapers, new governmental agencies will be formed, old ones reorganized, the experts will arrive and everything will be explained, the relief agencies will set up their tents and everyone will be relieved. English ladies will arrive in tweed skirts and sensible shoes and American women in jeans and high boots. But nothing will be done. There will be no warning system, no computers to coordinate the readings of the hydrometers along the river. His neighbors in Sante Croce, the *popolo minuto,* the little people, would continue to suffer, their houses defiled and broken, their workshops destroyed, their lives in shambles.

This is what it will be like at the end of the world. And all because of human stupidity. Human beings are as stupid as that dead cow. And not just the Florentines, not just the Italians, all human beings. They cut down the rain forests in South America, poison the earth with pesticides, the rivers with chemical effluents, the atmosphere with hydrocarbons. . . .

And yet, Dottor Postiglione has an instinct, an instinct that enabled him to survive the prisoner-of-war camp in North Africa and to endure a difficult marriage without losing the sweetness of his disposition. It is an instinct—almost an inner voice, like Socrates' *daimon*—for happiness. Guided by this inner voice he makes for happiness in any situation, however desperate, just as surely as an experienced air traveler makes for the aisle seat by the overwing exit.

This instinct did not desert him as he stood at the window of the Vasari Corridor, looking down at the dead cow batting against the pier. It spoke to him of occasions for charity and nobility of spirit and for inspired acts of heroism such as those just performed by the aging *soprintendente,* Signor Giorgio, a man who in all the years the *dottore* had known him had thought only of his own comfort and ease; it spoke to him of the possibility of priests and communists and *carabinieri* working side by side to clean up the mess and alleviate suffering; it spoke to him of vast sums of money that would pour in from England and Germany and America, especially from America, the land of plenty; it spoke to him of a giant step forward—even a leap forward—in the science of conservation, as leading conservationists—men like himself—struggled to deal with the problems posed by the flood.

"Postiglione? Postiglione?" A voice was calling to him, not the inner voice of his *daimon* but the voice of the *soprintendente.*

"Coming, Signor Giorgio," he shouted.

"Do you remember Vasari's complaint about the grand duke four hundred years ago?" The *soprintendente* was shouting, too, to make himself heard.

"Very well, Signor Giorgio. The grand duke didn't give him time to do the job properly when he built the corridor. He had to settle for inferior materials, inferior workmanship."

"So I wouldn't stand there any longer."

But Dottor Postiglione was in no hurry. He had mastered his own fear, or rather, he had forgotten about it—or perhaps the fear had just evaporated. In any case, it didn't concern him. In fact, he had never been less afraid in his life. What he felt was exhilaration, as if the trembling beneath him were the trembling of a horse and he a triumphant *condottiere,* as if the trembling beneath him were the trembling of the goddess of love, and himself the great Mars astride her. All thanks to his instinct.

Now, a month later, he can say to himself, And look what has happened! There has been a great noise in the papers. The problems of the weirs and the reservoirs and the hydroelectric dams at La Penna and Levane, and of the embankments, and of the deforestation of the surrounding countryside, of the need for a river regulation plan, have been rehashed. The engineer who opened the Levane dam has committed suicide. Everybody who had anything to do with anything has found someone else to blame. The Germans have sent equipment and money. The English have sent warm clothes and tea. The French have sent nothing. The Japanese have sent absorbent paper. The Americans have sent clothes and supplies. Even the Russians have gotten into the act with a boatload of toys for the children at Christmas. And the Americans have sent money, especially money. Every American who ever bought a leather purse or a wallet in Santa Croce, or a gold necklace on the Ponte Vecchio, or a cheap scarf at San Lorenzo has reached for a checkbook and given, given, given money, money, money. Such a generous people, and so charming. Especially the women.

On the upper loggia, now enclosed, of the Palazzo Davanzati is a trap door through which it was once possible to pour boiling oil on those—presumably enemies—in the courtyard below. It would still be possible, of course, if one had a supply of boiling oil at hand, which Dottor Postiglione has not, though there is enough prussic acid in his newly established laboratory to make up a solution powerful enough to discourage all but the most determined visitors.

But whom does the *dottore* wish to discourage? The list is too long; the *dottore* himself couldn't get to the end of it. But at the top of the list is his immediate (and, in a sense, only) superior, the *Soprintendente del opificio delle pietre dure,* Signor Giorgio Focacci, whose heroic deeds during the flooding have given him an exaggerated sense of his own importance. Second on the list is the abbot Remo from the Badia, who has been making urgent telephone calls to the laboratory since nine o'clock in the morning. The *dottore* is not pleased, then, to see the abbot and Signor Giorgio approaching together, the abbot gesticulating wildly, Signor Giorgio nodding his understanding and sympathy.

There is nowhere to hide. Oh, there are plenty of places to hide physically, but not conveniently. Dottor Postiglione does not wish to spend the day in the Lace Museum on the fourth floor, for example. He hasn't the stamina for it. Lace does not interest him; it is an oppressive business, lace. Not worth the trouble. It is the product of slave labor and the opposite, therefore, of true art. Besides, he has pressing business to attend to. At any moment the Donatello *Magdalene* from the Opera del Duomo will be arriving. A space has been prepared. Instructions have been given. He is sorry that he did not go directly to the Opera del Duomo himself, doubly sorry now that it is too late to escape Signor Giorgio and the abbot.

He is bending studiously over a Madonna and Child, scuola

Dürer, when they enter the laboratory. Not only is the abbot still gesticulating, he is crying, actually sobbing out loud.

Good, thinks Dottor Postiglione. The abbot is a man who has had things his own way too long. But what can the matter be?

"Signor Giorgio, Abbot Remo." Dottor Postiglione offers a slight bow.

The abbot, without prefacing his remarks or giving the slightest indication of what to expect, begins to apologize in the typical Italian manner, with copious tears, self-abasements, self-deprecations, mea culpas. He is sorry for any distress he may have caused Dottor Postiglione in the past . . . , upon mature reflection . . . , realizes that Dottor Postiglione had very good arguments . . ." (which was not the same thing, the *dottore* notes, as admitting that he, Dottor Postiglione, was right and the abbot wrong).

"Yes, yes, Abbot Remo. It was silly to have quarreled, but come to the point, please."

The abbot dries his tears on the long sleeve of his habit. "Saint Francis . . . ," he says. "The frescoes . . ."

The abbot is a father with a sick child, pleading with the doctor: "What is to be done? What can we do? You must come at once."

"Yes, yes, of course, but you must describe the symptoms."

"The frescoes, the frescoes," he cries in anguish. "They are growing off the wall. If you don't do something we shall be ruined."

" 'We,' Abbot Remo? You mean the frescoes will be ruined."

"Yes, we shall be ruined."

"Yes," Dottor Postiglione repeats. "I see. You mean that if

the frescoes are ruined your principal tourist attraction will be gone and you'll have to start manufacturing one of those dreadful aperitifs that monks specialize in. Something with ninety-five degrees of alcohol, like that nasty stuff they make at the Certosa."

"You are too severe, Dottore; even monks must eat."

There are many frescoed chapels in Florence that could fall to the wrecking ball without eliciting tears of regret from Dottor Postiglione, but the Lodovici Chapel in the Badia Fiorentina is not one of them. Quite the opposite, in fact. Its frescoes are, in their own way, as fine as those in the Carmine, and every bit as dramatic, though a recent (and highly controversial) restoration, carried out against his advice by a charlatan from the ministry in Rome, has rather tarted it up and destroyed some of the original charm.

"The brothers are praying in the chapel."

"You're hoping for a miracle, is that it?"

"God is good, Dottore, God is good."

"But tell me, Abbot Remo, what exactly has happened? The water damage was minimal, wasn't it? And I thought the *nafta* had been removed with great success?"

Signor Giorgio intervenes. "The heat lamps are your only hope, Abbot Remo. Believe me, you're too impatient. You have to pull the moisture out from behind the walls. You can't just snap your fingers and it's done. No. It takes time and patience."

"You command my greatest respect, Signor Giorgio," says the abbot, "but the situation is desperate and I must ask Dottor Postiglione to assist me."

"Very well, Abbot Remo, I wash my hands of the matter."

Signor Giorgio, fortunately, is not a man to hold a grudge.

As long as he receives a salary commensurate with his exalted position as a *soprintendente* he will not take umbrage at trifling insults.

"See what you can do, Sandro," he says good naturedly to Dottor Postiglione to show that he is not annoyed as he leaves.

The abbot *in extremis* is more painful to Dottor Postiglione than the abbot *in furore.* It is hard to believe that this is the same man who denounced him, in a letter to *La Nazione,* as an enemy of art and of progress.

"Everything that can be done will be done, I can assure you, Abbot Remo. I shall come myself. I have already telephoned for one of the vans. You should never have used those heat lamps; they work too fast."

"But Signor Giorgio—"

"Yes, Signor Giorgio and I don't see eye to eye on this question. Remember, Signor Giorgio is an administrator. But don't give up hope. We shall find something."

The abbot groans, and continues to groan, in the taxi that takes them to the Badia.

The church of the Badia Fiorentina has undergone many reconstructions. It was enlarged by Arnolfo di Cambio, architect of the Duomo, in 1282. The ruined campanile was reconstructed in 1330. The Cloister of the Oranges was added in 1435–40 by Bernardo Rossellino, who also constructed, in 1495, the portal that opens onto the present-day Via del Proconsolo. And finally, in the seventeenth century the entire structure was remodeled in the baroque style by Matteo Segaloni, who completely changed the orientation of the church, which is in the shape of a Greek cross, so that the high altar, once on the west end of the cross, is now on the east.

The Lodovici Chapel, which one reaches through a door in the west wall, was frescoed by an unknown painter (the "Master of the Badia Fiorentina") in the early fifteenth century, miraculously survived the radical reorientation by Matteo Segaloni and (even more miraculously) the attention of the nineteenth-century restorers, the same experts who repainted the Giotto frescoes in Santa Croce.

Dottor Postiglione pays the taxi driver—the abbot carries no money—and they enter the church, which is damp and chilly, through the portico on the Via del Proconsolo, and make their way to the Lodovici Chapel. The *dottore* experiences what a sinner who has frozen to death might feel upon waking up in hell, a pleasing warmth that almost immediately becomes intolerable. Two fantastical heating machines, like diabolical engines, have been trained at the base of the dado in an effort—evidently unsuccessful—to keep the moisture from rising to the level of the frescoes. This is the first time Dottor Postiglione has actually seen one of these machines, which the Committee to Rescue Italian Art has imported from Germany. The fires roar. The flames shoot blue and orange, licking the *pietra serena* panels of the dado, like the flames that tickle the feet of Pope Boniface VIII in the *Inferno.* They provide the only light in the room. Hellish. The noise is equally infernal, a roaring, mingled with the sound of the assembled monks, who have congregated to pray for the salvation of the frescoes. One of the brothers reads from the Ordinary, and the others give the responses in unison. The smell, too, is infernal. Electric, sulfuric, human. Twenty large, sweating, unwashed monks. (Dottor Postiglione suspects that they have congregated in this small room to get warm, the way people used to go to the movie theaters to get warm.) It is impossible to think in such circumstances. The *dottore* fishes in his pocket for some change and deposits one hundred lire in a little coin box. The electric light goes on and stays on for three minutes.

Art restorers, like plastic surgeons, learn to steel themselves against the power of painful visual stimuli: harelips, cleft palates, webbed hands and feet and other deformities for the one. For the other: mutilated canvases, deteriorating marble, crumbling stone, flaking pigments. But sometimes even the most hardened professional is caught by surprise, by a visual blow, as it were, to the solar plexus. The wind is knocked out of him, and he experiences a physical convulsion that is impossible to conceal. This is what happens to Dottor Postiglione when the light comes on and he catches sight of the frescoes.

He switches off the heaters and asks the abbot to dismiss the monks, who leave the warm room reluctantly and resume their prayers in the church itself. The light goes out and he fishes in his pocket for more change.

"You have to get some light in here," he snaps at the abbot.

"Yes, right away. I'll see to it immediately."

"Isn't there a switch to turn the light on so you don't have to keep putting change in the box?"

"Brother Sacristan will know, I'm sure."

"Get those heaters out of here." The *dottore* mops his high forehead with a handkerchief.

The abbot was right. The frescoes seem to be growing off the wall. They are moving, shimmering masses, like one of those idiotic religious cards you can buy at San Lorenzo: when you shift the angle slightly the picture changes from (say) Christ on the cross to (say) Christ ascending into heaven.

Though he is not a religious man, Dottor Postiglione crosses himself in the dark, still holding the handkerchief in his hand.

The watermark in the chapel is about two meters high. Some fuel oil remains on the lower part of the frescoes and on the clear gray stone at the base. The real problem, however, is not the water damage, or the oil slick, which can be removed. The real problem is that moisture rising *through* the tremendous walls of the old building not only carries with it salts from the ground, it dissolves the soluble salts that it encounters within the walls themselves, bringing them to the surface, where the water evaporates. The salts then crystallize, forming either superficial excrescences on the surface or cryptoflorescences within the actual pores of the wall. Various types of disintegration can occur at this point, depending on the nature of the salts themselves and the nature of the surface. As the crystals expand, something has to give way. Either the pores of the wall will break, causing the surface of the paint to disintegrate, or the crystals will be extruded in crystalline threads, like cotton candy. This is what is happening now. The crystals are growing so rapidly that you can almost see them forming, like whiskers. Not dark stubble, however, but translucent filaments, so that the surface of the painting, viewed from an angle, looks like a vertical field of wildflowers, something from the brush of an impressionist. But if the pressure exerted by the growing crystals becomes too strong, the paint surface will begin to crumble, and a work of art that has ministered to the needs of rich and poor alike for six centuries will disappear. As if someone were erasing a blackboard.

You can tear up a musical score without destroying the music. You can burn a novel without destroying the story. But a painting is itself, has no soul, no essence other than itself. It is what it is, a physical object. If it is destroyed it is gone forever. *Sic transit gloria mundi.* This is why Dottor Postiglione prefers it to the other fine arts.

"Calcium nitrates," Dottor Postiglione says to the abbot. "Too many dead bodies in the crypt. Too much nitrogen in the soil. You should have installed a moisture barrier as I recommended."

"Yes, Dottore, but where were we to find the money? You yourself know how difficult and expensive . . . What were we to do?"

The *dottore* sighs. The problem at hand won't be helped by getting into another argument with the abbot.

He tries to conceal the depth of his concern from Abbot Remo, but the abbot, like an anxious father, reads the *dottore*'s mind easily and resumes his pleading: "Dottore, you must *do* something."

The *dottore* looks at his watch, an uncharacteristic gesture, for he has never been an impatient man, not a man who got into a frenzy waiting for his wife to get dressed, or to return with the car, though when his wife moved to Rome she took the car. Since then something of the balance of life has been lost. The *dottore*'s work has become too important. Great works of art in the past have been lost. There are probably too many of them anyway, just as there are too many churches in Florence. But he doesn't like to see them go, and the Badia is a special place, a nice place to slip into and sit for a while if you're in the *centro*. There's a nice quiet cloister that's difficult to find unless you know where you're going. No one's likely to wander in there, not even the monks.

The abbot, unable to locate a light or an extension cord, stations a monk by the door. The monk keeps feeding hundred-lire pieces into the box to keep the lights on until the hastily assembled restoration crew arrives with floodlights and extension cords and the chapel begins to look like the scene of the crime in a detective show. A photographer starts snapping shots; the carpenters begin assembling a scaffolding; the technicians measure the humidity and the temperature. But there is no time for careful measurements and serious photographs to document the problem and the work. No time, even, for proper analysis of the salts, which is crucial in order to determine their exact composition. Something has to be done at once to retard the capillary action that is bringing the salts to the surface. A dramatic trial of strength is being enacted before their very eyes. If the crystals prove stronger than the pores in the wall, the intonaco itself—the surface coat of plaster that actually holds the paint—will begin to disintegrate and the painting will be lost. Student volunteers are bringing in ladders and a portable sink from the truck, and heavy glass bottles of various solvents and gels and fixatives, and boxes of Japanese tissues.

"Calcium sulfate?" Dottor Postiglione, altering his diagnosis, ventures a tentative opinion in the form of a question to one of the students. "I'm afraid so," he says, answering his own question. The sulfates are less soluble and therefore more dangerous than the nitrates. "Look at that patch there, and there." A white, opaque film has begun to form in several places near the lower edge of the fresco, where the donor, a Renaissance merchant, Francesco Lodovici, and his wife, kneel. The patches indicate the conversion of calcium carbonate into calcium sulfate within the intonaco itself, a cancer growing before his very eyes.

"Where's the nearest source of water?" he asks the abbot, who has returned with a small table lamp.

"In the *gabinetto,* Dottore, behind the sacristy."

"We'll need water. Some of your men will have to carry it. You have buckets?"

"Yes, Dottore. Brother Sacristan will know."

Dottor Postiglione lights a cigarette and throws the match on the floor. Holding his cigarette at arm's length, he inspects one of the white patches. "I've never seen anything like this," he says to one of the carpenters, an older man with small wide-set eyes. "I mean happening so fast. I warned Signor Giorgio about these heating machines. They're pulling the moisture up faster than it can evaporate, so the whole process is accelerating."

The carpenter touches his cheekbone to show that he appreciates the gravity of the situation.

A monk enters the chapel with a leaky wooden bucket of water from the *gabinetto.*

Dottor Postiglione, his cigarette dangling from his lips, removes his coat, rolls up his sleeves, washes his hands. Monks, gathered around the door, still chant and respond in a repetitive tribal ritual. Their chanting reminds Dottor Postiglione of the Buddhists who congregate in the apartment beneath him twice a day to chant wordlessly and meditate.

He measures thirty grams of ammonium bicarbonate into a wide-mouthed beaker. One of the carpenters drops a wrench and curses. A monk pours another bucket of water into the portable sink. The student volunteers watch in silence. Fifty grams of sodium bicarbonate. The bicarbonates form a base that will, if all goes well, dissolve the newly formed crystals. Twenty-five grams of Desogen (ten percent strength). The Desogen will "wet" the solution so that it will not form into droplets (like water droplets on a newly waxed car) and run down the surface of the painting. Six grams of carboxymethyl cellulose. To retain moisture.

Dottor Postiglione tears a sheet of Japanese tissue into small pieces, which he dips into the solution and applies to different areas of the painting, like small Band-Aids. The abbot, who has joined the monks in prayer, keeps popping back into the small chapel to see what's going on.

"How does it look, Dottore?"

Dottor Postiglione holds out his hand, palm down, and moves it from side to side, like a man trilling an octave on the piano, but slowly.

"I was too proud," the abbot says, "to listen to you before. I've learned something from—"

"Please, Abbot Remo. Let's forget the past."

"If I can help in any way . . ."

Dottor Postiglione puts an arm around the abbot and gently leads him to the door. "You belong here," he says, "with your children. Pray without ceasing, Abbot Remo, pray without ceasing."

8

Una cittadina

On the way to the Piazza Goldoni my natural curiosity got the better of me. The streets were full of people. A lot of shops were selling goods that had been damaged by the flood, and I tried to distract myself by buying a blouse, and then a scarf, and then a little sundress—all very cheap. And then I tried on a pair of shoes, but I knew, as I was trying on the shoes, that I was going to look at the book, just as I had known, once Molly told me about it, that I would look at the *Manual of Modern Marriage* that was hidden in the bottom of Papa's underwear drawer. I'd been too embarrassed, in Madre Badessa's presence, to really look; the pictures had been like flashbulbs popping in my face. But now I had them all to myself.

I went straight to the bar in the Piazza Signoria where the schoolboys had sung " 'ome on the Range" and settled myself, with an espresso, in an inconspicuous corner where no one could glance over my shoulder.

I took the book out of my book bag and placed it on the table next to my coffee. Though the embroidered binding was beyond repair the book itself had not suffered greatly. Like many of the books in the library, it had been squeezed so tightly in one of the massive oak presses that the paper hadn't absorbed much water. The sheets of absorbent paper, which had been properly inserted every twenty pages or so, would absorb what remained. Mold would be a more serious problem. It would need to be treated with thymol as soon as possible.

The second part of the book—not the prayer book but the Aretino—consisted of two ottavo gatherings. The sonnets were printed on the verso of each leaf, the engravings on the recto. There were sixteen of each.

I started at the beginning and tried not to rush forward too rapidly, but the sonnets turned out to be a nasty piece of work —coarse, crude, disgusting—enough, almost, to make me lose interest in looking any further, though in fact I read them all. In many of the sonnets, interestingly enough, the women speak out as forthrightly as the men. But such language! I kept my face in the book to conceal my blushes.

SHE: What a beautiful *cazzo,* how long and thick!
        If I matter to you, let me view it.
HE: Why don't we try, with me on top,
        To see if you can hold this *cazzo* in your *potta?*

SHE: What do you mean "Why don't we try?" "If I
        can hold?"
        I'd rather do that thing than eat or drink.
HE: But if I crush you with all my weight
        I'll hurt you. SHE: You're reasoning like Rosso.

Throw yourself on top of me
On the bed on the floor. If you were Marforio
Or a giant, it would make it even more thrilling;
   Just as long as you reach my marrow
With this oh-so-venerable *cazzo* of yours
Guaranteed to cure *potte* of their "itching."

HE: Open wide your thighs.
There are women around dressed more fashionably
But none so well *fottuta* as you.

The drawings themselves, however, told another story. The repertoire of poses, I suppose, was essentially the same as that of Mama and Papa's *Manual of Modern Marriage,* or of the *Kama Sutra,* or of Japanese pillow books, but it seemed to me that whoever had executed these engravings had transcended this abstract schema and produced something that the spectator . . . no, "spectator" is the wrong word. "Spectator" suggests an outside observer, a peeping Tom, and this is precisely the opposite of what I felt myself to be.

"Drawing is discovery," Mama used to say, but like most of the things Mama said about art, this maxim never made too much sense to me. But in this case I could see what she meant. The drawings struck me as private rather than public, not illustrations of something fixed and finished, not a record of completed experience, but something tentative, exploratory, as if the artist were in the process of discovering what the lovers were themselves discovering. I felt that I was included in this process, rather than just being a spectator. I felt that I was in motion, that my consciousness was expanding in a way that nothing in my actual concrete experience had prepared me for. And of course it was a visual consciousness, not a verbal one, which is why it's so hard to communicate it in words.

It wasn't till the bar filled up, about eleven o'clock, that I finally noticed the time. I'd been sitting there for more than two hours.

On my way to the Piazza Goldoni I noticed a sign in a store window that said: *Chiuso perché sono nervoso.* "Closed because I'm nervous." I was nervous, too. There was too much hustle and bustle, too much traffic, too much noise, and I felt as if everyone I passed in the street knew what I had in my book bag, and that if they looked me in the eye they'd see the images that had been imprinted on my brain. I wanted to retreat, to get back to the convent.

I pressed on, however, forgetting that the Piazza Goldoni, which is right on the river, was in one of the most severely damaged areas in the city. The Arno, turning in on itself, had chewed up the embankment the way a sawmill chews up trees. There wasn't much left of the bookstores. A tall man in a gray overcoat was standing in the piazza, smoking a cigar and crying openly. I wondered if he might be Signor Giustiniani, but I didn't have the heart to approach him.

My first thought was to try Feltrinelli or Marzocco, the big bookstores downtown. My second was to try Dottor Postiglione at the Palazzo Davanzati, which was much closer.

I made my way to the Palazzo Davanzati, where I learned, with some difficulty, that Dottor Postiglione was at the Badia. A secretary who was overdressed, at least for my taste, looked me over, decided I wasn't important, and told me to leave the book with her, which I was not about to do. Instead I made my way to the Badia, which was one of my favorite spots in the city. It had always been the third stopping point on Mama's tours, which proceeded chronologically rather than spatially, starting down at the Ponte Vecchio, to demonstrate why the city was built here (at the narrowest spot in the river between Pisa and the mountains) rather than somewhere else, moving on to the Piazza Repubblica (site of the original Roman camp) and then heading straight west to the Badia, located on the edge of the old Roman city. Mama had a specially dramatic way of entering the Badia, which is one of the reasons I liked it. There's an unobtrusive door on the Via Dante Alighieri, which is dark and no wider than an alley, a door that might be the back door to a warehouse or a police station (and in fact the Badia does house the Prefettura di Polizia). Mama would suddenly pause, and then, without warning, as if she were acting on a sudden impulse, turn and lead us (by "us" I mean myself and a group of American students) through the door and down a long narrow corridor that leads to the church itself. She would then stride across the church, up the steps that led to the high altar, through another obscure door on the right, and up a flight of unlit stairs. The effect was always the same. You felt you were being led into an inner sanctum where maybe you weren't supposed to be, and that some monk was going to appear mysteriously and block your way. Of course, any tourist with a good guidebook could have done the same thing, but very few did.

At the top of the stairs was another door, also mysterious. This door opened onto the upper portico of the Chiostro degli

Aranci, the Cloister of the Oranges. There hadn't been any orange trees for years, and the grass had gone to seed, but it was a peaceful place, partly because very few people found it. You couldn't hear the noise of the city from here. A sequence of frescoes depicting the life of Saint Benedict offered several amusing scenes. In one a glass of wine, poisoned by one of the monks, shatters in Saint Benedict's hand just as he is about to drink it. In another a crow knocks a poisoned loaf of bread out of the saint's hand. In another a brother who has fallen into the lake is rescued by the saint, who is able to walk on the surface of the water.

The visit to the Badia was always a success. I sometimes stopped at the cloister. I practiced Mama's dramatic way of entering the church and surprised some of my Italian friends, who had never been inside.

There was another thing about the cloister that I liked. There was, on the lower level, a "foosball" game, one of those table games where you knock a ball back and forth by rotating levers with little men attached to them. Completely incongruous, but there it was. Was there some kind of youth group that met in the Badia? Did the monks themselves play "foosball," which the French call "babyfoot"? All the students had to take a picture of the "babyfoot" game. It humanized the whole place, made it more real, somehow. Mama and I also had lots of pictures that managed to include that "babyfoot" game.

Mama's tours always concluded with brief stops at the tomb of Ugo, marchese of Tuscany, and Fra Filippo Lippi's *Appearance of the Madonna to Saint Bernard,* and finally at the famous Lodovici Chapel, which is what everyone comes to see, and which is where I found Dottor Alessandro Postiglione.

When I first entered the church, from the Via Dante, I heard the sounds of chanting and was reluctant to interrupt a service. I could see, however, that there was no one behind the high altar. I poked my head around the corner and saw an astonishing sight: about thirty monks on their knees in three rows, half circles, around the door that led to the Lodovici Chapel. I couldn't make out what they were saying. The church was dark, but there was a bright light in the chapel itself.

On my way past them I was accosted by a monk who turned out to be the abbot. "I'm sorry, Signorina, the chapel is undergoing restoration."

"I'm bringing something to Dottor Postiglione," I said, undeterred.

"Please, Signorina, you can see that we are suffering a terrible tragedy."

"It will only take a moment," I insisted. I wanted to see what in the world was going on. If I'd been a man I believe the abbot would have stopped me forcibly, but I think he was afraid to touch a woman. At least he drew back as I pressed forward.

I did not have a very clear visual memory of the chapel from my earlier visits—I tended to remember Mama's enthusiasm more than actual details of what she was enthusiastic about— but the scene that I saw when I entered this time has stayed with me in minute details. A wooden scaffolding. Bright floodlights, like the ones Papa used to get out at Christmas when he wanted to take movies. Dottor Postiglione's shiny bald head reflected the light. There was a bronze cast to it, as if it were getting some sun. But the main shock was the row of white bandages plastered all over the two lower frescoes, so that they reminded me of the figures you see in cartoons (and perhaps in real hospitals, too), completely bandaged up. It was physically painful to look at.

It took me a while to grasp what was going on. An old man in dirty clothes that suggested some kind of uniform was coating the bandages with a transparent jellylike substance—sort of like Vaseline—and handing the strips to Dottor Postiglione, up on the scaffolding, who applied them with infinite care, pressing them with his fingertips, following the contours of invisible wounds. It was impossible to determine the subject of the two lower frescoes, not simply because of the bandages but because the surface had become cloudy, as if giant cataracts had formed.

I watched silently, listening to the rhythmic sound of the chanting monks, till Dottor Postiglione climbed down the ladder propped against the scaffolding and began to mix another batch of the salve or ointment—whatever it was he was applying to the surface of the painting. His face was strained, though like the young man leaning against the wall, he was smoking a cigarette as he worked. (I had to remind myself that this was Italy, where doctors smoke in hospital wards.) He looked past me at the abbot, who was standing behind me in the doorway, apologizing for my interruption, and then at me. Then he smiled and tilted his head.

"Ah, Signorina, what an unexpected pleasure. Now you can see that I earn my living like an honest man."

"I never thought otherwise," I said, though in fact I had, somehow, been thinking otherwise.

"Like a bricklayer, as you can see, or a plasterer, really—*un artigiano.*"

"Can I help?" I said, forgetting, for the moment, the purpose of my visit.

"*Che fortuna!* But of course, Carlo," he turned to the old man, "please show the signorina how to prepare the compresses, and then maybe you could bring us some coffee."

And that was how I spent the rest of the day. Dottor Postiglione applied the compresses as rapidly as I could prepare them. Carlo returned in half an hour with two cups of espresso on a tray with a sugar bowl and some little spoons and then settled himself comfortably on the floor. The room was strangely warm from some fantastic space heaters, though these had been turned off.

Four scenes from the life of Saint Francis had been frescoed on the wall above the altar: Saint Francis disrobing in the public square, casting off his rich man's clothes in order to go naked, while the bishop, at his father's orders, rushes to cover his nakedness without quite succeeding; Saint Francis preaching to the birds; Saint Francis dancing before the pope; and finally Saint Francis receiving the stigmata. The two lower frescoes had been completely filmed over with—as I learned from Dottor Postiglione—salts that had been carried upward by the moisture rising up through the thick walls. The upper two frescoes weren't so bad, though you could see that they were starting to cloud over too.

We worked without talking, without thinking. At least I wasn't thinking. I was drifting and dreaming even as I followed Dottor Postiglione's instructions for a new batch of the solution. I'd been doing a lot of thinking and it was nice to turn my mind off for a while. The only interruptions came from time to time from the anxious abbot. "Pray without ceasing,"

Dottor Postiglione would say cheerfully. "Pray without ceasing, Abbot Remo, and all will be well." I thought that this was the sort of joke a doctor might make during an operation to relieve the tension.

I've always felt intimidated in the presence of great art. I've always felt that my responses were inadequate. "Just sit quietly and look," was Mama's advice. But sitting quietly and looking always made me nervous. Like many people, I'd rather read about a painting than look at it. Or I'd rather hear someone talk about it. But working with Dottor Postiglione gave me a new perspective. The pressure was off. There was no need to work up an intense spiritual experience. No one was going to quiz me to make sure I'd appreciated them properly. The job wasn't to appreciate them but to keep preparing the compresses. I saw the frecoes as things, pieces of this world rather than venerable icons pointing the way to some remote metaphysical realm called Art, physical objects that could wear out, like a shirt, and then be mended, and as things I found them easier to like. Like old shirts. Saint Francis dancing before the pope, Innocent III, who has just given him permission to found a religious order. What a wonderful image. I'd seen it a dozen times before, but this was the first time it made me want to dance, too.

At one o'clock old Carlo disappeared for his siesta. He returned at three and then went for more coffee. Each trip took about forty-five minutes, though there was a bar just across the street, on the Via del Proconsolo, where Mama had always stopped with the students for hot chocolate. About five o'clock a reporter from *La Nazione* arrived, took some pictures, asked Dottor Postiglione some questions and then turned to me.

"Are you a member of the emergency restoration team?" he wanted to know.

"Oh, no," I said; "I just wandered in off the street."

"Just wandered in off the street? And you're helping like this? *Favoloso!*" He grabbed my hand and kissed it, notwithstanding the rubber gloves and the caustic paste, which must have burned his lips.

By this time the worst areas had been done and I had made up a new solution, following Dottor Postiglione's instructions carefully, that was slightly less caustic, for areas of the painting that were less heavily encrusted with salt, like the crystals you'll find on a dish if you fill it with salt water and allow the water to evaporate. Not sodium chloride, though, but calcium sulfate (the worst) and probably other salts too, nitrates, and so on. The gel was a solvent that worked on all of them, though at different rates, depending on the nature of the salt. Nitrates were the easiest to dissolve, calcium sulfate the most difficult. There was no way of telling them apart just from looking. Every once in a while Dottor Postiglione would remove a compress and gently probe the surface with a wooden spatula. The solution, mildly caustic like strong laundry soap, caused a slight burning on my arms at the tops of my rubber gloves, but nothing really uncomfortable.

At seven o'clock Dottor Postiglione climbed down from the scaffolding for the last time, stripped off his rubber gloves and called for the abbot. The monks were still praying, their enthusiasm, if that's the right word, undiminished. (Was it still the same team or had replacements been sent in from time to time?

I couldn't tell.) Dottor Postiglione lifted one of the compresses and probed with his spatula, showing the abbot how the salt crystals were beginning to soften.

"I'll be back in three or four hours," he said, "and then we shall see."

"Is everything going to be all right?"

"Be happy, Abbot Remo. One way or another."

"Shall we continue to pray?"

"Oh, I think so, yes, it won't hurt."

"But is it necessary?"

"For insurance, Abbot Remo, for insurance. I shall return tonight. How will I get in?"

"There's an entrance through the police station, Dottore. Let me show you. There's a bell you can ring. They'll let you in. The night *capitano* knows me, you won't have any trouble."

"Very good, Abbot Remo. Just leave everything as it is for now. Please don't touch anything. And don't turn on the heaters, please."

"As you wish, Dottore."

We followed the abbot up the set of stairs that led to the upper level of the cloister, down a winding corridor, and out through a door that admitted us into a large room filled with desks, empty now. Two *poliziotti,* in smart uniforms, gave us a funny look as we said goodbye to the abbot.

We went down another set of stairs and out into the night, which was cold and starry. I was thinking to myself how much Mama would have appreciated this exit through the police station, when I suddenly realized that I'd completely forgotten about the book of drawings. I'd left it in my book bag in the chapel.

"*O Dio!*" I said. "I've forgotten my *borsa*."

"*Niente,*" he said. "You can come to dinner with me, it's the least I can do. Then we come back here, you can retrieve your *borsa* and all will be well."

"Oh, no, I couldn't, really I couldn't. I must get back to the convent."

Actually I wanted to, but the prospect of showing him the Aretino book was beginning to seem more problematic. I couldn't quite picture the scene, his response. Not after the labor of this particular day. What would he think? I had imagined something more businesslike, handing the book to him across a busy desk, in a room full of people. And it was late. Madre Badessa would be worried.

"So convent life is agreeing with you?"

"Very much so. You were right, it's much more interesting than I anticipated. Madre Badessa is a wonderful woman. And I feel very useful."

"And you don't feel useful at home?"

"Not in the same way. I like the feeling of urgency, of everyone pulling together, the sense of purpose. I don't feel lost in the convent."

"You've discovered your vocation, perhaps?"

"Do you always speak in questions?"

"Only when I have so few answers."

"But what about my *borsa?* Will it be safe? I'll come by tomorrow, first thing in the morning. Will you be here?"

"*Dipende.* Yes, I'll be here, but I don't know when. I have to look at the frescoes again tonight. But don't worry, your *borsa* will be perfectly safe."

"Listen, there is something."

165

"*Mi dica.*" Tell me.

"There's a book in the *borsa.* Madre Badessa thinks it's very valuable and wants to dispose of it. She wanted me to take it to a dealer, but his shop is closed because of the flood. I thought you might be able to help."

"Books are hardly my line, Signorina."

"But you would know whom to ask, wouldn't you?"

"Well, yes, but . . ." He shrugged his shoulders, one of those full-bodied Italian shrugs. "A book, it can't be difficult. All right. I'll take it to my place and have a look at it. But tell me something about this book. I know my cousin was up in arms because the monks at San Marco were trying to get their hands on the library. This must be a very special book, to dispose of it . . . *così furtivamente?*"

"You'll see when you look at it. But you're sure it's safe? I wouldn't mind going back for it now."

"Believe me, there's not a safer place in the entire city."

I assumed I could trust him—because he was Madre Badessa's cousin, and because I liked him.

"You're a woman of mystery," he said. "But even women of mystery have to eat."

"No, really, I couldn't. Thank you very much; it's been a very interesting afternoon."

"*Molto interessante, Signorina, molto interessante.*"

The next day a special messenger delivered my book bag to the convent. The Aretino volume was gone, but there was a clipping from *La Nazione* in its place, a photograph of the monks on their knees in the nave and of the bandaged frescoes, and a brief account of the heroic efforts of Dottor Postiglione, and—to my surprise—his volunteer assistant, an anonymous *cittadina* who had just wandered in off the street. I was as pleased as if Mayor Bargellini had presented me with the key to the city.

9

Non voglio morire

Sister Agata Agape became ill. A week passed. I was very busy, but I missed her cheerful presence in the evening sessions and was sorry to learn that she wasn't expected to live. Old contemplatives, I was told, can generally predict their own deaths, sometimes right to the minute, but apparently this wasn't the case with Sister Agata, for Father Francesco had been summoned twice in the middle of the night to administer the sacrament, and both times Sister Agata had rallied by the time he arrived.

I was also sorry to learn that Father Francesco, whose apartments were at the opposite end of the convent from the infirmary, had made it clear to the novices, whose job it was to sit up with Sister Agata, that he didn't want any more false alarms. He had, in fact, scolded Sister Maria in front of Sister Agata and accused her of crying wolf.

No one talked about anything else during the evening session in the *sala comune*. Nuns, you know, are not self-sufficient. Monks can get on by themselves, as long as one of them is ordained, but nuns need a man to say mass. And to anoint the sick. But Father Francesco was not popular. When he entered the *sala comune,* which was not often, the nuns knelt and asked his blessing, but behind his back they criticized him freely. What if Sister Agata were to die before he got there to administer the last rites? It could happen. And if it could happen to Sister Agata, then it could happen to any one of them!

I could share the indignation of the nuns at Father Francesco, but not their professional concern for the well-being of Sister Agata's immortal soul. What if Sister Agata *were* to die before Father Francesco administered the last rites? What difference could it possibly make? The notion that God might deny salvation to a soul on some technicality is so morally repugnant that I found it painful to think about.

I tried to turn the conversation back to more congenial issues: the new habits, Sister Chiara's second book, the ongoing struggle with the bishop, the cleaning of the frescoes, the construction of the new library on the second floor. But without success. I'd come up against something primitive and irrational that took precedence over these enlightened concerns.

Determined to stay out of it, I kept my opinions to myself and thanked God that I still had enough detective novels to last another week. I was planning to go home just before Christmas, but before I went I wanted to stabilize the Aretino volume so that it could be sold. I'd set up a little workshop for the purpose in Dottor Postiglione's apartment in Piazza Santa Croce. Dottor Postiglione—Sandro—had a friend in Rome, a rare book dealer, who had offered to dispose of it for a small commission.

I visited Sister Agata once in the infirmary, as was the custom, to say good-bye. We were both, I thought, in our own ways, preparing to go home. I found her lying flat on her back on a narrow bed. Out of her habit she looked very different. The fine white hair on her old head was cropped short and stuck out in tufts. She reached for the hand that I extended and took it. I'd thought of her as a large peasant woman, but she looked thin and frail under the coarse sheet. There was no strength in her grip.

"Is it true that you're a *protestante?*" she asked.

"Yes," I said, "but you mustn't worry."

"I'm a foolish old woman," she said. *"Una vecchia sciocca."*

"Don't be silly," I said. "You're a lovely old woman. You make me think of my mama." This was true, not because of any particular resemblance, but because I had stood by Mama's bedside so often.

"A *protestante* came to our village once, to help the sisters with the *scuola materna.* No one would rent to her; everyone was afraid. But she stayed five years anyway, and when she left everyone was sorry. She was a good woman." She sighed. *"Tutto è possibile."*

She gave my hand another feeble squeeze.

I had finished the prayer book she'd been working on and showed it to her. She seemed pleased with the blue-and-white headband and asked me to leave it with her, which I did.

"Is there anything else, Sister Agata?" I asked her.

"Yes," she said. *"Non voglio morire*—I don't want to die—but don't tell the others."

I wouldn't have seen her again if it hadn't been for Sister Gemma.

When it came Sister Gemma's turn to sit up with Sister

Agata, she was very nervous. It was the first time I'd seen her upset.

"How can you tell when she's dying?" she asked me. "I've never seen anyone die. What if I call Father Francesco again and then Sister Agata doesn't die?"

"Better safe than sorry," was my advice.

"But he's such an unpleasant man," she said. "And he made such a fuss when Sister Maria called him. He scolded her right in front of Sister Agata."

"Why don't you just get rid of him and find somebody else?"

"He's appointed by the bishop."

"Ah, yes," I said knowingly, "the bishop. Well then, it can't be helped, can it? You'll just have to use your own judgment."

"Would you sit up with me?"

I give her my "Who, me?" look, like the Madonna at the Annunciation. "What good would *that* do? I've never seen anyone die either. I wouldn't know anymore than you do."

"Are you afraid?"

"No, of course not."

"Please?"

I had no particular wish to see someone die, but I didn't want to seem afraid either.

"We'd have to ask Madre Badessa."

"I'll ask her. I'm sure it will be all right."

Of course it was.

In the corridor on the way to the infirmary I encountered Dottoressa Bassani, who didn't expect Sister Agata to last the night.

"Sicuro?"

"Sicuro."

The *dottoressa* was a young woman, cheerful, professional. Her scientific confidence was reassuring. Death, after all, is a perfectly natural physical phenomenon. There was nothing out of the ordinary going on.

"Her heart isn't strong enough to keep the blood circulating," she explained. "Either she'll suffer another myocardial infarction or the heart will simply slow down gradually and stop."

"How will I know when to call the priest?" I smiled to distance myself from the superstition.

She smiled back. "You won't need to. She doesn't want one."

The infirmary was a series of small rooms, all empty except one, like hospital rooms, but there were no nurses' stations, no hustle and bustle as in a hospital corridor, no bright lights. Deep-set windows opened onto the upper loggia of the cloister. There were four beds in Sister Agata's room, and four small tables. On one of these tables, spread with a white cloth, were the mysterious necessities for the last rites: a crucifix, two lighted candles, a glass of water (half full), a small bowl of water, a linen napkin, a bottle of holy water, balls of cotton on a white plate, another plate with a bit of bread.

Sister Gemma was waiting for me at the door, looking pale and grim.

"I saw Dottoressa Bassani in the corridor," I whispered.

She nodded.

"She says it will be tonight."

Sister Gemma continued to nod her head slightly.

Sister Agata was neither sleeping nor awake, but present. She opened her eyes when I took her hand. *La protestante.* Moving her fingers slightly in my hand.

I sat down on a wooden chair next to Sister Gemma. We were both uneasy. "I saw Dottoressa Bassani in the corridor," I whispered again.

Sister Gemma nodded again.

"She told me Sister Agata doesn't want us to call Father Francesco."

Sister Gemma gave me a frightened look, and I tried to reassure her. *"Boh,"* I said, an all-purpose Florentine noise made by suddenly opening one's mouth and taking in a lot of air (while keeping the nasal passages closed). And then: "You can't really blame her, can you, after what happened?"

"No, but what if . . . what if she's slipped, fallen into a state of sin?"

"I don't think that's likely, do you? Sister Agata? She hasn't had much opportunity, after all."

"But what if she's *angry* with Father Francesco? What if she hasn't forgiven him? If she's carrying a grudge against him she could be in a state of sin."

I hadn't thought of this dimension of the problem. I'd thought Agata was perfectly safe.

"What legalistic nonsense," I said. "You can't really believe that God would let Sister Agata go to hell on a technicality?"

Sister Gemma didn't answer me, she just sat quietly with her hands folded in her lap.

"My mother," I said, "refused to see a priest before she died."

"O Signora!" Sister Gemma took in a short, sharp breath. I was surprised at the strength of her dismay and didn't press on.

Mama was, in fact, an Episcopalian but hadn't been to church for years, and her sense of honor prevented her from accepting a visit from Father Brady, the rector of the Church of the Redeemer, where my sisters and I had been baptized, even though Papa had called him and he was standing downstairs in the front hall in his shirtsleeves, taking in the central air-conditioning.

"I'll take my chances," she said, and she did, though afterwards Papa called Father Bob again and asked him to conduct the funeral service. He did it, but without much enthusiasm, not that you could blame him. Papa gave him a hundred dollars for his trouble and made a substantial donation to the building fund. We lapsed Protestants are funny things, aren't we?

Our "watch" had begun at nine o'clock, directly after compline. It was now eleven. The *silenzio maggiore* was in effect. I didn't think it applied to us, but we had stopped talking anyway. Another hour elapsed. Twelve o'clock, and then another. Sister Agata had been lying still and breathing easily, but now she began to struggle a little, and her fingers began to pluck at the coarse sheet that stuck out from under a heavy, standard convent-issue blanket. They moved rapidly and unceasingly, back and forth, as if checking the hem of a fine garment for loose threads or for some unevenness in the stitching.

Sister Gemma was agitated, too. "Do you think it's time?" she asked.

"Not yet."

I put my hand on Sister Agata's papery dry forehead but couldn't notice any sudden drop in temperature.

"Sister Agata," I said, just to be sure, "do you want me to call Father Francesco?"

Sister Agata, who was beginning to breathe more shallowly and more rapidly, opened her eyes for a moment and shook her head. Her lips moved without sound, no.

I sat down on the edge of the bed and rested my hand on her shoulder. Her fingers continued to pluck at the hem of the sheet. I closed my eyes so I wouldn't see them, and I realized now what I'd known all along—that Father Francesco was quite superfluous. That it was all superfluous, the whole enormous superstructure that had been erected, like the walls of an imaginary prison, to incarcerate our deepest hopes and fears, to keep them in place. What need did Sister Agata have now of holy water, holy bread, holy oil? What Sister Agata needed was someone to hold her hand, which I did.

Sister Gemma was sitting ramrod straight on her chair. What could I say to *her?*

I was trying to think, but Sister Agata's fingers continued to move under my hands and for some reason this nervous reflex—that's what I called it, a "nervous reflex"—was terribly upsetting. The energy it displayed was almost violent. You couldn't *not* be aware of it. I couldn't ignore it any more than I could have ignored a bat flying around the room or a rat stirring in the corner.

It's odd, isn't it, how you can suddenly settle on something, see it perfectly clearly, and then the next minute your imagination runs away with you. I'd been telling myself that death is the most natural thing in the world, but suddenly it didn't feel natural at all. A person crosses an imaginary line and you can't see her any more. Is that perfectly natural? Mama crossed that line in the night, alone, and now she's gone. Forever. And now Sister Agata was about to cross it, too, and I was there, right next to her, on one side of the line, and I thought I ought to be able to catch a glimpse of what lay on the other side. But I couldn't, and I suddenly thought of Hamlet's father, dying unhoused, and of that chilling scene in the *Inferno* when Saint Francis comes to gather in the soul of Guido da Montefeltro at the moment of death, only to learn that Guido had spoiled everything at the very end by putting his trust in the evil pope —lapsed from a state of grace, nothing to be done about it. My imagination, in spite of my express commands, began to fill the room with angels and devils, waiting just beyond the spectra of human perception, to pounce upon the naked soul of Sister Agata Agape, whose breathing was becoming more rapid and shallow. The fingers were suddenly still. I tried her forehead again. Cool and damp now.

Sister Gemma seemed calmer now. "You should say a prayer," she said.

"Agata Agape," I said. Sister Gemma crossed herself. "Agata Agape," I said again, "go without fear. Go with our love. We will hold you in our hearts. Good-bye."

And with no more noise than a canoe makes when you shove off from the dock in still water in the night, Agata Agape crossed over an imaginary line and we could see her no more.

"You can call Father Francesco now," I said to Sister Gemma. "Tell him it's no false alarm this time. It's the real thing."

10

The Sixteen Pleasures
of Pietro Aretino

I stopped by Alessandro Postiglione's apartment every afternoon to check on the Aretino, which I'd taken apart and
washed before interleaving it with absorbent paper and putting
it in a gerry-rigged thymol chamber. The apartment was
sparsely furnished—Sandro's wife had taken most of the furniture when she'd moved to Rome a dozen years earlier—but
there was a long table that I used for my workbench, and an
orange crate to sit on, and there was (at last) running water (not
hot, but running).

Sandro, who had given me a key, generally turned up just
after I'd arrived or just as I was about to leave, and in either
case we'd brew a small pot of espresso and drink it while we
talked—about the flood and its aftermath, about the magnitude
of the restoration effort, about the incompetence of the government in Rome and the latest political scandal, and about personal matters, too, though Sandro didn't say much about his
wife, except that she'd found Florence too provincial and that
annulment proceedings, after spending several years in the

lower courts, had finally found their way to the highest court of all, the Sacred Roman Rota. I had nothing comparable to reveal or to conceal, but Sandro seemed to find the details of my childhood in Chicago as exotic as I found the details of his in the Abruzzi. Our favorite topic, however, was neither the great world of public affairs nor the details of our respective childhoods. Our favorite topic was the book itself, the Aretino: How had it escaped the pope's wrath in the sixteenth century? How had it found its way into the library of Santa Caterina Nuova? Who had bound it with the prayer book? Had Lucia de' Medici known of its existence? And above all, How much money would it bring?

The latter question was the only one that was likely to be answered with certainty, but not till Sandro's friend in Rome— the antiquarian book dealer—had actually sold the book. Like Madre Badessa, he refused to name a figure, but he was eager to see the book, and in fact after it had been in the thymol chamber for two days, there was no reason not to send the loose gatherings to him in the solander box I'd constructed to hold them. But I wanted to be absolutely certain that all the mold spores had been destroyed, and besides, I didn't trust the Italian postal service. Sandro had to go to Rome in January or February, to put in an appearance at the ecclesiastical court, the Rota, and offered to take the book with him then. By that time, I'd be back in Chicago.

Everyone knows the story of Paolo and Francesca, but let me set it down anyway:

On a day for dalliance we read the rhyme
   of Lancelot, how love had mastered him.
   We were alone with innocence and dim time.
Pause after pause that high old story drew
   our eyes together while we blushed and paled;
   but it was one soft passage overthrew
our caution and our hearts. For when we read
   how her fond smile was kissed by such a lover,
   he who is one with me alive and dead
breathed on my lips the tremor of his kiss.
   That book, and he who wrote it, was a
   pander.
   That day we read no further.

Well, Sandro and I read no further either. Our go-between was
not so high-toned, I suppose, as Paolo and Francesca's French
romance, but then ours is not such a high-toned age. But not
without its own graces and little courtesies. Sandro led me into
the bedroom and undressed me in front of a cheval glass, which
is called a *psiche* in Italian, which is also the word for soul. I had
been in love before but I'd never really experienced lust. At
least not like this. All the imperfections, with which I was all
too familiar, of my stocky, serviceable little body, seemed to
disappear in that glass. I was like a statue coming to life, just
breaking out of its rigid pose. And my face was suffused with a
kind of radiance, not the kind you try to cover up with powder,
either.

   It was broad daylight and the figures carved on the frame of
the mirror stood out clearly: the Judgment of Paris. Aphrodite,
Hera, and Athena were all naked as jaybirds.

I reached out and touched them with my finger. The wood was smooth and cool.

"Which one would you have chosen?" I asked.

"Let me see," he said. His face wore a serious expression, as if he were performing some difficult calculations in his head.

I was down to bra and panties by this time, wondering which he'd remove first. Aware of his face in the mirror, peering first over one shoulder and then over the other. He had removed his jacket and rolled up his sleeves, like a man about to get down to serious business, but he still had his tie on.

"Signorina," he said, "I would choose you."

He removed the rest of my clothes and then I, too, was as naked as a jaybird, as naked as I'd been when I stood on the rock overlooking the sea in Sardegna, ready to take the plunge again.

Back at the convent I was sure that everyone would be able to tell what had happened, but nobody seemed to notice and our work proceeded on schedule. The only difference was that my afternoon excursions became more numerous and lengthier. And then one night I didn't return to the convent till eleven o'clock. This was late for Florence, which is not a late-night town. And it was late for me. It was the first time I'd stayed out, the first time I'd skipped supper. No one had ever said that I had to be in by such and such a time, but I was a little uneasy. I didn't know if the *portinaia* would let me in or not. There was nothing to do but ring the bell, which I did.

The door was opened immediately, not by the porteress but by Madre Badessa. Startled, I tried to read her face.

"I've been worried," she said, turning away from me, straightening something on a table that held some pamphlets, information about the convent. The room was a small one, like the little room in a funeral parlor where you sit down to do business with the undertaker. It was lit by a bulb that couldn't have been putting out more than ten watts. The dampness hadn't left the walls yet. All the carpeting had been taken out.

"May I speak to you?"

I thought she was going to ask me where I'd been, the way Mama had when I'd come home too late. She'd always been awake, no matter how late it was and no matter how quietly I moved. But it was nice. We'd always have a little talk, and I'd tell her everything that had happened. I never felt I really had to lie to her, though I sometimes spread a thick coat of varnish over the truth.

"Of course."

"Not here."

I followed her upstairs to her office.

"Please sit down." Something formal, distant, odd, between us.

"You wanted to ask me something?" I thought: She knows what's happened just by looking at me, or by the way I smell.

Madre Badessa was not perfectly at ease.

"May I ask what your plans are?"

"I'll have to leave soon."

"You're going to Rome?"

"No, to Luxembourg. I'm flying Icelandic. To Reykjavík, then New York, then home."

"You haven't thought of staying longer?"

"I've thought of it, but I have a job to get back to, I hope, and Papa's expecting me for Christmas."

"Because you've very welcome to stay with us, you know. You can stay as long as you like."

"Thank you, Madre Badessa. You're very generous."

"Maybe selfish rather than generous."

"You mustn't think so."

"You've been happy here? Reasonably?"

"Reasonably." I was uncomfortable. "No, more than 'reasonably.' "

"And you don't find our way of life quaint or repulsive?"

"No, how could you say so?"

"Because the world objects to us very strongly. I've lived in the world—I used to think that way myself. I thought that the monastic life was a kind of escapism, a running away from responsibilities. But don't look so alarmed, I'm not going to ask you if you've felt a vocation!" She smiled.

I felt more at ease. We were getting close to something.

"When I married," she said, "I thought I'd never be lonely again. But it wasn't like that."

I didn't know what to reply to this.

"My husband and I were very successful," she said. "We put together these sewing machines and bought up the local wool, which was usually sent off to Milan. . . . He was never unfaithful to me. . . ."

A series of false starts. I couldn't figure out what she was trying to get at. She was like someone trying to join two magnets together, positive to positive or negative to negative. They kept jumping apart. I wasn't much help.

"We had no children. That was a disappointment. Like Sarah

—Abraham's wife. We tried everything, doctors in Milan and in Switzerland, but nothing worked. I had to accept the fact that I was barren. That changed the direction of my life. What I wanted most was denied to me. You come up against something, a roadblock, you're so sure of the direction you're going in, the road you want to take, that it's inconceivable. But a bridge has been washed out. You have to find some other way."

The light was dim, the desk bare. There was absolutely nothing on it, not even any scratches.

"And now look. God has given me these children, my daughters, you see. I could never have foreseen it. Daughters in abundance. That's what I wanted to say to you. People say that God works in mysterious ways when they really mean that life, or something in their own lives, doesn't make any sense, but I think that's wrong. I think it means that we can't make any sense out of life until we give up our deepest hopes, until we stop trying to arrange everything to suit us. But once we do, or are forced to . . . That's what's mysterious."

I wasn't prepared to agree or disagree. I was too busy wondering how this applied to me. No, I wasn't really wondering, but I wasn't prepared to face the issue clearly.

"It's a joy, but it's also a terrible responsibility. I am their *superiora*. I act as their spiritual mother in the place of Christ. Mistakes can be costly."

"I'm sure you don't make many mistakes."

"Oh, child, you don't know. But what I want to say is that I think of you as my daughter, too. I wish you well, more than I can say. Maybe it's because you're different, or in a different situation. You're bound by no vows, no obligations. But I fear that in your case I've made a mistake, and I hope it's not too late to rectify it."

"A mistake, Madre Badessa? You've been wonderful."

"You're very kind, but . . . but the bishop is very unhappy."

I made a face when she mentioned the bishop.

"The bishop doesn't make things easy for us," she went on, "and I'm afraid now that he'll want to speak to you. I thought I ought to warn you. The bishop can be very unpleasant."

"Is it about Sister Agata?"

"Yes, but there's something else, too."

"The book?"

"Yes, the book. I shouldn't have asked you to take the responsibility for the book."

"But it was no problem."

"It's not just the book; it's what I've asked you to do or what I can't *ask* you to do. I can't ask you to lie to the bishop for me."

Deep breath. "Yes, I see. The bishop wants the book."

"Where is it now?"

I saw now where I stood: between the abbess and the bishop. But I didn't know what to say.

"Please don't lie to me, too. It's not necessary."

"It's at your cousin's, Dottor Postiglione's. I'm stabilizing it so that it can be sold. He has a friend in Rome who deals with rare books. I won't have time to rebind it properly myself, so it may take a while. Sandro, your cousin, will bring you the money after it's been sold."

"Bless you." She put her hand on my head and let it slide

down side of my face, like a blind person feeling me, trying to figure out what I looked like.

She opened a cupboard and brought out a bottle of *vinsanto* and some *biscotti*. She poured two small glasses and we drank.

"Tomorrow morning you will bring it back to me and we can begin again. We can wipe the slate clean."

"Begin again?"

"God willing. I should never have gotten you involved. It was a mistake."

"I can't bring it back tomorrow. I've taken it all apart."

"Then as soon as possible."

"Yes, Madre Badessa, but what is it you're worried about?"

"I don't want to have your lies to the bishop on my conscience, nor do I want to have my cousin on my conscience."

"I rather like your cousin, but there's no reason to have him on your conscience."

"There's no one I like better. No one more charming, and not in that slick way some Italian men have. He's unpretentious, open hearted, generous."

"But you don't want me to see him? You're afraid he'll seduce me? Ruin my reputation?"

Madre Badessa laughed. "Of course he will, if he hasn't already, but that's not what worries me. Sins of the flesh have a bad reputation, but they aren't so very terrible. But he's a man with no center, no soul."

"Whatever do you mean by that?"

"I mean that he's a very agreeable man, but, but, but—"

"But you can't count on him in a pinch?"

"Something like that. He's fundamentally unserious. There's no inner core."

"Is that so bad?"

"For you, yes. He'll devour you. He'll feed on you, use you up."

"You don't trust him?"

"Not at all, and you mustn't either." She gave me an embrace, a good hug. Smelled sweet, warm, womanly. "And don't repeat anything I've said, please! Now, good night."

The bishop of Florence, short and red faced, was dressed in a flowing black cassock, the word for which in Italian is the same as that for petticoat.

Underneath which, I reminded myself, he's just a man, though Madre Badessa had instructed me to call him *Eminenza*.

We met in Madre Badessa's office.

"Let me say that we have been greatly honored by your presence."

"Thank you, *Eminenza*."

"What do you think of the collection?"

"It's hard for me to say. I'm a conservator, not a collector."

"But you must have formed some impression."

"I'd say it's a very unusual collection. Such a large number of incunabula."

We talked about the library for a while, and I soon realized that the bishop, despite his red face and roundish figure, his cassock with a thousand buttons down the front and his red biretta, was a powerful man, not a dry stick like Father Francesco.

"But let me speak openly."

"Please do."

"You have your vocation, and we have ours. Father Francesco tells me that you took it upon yourself to let Sister Agata Agape die without . . . without the benefit of extreme unction."

"It's difficult to know just when someone's going to die, *Eminenza,* and Father Francesco made it clear that he didn't want any false alarms. He was summoned twice, you know."

"Priests are only human. Unfortunately. But is it true that the novice whose duty it was to sit with Agata Agape wanted to call Father Francesco and that you kept her from doing so?"

"The fact is this, *Eminenza:* Sister Agata did not want to see Father Francesco again."

"What Sister Agata Agape may or may not have wanted, or thought she wanted, in her condition, is not the issue. The issue is that you took it upon yourself to interfere with the proper administration of the sacraments. You, a visitor, an outsider. Not even a Roman Catholic. But you take it upon yourself'—a phrase he kept repeating—"to decide who shall receive the sacrament and who shall not. Not even the pope has the authority to refuse the sacrament to the dying." He paused. "You know that Father Francesco administered the sacraments anyway?"

"Yes, I'm aware of that."

"So you didn't really accomplish anything."

"I wasn't trying to *accom*plish anything, and anyway, if the sacraments work after death, then there's no point in kicking up a fuss, is there?" (I was getting angry, or trying to work up a reserve of anger, like having a drink, to keep me going.)

"Why take unnecessary risks?"

"Do you really believe that Sister Agata's soul was at risk?"

"It's unlikely, I admit. But when the stakes are so enormous, you want to do everything possible to avoid eternal damnation."

I didn't say anything more. I just sat there passively aggressive.

The bishop didn't say anything more either, and there was a long, awkward silence. It's difficult enough to find your way in *this* world without worrying about the next.

Several minutes went by. The bishop walked up and down, like a caged animal in a zoo. But not one of the cats. More like a large bear. Awkward. I stood and looked out the window. As far as I know it's the only window in the place that looks out onto the street, the piazza, where Mama and I used to shop: cheese, milk, bread. Sitting down I could see the top of one of the Donati towers, which had been turned into a fancy apartment. Mama went there for drinks once and told me all about it.

The bishop turned and stopped. "There's something else too. A book, possibly quite rare. I learned about it only by chance, when I was hearing confessions. Madre Badessa says she gave it to you to dispose of." The bishop fixed me with his eyes: "And have you done so?"

"Yes, as a matter of fact."

"To whom, may I ask?"

I wasn't sure what to say. I'd told Madre Badessa that I'd return the book to her as soon as possible, but I didn't want to cave in to the bishop. "To a bookseller in the Piazza Goldoni," I said, thinking of the man I'd seen standing in front of one of the shops, tall, gray, smoking a cigar and crying.

"Rubbish. The Piazza Goldoni was completely destroyed by

the flood. You couldn't possibly have found anything open there."

"One of the owners was standing outside his shop," I said. I was in for it now. I was not accustomed to lying, but I knew enough to keep it simple and stick to my story.

"What was his name?"

"I have no idea."

"Which shop?"

"I don't remember."

"This man told you he was the owner?"

"Not exactly."

"But you sold him the book?"

"Yes."

"You asked him if he was a dealer in rare books?"

"Yes."

"And he said he was?"

"Yes."

"And you showed him the book?"

"Yes."

"And he offered to buy it from you?"

"Yes."

"I won't ask how much he gave you."

"No."

"Do you know why?"

"No."

"Because it's patently obvious that you are lying through your teeth."

He suddenly became very animated. His face grimaced. He tipped his head back and began to stroke his chin violently with the backs of his fingers.

I didn't deny that I was lying. There was nothing he could do. Maybe.

"Madre Badessa has no right to alienate *any* convent property, not a stick, do you understand? The books in the library are not her property."

"I think she was mainly concerned to get the book out of the convent. It was very salacious. It doesn't belong here."

"You looked at it then?"

"Just enough to see what it was."

The bishop leaned back, drummed his fingers on the table. There were rings on every other finger.

"You must return the book," he said at last. "You may return it to me, to spare Madre Badessa's feelings. It is illegal, you know, to take works of art out of the country. If you do not return the book to me, I shall notify the Vigilanza ai Beni Artistici in Rome to search your luggage, and your person, before allowing you to leave the country. You will not be permitted to take the book with you." The bishop didn't strike me as a man of empty threat, but . . .

"But I don't have it."

"But you know where it is, don't you? And you're planning to take it with you."

"*Boh,*" I said—getting as much nose into it as I could. "Why is it so important? A work of pornography. I'm surprised you're so interested."

The bishop was evidently ready for this question. "It may be of great historical interest. But that's beside the point. The point is that you must return the book at once. Immediately, do you understand? There's nothing more to discuss."

190

And that was the abrupt end of my interview with the bishop of Florence. I don't think I've ever been so glad to see a man leave a room as I was then. Not even Jed Chapin. I won't pretend that I wasn't upset, but when Madre Badessa came into the room I told her that everything was fine. She didn't ask me any more questions, so I didn't have to tell her any lies.

According to the art historian Giorgio Vasari, Giulio Romano, Raphael's greatest pupil, employed Marcantonio Raimondi to make a series of engravings of sixteen erotic drawings, sometimes known as "The Sixteen Pleasures," and Pietro Aretino made matters worse by writing a sequence of indecent sonnets to accompany the engravings. The original drawings *may* have been executed in the Vatican, on the walls of what is now the Sala di Costantino, in order to embarrass Pope Clement VII, who was too slow in paying Giulio for some previous work. The room was later frescoed over with scenes from the life of Constantine. And in fact there is contemporary evidence to suggest the engravings (which are mentioned in Ariosto's *Supposti* [1526]) were originally published separately in 1523, not 1525, which is the date of the Aretino volume. In any case there was a scandal of terrific proportions. Marcantonio was thrown in prison, Giulio was forced to flee to Mantua. The original plates were destroyed, and every effort was made to destroy all existing copies. The effort was apparently successful. No copy is known to exist. Except one, which evidently found its way into the library of Cosimo I, grand duke of Tuscany, at Poggio a Caiano, perhaps through the agency of Cosimo's brother, Cardinal Francesca Maria, a well-known libertine. The shelf number on the flyleaf is in the same hand as that on many of the books in the convent library, which had come to the convent as part of Lucia's considerable dowry. It is, however, impossible to say who was responsible for binding it together with the *Preghiere cristiane,* though one can easily imagine the motive.

A unique copy, then, of the most famous example of Renaissance erotica. You didn't have to be an expert to realize that this was a valuable piece of property, but not even an expert could have given a trustworthy estimate. There was no way to estimate it, really, since the book had never been sold at auction and therefore had no track record. There was nothing to compare it to. In Sandro's judgment the work had either been printed from the original plates (which had supposedly been destroyed), or else Marcantonio had re-etched them. In any case the quality of the engraving, according to Sandro, was very fine.

Vasari himself had not been able to conceal his disgust: "I do not know which was the more revolting, the spectacle presented to the eye by the designs of Giulio or the affront offered to the ear by the words of the Aretine." Initially—sitting in Madre Badessa's office, that is—I might have been inclined to agree with Vasari. But the more I contemplated the drawings—or perhaps I should say the more Sandro and I contemplated them —the more I came to believe that they told the truth, or at least *a* truth. The figures were not romanticized. There was a definite sense of stress and strain as odd curves of the body were exposed, curves that we tend to forget about because we almost never see them. These lovers, instead of confirming our prejudices and expectations, startled and astonished; they seduced and illumined, giving visual definition, as they did so, to . . .

You know how art historians talk about Leonardo or Michelangelo exploring the limits of the human condition? That sort of thing? Well, something like that was going on in these engravings. In the faces as well as the bodies. There was none of the vacuity that characterizes the expressions of professional models. These faces had been drawn with great care, not like Dutch realism but like the faces of Leonardo's angels, and like Rembrandt's side of beef they spoke with a strange urgency. Turning back and forth from one to another I felt myself suffused, if that's the word.

But you mustn't think that I'm trying to conceal the sheer erotic impact of these drawings behind this fancy language. Sandro had heard about an electronic device marketed by a Japanese firm that's guaranteed to produce an erection even in a dead man, if he hasn't been dead too long. These drawings might just be equally effective—if you could get the dead man to open his eyes. If I had a favorite it was a representation of cunnilingus. It was my favorite because, after all these years, it was such an unexpected gift. And besides, it reminded me of Sandro. How funny he looked, in the cheval glass, how different from all the passionate love scenes I'd ever seen or imagined. What could it mean, this strange conjunction of the human face and the human bottom? The seat of reason, and the seat that one sits on? Reason and appetite. Nonanimal behavior. Nonpurposive. Mama used to say that Papa loved life and therefore didn't mind looking foolish, and I thought the same thing applied to Sandro. He loved life and therefore didn't mind looking foolish. And it does look foolish, doesn't it? Imagine a grown man on his knees shoving his snout into a woman's crotch. Lying on my back, my legs over the side of the bed, I could look straight down between my breasts and see the top of his shiny bald head between my legs, crowning like a baby's head, as if I were giving birth.

11

The Sixteen Pleasures
Restored

On Tuesday the twentieth of December at nine o'clock in the morning I left the convent of Santa Caterina Nuova. In tears. I'd been happy there, happier than I realized, and I felt close to many of the nuns, especially to Sister Gemma, who gave me the Saint Christopher medal she'd worn since she was a child, and to Madre Badessa, who gave me her blessing, held out her hand for me to shake, which I did, and then took me by the shoulders and looked as far down into my eyes as anyone had ever looked in my entire life. I had not yet returned the Aretino to the bishop, but Sandro was going to do so for me.

I let everyone think that I was going to take an express train that morning to Luxembourg, but in fact I wasn't planning to leave Florence until the *following* morning, and as soon as we were out of sight of the convent I told the taxi driver to take me to Piazza Santa Croce. I wanted to spend an entire night with Sandro before I went home, and this was the only way I could think of to arrange it.

Sandro had some things to look after at the Uffizi, which was reopening in a couple of days, and I didn't expect him until noon or so, so I removed the Aretino from the thymol chamber and checked it for the hundredth time for traces of mold. There were none. I put the signatures in order and placed them in the solander box I'd made to hold them. Then I took them out of the box and had another look. The engravings had not lost their power to astonish me. If anything I'd learned, by looking at them through Sandro's eyes, to appreciate them more fully. It's unusual for a great artist to concentrate his energies so intensely on the erotic, and though Marcantonio is not usually considered an artist of the very first rank, I was learning to see in the dynamic composition of the figures and in the heavily worked contours and dark cross-hatching that gave them a soft luminous quality, the influence of Raphael. I put the signatures back in the box, put on most of the clothes I'd brought with me, because it was cold, and sat down on my orange crate by the window to wait.

Piazza Santa Croce was in a state of disrepair. The buildings were discolored, stained by fuel oil from the thousands of furnaces that had been flushed out by the floodwater. A few had even been abandoned because they were threatening to give way and had been shored up with temporary supports. But I was drawn to it anyway.

It was cold, about as wintry as it gets in Florence. There was no snow in the city, but there was snow on the cars that had come down from the surrounding hills. Some of the leather shops had reopened, and the bars were doing a brisk business. BUON NATALE signs appeared here and there, and signs announcing Christmas sales. There was still no central heat, but electric heaters took the edge off the chill. I watched a group of students—mud angels—cross the piazza on their way to the Biblioteca Nazionale. Soon they would be at work in the freezing cold basement, digging the archives of the city out of oil-impregnated muck, but they were laughing and happy because they were young and because, like me, they'd stumbled into a great adventure. But my part in the adventure was coming to a close, and I was feeling a little melancholy. Leaving the convent had been difficult enough, though the restoration operation was in good hands: the nuns were perfectly capable of treating the books and resewing them, and thanks to Sandro there were plenty of thymol crystals and absorbent paper. Sisters Angelica and Maria had managed to salvage much of the wood from the old library and the new bookpresses on the second floor would soon be ready.

But in a sense I'd already left the convent when I made love to Sandro the first time, and it was Sandro I was more concerned about leaving. I'd never had a man like that before, all to myself. And such an attentive man. I didn't believe half his compliments, but he valued me enough to make them, that's what counted. He was an old-fashioned man in many ways, a courtly man, a romantic man. And lots of fun, too. But it wasn't till I saw him coming out of the Via Verdi with a bouquet of flowers in his hand that I knew I was in love and that even though my old life was calling me home, I didn't want to leave him.

Imagine this man if you can: how fresh he looks, even at a distance, fresh as the flowers he's carrying in his hand. Now he's going out of his way to speak to an old man sitting at the base of the horrible nineteenth-century statue of Dante that disrupts the middle of the piazza, glaring at everything, perpetually angry at everyone. The old man gestures and Sandro gestures. They might be speaking to each other in sign language. You can almost tell what they are saying. The old man offers a cigarette, which Sandro accepts, though he's not a regular smoker. He lights it. The old man gestures some more, spreads out his fingers, touches his Adam's apple with the tip of his index finger, then makes a rapid pecking motion with his hand, as if his hand were a bird pecking at his throat. And finally, with his other hand he makes a long scooping motion just under his rib cage. It's a gesture I've seen only once before, on the train to Pisa with Mama, shortly after we arrived in Italy. We were sitting in a third-class car with wooden seats, like the old streetcars in Chicago. We never knew what it meant. I asked all my friends, but they'd never seen anything like it. Sandro moves on. He can't cross a piazza without talking to half a dozen people. Every tenth person stops to talk. Now a young woman with a baby, now an elegant woman in a fur, a countess (I imagine). He whispers something in her ear and points toward the window where I am standing. She looks up at me and touches her lips with one finger. A boy kicks a soccer ball in Sandro's direction. He catches it with his foot and, magically, the ball rolls up and around his leg. He shoots it on its way and moves on, always in slow motion. You can't get this man to hurry. Now he has to have an espresso and buy a lottery ticket. I wait. Now he stops to admire a display of leather purses outside a *monte di pietà,* a pawnshop. He opens one, looks inside, puts the strap over his shoulder, feels the weight, speaks to the pawnbroker, signs a receipt, it's a going-away present. For me. But I've just decided that I'm not going anywhere. I've just decided that I'm going to stay right here.

* * *

I decided to stay in Florence because I was happier than I'd been in years. I stayed because I was in love. But there was another reason, too, which was perhaps equally important. I did not want to return the Aretino to the bishop. The nuns were the ones who deserved the money, not the bishop. I had no idea what the book would bring, but whatever it was could be used to help preserve the convent library. Besides, I wanted to restore it myself. I wanted to put my stamp on it. Every profession has its peaks: the baseball hero steps up to bat with the bases loaded with two outs in the ninth inning in the final game of the World Series; the diamond cutter brings his hammer down on a rough diamond worth millions if only it doesn't shatter into bits; the surgeon severs a nerve that will lead to blessed relief or excruciating agony; the lawyer pleads a case that will exonerate her client or condemn her to the electric chair, and so on. Book restorers seldom if ever enjoy the limelight, but they have hopes and fears nonetheless real. It was an opportunity I couldn't pass up.

I was worried about the bishop, of course. I was afraid that he'd pester Madre Badessa about the book. But Sandro called his friend in Rome—the antiquarian book dealer—who sent us a small, inexpensive volume of nineteenth-century pornographic engravings. I soaked it overnight in a bucket of dirty water to simulate flood damage and Sandro delivered it personally to the bishop at the Episcopal Palace along with a note saying I'd asked him to return it to its rightful owner. It was an outright lie, but what was I to do? Technically the Aretino might belong to the bishop, or even the pope, but as far as I was concerned it was the exclusive property of the sisters of Santa Caterina Nuova.

"Do you think he was convinced?" I asked Sandro who had puffed himself up and was demonstrating how the bishop had paced up and down with his hands behind his back.

" 'A matter of great historical interest,' " he boomed. " 'The signorina has done the right thing.' "

"Did he look at it?"

"Not while I was there."

"I hope he's not too suspicious."

Sandro shrugged. "What does he know for sure? That the nuns found a book of dirty pictures, that's all. A book that you read—how do the French say it—with one hand."

"Do you think he'll read it with one hand?"

Sandro laughed. "I'd rather not picture it."

This worry out of the way, I set to work. I'd already made out my worksheet:

Sonetti lussuriosi di Pietro Aretino. Roma, 1525.

Owner: Convento di Santa Caterina Nuova.

Provenance: Shelf number on flyleaf indicates that the book is from the library of Cosimo I at Certaldo, which supplied the bulk of the volumes brought to Santa Maria Teresa Nuova by Lucia de' Medici as part of her dowry. No similar markings on the prayer book with which it was bound

Description: Bound together with the *Preghiere cristiane preparate da Contessa Giuliana d'Arezzo,* Venezia, 1644.

8vo, 120 × 18.5 × 22mm, slightly out of square

16 engravings by Marcantonio Raimondi

Embroidered textile binding; velvet covering fabric (embroidered with metal thread in four different configurations) has suffered irreparable water damage

Beech boards (1.5 mm thick), badly warped, broken at corners; All sewing cords broken

Paper of good quality, external pressure on book kept water out of the center of the text block, needs thorough cleaning, mending needed on several signatures

The Aretino volume consists of two signatures only, on good quality Venetian paper. The *Preghiere cristiane* consists of 14 signatures, A-N6. The pagination of the third signature is irregular (the compositor evidently placed the sheet upside down in the press before it was folded).

Notes: The following calculation appears on the recto of the first leaf:

Per scudi tre d'oro	22:4
Per grandoppia di Spagna	14:16
Per altre	10
Per altr[e]	49
	96:0
	4
	100:0

Several notes in pale brown ink, some indicating approval (*posa bellissima, bella comp{arazion}e);* others noting similarities to other drawings and paintings.

Ink sidelinings by some of the sonnets (black ink)
Binder: unknown
End leaves: one plus pastedown at beginning; two plus
   pastedown at end. Watermark: a large free fleur-de-lys.
Treatment:
   1. remove text block from cover *(completed)*
   2. remove boards and lining papers *(completed)*
   3. remove endpapers *(completed)*
   4. clean entire volume
   5. wash
   6. repair tears in second and third signatures and on
      final two signatures (Aretino)
   7. recover original boards (w. ?)
   8. finishing ?

The decision to bind the two books together again was a difficult one. There was no intrinsic reason to do so, and yet the yoking together of such unlikely bedfellows, from different historical periods, appealed to me for two reasons: First, the fact that they had been bound together was not a simple accident, it was an integral part of the book's history; and second, the fact of the conjunction seemed to me to embody the central paradox of the human condition. Who was I to terminate such a long-standing union of spirit and flesh? I suppose there was a third reason, too: aesthetically the result would be more pleasing, for the Aretino by itself was only thirty-two pages, more like a pamphlet than a book.

* * *

On Christmas Eve a great crowd gathered in the piazza, like the crowds that once gathered to hear the great medieval preachers or to see the jousting tournaments put on by the Medici, presided over by the beautiful Simonetta, who was the inspiration for Botticelli's most beautiful figures, and in fact for a whole new type of female beauty. Sandro and I watched the festivities from the window of his apartment. At ten o'clock the pope appeared, in a closed car. He addressed the crowd briefly and then proceeded to the Duomo, where he was going to celebrate midnight mass for the *alluvionati,* the victims of the flood. In a little while the crowd thinned out, and we went out for a hamburger at a fast-food restaurant, behind the central market, which had just reopened. Sandro had invested a lot of money in this restaurant, so we didn't have to pay for our meal, and it was nice to have an *'amburger con tutto.*

On Christmas morning we opened our presents—a scarf and a new wallet for Sandro, jade earrings and a necklace for me— and then wandered around the city. European cities really know how to close down. Stores, bakeries, delicatessens, butcher shops, restaurants are all covered by solid metal grates like garage doors. Familiar streets take on a strange, guarded look.

The Italians have a saying that hit home as we wandered around the empty city: *Natale con i tuoi e Pasqua con chi vuoi,* Christmas with your family, Easter with whomever you want. I suddenly wanted to call home, where Christmas was going on without me, so we went to the post office. I was a little apprehensive because I hadn't written to Papa, except for one postcard, and I hadn't called either. But then, I'd been planning to be home for Christmas, so there hadn't been much point in writing.

I told the girl at the counter that I wanted to call the United States, gave her the number, waited in a glass booth for her to put the call through. There are time clocks on the wall with the numbers of the booths on them so you can keep track of how long you've been talking. Sandro chatted with the girl for a bit and then stepped into one of the booths himself.

When I heard Papa's voice I started to choke up a little.

"Hello?" he said. "Hello? Hello? Margot, is that you?"

"Papa, it's me."

"Are you all right?"

"Oh, Papa, I'm so happy. I'm in love, really in love. Head over heels. Can you hear me all right? I don't want to say it too loud."

"Where are you?"

"At the post office."

"In the middle of the night?"

"It's nine o'clock in the morning here. Why? What time is it there?"

"It's two o'clock in the morning."

"Oh Papa, I thought it would be afternoon. Is it Christmas yet?"

"It's still Christmas Eve. I'm filling the stockings. I gave yours to Molly's boyfriend. His name's Tejinder and he's from the Punjab. He's a Sikh and he wears a turban."

"Do you like him?"

"He seems like a nice guy."

"Did you get my card?" I'd sent him a card of the Martini *Annunciation.*

"It's on the refrigerator." There was a pause. "Who's the lucky guy?"

"He's an Italian."

"Married?"

"No, Papa. Well, yes, but he's getting a divorce. He's from the Abruzzi. He's the head restorer for the whole region of Tuscany. He's working on the frescoes in the Lodovici Chapel in the Badia. You remember the Badia? The monastery, where they had the foosball game in the cloister? It's still there."

"I remember the foosball game, but that's about all."

I could see him sitting at the kitchen table, filling the big red stockings with raisins and dried apricots and paper clips and rubber bands and ballpoint pens and nonsense toys.

"What are your plans? I mean, are you coming home or what?"

"We're going to the Abruzzi at the end of January to see Sandro's parents, and then to Rome."

"Have you written to your boss at the Newberry? He called here the other day. He's been back for a while, and, to tell you the truth, I don't think you've got a job anymore."

"Listen, Papa. I'm working on a really important book here, it's a wonderful opportunity professionally, really. I'd never forgive myself if I passed it up."

Another pause. "I thought you couldn't get a divorce in Italy?"

"It's an annulment. It's the same thing. You'll see. Don't worry, Papa, I'm all right, I'm fine. I'll write to you, Papa, I really will. I have to go now."

"I'm thinking of putting the house up for sale."

"The house? Our house?" Sandro had finished his call. I could see him talking to the girl at the counter. "Where will you live?"

"I might go to Texas," he said. "Raise avocados."

"Have you talked it over with Meg and Molly?"

"Sort of. But it didn't come clear to me till tonight. Maybe it's time to move on. Try something else."

I had to resist an impulse to scold him. "Do you know anybody in Texas?"

"Some of the growers, some of the shippers. I've done business with them for years over the phone."

"Well, Papa, I don't know what to say. I'm pretty amazed."

"You don't need to say anything. We'll just see what happens."

"I've got to go. Take care of yourself, Papa."

"You take care of yourself, too."

"Papa, I love you. Tell everyone I love them. The dogs, too."

"They miss you. I miss you."

"I miss you, too, Papa. Good-bye."

When I got out of the booth, Sandro was on the phone again. I was so preoccupied with Papa's news that it didn't occur to me till we went to bed that night that I wasn't the only one who hadn't gone home for Christmas.

Except for the finishing, there was nothing I couldn't do, with my own tools and a little Yankee ingenuity, right in Sandro's apartment. I rigged up my own sewing frame and sent Sandro to Santa Caterina to collect a small nipping press. I told him to say that Signor Cecchi, the binder in Prato who had been so generous, needed it back. The nipping press would have to double as a backing press. Backing boards, thread, leather—a piece of gorgeous dark red morocco—and glue I was able to find in Florence.

If I were to describe an ideal day, it would be this: up early, out for fresh bread and fruit, drink *caffelatte* with Sandro, boiled egg for me, say good-bye to Sandro; work on the Aretino until noon (wash and clean every page, mend every tear, pare down leather), salami and cheese and *pane toscano* for lunch, with maybe a small glass of Chianti; lie down on my back for an hour and relax till my mind becomes perfectly calm, like the smooth surface of a pond, so that it can reflect the divine radiance (I picked up this idea in Santa Caterina); resume work; take a long walk with no destination in mind; sit on orange crate by window and watch piazza till Sandro comes home; mess around, go out to dinner, talk about the day's work, come home, mess around some more, read, sleep.

I stuck to this routine, more or less, till the middle of January, when it was time to finish the Aretino, which I was going to do in Signor Cecchi's workshop in Prato. On my walks I sometimes visited Sandro at the Pitti Palace where damaged paintings—many of them bandaged up—were laid out in the Limonaia like patients in a hospital ward, or at the Badia, where preparations were under way for detaching the frescoes from the wall of the Lodovici Chapel, an operation called a *strappo.* Sometimes I walked up to Piazzale Michelangelo, and sometimes I took the bus up to Fiesole and took my favorite walk to Settignano, where I'd stop at the Casa del Popolo for a glass of wine before taking the bus down to the city. Home. I was a *cittadina,* remember?

* * *

I persuaded Signor Cecchi to let me use the gold-tooling equipment that I would need to finish the binding. These tools are both delicate and expensive, and normally I would no more have asked him if I could use them than I would have asked him if I could use his toothbrush. But when I explained the circumstances and showed him the book, he understood perfectly and even offered to do the work himself, *gratis.* Perhaps that would have been the sensible thing to do. He'd had much more experience than I, and he showed me some examples of his work that were strikingly beautiful. But I wanted to do it myself. He understood this, too, and promised to assist me in any way he could.

His workshop was beautiful. His tools were beautiful and absolutely clean, his brass typefaces were of the highest quality, and the gold he used was deep XX, which is superior to the more commonly used red or green gold. I settled on a design that featured a few simple ornaments.

The morocco I selected had a prominent grained surface, and I spent a morning polishing it with a warm polishing iron, smoothing out all the irregularities. In the afternoon Signor Cecchi helped me select the type and set it up in pallets: *Le preghiere cristiane preparate da Santa Giuliana d'Arezzo.* After much agonizing I had decided to use *Preghiere cristiane* rather than *Sonetti lussuriosi* for the title on the spine.

The aesthetic problem I'd set myself was to incorporate the curve of the Santa Trinità bridge into the design of the front cover, but as Signor Cecchi pointed out, because of the limitations of the tools, long curves like the ones I had in mind tend to look thin and weak unless properly supported. We settled at last on two rectangles, one enclosing the other, surmounted by four of the Michelangelesque curves, one on each side, with simple floral ornaments at the four corners. There was a technical problem, too. The curve is a complex one. When the bridge was rebuilt after the war—it had been blown up by the Nazis —the engineers could not find a formula to express the curve mathematically, and I wasn't having much luck figuring out how to express it with finishing tools either. But Signor Cecchi came up with the solution. I would have to use a very small fillet—a tool not unlike the wheel used to cut a pizza into slices or to trace the design on a dress pattern onto the fabric—to describe the long, flat part of the curve, and then finish off each end, where the curve starts to curl in on itself like a spring, with two separate gouges, which are bronze tools designed to stamp out different-size arcs.

On Monday the sixteenth of January I did the blind tooling, that is, I marked up the cover of the book using a bone folder for the straight lines and a paper pattern for the curves and the ornaments. Then I blinded the design into the leather with heated tools. I'd been practicing the curves for several days on some scrap leather and was feeling confident, but I proceeded slowly and cautiously nonetheless—because I was afraid of burning the leather—and probably took four hours to do what Signor Cecchi might have done in thirty minutes.

I washed the cover in vinegar and set it aside to dry. Everything had gone well—the lines had gone down where I wanted them to go, and I hadn't burned or cut the leather—but I was exhausted from concentrating so hard, and I was nervous about the gold, too nervous to eat the sandwich that Signora Cecchi brought for me. I mixed up a batch of fresh glair from egg whites and vinegar and put it aside to settle while the book dried. It was the goldwork that would reveal, to the trained eye, the difference between the amateur and the professional craftsman; it was the goldwork that would justify (or expose) the risks I'd taken in binding the book myself, and especially the risk posed by the Santa Trinità curve. I was beginning to think I should have been satisfied with a simple diaper, a small repeating overall pattern, that is. But by the time I reached this point in my thoughts, it was too late, for the book was almost but not quite dry: time to begin.

I used a very fine brush to paint the design with a thin coat of glair, let it dry, and applied a second coat.

Signor Cecchi returned from his lunch and came to have a look. Unlike some of the teachers I'd had in the past, he didn't make me feel self-conscious about every move I made. He was more like an insurance policy than a teacher, more like a safety net.

He closed and locked the doors to the workshop and stopped up the cracks under the doors with strips of foam rubber cut to size. When you're working with gold leaf there must be absolutely no drafts whatsoever.

I rubbed some Bath brick into the gold cushion to make it easier to cut the gold cleanly; then I rubbed both sides of the gold knife on the cushion. The knife must be absolutely free of grease or the gold will stick to it. My guess was that the blade of Signor Cecchi's knife had never been touched by human hands.

I opened the book of gold—double-thick pure gold—slipped the blade of the knife under a leaf and turned it over onto the cushion. I blew on it lightly, in the center, and it detached itself from the blade and settled flat on the cushion, where I cut it into the thin strips that would be laid over lines of the design. I dabbed a small piece of cotton in a smear of coconut oil and rubbed it over the surface of the design and then over the back of the middle finger of my left hand. I picked up the first piece of gold with the back of my finger—the gold sticks to the grease—held it over the straight line at the top of the cover and blew lightly. The gold settled into place on the cover, directly over the line. I did the same with the second and third pieces. The fourth piece cracked, and Signor Cecchi told me to put a second thickness directly over it.

By the time I had half the pattern covered I was exhilarated. It was as if I could will the gold into place almost without touching it.

When the entire design was covered I used a clean piece of cotton to press the gold down firmly into the grooves of the blind tooling. I went over the entire surface several times until I could feel each line clearly and distinctly beneath my fingertips.

Signor Cecchi had lit the finishing stove, but the stamping tools weren't hot enough yet, so I had a little break. I told myself that I'd worked with gold before and that nothing I did could do real damage to the book, but I desperately wanted to get it right. I didn't want any blurred impressions. I didn't want the gold to flake because the tools hadn't been hot enough, or to have a frosted look because they'd been too hot or because I'd pushed down too hard or too long. And above all I wanted the long graceful curves to *look* like long graceful curves, not a bunch of separate curves that had been cobbled together.

I took the small bronze fillet from the stove, laid it on the cooling pad until it stopped hissing, put my thumb on top of the handle, steadied it with my left hand, brought my right shoulder up so I could use the weight of my body as a press (better control this way than trying to do everything with your arms), ran the fillet up the long vertical line closest to the spine of the book. It didn't feel right, so I went over the line a second time, being careful not to twist the fillet and double the impression. But the gold didn't stick.

"You left the fillet on the cooling pad too long," Signor Cecchi observed.

I tried to conceal my disappointment by a businesslike demeanor as I scraped off the old gold and cut strips of new, but I was moving too fast and Signor Cecchi had to slow me down. *"Piano, piano,"* he said. "This isn't a race. This isn't a job to be done in haste and fury, *in fretta e furia.* Do the rest and come back to this line when you're done. You have to add more glair anyway."

Once again I took the fillet from the stove and touched it to the heating pad. This time I kept an eye on Signor Cecchi, and though he didn't give me a visible signal, I could tell from a slight twitch in his face when the bronze reached exactly the right temperature.

I tried a second line, getting some body weight into it. It felt good. It was an athletic feeling, like knowing you've swum the hundred-meter freestyle in less than seventy seconds even before the times are posted, or knowing you've bowled a strike before the ball is even halfway down the alley, or that your backhand drive is going to hit three inches inside the baseline. I had no further problems with the straight lines or with the ornaments at the corners.

The Santa Trinità curves, however, remained. My instinct told me to start with the long flat part of the curve and then add the smaller arcs, but Signor Cecchi pointed out that it would be easier to match fillet lines to gouge lines than vice versa, which seems obvious once you think of it. I still had to articulate the two smaller arcs at each end of each curve so that the arcs met exactly, forming a single line.

The trick in using a gouge is to "sight" it from the inside of the curve and then apply the pressure quickly and evenly so that neither end of the stamp cuts into the leather. I was getting a feel for the tools now, and I had a certain momentum going, too, carrying me along like a boat on a river. All I had to do was steer.

I won't say that I did a perfect job, and I won't claim that *I sonetti lussuriosi* put me in a class with Thomas Berthelet or Roger Payne, or with the great modern binders like Douglas Cockerell and Roger de Coverley, but I will say that those curves were enormously satisfying. It was as if Michelangelo had created *ex nihilo* a curve as satisfying as some of the curves of the human body. It was gratifying to know that I had added to the small store of these curves.

Only one thing went wrong. I'd begun to sweat profusely, and as I was about to join the long, flat arc of the last curve to the sharper arc at the end, a drop of sweat fell from my forehead and landed on the hot fillet. The fillet hissed; I jumped, as if I'd been stung by a bee, and overshot the mark slightly. Instead of meeting end to end, the two arcs intersected. I don't suppose the overlap was more than three or four millimeters, but as far as I was concerned it was enough to spoil the curve.

Have you ever had the impulse, when you're working on

something, to destroy it completely if you make even the tiniest little mistake? You hit a wrong note that no one would notice, but instead of going on, you start banging on the keyboard? You write an *a* instead of an *e* in copying out a poem and instead of whiting it out and going on you crisscross the paper with great big X's? Signor Cecchi must have realized what was going on in my mind, because he reached over and took my hand in his.

"*Niente*," he said. "It's nothing. No one will notice a thing. When you come back tomorrow you won't notice it yourself."

They say that chess players lose as much as ten pounds during a match, even though they aren't exercising physically, because they concentrate so hard. That's the way I felt—as if I'd lost ten pounds. I was drained. I was too tired to redo the first line I'd attempted.

"*Domani*," I said. "Let's finish up tomorrow."

I wiped off the excess gold with a rag dampened with a bit of coconut oil. The tooling was perfect except for the first line, which could easily be retooled, and the one mistake, which stood out like a proverbial sore thumb or, as the Italians say, a sore nose.

But Signor Cecchi was right. The next morning I didn't even notice it, and it wasn't till I was showing the finished book to Sandro a couple of days later that I realized what had happened: not only had Signor Cecchi picked out the gold where the lines had intersected instead of joining, he'd dampened the leather, picked up the impression with the point of a pin and retooled the join. He'd left his mark, too, in his own way, and I was very grateful.

12

Gli Abruzzi

In the third week in January we went to visit Sandro's family in Montemuro, in the Abruzzi. It was a cold, crisp day and the car, an old Fiat station wagon that Sandro had borrowed from a friend, was leaking air. The heater didn't work properly, but we generated our own heat. Sandro's face was as fresh and shining as if he'd been driving an Alfa Romeo. He was dressed for the occasion in old clothes, like a very rich man who doesn't have to dress fashionably.

The more I got to know this man, the more I loved him. I loved him for himself, and for his bald head and for his uncircumcised *uccello* (his little bird that sang so sweetly in the night); I loved him for his attentiveness; I loved him because he seemed so at home in this world and because at the same time he was so hopelessly unworldly; I loved him because he never opened unpleasant mail and because he'd invested half his money in a fast-food restaurant and the other half in a scheme to export low-calorie wine to the United States; I loved to see him crossing the piazza, I loved to find him waiting for me in the station when my train came back from Prato; I loved to come home and find him waiting for me in his old silk robe; and I loved him for the things I learned about him from others, which seemed great and heroic: on the night of the flood, for example, he opened up his apartment to all the people living on the lower floors who had no place to go, and he waded to the Uffizi to help rescue the paintings in the restoration rooms in the basement and the self-portraits in the Vasari Corridor, which was in danger of collapsing into the Arno.

And I loved him for being so good at his work, for being a true craftsman. He was a man who cared about things, who cherished them, who spent his life preserving them.

"When was the first time *you* fell in love?" I asked him, thinking out loud.

He laughed and adjusted his sunglasses.

"You mean *really* in love?"

"Really, really in love."

"November 1928."

No hesitation!

"What day of the week?"

"It must have been a Wednesday, because the truck from Sulmona had come—"

"What time?"

"Oh, I'd say about three o'clock, because Papà'd just gone across the street to have coffee with Zio Franco and Signor Spettini at the bar."

"Who was she, a shepherdess coming down out of the mountains?" (I'd seen plenty of pictures of Abruzzi girls in fancy peasant costumes.)

"Not at all, though believe it or not I knew lots of shepherd-esses, and some of them were very pretty, and I'd fallen in love with some of them, too. But not *really* in love."

We were on the outskirts of Florence, just passing the Certosa.

"Someone from the village?"

"No."

"I give up."

"Her name was Sybil Connelly, and she was an American."

"Sybil Connelly?"

"The film star."

"Never heard of her."

"Before your time, I'm afraid. She starred in the first sound film made in Italy. It was an American company, I think."

"You saw her in a film?"

"In the flesh, *cara mia,* in the flesh"—he touched my leg with his fingertip—"like this. It was November, getting cold, we'd just had the first snow. I was minding the store when a red car drove by. You have to realize that there were about as many cars in Montemuro as there were flush toilets, about half a dozen, and most of those—the cars, not the toilets—had been put away for the winter. And none of them were red, believe me. No one had ever seen a car like this one. A Hispano-Suiza. For the most part all we saw was the truck that brought supplies from Sulmona. And motor cycles. There were some paved highways outside Rome—I know because my brother had been called up to work on them—but in the Abruzzi, no. So when this car drove by, I was all eyes and ears. I ran out of the store to look, but all I saw was a cloud of dust. Ten minutes later it came back. A woman got out, and she was even more remarkable than the car. She was cream colored. We didn't have women like that around. She must have lost her way or gotten off the highway. She looked like a movie actress, and of course she was. But there was no movie theater in the village, so nobody recognized her.

"She stopped the car, got out, looked into the bar, changed her mind, and came into the store. Her skirt was so long that it caught in the door when it closed behind her. She didn't speak Italian, but I'd won the English prize in the fifth grade and spoke a little.

"American," she said.

"My first impulse was to run across the street to get Papà or Signor Spettini, who owned the bar and who had been to New York. Actually he'd never gotten past Ellis Island, but it was an experience that had served him well, and he was sometimes known as the man who'd been to New York. He didn't speak any English, though, and the woman was so beautiful I was mesmerized. I wanted to have her all to myself.

"She was the most beautiful woman I'd ever seen, not that I'd had wide experience. The farthest I'd ever been from home was Sulmona, but I'd arrived at the age when boys start to notice these things. Not only was she blond and cream colored, she had red fingernails that matched her red lips. But was sweating, little droplets of crystal-clear liquid. She was in distress. Only I could save her.

"She looked around as if she didn't notice me and was waiting for someone more substantial. But finally she spoke, a mishmash of sounds, nothing at all like the English I'd heard in

218

school from Signor Dieci. She spoke louder and louder and faster and faster, and finally she pointed between her legs and made a shishing sound. She needed to use the toilet.

"It just so happened that we had a toilet, at the back of the store, of which Papà was justifiably proud. It attracted customers.

"I showed her the little room, a toilet only, and waited outside the door. I wanted to stay close to her. She made noises, just like a real person, not at all what I expected from a cream-colored angel. She seemed surprised, when she opened the door, to find me standing right there.

"Mamma appeared at this point, up from her siesta. The two of us stood there, staring at the radiant American. Mamma, who'd always seemed beautiful to me, looked old and shriveled.

"I could speak enough English to communicate, though the *americana* didn't make it easy. She couldn't seem to speak slowly, and I was shy.

"She was lost, she said. She needed someone to drive with her back to Rome. If I understood her correctly she had come to Italy to make a film, but the director had treated her badly and she had taken a car from the studio and driven as far as she could.

"By this time the men in the bar had noticed the car and come over to the store. None of them could speak English, and they were all as shy as I was in the presence of this woman. They might as well have been struck dumb, but they were indignant at her story of mistreatment, ready to go to Rome to avenge her.

"It wasn't so easy to get down out of the mountains in those days. There was no major highway to Rome, and you couldn't drive on the roads around Montemuro in the winter or in the spring. So you had to admire her daring and courage, though I suppose now that it was just foolishness. Whatever it was, she had driven to the end of the paved roads and then just kept on driving.

"I was the only one there who knew any English, so I was elected to accompany her back to Sulmona. At Sulmona she could pick up the highway and drive back to Rome with no problem. I didn't have a choice and didn't want any. I knew the way to Sulmona because my mother's sister lived there and we went to visit once a year.

"By the time we'd sorted things out and filled the car up with petrol from the storage tank behind the bakery, it was too late to start out. It was getting dark, and though the car had electric headlights, it was too dangerous. I explained, with considerable difficulty, that she would have to spend the night.

"That afternoon we sold our entire stock of pens and pencils and paper and envelopes to the people who kept coming into the store to see her. She was resting on the sofa, but Papa would open the door to let customers have a peek.

"At supper she asked a lot of questions and I translated. We were too shy to ask her much, so we stuck to questions about the film, which was called *The Villa of Mystery* and was unlike anything we'd ever heard of, since the nearest movie theater was in Sulmona, ten kilometers away.

"But what I remember wasn't her conversation, it was her tremendous erotic presence, which was so overwhelming that no one would have dared even to touch her. Even Mamma was affected. Everyone wants a little romance.

"She didn't seem particularly grateful for our hospitality, but then, we weren't asking for gratitude. It was enough that she'd condescended to visit us. She was a princess among peasants and assumed that the best we had to offer was no more than her due.

"We set out early the next morning, furnished with two loaves of bread, a tremendous chunk of local cheese, and little salamis made from wild boar meat.

"We reached Sulmona without any problem. I was supposed to go to my aunt's house and then take the bus back to Montemuro. But she—Sybil Connelly—asked me if I would go to Rome with her. She said she was afraid to go by herself and that she'd have someone drive me back all the way home.

"I was in love with her and she knew it. She stopped the car in front of the cathedral, where she was supposed to let me off, and looked at me with eyes as blue as ultramarine. I was as nervous as if we were eloping or embarking on an affair. I didn't know much about women. I now recognize her as a type: she was modeling herself on Greta Garbo, but I didn't know that then. I was torn between fear and desire—fear of the unknown and desire for the unknown. Didn't know anything about Roma either. I'd heard it mentioned, and I'd heard about Mussolini, and my older brother, Franco, had gone off to build roads, and I could probably count on a whipping when I got home, but I told her I'd go with her wherever she wanted to go.

" 'Tell your mamma I was afraid,' she said. 'Tell her I needed a man with me.' She put her hand on my leg, above my knee, and dug her fingers into my flesh. Her hand felt like a cattle prod or like a bunch of nettles. Like this." Sandro used any excuse to put his hand on my leg.

"Rome was further away in those days. She drove faster and

faster as we got closer to Rome and the roads improved, and she talked all the time. About her life. About love. How wonderful it was. And how terrible, too. And every once in a while she'd reach over and tousle my hair or put her hand on my leg again.

"It was mid-afternoon when we got to what must have been the outskirts of Rome, but she had no notion where the studio was and it was almost dark by the time we found it. It was north of what later became Mussolini's Cinecittà. At the gate an Italian *portinaio* picked up a phone, and pretty soon there was a crowd, everybody swarming over the car, over *la bionda.* It was pandemonium, which, I understand now, is exactly what she wanted. I waited by the car, and when she disappeared through the gate, I knew I was in trouble. I tried to explain to the *portinaio,* who told me to get lost. I waited around, demanding to see her, but it was no good. The *portinaio* threatened to call the police if I didn't make myself scarce.

"It took two days to get home. I spent the night in the station in Rome, and I had just enough money to get as far as Avezzano. When I got on the train I went straight into the *gabinetto* and locked the door and didn't get out till the train got to Sulmona, which I recognized by the station sign. I spent the night with my aunt, who put me on the bus in the morning.

"Had I done the right thing or not? Opinion was divided. Most of the men thought yes, and most of the women thought no. But Mamma sided with the men and took my part. Everyone, of course, was angry at *la bionda,* but when the film came to Sulmona everyone wanted to see it, and I was a hero, just as if I'd been in the film myself."

"Did you ever see her again?"

"I saw all her films, though there weren't too many. She never became a big star."

"Do *you* think you did the right thing?"

"I've never been sorry."

"She was very beautiful?"

"Oh, yes. But her voice was no good. I think that's why she didn't do too well in talking films."

"But what do you mean when you say you were in *love* with her? *Really* in love?"

"That kind of love is very powerful, but it's a fantasy. You're in love with yourself, actually, an image of yourself (or the opposite of yourself) that you project onto someone else. The psychologists know all about that sort of thing nowadays; you can read about it in all the magazines. It's not so mysterious as it used to be. Biological versus psychological. The same thing in the end."

"But she was very beautiful?"

"Very beautiful."

What did I know about the Abruzzi? Everything and nothing. Everything: because of the stuff I'd memorized in school—detailed information about each province—for the *interrogazioni* in geography, a subject the Italians take more seriously than we do. I couldn't call up this information at will, but if I got started I could reel it off as easily as sliding down a hill on a sled. Nothing: because I'd never imagined mountains, real mountains, snow-capped peaks, like Switzerland. And I'd never driven past the cathedral in Sulmona where a twelve-year-old boy had told an American actress that he'd go with her wherever she wanted to go, and I'd never looked in the window of the little *cartoleria* in Montemuro where that same little boy had been minding the store when the actress appeared out of nowhere, needing to use the toilet. The window was full of pens and pencils, paper and envelopes, mechanical drawing sets and T-squares, just as it had been on that day. Sandro tried the door, but it was locked. We got back in the Fiat and drove on.

It was odd to think of Sandro as someone with a home to go to, with a mama and a papa, and an older brother who ran the *cartoleria,* and a widowed sister who worked in an office in Sulmona and had three children, two still at home. And who was I?

I suddenly realized that I hadn't given a thought to my own role. "Who am I?" I asked. "Friend? Assistant? Mistress? Girlfriend? What did you tell your parents?"

"Don't worry," he said. "I've explained everything."

"But what did you explain?"

"Please don't worry." But I thought I detected a note of uncertainty in his voice.

"Will we sleep in the same room?"

"No, but I'll come to you in the night, like Cupid coming to Psyche."

The entire family was waiting for us in the kitchen, where a huge leg of lamb was cooking on a grill in the large fireplace. There was a lot of hugging and kissing, on both cheeks, and I felt an instant rapport with Marissa, Sandro's sister, and her handsome children, a boy and a girl in their early teens. Sandro's father was a little remote, but he had reached a time in his life when he didn't worry too much about things. If he hadn't made his peace with them at least he had surrendered gracefully. He was placid, calm, peaceful; not senile, but he had no agenda beyond his birds and his tame fox and his two dogs—two short-haired pointers. I was reminded of the old problem of getting a fox and a duck and a sack of grain across the river in a boat that's not big enough to take more than one item at a time. His hair was perfectly white and his face was covered with white fuzz, as if his whiskers had lost their mettle, their stiffness. There was just a touch of pink in his cheeks, and his eyes were watery. He wore light-colored trousers and two flannel shirts, which didn't match. The cuffs of both shirts were unbuttoned and flopped around his wrists.

Sandro's mother, on the other hand—*la nonna*—was a handsome woman with gleaming silver hair pulled back tight on her head and fastened in a bun. But witchlike, too, in a dressing gown of raw silk. She was just as dark as her husband was light. Her skin was wrinkled, but the wrinkles were fine. She struck me as tough and sharp, the one I'd have to watch out for, if I had to watch out for anyone. She'd been a French teacher and for some reason insisted on speaking to me in French, which I couldn't understand very well. I answered her in Italian.

The news of the flood in Florence neither upset nor interested Sandro's father. He was glad that Alessandro was well and happy and safe, that was enough. But *la nonna* wanted to hear everything—how the water had come rushing through the streets at sixty kilometers an hour, and how the people were eating, where they got their drinking water, etc. She asked about everything but was careful not to ask about me.

The house was an old olive-oil factory that had been con

verted into four large apartments—one for Sandro's parents, one
for his widowed sister and her children, one for his brother, and
another that was rented out to the family that owned the new
olive-oil *fattoria*. The conversion was so skillful, with four separate entrances on two different levels, that I wouldn't have been
aware of it if Sandro hadn't pointed it out. There was a large
courtyard with a stone table where the family ate *al fresco* in
good weather. Behind us the Apennines rose really steeply; below us in the valley we could see Sulmona.

   Dinner, prepared by Sandro's sister, was superb: a risotto
made with locally grown saffron followed by a leg of lamb
seasoned with garlic and basted with honey, which we ate with
potatoes, also cooked on the grill. I sat next to *la nonna,* who
had begun to address me in Italian and who seemed to know a
great deal about me. I gathered that Sandro had described me
as an important curator from the United States. I felt more
comfortable when she turned to Italy. How did I like Italy?
How did I like the Abruzzi? I told her that I had learned a
great deal about the Abruzzi in the Liceo Morgagni, and that
I'd always wanted to visit the Abruzzi, but when she asked
what I'd learned, my mind suddenly went blank. I couldn't
remember a thing. Everyone waited. Someone asked for the salt.
Marissa poured more *vino rosso* for me, though my glass was still
half full. Sandro picked up a loose thread from the previous
conversation and began to pull on it, and suddenly it all came
back to me, just as if I were standing in front of my former
classmates at the *liceo:* the borders, the principal rivers, lakes,
and mountains, the average temperatures (in Celsius), the principal cities, the population density, the principal railroads, typi-

cal products, the timber harvest, the flocks of sheep and *tonnel-late* of fish . . . I went from beginning to end without stopping, astounding everyone, especially myself.

After dinner Sandro and his father disappeared while Marissa and *la nonna* did the dishes. I was not allowed to help. There was a piano in the living room. For some reason I'm always surprised to see a piano in Italy. I was especially surprised to find one in the Abruzzi, since I had in my head the notion that I'd come to a wild place inhabited only by shepherds and, along the coast, fishermen—certainly not by members of the middle class. It was a small grand with music set out on it, but the arrangement of the music was so precise that it looked to me like a display of culture rather than the sort of jumble that generally results from regular practice sessions. As I paged through an edition of Chopin mazurkas, looking for something I could play, I was struck by some interesting comments that had been written in the margins with a fine pen in black ink. The ink was faded but still clearly legible. The comments, which were in English, were astonishingly romantic.

When I asked *la nonna* about them she said she'd written them herself; she'd copied them from a book that had belonged to her piano teacher, but so long ago that she'd forgotten what they meant. She asked me to translate them for her, which I did. She sat on the bench next to me and turned the pages, listening closely with her eyes closed:

> Still on the village green, & boys & girls romping
> in the dance. We hear a drone bass & the chatter
> of the gossips, the bustle of a rural festival.
> The harmonization is rich, the rhythmic life vital.

Bold, chivalric, with the swish of the warrior's
    sabre. The peasant has vanished while his master goes
      through the paces of a courtlier dance.

Its scale is exotic, its rhythm convincing, its tune a
    little saddened by life, but courage never fails.

    Bleak & joyless, modulating into a sort of desperate
gaiety . . .

That night we were shown to separate bedrooms. *La nonna* was
very clear about showing me mine. I had no idea where Sandro
was to sleep, but I expected that he knew where I was. It was a
comfortable room given some character by beautiful French
doors that opened onto a balcony. The doors were closed, of
course, and I couldn't see out through the curtains, so I didn't
know if I was facing the mountain or the valley. I thought of
Ruth and Yolanda on the train from Luxembourg and wondered
if their adventures had turned out as well as mine.

The room was cold, but there was a heavy *piumino,* or eiderdown. I undressed completely, popped under the *piumino* and,
excited by the prospect of a forbidden tryst, was soon warm as
toast. I was toasty and sexy, positively steaming by the time I
finally heard Sandro's gentle tap-tap-tap. I pulled open the door
as I was, without a stitch, but it wasn't Sandro, it was *la nonna,*
in a heavy wool robe.

She looked me up and down: "You should have a nightgown," she said. "It's too cold to sleep *nuda come un verme.*"
Nude as a worm. I'd never heard the expression before. "I'll
bring you one of mine. But get back in bed."

I climbed back in bed and pulled up the covers. "It's nice

and warm under the covers," I said. "This is a beautiful *piumino*." I ran my hand over the eiderdown.

"I want to speak to you," she said.

"The morning might be better."

"No, now is a good time. In the morning, who knows? Some things it's better to talk about at night."

"*Sì.*" Just an acknowledgment.

"My son has had bad luck with women," she said, pushing the *piumino* back to make a place for her to sit on the edge of the bed. "Right from the very beginning. There was an American actress who took him to Rome and then left him on the street. The poor boy was only twelve years old. And Signora Colonna! *O Dio.*" Signora Colonna—Isabella—was Sandro's wife. "And so many others too. He's too kind. He has a large heart. They take advantage of his good nature."

I had nothing to say to this.

"When he didn't come home for Christmas for the first time in his life—even when he was living with Signora Colonna he always came home for Christmas—I knew there was another woman. And I asked him on the telephone: 'Who is she?' 'This is different, Mamma,' he told me. 'This is different.' 'You be careful,' I said. 'Pay attention. Don't lose yourself in the mountains.' "

I was pretty astonished at this view of Sandro as the victim of designing women. And at being cast in the role of a designing woman myself. But she was his mother, after all. Maybe all mothers feel this way about the women their sons get involved with.

"You have a book," she said, in same tone of voice. "May I see it?"

"A book?"

"Yes. A book of poems. With engravings. You always keep it with you."

She turned on the light by the bed.

I didn't know what to do. Should I lie directly? Simply say there was no book? But obviously Sandro had told her about it, so she *knew* there was a book. It was in my book bag on a chair. (It was true, I always kept it with me.)

"Are you sure?"

"Of course I'm sure. Where is it?"

I pointed to the chair. She got the book, came back to the bed. She held it out at arm's length under the light, then put it down on the edge of the bed and took a pair of reading glasses from a pocket in her robe.

"You did this yourself?"

"Yes."

"It's very beautiful." She ran her fingertips over the red morocco cover.

I tried to make myself small as she turned the pages in silence. She kept turning, a few pages at a time, till she came to the Aretino. She looked at the pictures one by one.

"You do these things with my son?"

"Not all of them."

"But this?" She held up one of the drawings for me to see. I nodded.

"And this?" I nodded again.

"And this?" She had arrived at a drawing in which the bodies of the lovers form a gondola or perhaps a bird in flight—it was hard to tell. I shook my head. (We'd tried, but I think it was physically impossible.)

She sighed. "My son says this is worth a lot of money."
I nodded.

"Do you know how much?"

Now I was on safe ground, for this was something I'd been over and over in my own mind. "You can't really tell with something like this. It's unique. You don't know how many people want it or how much they're willing to pay. There's nothing comparable."

"I wanted to see it for myself," she said, putting her hand on my face. She sighed again. "Maybe my son's luck is changing," she said.

That was the end of the discussion. Ten minutes later there was another tap on the door, which I answered as I had before —*nuda come un verme.* I was still expecting Sandro, but it was *la nonna* again, with a flannel nightgown for me.

When I woke in the morning I heard voices out in the court-yard. I threw open the French doors to see what was going on. The ground was covered with new snow. Sandro and his brother Franco were tromping up and down and stomping the snow off their boots. They were dressed in hunting clothes and carrying large rifles, bigger than Papa's thirty-ought-six. The dogs were turning in circles and whining.

"Where are you going?" I shouted.

"We're going after a *cinghiale,*" Sandro shouted back. Wild boar. "We're waiting for our cousins."

It was so cold that steam was coming out of their mouths.

I'd seen the boars hanging in the *polleria* in the Piazza San

Pier Maggiore, but I'd never really thought about where they came from. Now I knew; they came from the Abruzzi.

"I want to come, too," I shouted, but they just laughed, and by the time I got downstairs, they had gone.

It was a Saturday morning. Marissa, who'd taken the morning off, gave me a pair of boots and we walked together to the olive-oil *fattoria,* about half a mile down the steep road Sandro and I had driven up the night before. Two men were standing in a pit right in the oil, which came up almost to the top of their waders. Actually the oil itself was floating on the surface of about three feet of water. The men skimmed it off with large shallow spoons as big as shovels. Marissa filled a tin from a barrel of oil that had been pressed the day before. Back in the kitchen *la nonna,* Marissa, and I toasted chunks of bread in the fireplace, rubbed them with garlic, and poured the fresh oil over them. It was a wonderful breakfast. Fresh unprocessed virgin olive oil is to regular olive oil what Chateau Lafite is to Gallo.

"This is delicious," I exclaimed. "Do you do this often?"

La nonna laughed. "About once every twenty years," she said. "But Sandro said you'd like it."

Marissa blushed at the deception.

But it really was wonderful, and sitting there before the fire with those two women I really let myself go for the first time. I mean I let the fantasies I'd been holding in check run loose. All my expectations about life seemed to be coming to a head: love, marriage, maybe even a family of my own. All the things that I'd put aside, that I'd tried to put out of my mind, seemed to be within my grasp.

When Sandro came back from the boar hunt I was sitting at

the piano stumbling through a Chopin mazurka with too many flats in it for me to handle comfortably, but I was taken by the comment in *la nonna*'s fine hand:

A gem, a beautiful exquisitely colored poem.
Figuration tropical. When major is reached & those
    32nds assail us we realize the seductive charm of
Chopin. Last 2 bars ineffable sighs.

13

Impotentia coeundi

From Montemuro they drive on snow-covered mountain roads to Popoli and then follow the *autostrada* across the Apennines to Rome, where Dottor Postiglione is to be interrogated by the Sacra Romana Rota Tribunalis regarding the annulment of his marriage to Isabella Colonna. They take a room in an old hotel in an old piazza, the Piazza Campo dei Fiori, a room with a bare tiled floor and a *matrimoniale*—a double bed—also old, and noisy, and so soft that it is impossible for the *dottore* to mount her in the ordinary way without straining his back. So Margot mounts him instead, and the weight of her pushes his rump so far down into the bed that he is sitting almost straight up. Tête-à-tête they talk the love talk they love to talk, love, talk to love, then lie listening: buzz of Vespas, shifting of gears, opening and closing of heavy doors, steady plash of fountain, deep masculine laughter, dreamy voices of women who've been drinking wine and smoking cigarettes, rumble of wheels on the paving stones, voices of porters who arrive at three o'clock to assemble the stalls: fruit, vegetables, cheese, meat, flowers, clothes, material, shoes, leather goods, vendors in full cry—it's morning.

Although he has hardly slept a wink, the *dottore* rises refreshed, shaves, disguises himself in an inoffensive old suit that has lost its shape—no point in antagonizing the old priests at the Rota by looking too sharp—kisses his sleeping comrade-in-arms on the head, just behind her ear, buys a small sack of clementines at a stall near the spot where Giordano Bruno was burned alive, peels one as he walks across the piazza on his way to the Cancelleria, a massive Renaissance—early Renaissance—palazzo that houses the nine-hundred-year-old Roman Rota, an ordinary tribunal of the Holy See, a sort of appeals court that hears matrimonial cases that have been referred to it by lower courts of the first and second instance. As he walks he wipes his fingers on a fresh handkerchief. At a bar opposite the main entrance of the palazzo, with its narrow bays and double order of pilasters—Florentine, he thinks, in everything but its size—he arranges the clementines on the table and drinks an espresso with his lawyer, who has been waiting for him, looking over a copy of *L'Osservatore,* the Vatican newspaper. The lawyer has a professional interest, for he is not an ordinary attorney but a consistorial advocate, a specialist in canon law who is licensed to represent those who have fallen into the hands of the Sacra Rota, the Sacred Wheel.

The lawyer, who is the same age as Dottor Postiglione, removes his sunglasses and puts them in a leather case. He fingers the lapel of the *dottore's* suit. He turns up his palms. "Not too bad," he says, "but you look too pleased with yourself."

"I can't help it."

The lawyer, Gianozzo, smiles and touches the back of the *dottore*'s hand. Like Dottor Postiglione, he is from the Abruzzi. They share a taste for mountain dancing and lamb roasted with eggs and cheese.

"Your wife tells me that you are traveling with a young friend."

Dottor Postiglione inclines his head to one side, and draws a thumb across his freshly shaven cheek.

The lawyer holds up a cautionary hand. "*Va bene,* but you're going to have to stop smiling."

The *dottore* tries to tug his face into a frown with his fingers, but once he lets go, his features spring back to a smile.

"Don't worry," says the lawyer, "you'll stop smiling soon enough when the old buzzards start digging their claws into you."

"Have one of these clementines, Gianozzo, they're delicious."

A scraping of chairs, a clearing of throats, the three judges—two Italians and an "Anglo-Saxon," English or Irish—enter the long room. Dressed in black cassocks—no purple pomp here—they sweep their skirts under them as they take their seats. The Sacra Romana Rota Tribunalis wishes to interrogate Alessandro Antonio Postiglione whose case has been referred to the Rota by the defender of the bond of the diocesan court of the second instance in Turin (whence it had been sent by the defender of the bond of the diocesan court of the first instance in Florence). On the long table behind which the judges are seated the clerk has laid out the folders containing the documents of the case, which are called "judicial acts." What is not contained in these acts, according to a judicial maxim, does not exist: *Quod non est in actis, non est in mundo.*

The room is poorly lit and Dottor Postiglione has to quell an impulse to tear open the purple drapes that cover the high windows. He is still smiling, though imperceptibly. The faces of the judges appear neither cordial nor hostile. Their duties— their expressionless faces seem to say—are unpleasant and even, from the point of view of the church, unnecessary: a concession to weaknesses of the flesh and spirit that almost two millennia of discipline have failed to correct. But they are interested, too, for all their feigned indifference. They are professionals, experts in the legal, psychological, theological, metaphysical, and physiological aspects of the mysterious bonds of holy matrimony that make one flesh out of two. Indivisible, except under certain conditions.

The Anglo-Saxon, like Dottor Postiglione, is bald. The *dottore* tries to catch his eye, succeeds, thinks he detects a faint response.

Also present are a notary and the *defensor vinculi*—that is, the defender of the bond, tall and thin, almost emaciated. It is his job to defend the bond of marriage against those who would attack it, namely, Dottor and Signora Postiglione. He is the adversary who can never be defeated, but who may be circumvented.

What God has joined together, no man can put asunder, unless there was some flaw in the original joint, in which case there was no true marriage *(conjugium ratum)* in the first place. Such flaws, called impediments, are (1) insanity, (2) false identity, (3) constraint, (4) conditional consent, and (5) *impotentia coeundi.*

Dottor Postiglione would have preferred another line of attack, but at the advice of the best lawyers, he has agreed to take advantage of the fact that he and his wife have had no children and plead impotence.

Unfortunately the testimony of the principal parties is never sufficient to establish *impotentia coeundi,* and it has been necessary to take depositions from Isabella's brothers (who cooperated without much enthusiasm), from the *dottore*'s closest friends, from psychoanalysts, and from medical experts, appointed by the court, who specialize in conducting the humiliating visual, digital, and instrumental examinations prescribed by canon law in cases of this sort, who know how to describe to the court's satisfaction the length, diameter, circumference and other distinguishing features of the penis in question, and the shape, thickness, and elasticity of the hymen, and to note whether the latter has been notched, scarred, or ruptured in any way; and who also know how to encourage the woman they are examining to recount the intimate details of any experiences that may have affected her physical integrity (in order that the court might be in a better position to pass judgment on the case); and who must also be alert to the possibility that physical integrity may be craftily faked by means of new surgical techniques.

It is also necessary in cases of *impotentia coeundi* to establish the antecedency of the impotence, for impotence that develops *after* a marriage has been contracted does not constitute a true impediment and the marriage remains valid. Antecedency is presumed only if the complaint is issued shortly after the marriage has been contracted. If a long interval precedes the allegation of impotence, the condition is presumed subsequent. In

order to establish antecedency Dottor and Signora Postiglione
have submitted as evidence a number of postcards, which Signora Postiglione presumably sent to her husband shortly after
their marriage, in which she complains to her husband about
his failure to consummate the marriage. Fortunately old postcards, suitably franked (with old stamps) and canceled (with
whatever date and location are required) can be purchased for
these purposes in any major Italian city, along with the appropriate writing instruments and inks. Modern couples often take
the precaution of sending postcards to each other from the time
of their engagement, leaving the message space blank so that it
can be filled in later if the couple wishes to establish grounds
for an annulment. The wife will write, for example: "Dear Giovanni, I'm so glad you're going to be a lawyer. I could never
love a man who is not a lawyer . . ." The stipulation that
Johnny is going to be a lawyer becomes a necessary condition
for a true marriage. Johnny is a plumber, however, not a lawyer. Ergo his marriage is invalid.

It is about these postcards that the judges of the Rota, always
suspicious of collusion in cases of impotence, wish to interrogate Dottor Postiglione.

The interrogation is carried out informally. The *officialis,* or
chief judge, begins by reviewing the pertinent facts:

"According to your initial deposition, Dottor Postiglione,
you failed to consummate your marriage on your wedding
night."

"That is correct."

"And that despite repeated attempts, made in good faith, at
no time did the external meatus of your penis permeate beyond
your wife's hymeneal membrane?"

"That is correct."

"Rendering it impossible for you to deposit even a small amount of seminal fluid in your wife's vagina?"

"È vero."

"And that you continued to live together for nineteen—excuse me, twenty—years before separating?"

"È vero."

"And that a thorough medical examination of both you and your wife revealed no organic impediments to intercourse."

"È vero."

"And that in fact the condition of your wife's vagina indicated that she had experienced intercourse regularly for a number of years?"

"Vero."

"But that by her own admission she had consorted with other men?"

"Vero."

"And that you yourself, in fact—though your original testimony on this point was somewhat confused and contradictory—have consorted with other women?"

"Vero."

The *officialis* puts down the piece of paper from which he has been reading as he turns from specific evidence to general principles: "In order to stand as an impediment to marriage, Dottor Postiglione, impotence must be (a) antecedent, (b) permanent, and (c) certain. Doubtful impotence, either of law or of fact, is *not* an impediment."

"Permit me, Your Reverence"—Dottor Postiglione's lawyer speaks for the first time—"to say that all three conditions were established to the satisfaction of the diocesan tribunals."

The defender of the bond is moved to answer: "That is true, Signor Avvocato, but in cases of *impotentia relativa*—that is, impotence experienced with one person only—as opposed to *impotentia absoluta,* it is always proper for the court to exercise particular caution. The defender of the bond in the diocesan court in Turin was quite right to refer the case to us in spite of the court's decision."

"But according to the rule," the lawyer responds, "laid down by Canon 1979.2, which provides the norms for resolving cases of *impotentia relativa,* when the independent testimony of two psychoanalysts confirms what must be evident to a hypothetical prudent man—"

"Excuse me," the defender of the bond interrupts, "but it is a point of fact, not of law, that causes the court to . . . ah, wonder. Surely a prudent man will have cause to doubt—reasonable cause—that a man with your client's reputation for virility will be incapable of penetrating his new bride."

The lawyer stands, adjusts his coat with both hands, tugging at the lapels: "To begin with, my client's virility is not a matter of record and as far as this court is concerned, does not exist. Secondly, you will recall that at the time of the marriage my client was a young apprentice at the Galleria Colonna. He was new to Rome. He was marrying a wealthy woman against the wishes of her powerful family. She had been brought up in a palace and was accustomed to every luxury. He was a peasant lad from the Abruzzi. It should not be hard for a prudent man to grasp the difficulty of the situation. Nor to understand that the trauma of the first night—the bride's family waiting outside the bedroom door for an announcement, for the presentation of blood-stained sheets. It's no easy thing, under the circumstances, to perform that most delicate act, an act requiring trust, grace, tact, and—may I say it?—exceptional courage. Having failed once . . ." Up go the shoulders and the palms, as if the lawyer is being carried upward toward the ceiling, which is lightly frescoed with pink putti in the manner of Bronzino. "And the fact remains, of course, that there has been no issue."

The *officialis,* eyes sparkling, intervenes: "No mention was made in any of the depositions of the family standing outside the bedroom door."

"I was speaking figuratively, Your Reverence."

And now the court hears from one of the assistant judges, who speaks with a rich Irish singsong that is not in fact uncommon in ecclesiastical courts: *"Quantum a rerum turpitudine, tantum te a verborum libertate sejungas."* ("If you want to avoid the corruption of things, you've got to avoid corruption of language." It's the closest thing to a joke you're likely hear in the Rota.) The *officialis* gives his colleague a disapproving look.

"Cicero," says the Irishman. *"Pro Coelio."*

"Let me turn now to the matter of the postcards," says the *officialis,* "which are the principal issue. The first is dated 5 August 1937, shortly after the invasion of Ethiopia. It is addressed to you at the military training camp in Lucca."

Dottor Postiglione's lawyer interrupts: "These postcards, Your Reverence, express the anguish of the signora's condition —a wife but not a woman . . . no, not yet a wife. Perhaps I should put it the other way round: a woman but not a wife. Not yet a wife. Married, no . . . ." The lawyer, who has confused himself, abandons this line and takes up another. "In the later ones, Your Reverence, we see her losing hope, threatening to take a lover."

"The court," says the *officialis,* "has examined these postcards with some care. The issue is not what they say but whether what they say can be corroborated. It seems odd to the court that a woman would express herself so freely in such a public way, especially when she had ample opportunity to express herself *viva voce.*"

The lawyer embarks on a lengthy explanation.

"There are others who have seen these cards?"

"Yes, Your Reverence."

"At the time? Someone who can remember them at the time they were sent?"

"They're not the sort of thing a man shows to his friends, Your Reverence, but yes, my client did in fact show them to several close friends at the time."

"We will need depositions from these friends."

"Of course, Your Reverence."

"I must remind you that these depositions should have been taken by one of the lower courts, and it is only with the consent of the defender of the bond that the Rota has agreed to proceed with the case instead of sending it back to Florence or Turin."

"We are very appreciative, Your Reverence."

"And you must also remember, Signor Avvocato—and Dottor Postiglione, I include you, too—that the presumption of the law favors the validity of the marriage, and for this reason the court suggests that you, Dottor Postiglione, make a further attempt to have intercourse with your wife. It may be that in the twelve years during which you've lived apart your disposition will have been altered sufficiently to overcome your incapacity. In the meantime you cannot expect the court to smile indulgently on the habitual adultery of either party."

"Out of the frying pan into the fire," says the Irish priest, in English, provoking another disapproving look.

"But that's quite impossible." Dottor Postiglione, who has been shaping his own version of the proceedings into a one-act *opera buffa* in the manner of Pergolesi's *La Serva Padrona,* with the old priests taking the *parti serie,* expresses his incredulity by giving his hand three firm shakes, as if he were trying to detach it from his wrist. "I . . . why . . . our differences are . . . It's simply out of the question."

"Out of the question, Dottor Postiglione, that husband and wife, with the blessings of Holy Mother Church, should knit themselves together into one flesh?"

"You're dealing with human beings, Your Reverence."

"Precisely."

"You need to consider the needs of human beings. You need to consider human dignity. You need to consider simple human decency."

"Dottor Postiglione, that is precisely what the church must ignore if she is to do her work: *human* needs, *human* dignity, *human* decency. What *you* mean, if I may translate, is that *you* find the teachings of the church inconvenient. Of course you do, Dottor Postiglione. The church is very inconvenient. She stands in our way—mine as well as yours—and says 'Turn back, O man, forswear your foolish ways.' Two souls have been intertwined, Dottor Postiglione, in a most complicated way, like two pieces of string that have been wound up into a tangle. You would like us to cut through the tangle with a pair of scissors, snip, snip, snip"—he makes little snipping motions with his fingers—"but that is precisely what we will not do. It may be that the pieces of string can be untangled without damage to either of them, but that requires time and patience. If the pieces of string have been properly knotted, then it will not be possible. What God has joined together, let no man put asunder. It is our office to examine the knots, Dottore, not to cut the string." More snipping motions.

The *dottore*'s lawyer and the defender of the bond both have a good deal to say about strings and knots and the distinctions made in canon law between *impotentia relativa* and *impotentia absoluta.* Dottor Postiglione himself, who regards the matter with extreme distaste, has brought his *opera buffa* to a fine point, but just as his wily conniver—portrayed by a *basso buffo,* himself—is about to confound the court of old men with a dazzling *deus ex machina,* the audience falls silent. The *officialis* is speaking to him, repeating himself: "Dottor Postiglione? Dottor Postiglione? Let me remind you again, Dottor Postiglione, that doubtful impotence is no impediment, nor is subsequent impotence. The court will ask the bishop of Florence to appoint a commission to take the depositions regarding the validity of the postcards; the commission will prepare the interrogatories and begin to summon the witnesses within three months' time. And let me remind you, Dottor Postiglione, that until you have complied with the court's suggestion, the court will continue to regard your case as one of *impotentia coeundi dubita et relativa.* A deposition from your wife will be required as well to establish the fact that you have carried out our suggestion in good faith. And one final point: If the new depositions furnish proof of nonconsummation that are stronger than the proofs of impotence, then the Rota will declare itself in-

competent to rule in the case and all the records will be sent to
the Sacred Congregation of the Sacraments, along with the
written opinion of the *defensor vinculi,* and you will have to
petition the Sacred Congregation for an apostolic dispensation,
which the church may grant *as a favor* she accords her subjects.
There will be no appeal against the decision of the congregation, of course, since it is a purely administrative matter, not a
judicial one. That will be all."

The judges rise. The defender of the bond rises. The notary
rises. Dottor Postiglione and his lawyer rise.

Where is the *deus ex machina?*

"Go in peace," says the *officialis,* smiling.

Margot is full of questions.

"How did it go?"

"Not too badly."

"But not too well?"

"One can't expect too much from those old crows."

"Tell me everything."

"You don't want to know, and you wouldn't believe me if I
did tell you."

"Try me."

He tries.

"Where did you get the postcards?"

"At a place behind the Pantheon."

"Behind the Pantheon?"

"A specialty shop, everything you need to manufacture evidence: old postcards, old inks, old-fashioned fountain pens, old
stamps, a machine that does any kind of cancellation you want,

any date and city." Dottor Postiglione pretends to pluck out an eye, which he places on the railing of the balcony, to indicate how much the place charges for its services.

"Why not letters?"

"Because the postmark is only on the envelope, not on the letter itself. You need something with the date stamped right on it. It's like insurance."

"And what about your wife?"

"She'll have to make another visit to the Rota."

"You're not really going to . . . ?"

"Of course not."

"But those old men will ask her about what happened when you . . . ?"

"Exactly. And she'll tell them . . . ?"

"Everything?"

"All the juicy details."

Margot shudders.

"It's the only chance the church has left to squeeze you by the *coglioni,* legally. Now in the old days there were a thousand ways the priests could get at you. If you looked cross-eyed they could put you to the test. Look"—with a sweeping gesture of his arm he invites her to take in the entire piazza, the noisy market at their feet; the pushcarts and large umbrellas; the fountains, the restaurants; the old, crumbling palazzi; the schoolchildren on their way home for lunch; the great hooded figure of Giordano Bruno, towering over the market stalls. "This was the place of public executions. Bruno was only the first. Burned alive. February 17, 1600. That's what those old crows would do to me if they could. Public torture too. Right over there. You see that *banchetta* with all the scarves? Just beyond the fountain? This was the city center, you know. Everybody came through here, all the religious processions, all the notables. They'd hoist you up by your arms—especially if you were a Jew or a heretic—tie weights on your feet, and then drop you just enough to pull your arms and legs out of their sockets. It gave the place a bad name."

"'Bruno,'" she says. "That's my dog's name, and Mama had a lover named Bruno, Bruno Bruni. Do you know him?"

"Of course, everybody knows Bruno Bruni. But I'm hungry. Let's eat. You can tell me about Bruno and your mother while we eat."

After lunch the piazza will remain quiet for an hour or so. Back in their room the *dottore* is drowsy, ready for a siesta, but Margot is ripe for play, for love. He allows her to undress him.

"What's the *meato?*" she asks, tugging his shorts down.

"It's an obsolete word that means orifice or opening."

"Oh." She kisses, pinches, pats, tickles, fondles him, but he is incapable of (a) erection, (b) penetration, (c) semination. He has become, at least for the moment, what he has been pretending to be.

14

An Instinct for Happiness

Dottor Postiglione looks sideways at the woman sitting in the taxi beside him blowing on her hands from time to time to keep them warm and then tucking them between her legs. With her hair tied back in a yellow scarf, she is especially beautiful. And strong, full of strength, like a young heifer. High spirited without being high strung. So different from the hesitant young woman he remembers standing on the steps of the Uffizi, abandoned by her idiotic American colleagues. He runs through all the clever things she's said in the past months, and remembers the way her eyes widen in surprise, though she knows it's coming, when he caresses her in a certain way. She is intelligent; she is interested in his work, as he is in hers; her fundamental outlook on life is, like his, romantically realistic or realistically romantic. They take the same pleasures in the same small things: the plaques on the walls of the palazzi that mark the levels of the great floods of the past or that indicate that some great man worked here: "Here Fyodor Dostoyevski wrote *The Idiot*"; "Here Luigi Bertoli conducted his immortal experiments on vermin." She is delighted by the old rosemary plant on his balcony, the tiny artichokes they eat with lemon and oil at the Trattoria Maremmana, the freckled brown eggs she boils every morning for her breakfast. She herself is as zingy as the artichokes, as fresh and smooth and delicate and delicious as the eggs, which he tastes from time to time, though he seldom takes more than coffee and milk in the morning.

I've been disappointed in love, of course, he says to himself. Who hasn't? As a young man I fell in love with and married Isabella Colonna, the daughter of a Roman banker, Ignazio Colonna, against the wishes of her family, but her brothers eventually came round and with their help I was able to follow my inclination and pursue my studies at the Istituto per Restauro in Florence, and then, after the war, at the Courtauld Institute in London. When it became clear, after several years, that Isabella would not be able to have a child, I did what I could to comfort her. When, in a desperate attempt to become pregnant, she took a string of lovers, I closed my eyes and ears. When, after almost twenty years of marriage, she decided that Florence was too provincial for her and returned to Rome, I shrugged my shoulders. I had done what I could do. I never let it get me down, you see. And besides, for reasons which I've never fully understood, I've always been, without making any special effort to be so, attractive to women. Even after losing my hair. Or perhaps especially so. And so . . .

They are crossing the Tiber on the Ponte Umberto I and Dottor Postiglione is rehearsing in his mind a speech he has been composing ever since they left his parents' home in the Abruzzi. It is his *daimon,* his instinct for happiness, that has prompted him to compose this speech.

I've always been happy, Margot. I was happy as a child in the mountains; I was happy minding the *cartoleria* for Papà and running errands for Mamma; I was happy when I went to Rome, and when I fell in love with Isabella, and when I first put on a soldier's uniform. I was even happy in the British prisoner-of-war camp in North Africa, which is where I really learned English, and I was happy when I was able to study in London at the Courtauld Institute, and when I was given my first painting to clean—a nineteenth-century landscape by Giovanni Boldoni, not one of my favorites, but . . . It's up on the top floor of the Uffizi; no one ever sees it except the guards. But I've never been as happy as I am now. Only one thing could make me happier: if you would agree to be my wife.

If it is his instinct for happiness that has prompted him to compose this speech, it is also his instinct for happiness that has prevented him from delivering it prematurely. He has to bring the business of the Aretino to a successful conclusion first, and besides, he's not satisfied with the bit about "being attractive to women without making any special effort to be so." It's true, but it sounds too much like . . . like Zeus boasting of his conquests just as he is about to bed Hera on the gentle slopes of Mount Ida. He'll have to work on it.

They've had a siesta and are on their way to the rare book dealer to dispose of the Aretino. The *dottore* would prefer to go alone, but he knows better than to suggest it.

"How do you know you can trust him?" she asks as the taxi accelerates on the Lungotevere Castello.

"We were in North Africa together, in a prisoner-of-war camp. That was before Italy switched sides. The lot before us

was wiped out completely, and we'd have been wiped out too if
the British had waited any longer."

"Army buddies," she says in English.

"Buddies?"

"Old friends."

He nods. "Besides, *è finocchio.*"

"Finocchio?"

"Homosexual. He can be objective about the drawings as art
per se."

"What do you think he'll offer?"

Dottor Postiglione shrugs and remains silent as the taxi
slows down and then stops in front of one of the high-rise office
buildings that have begun to spring up like mushrooms along
the west bank of the Tiber.

The elevator that takes them up to the sixth floor does not
open onto the sort of corridor one expects in an office building
but onto a small foyer. On the left, in a handsome display case,
a leaf from a Gutenberg Bible; on the right, a book of hours,
open to a genre scene—peasants drinking wine and baking
bread. Opposite the elevator, a heavy door with a small bronze
plaque:

SIG. VOLMARO MARTELLI, ANTIQUARIO
ESERCENTE DI LIBRI RARI
SOLTANTO PER APPUNTAMENTO

The door is opened by a young man with an American haircut, very short, and Dottor Postiglione follows Margot into
what appears to be a gentleman's library, English rather than
Italian, though the grisaille paneling has undoubtedly been

chiseled out of some old palazzo. Volmaro himself, a beefy man in a linen vest that fits him like a girdle, returns a book to its place on a shelf just slightly higher than he can reach comfortably, and turns to greet his guests.

"Champagne," he says to the young man. And turning to Dottor Postiglione: "We've been expecting you."

Volmaro greets him warmly with a double hug, left cheek to left cheek, right cheek to right cheek. Margot, evidently not wishing to hug or to be hugged, extends a hand, which Volmaro grasps firmly—the whole hand, not just the fingers. He raises it halfway to his lips and then, as if meeting some subtle resistance, releases it with a smile.

"*Piacere.*"

The *dottore* is not a jealous man by nature and does not begrudge his old acquaintance his success, but he always feels uneasy in this splendid room, which—because of the arrangement of the bookshelves in a series of bays, some of which are subdivided into additional bays—cannot be taken in at a single glance.

"I hear about you from your brother-in-law." Volmaro motions his guests to sit down, which they do. He sits down himself. "You're going to be pulverized by the Rota, ground to fine powder." His eyes sparkle. "You'll pay and pay and pay," he says. "Believe me, it's not worth it. Better to live in . . . sin, if you'll pardon the expression."

"Not if you want children," the *dottore* replies.

"At your age?" Volmaro laughs. "I've been reading about you in the papers, too," he continues, changing the subject. "You're quite a hero. First the Vasari Corridor, now the

Lodovici frescoes. I hope the *soprintendente* has learned to appreciate you properly."

Dottor Postiglione, pleased to hear his actions spoken of before Margot, holds up two fingers to indicate that he and the *soprintendente* are on good terms. "And Abbot Remo, too. The good abbot is eating out of my hand right now."

"You're going to go ahead with the *strappo?*"

"As soon as I get back to Florence."

"You restorers are like surgeons: always eager to use the knife. You pretend to be cautious, but you have an appetite for drama, for drastic intervention."

The *dottore,* though he is anxious to get on with the business at hand, begins to defend the decision to detach the Lodovici frescoes, but Volmaro laughs. "Not you, I didn't mean you. You are the exception. You approach the matter in an entirely different way. But tell me," he says, leaning forward in his chair; "you're doing well?"

"I've found my niche, you might say, and it's a comfortable one."

"You and I," says Volmaro, eyeing Margot, "after what we've been through, we deserve a little comfort."

The young man with the American haircut returns with three champagne flutes on a silver tray that he places on Volmaro's leather-covered library table. Volmaro lifts a glass and proposes a toast: "The Sixteen Pleasures."

They drink.

"You have the book with you?" He addresses Dottor Postiglione.

"Che bella . . ." Margot, rummaging in her *borsa* for the

Aretino, swings her head around at her surroundings. "What a beautiful . . . room. I hardly know what to call it."

"*Libreria,* Signorina." He shrugs, inclining his head toward the cases of gleaming leather volumes. "I sell these by the meter." He indicates a row. "The decorator calls and says, 'I need ten meters, browns and reds, no blues.' He doesn't ask what they cost." He pauses. "Please," he says, "look all you want. Then when we're through I'll show you the vault: climate control, humidity, temperature, the door opens only when it recognizes my palm print. You'll see."

Margot places the book on the table.

"Where did *this* come from?" Volmaro taps the protective box.

"The solander case? I made it."

They both reach for the book and their fingers touch. "Allow me, Signorina. Giulio, bring me a cloth, please."

Giulio produces a soft cloth.

Volmaro rubs the box carefully before opening it. "Dust, you know, is the enemy."

Margot nods.

"Dust and water."

"Yes," says Margot. "And acid and fire."

"Of course." He lets the book fall open in his hand, catches the edge of a page on his thick thumb and turns it, then another, then another, till he arrives at a print. *"Porcamadonna!"* He continues to page through the book. "And you did the binding as well as the box?"

"Yes."

"Very fine indeed."

Volmaro shakes his head, purses his lips. "Well," he says,

closing the book. "I won't haggle, but I won't give you any reason to complain. Eight million lire. There you have it. Eight *million*, 'in cash,' as you Americans say. No questions asked." Volmaro opens a drawer—"That's more than five thousand American dollars"—and begins to count out hundred-thousand-lire notes.

"*Momento.*"

Volmaro looks up, a finger separating the banknotes he's already counted from the pile in the desk drawer.

"Could you explain how you arrived at *otto milioni*?" Margot asks.

Volmaro looks at the *dottore,* incredulous. "I arrived at that figure out of the goodness of my heart, Signorina, out of a kind of inborn generosity. I arrived at that figure because this man" —nodding at the *dottore*—" gave me his cigarettes when we were prisoners of the British. We each got four cigarettes a day and a book of American matches. That's how I arrived at that figure."

"I was thinking more in terms of market value. I mean, this is an *unico,* unique. No one has a copy. And it's erotic. And it's famous. There's nothing like it. I'd think there'd be collectors willing to pay through the nose. I mean, someone just paid almost one million dollars for a Monet. There's a lot of money around."

"You're confusing your markets." Volmaro laughs and gives another eyes-rolled-up-into-the-top-of-his-head look at Dottor Postiglione. "Art is art, books are books. Besides," he says in English, "I'm already paying through the nose. I'm paying through the arse."

"But sixteen drawings by Marcantonio Raimondi, that's art, too."

"Prints, not drawings. Nothing original."

"Engravings. What do you think it would bring at Sotheby's?"

Volmaro pulls himself up, slides backwards in his chair, leans forward: "Sotheby's won't touch it unless you can establish your title to it. They'll want a clear provenance and a *licenza d'esportazione* from the Italian government. They're not going to sell something that might have to be returned if someone brings a claim against it. No reputable auction house will touch it without papers. You can't sell it out of the country. There'd be too much publicity. This is a national treasure. You don't just walk out of the country with it."

"And what do you plan to do with it? How will you establish *your* title to it?"

"I don't think that's important now. What's important is that I'm risking my neck to do you a favor, and paying handsomely. Through the nose," he adds in English, "for the privilege."

"But you stand to make a handsome profit?"

"Not as handsome as if you'd kept your hands off it. You should have left it as you found it, you should know that. You shouldn't have touched it."

"Nonsense. The binding was completely gone. The textblock was starting to mold. If I hadn't intervened it would have been ruined. There wouldn't be any book."

Volmaro speaks in English: "I'm sorry, miss, we've already reached an agreement." Laughing, he pushes a stack of banknotes across the table toward the *dottore.* "You didn't tell me she was so spirited."

Dottor Postiglione, who has been watching, like a man watching a street quarrel, from a distance, is uneasy. But what is he to do? His fast-food restaurant behind the central market is as empty at noon as it is in the evening; his low-calorie wine is sitting in a warehouse in a place called New Jersey while two different unions decide who has the right to distribute it. He has to have money. Money for his lawyers, for Gianozzo in Rome to press his case in the Rota; for other lawyers in Florence; money to pay off the note on the restaurant, which is coming due; money to pay off the union officials in New Jersey. His parents have refused to lend him more money; his older brother has refused him; his sister would give him anything, but she has no money of her own. His only hope is the Aretino, however distasteful to his open and honest nature his plans might be. If he is to marry, he must have more money. He has been hoping, with Volmaro's help, to clear eighty million or so by disbinding the book and selling the engravings separately, though even with eighty million he wouldn't be out of troubled financial waters. But at least he'd be in a position to maneuver. He wouldn't be in immediate danger of drowning. But now he feels that Volmaro is deliberately jeopardizing their plan by refusing to deal directly with Margot. He feels that Volmaro is deliberately putting him on the spot, reminding him that he is not the master of the situation, that he has not been able to bend this young woman to his will. But that wasn't what he had wanted to do. What he had wanted . . .

"You didn't make an agreement with me," says Margot. "And I'm the one who has the book."

"How much do you want?" Volmaro addresses the question to Dottor Postiglione.

Margot: "The book is not for sale."

"Really," says Dottor Postiglione, "this is beyond me, I hadn't expected, I had no idea . . ." He is aware that he is making *brutta figura,* but he is at a loss, taken by surprise, can't help himself.

"Twelve million," says Volmaro.

"Not for sale," Margot says in English.

Non è in vendita. Dottor Postiglione repeats the words to himself in Italian. What he wanted was . . . He is no longer sure what he wanted, but he is experiencing a feeling of relief. He has attempted to betray Margot, and she is probably well aware of it. But he has not betrayed her de facto. He may still be able to redeem himself.

"Piano, piano," he says. *"Il libro non è in vendita."*

"I can assure you," says Volmaro, ignoring him and speaking now to Margot, "that if you don't sell to me now, there's not a dealer in Italy whom you *can* sell to. I give you my word."

"I don't intend to sell it in Italy."

Volmaro, leaning back: "You are prepared to violate international law?"

"Perhaps."

"Be careful; be very, very careful."

Margot stands up. "You were going to show us your vault?"

"Another time, Signorina, another time. Sandro, *mi dispiace,* but you have a tiger by the tail. Let go now before it's too late. And don't forget, there's the small matter of the French engravings I furnished you on credit. I'll expect payment by the end of the month. Sixty thousand lire. A small sum, perhaps, but I can't afford to overlook it. Thank you."

That evening, en route to a Chinese restaurant Margot is inexplicably drawn to, the *dottore* suggests a stop at the French church, San Luigi dei francesi, to have a look at the Caravaggios. He has once again failed to achieve an erection, to say nothing of penetration and semination, and though he is too experienced a traveler on the pathways of love to panic simply because he has lost his way for the moment . . . even when his vulnerability is the occasion for such tenderness and generosity on Margot's part . . . well, what man in his fifties will not see in such a failure an ominous sign of things to come?

He has never eaten in a Chinese restaurant, does not know anyone who has, and has no desire to do so himself. What he wants is not an exotic Oriental dish but a friendly plate of pasta or a comforting bowl of minestrone. Maybe the Caravaggios will change her mind.

The church is dark; a few candles burn here and there at an altar, but no one will accuse the *sacristan* of wasting electricity. They feel their way to the Contarelli Chapel and Dottor Postiglione locates the light box, hidden behind a pillar, and inserts a hundred-lire piece. Three minutes of light for one hundred lire, reasonable enough.

He watches Margot as she takes in the three large paintings in the chapel, which tell the story of Saint Matthew.

All his life, he thinks, he has been content to let his little boat drift wherever it would. He has been accustomed to smile at the frantic efforts of others whom he sees struggling against the current—their faces distorted by the strain, troubled, clearly unhappy—but now he himself has drifted too long and he realizes at last that he will have to exert himself if he is to arrive at his destination.

Behind the altar Saint Matthew, a dignified patriarch with a shining bald head and a long gray beard, takes dictation from an angel suspended in the air over his head. The angel is so foreshortened that you can see only the upper half of his body. The lateral paintings are more dramatic: on the left Matthew, counting money in a tavern, is summoned by Christ to become a disciple; on the right he is murdered by a gang of ruffians.

Dottor Postiglione keeps feeding the meter. Two, three times. Nine minutes. Most people can't look at anything that long. Margot's mother may not have succeeded in teaching her the principles of art history, but she did teach her something more important: not to fake her responses. He says nothing. He doesn't believe in talking too much about art, especially while you're looking at it. The pressure to appreciate is the great enemy of actual enjoyment. Most people don't know what they like because they feel obligated to like so many different things. They feel they're supposed to be overwhelmed, so instead of looking, they spend their time thinking up something to say, something intelligent, or at least clever.

While he is thinking these thoughts he is also, on another level, revising his speech, the things he must say to Margot before the evening is over: Margot, this has been one of the most difficult days of my life. I've been humiliated by the Sacra Rota, which has placed still another obstacle in my path, I've been humiliated by my own failure to make love to you, I've been humiliated by an old "buddy," Volmaro Martelli. And what is more, I was—as you've probably guessed—intending to deceive you. I was cutting a deal with Volmaro. The Aretino is worth much more than eight million or twelve million. We were planning to disbind the book and sell the engravings separately. I won't try to excuse myself, but I will say that I thought that without the money I could never ask you to be my wife. The Sacra Rota turns very slowly, and it takes a great deal of money to keep it turning at all. You have to keep feeding it just as I have to keep feeding this light box. My own investments have been unsuccessful, and though my wife could easily afford the expenses, she, too, wishes to humiliate me. But now I see that none of these things matter. What matters is that I love you, and I believe you love me too. If you can forgive me . . .

The light goes out and he inserts another hundred-lire piece, but Margot has had enough.

"Mama and I came here," she says, "with all the students. It's coming back to me. But the only thing I remember are the feet. The feet are superb."

"Caravaggio had a fetish, you know."

"No, really?"

The *dottore* laughs.

She takes his arm. "Say something clever," she teases.

"I'm not feeling clever," he says. "Do you *really* want to go to this Chinese restaurant? I'm not sure I'll survive it. Those plastic replicas of the dishes didn't look too tempting. And the names: 'Plum Blossom and Snow Competing for Spring' . . . What kind of a name is that?"

"You're so provincial," she says, "I can't believe it. Your idea of foreign cooking is something from Naples."

The restaurant has lots of smooth surfaces that are either red or black, lacquered and shiny. Instead of bread and wine the Chinese waiter—who, much to Dottor Postiglione's surprise, speaks Italian—brings a pot of tea and two small cups, slightly larger than espresso cups, and thicker.

Margot pours for herself; Sandro declines.

"I can't drink tea," he says. "That's all the British gave us in the prison camp. Tea, tea, tea. Morning, noon, night. Afternoon, too. They were mad about tea. That's the only thing that wasn't in short supply."

"This is green tea," she says. "It's not the same at all. You could at least try it."

"Margot," he says, "this has been one of the most difficult days of my life . . ."

"Don't be silly," she says. "You'll survive."

She orders for both of them from a menu which is printed in Chinese, Italian, English, German, and French, in that order—each dish is numbered—and the waiter brings them some of the little *bacchette* the Chinese use instead of knives and forks. He doesn't know the word for them. With a *bacchetta,* he thinks, a conductor directs an orchestra, a drummer strikes a drum, a magician causes pigeons to fly out of a hat, a *rabdomante* divines underground sources of water, a teacher whips a disobedient pupil.

"Chopstick," she says in English, holding up a *bacchetta.*

"You liked the Caravaggios?" he asks, moving the conversation back to familiar territory.

"Very much. Did you notice," she asks, "how the violence of the assassination is softened by the graceful S-curve that runs through the body of the angel and down his arm to the palm branch and then through Saint Matthew's outstretched arm?"

"Beautiful." He frowns, thinking, and then laughs. "You've got the hang of it," he says. "Keep it up and they'll make you a professor at I Tatti."

"You know what I really noticed?"

"What?"

"Saint Matthew—in the altarpiece—looks just like you except for the beard. And the halo!"

"Definitely not the halo." He laughs again. "But you know, that painting has always seemed rather tame to me, compared to the others. It's not the original, you know. I mean it's not the one Caravaggio originally intended for the altarpiece. The first one was rejected."

"Why's that?"

"Too shocking. Saint Matthew is an ugly old man—Caravaggio wasn't afraid of ugliness; his Saint Matthew's a laborer who doesn't even know how to hold his pen properly. The angel has to lean over and guide his hand for him. And the angel is luscious, very definitely a she-angel."

"Where's the original?"

"It was snapped up by the Marchese Giustiniani and stayed in the Villa Giustiniani till the Germans looted it during the war. I don't know the whole story, but it wound up in Berlin and was destroyed in 1945."

"Have you seen it?"

"I saw it when it was still in the Villa Giustiniani."

The waiter brings two sausage-shaped things, evidently deep-fried, on small plates. On each plate are little bowls of sauce, mustard (probably) and something orange and translucent, like apricot marmalade.

"What are these?"

"They're egg rolls."

"Egg rolls? How strange."

"And this is hot mustard, and this is duck sauce."

With two *bacchette* Margot lifts her egg roll—the entire thing —dips it in both sauces, raises it to her lips and takes a bite. He doesn't know where to begin.

"Egg rolls are hard to eat this way," she says. "The other dishes will be easier. But try it. Look: you lay the first one between your thumb and your first finger, like this." She demonstrates. "And hold it firm against your fourth finger." She reaches across the table and adjusts the *bacchetta* in his hand. "Then the second one you just hold like a pencil, see?" She holds up her hand with the two *bacchette* in them, clicking the tips together, like the pincers of a crab. He picks up a second *bacchetta* and tries to hold it like a pencil. He squeezes as tightly as he can, but the tips of the *bacchette* waver around helplessly, out of control, like an insect's antennae. Once again she reaches across the table to guide his hand, and as she does so he suddenly sees himself as Caravaggio's original Saint Matthew—not the dignified patriarch but a clumsy old man who doesn't know how to hold his pen, and she the angel sent to help him, to guide him, to show him the way. This is how he must look to the other diners. He looks around him. No one is paying the slightest attention, and yet it is impossible to say what he wants to say under the circumstances.

"You know," he says, "Caravaggio was the only one strong

enough to stand against the convention of representing all biblical figures as uniformly handsome or beautiful."

"What about Rembrandt?"

"Yes, Rembrandt, of course, later on."

All along he's been telling himself that the gap between them could be bridged. But now his instinct—the very instinct for happiness that has always guided his actions—sends him a sharp and distinct signal, a signal that is almost visceral.

He pushes her hands away and sets the *bacchette* down next to his plate. He eats his egg roll, and then the rest of the meal—thin strips of various meats mixed with vegetables—with a knife and fork. The duck sauce is sickly sweet, the mustard too hot; the different combinations of salt and sweet are offensive to his Italian palate; the soy sauce stuns the senses. He is relieved when the meal is over and the waiter brings them each a small dish of orange sherbet and a little twisted *biscotto.* The sherbet is cool and refreshing on his tongue.

Sandro is fifty-two, fifty-three in September. She's twenty-nine. He's December, she's May. She's in love with Italy, but so are a lot of American women. He's seen it too many times. They fall in love with Italy, marry an Italian man, settle down to live an Italian life. For six or seven years everything is wonderful and then the novelty wears off. They start to get homesick. They have a child and realize that the child isn't going to have an American childhood, isn't going to have any of the important experiences that they recall so fondly from their own childhoods. American Christmases, Thanksgivings, Independence Days, he can't begin to name them. Moreover, there won't be enough money. And how hard she was with Volmaro.

The little *biscotti* are called fortune cookies, because each contains a fortune, a prediction, a warning. He breaks open his cookie and reads his fortune with some trepidation, not because he is superstitious but because, when he is in this peculiar frame of mind, even the slightest breeze can cause him suddenly to change tack. They read their fortunes in silence and then aloud.

" 'Some wives don't get mad,' " she reads. " 'They get even.' Your turn."

His is equally pointless: " 'Talent, like the gout, sometimes skips two generations.' "

"Idiotic," he says, genuinely annoyed. "That's the stupidest thing I've ever heard of. It's ridiculous. What nonsense. What a way to end a meal. *Stupido.* I can't see what the point is of—"

"*Piano, piano,*" she says. "What's the matter? It's only a joke."

He will explain later, he tells himself. In bed, with his arms around her, he will explain everything. But no, he knows it is too late now for explanations. The current is too strong. The moment he has been anticipating has passed. He has drifted past his destination, and in the twinkling of an eye his life has been changed. He is in the same boat, drifting down the same river, but he has turned around. The boat is still traveling in the same direction, but instead of standing in the bow, looking straight ahead to see where he's going, he is standing in the stern, looking back at where he's been, and this is where he will remain for the rest of the journey.

15

Mont Blanc

Preparations for detaching the frescoes in the Lodovici Chapel had been under way for several weeks. Every square inch of the chapel had been photographed by a documentation crew. Paint samples had been subjected to a variety of tests by the chemists and X-rayed by physicists. Humidity had been monitored by technicians. Scaffoldings constructed by carpenters.

The original plan had been to detach the frescoes along with the arriccio—the lower layer of plaster or ground on which the intonaco—the upper layer of plaster that holds the paint—had originally been applied. But this process, which is called *stacco* or "detachment," is slow and costly and eventually proved to be unworkable because the paint itself was not attached firmly enough to the intonaco.

Sandro's decision to remove the paint layer alone—to lift the paint right off the intonaco, a process called *strappo* from the Italian word for "to tear"—had been made before our trip to the Abruzzi and Rome, but he was never perfectly happy with it.

I'd begun working at the Certosa, the Carthusian monastery on the outskirts of town where many of the books from the Biblioteca Nazionale had been taken for treatment, but I followed the preparations for the *strappo* with great interest. Sandro could talk about nothing else. It was the only time I had seen him nervous, but I could understand why. Can you imagine ripping four of the world's great frescoes off the wall on which they'd been painted six hundred years ago? I'd never seen it done myself and wouldn't have missed it for anything. It made me nervous just to think about it, because it seemed so impossible, though the process, which was first used in the eighteenth century, is perfectly straightforward. After the painting is cleaned it is coated with a layer of animal glue and then a layer of a facing is applied: strips of lightweight cotton gauze that have been steeped in more glue. The gauze is then covered with more glue and two layers of hemp canvas. Then the glue is allowed to dry for two or three days and the whole thing is "torn" off the wall.

Sandro fretted about mold and worried that it was too damp for the glue to dry properly. He monitored the humidity constantly, turning on, or sometimes off, a battery of infrared lamps. He came home every two hours or so at night but then turned around and went straight back to the Badia (which is only a ten-minute walk from Santa Croce).

On the morning of the *strappo* itself I took the day off and went to the Badia. The Lodovici Chapel was full of people, not simply the technical crew but reporters and photographers who had no business being there but once there were not easily dislodged. The abbot, who loved publicity, had called all the newspapers. Sandro was furious. It was the only time I saw him angry, and frankly I was a little worried that his anger might cause him to make a mistake.

He began by making a long, clean cut, with what looked rather like a gold knife, around the perimeter of the lower left fresco, Saint Francis preaching to the birds. Then, without wasting any time, he gave a firm tug at the bottom corners, and with the help of two assistants the hemp canvas was slowly "torn" from the wall, taking the paint with it—paint that had been laid on wet plaster six hundred years ago.

There was no sound except the tearing of the paint. Then complete and absolute silence, and then a round of applause. Sandro was dripping with sweat as if he'd stuck his head in a bucket of water.

The detached painting was then rolled out on one of several large tables that had been placed in the nave of the church itself, facedown on clean paper. Parts of the back were still covered with a thin layer of intonaco. In other places you could see the paint itself, the back of the paint.

The other three frescoes were detached in the same way, without incident.

Later in the day I watched Sandro remove the intonaco from the back of the paint layer by hammering it lightly with a rubber mallet until nothing but the paint itself remained and you could see the frescoes from behind, as it were, their images reversed as in a mirror. On the following day these images would be transferred to tightly stretched canvases.

The reporters and photographers had gone. The technical crew had gone home for the night. The abbot and his monks were in the refectory. We were alone.

"You must be pleased," I said. "The *strappo* was a great success. Your picture will be in all the papers tomorrow."

"That fool of an abbot," he exclaimed, "thinks the publicity will attract more tourists."

"He's probably right, don't you think?"

Tap-tap-tap. Tap-tat-tat. "I suppose."

I don't think Sandro had a metaphysical bone in his body—he was a man who loved things rather than ideas, surfaces rather than essences—but now and then he'd lapse into a kind of metaphysical mood when talking about the art he loved best, painting, and could conjure up a vision of universal decay that would bring tears to the eye: pigments fade or change color over time, details are lost in deepening shadows, paint layers fracture and flake. No one has ever seen a single painting from classical Greece, and the same inevitable fate awaits every single painting in the Uffizi and the Pitti Palace and the Louvre and the Alte Pinakothek, and so on, the modern paintings as well as those of the Middle Ages and the Renaissance, for most modern paintings are less stable, less firmly constructed as things, than the works of earlier ages.

"Well," I said, "tourists or no tourists, you've saved the frescoes, and I think it's fantastic."

"A *strappo* is always a defeat," he said, "not a triumph. We've torn these frescoes from their natural environment. We've turned them from architecture into easel paintings. And that's only the beginning: all the undulations and irregularities of the underlying ground, which gave them weight and density, will be smoothed out before I'm finished. The paint has been traumatized by the operation, and the new backing will create different optical properties, and as I'm tapping away here the crumbling intonaco is pulling away a fine skin of paint."

So gloomy! And yet Sandro was the most cheerful person I've ever known and these moods were as ephemeral as fruit flies. That night we went to the Trattoria Maremmana, one of our favorites, and ate lasagna *al forno* and grilled shrimp, and drank more wine than usual. On the way home Sandro sang, in English, "The Flowers That Bloom in the Spring" from *The Mikado,* and I was sorry I didn't know my Gilbert and Sullivan well enough to accompany him, though I did join in on the tra-la's.

It was, all in all, a period of pregnant calm and intense happiness. I knew from Papa's letters that he'd sold the house in Chicago and bought an avocado grove near Mission, Texas, on the Rio Grande, so I felt oddly cut off from my old life, my old self, like a planet without a sun. But I had a new life, a new self, a new sun, so I didn't let it worry me.

Sandro and I continued to live together as man and wife, except for one thing: we never quarreled. I don't recall a harsh word, in fact. He was always attentive, considerate and generous, even though his finances were going from bad to worse. His own lawyer—not Gianozzo but another—had threatened to "denounce" him. The fast-food restaurant had closed its doors, so there was no chance of recovering on the note he'd cosigned. The dispute over who had the right to distribute the low-calorie wine had not been resolved. But we ate out every night, and hardly a week went by without a present of some sort, small but expensive: a gold chain, a special lipstick, fancy under-things.

Sandro was a popular man, a man who knew everyone, and though we were never invited out as a couple, we saw other people, discreetly. I had my own circle of friends, too. Florence is a small town; it was only a matter of time before I started running into old friends on the street. The problem was not running into them but recognizing them. But once I'd met Silvia in front of the Marzocco I was in touch with everyone, including Fabio, who ran a butcher shop on the Via Pietrapi-ana, not far from Santa Caterina Nuova.

I didn't go back to Santa Caterina, though whenever I crossed Piazza San Pier Maggiore I felt a strange attraction and was tempted to knock on the door. Somehow, though, I didn't want to have to explain. I wanted to wait till I'd sold the Aretino, though I still didn't have a plan for doing so.

Two weeks after the *strappo,* Sandro told me that he had ac-cepted a position as director of conservation for the Vatican Museum. There was talk of cleaning the Sistine ceiling; it was a wonderful opportunity; he couldn't afford to turn it down; it gave him more scope, and it paid him more money. His broth-ers-in-law had arranged it. He would be going back to Rome and to his wife, who had, in any case, refused to submit to another vaginal examination. There was nothing he could do. But they would be keeping the apartment in Florence, he said, as a *pied-à-terre,* and I was welcome to stay there as long as I wanted.

It was eight o'clock in the morning and I was cooking an

egg; Sandro was drinking *caffelatte*. I felt hot tears boil up instantly, hot as the water in the pan on the stove. I looked at my watch and watched the second hand for three and a half minutes. I took the pan to the sink, poured out some of the boiling water and ran cold water over the egg. I didn't ask him any questions, like: "How long has this been in the works?" or "When did you decide?" I just said, "When will you be leaving?" as if he'd told me that he was going up to Milan for a couple days to offer his advice on the restoration of some fresco, something old and beautiful and priceless that wouldn't survive into the next century without his expert intervention.

"Not till the beginning of March," he said. "We've got another two weeks."

I cracked open my egg, spooned it into a dish, and ate it without salt or pepper. He finished his *caffelatte* and kissed me good-bye just as he did every morning. "I'll be at the Limonaia all day," he said.

I went to the window and watched him cross the piazza. He must have spoken to a dozen people before disappearing into the Via Verrazzano. I thought it was the worst moment of my life, but it wasn't.

I didn't make scenes. I didn't beg him to stay, I didn't ask him what was going to happen to *me*. I just kept on doing what I'd been doing all along: making my rounds: taking the bus out to the Certosa every day. I had even been given an official title: "Friend of the Italian People," though as a friend, unfortunately, I was not entitled to a salary. As the end drew near we stepped up the pace of our lovemaking, but even so, I began to have trouble sleeping: I'd lie down and then in a few minutes my whole body would start to freeze up and then to twitch, just as if I'd had too much coffee, way too much coffee. And I started talking to myself, telling myself that I was going to be all right, that I *was* all right. I went to the Certosa every day. I didn't miss a day.

I was even planning to go there on the day, the third of March, that Sandro left for Rome. But I went down to the station instead to see him off, and when he got on the train I got on, too. I couldn't stand to let him go. That's why I followed him onto the train even though he was trying to push me back, but there were people getting on behind me and he had to let me on. So we went to the club car and ordered two beers. Italian beer is good. It's got more taste than American beer, more taste than German beer, too, if you ask me. German beer and American beer are about the same.

I'd never asked Sandro what he and Martelli had been up to, but I asked him now, and he told me.

"That Martelli's a real prick," I said in English. "A first-class prick."

He didn't argue with me.

"What would you have done with the money?—not that you'd have gotten it—your pal Volmaro would have cheated you just the way everyone else has. You need someone to look after you."

"I'd have paid off my debts and asked you to marry me."

"Why didn't you ask *me* for the money? Why didn't you ask me to *give* you the book, instead of sneaking around behind my back, double-crossing me with that first-class prick?"

"You wouldn't have done it."

"How do you know?"

"Because I know you. I thought if I could get it away from you without you knowing . . ."

We ordered more beer.

"Was it just the money that stopped you?"

"Margot, listen to me. I'm glad we're having this talk, because . . . because I don't think you fully understand my position. I'm fifty-two, fifty-three in September. You're twenty-nine. I'm December, you're May. You're in love with Italy. So are a lot of American women. I've seen it too many times. You fall in love with Italy, you marry an Italian man . . ."

Everything he said made sense, but there was something stale about it, as if he'd gone over and over it in his mind so many times that it had begun to sound like a recording.

I finished my beer and ordered another. The train seemed to be going faster and faster.

"You're not going to make a scene when we get to Rome, are you?"

"No, I'm not the type."

The landscape was flat and unattractive, spotted with public housing developments, flat surfaces broken up by little balconies too small to sit on. I could see what was happening. I could feel it in my whole body. But I couldn't do anything to stop it, anymore than I could have stopped the train by willing it to stop. Thinking of Ruth and Yolanda, I looked around for emergency cord and there it was, at the end of the car. But it wasn't the *rapido* I wanted to stop. It was the train inside me. But this train had no brakes.

It was time to go home, but I didn't have a home. I think this was the first time it really hit me, like a blow to the stomach: I didn't have a home.

*   *   *

We got to Rome about noon, and that was the last I saw of Alessandro Postiglione.

I bought a sandwich in the station but didn't eat it. I wasn't hungry. I'd been to Rome a couple of times with Mama on student excursions, and then with Sandro, but I didn't really know my way around very well. The sensible thing to do would have been to get on the next train back to Florence. I had two hundred thousand lire (a little over a hundred dollars) in my book bag that Sandro, who suddenly had plenty of money, had given me to tide me over. I could afford to stay in a hotel. I also had my plane ticket back to Chicago.

But what I needed was to walk. I told myself I was going to be sensible. I was not going to waste the opportunity to see more of Rome, maybe see an old church, the way people do in English detective novels, or even go back to San Luigi dei francesi and look at the Caravaggios again. Even though I didn't know my way around very well, Rome felt familiar, like a big city, like Chicago, with traffic roaring down wide streets. Not like Florence, all dark and cramped.

I knew that the Via Cavour would take me to the Roman Forum, and that the Forum must be close to something, because I'd been there with Mama. It would be something to do. But the Roman Empire has never figured importantly in my imaginative scheme of things, and when I got to the Forum it didn't look like much and I didn't want to pay to get in. The beer had gone to my head and I was confused, but I wanted another one.

Drinking it, at a bar, I could remember parts of Sandro's

body, his way of holding a brush (between thumb and third and fourth fingers; so why couldn't he hold chopsticks?); little scars and nicks, the hair on his belly, his little *uccello,* uncircumcised, like Isaac's penis on the Ghiberti doors. And these memories were like memories of home.

Outside the Forum I had the feeling that someone was following me, that someone was looking at me. This was absolute nonsense, of course, but there it was. I wanted to call someone, but there was no one to call. I knew I shouldn't have come to Rome. I looked in the phone book. Several Postigliones. I looked at my watch. Only five minutes had elapsed since I'd left the Forum. Impossible. It must have been an hour and five minutes. I wound my watch, but it was already too tight. I'd overwound it. I had another beer at a bar, and then I went to another bar and ordered a cappuccino. I was warm from walking and thinking about Mama's funeral. I sat so near the casket I could have reached out and kicked it during the service. Suddenly I wanted to go to the Protestant Cemetery. It's not frightening, like the Protestant Cemetery in Florence. It's open and lovely. Keats is buried there, and Shelley, or Shelley's heart. I went with Mama. But I had no idea how to get there. I knew the Keats-Shelley Memorial was in the Piazza di Spagna.

What had it been like when Mama parted from Signor Bruni? Had she cried, too? But she'd had a husband and family to go home to. Home. That really bothered me. Where could I go that, when I got there, they'd have to take me in?

I tried to calm myself, but my mind was going in spurts and sprints. I could hear the sound of water, the sounds of the city blending together to make a sound like the ocean. Not a roaring. More like a growling. Like a waterfall.

Coming out of a bar on the Via Veneto, where I'd stopped for another beer, I almost walked into a car. There hadn't been any women in the bar; I had been uneasy. I had a headache, I could feel it pulsing, and there seemed to be a gaping hole in the sidewalk. Only a shadow, but I couldn't bring myself to step on it. I couldn't see what was making the shadow, what was coming between the sun and the sidewalk. I kept looking up in the sky. No trees. No skyscrapers. Just a spreading patch of dark at my feet, and a muffled sound.

I wandered around for a while, heading in what I thought was the general direction of the station, till I came to a huge church—which I now know was Santa Maria Maggiore. I climbed a long flight of stairs and entered. There was nothing handsome about the interior. It was just big. Not big like a Gothic cathedral, not "big" as in huge or immense or soaring or magnificent or overwhelming, but "big" as in bulky. There were long rows of confessionals on either side of the nave, like Porta Pottis at an outdoor rock concert, with LIBERO and OC-CUPATO signs on them, like the signs on the toilets in a train. And there were signs to indicate the language or languages spoken by the different confessors: not just English, French, Spanish and German but Russian, Polish, Hungarian, Chinese, Japanese, Hindi, Urdu. The place was an international cross-roads. At some of the confessionals people were lined up waiting, mostly foreigners. I had a sudden impulse to get in one of the lines, to confess. "Unload," I suppose, would be a more accurate description of what I wanted, but at the time I thought I wanted to confess.

Of course I didn't have the faintest idea how to go about confessing. I knew there was a formula—"Forgive me Father for

I have sinned," something on that order, but where did one begin? Should I try to fake it, or should I begin by explaining that I wasn't in fact a Catholic? Would I have better luck in English or in Italian? I decided on Italian because there was no one in the Italian line, though the little sign at the top said OCCUPATO. After ten minutes I began to think I'd made a mistake—the other lines were moving right along—but then the door opened and a woman emerged, dressed in a simple black sheath, very elegant, her hair pulled back in a chignon like Princess Grace. Her dark eyes, mysterious with grief, were downcast and she didn't recognize me but I thought I recognized her. Margeaux, my ghostly double, outdoing me even in grief! I banged open the door of the confessional without knocking. There was a bench seat and a kneeler. I sat down and began to explain: "Excuse me," I said. "*Scusi.* Padre, are you there? Yoo-hoo?"

"What is it?"

"Excuse me, Padre. I'm not really a Catholic, but—" and that was as far as I got.

"You Protestants!" he shouted. "You come to Italy and all of a sudden you want to confess your sins. I can't do anything for you. If you want to confess why don't you join the church?"

"Right," I said. "And why don't you join the human race?"

I hadn't gotten very far, but far enough to turn myself around. Instead of sinking I was soaring. I felt wonderful; I was flying in the upper atmosphere, not in an airplane or a space ship but with my own wings. I could look down on everything, take in the big picture. It was like being in tune with a man and knowing he's in tune with you, and it's coming, it's going to happen, nothing's going to stop it. Only I felt that way with the whole world.

I started walking. I didn't know where I was going, but every once in a while I'd recognize something that looked familiar, something I'd seen with Mama or Sandro: the Colosseum, the Trevi Fountain, the Castel San Angelo, the Pantheon. When I hit the Pantheon something clicked—Sandro's postcard shop. I wanted to buy some postcards with old postmarks on them so I could rewrite the past and make it turn out differently. I searched systematically, making larger and larger circles, like a dog trying to pick up a scent. I found it on the third circle: La Casa della Stilografica. The House of Fountain Pens.

The place was full of pens, literally thousands of pens. Mechanical pencils, too, but mostly pens. Ballpoint pens, roller pens, quill pens, drawing pens, and of course fountain pens, new and antique: Watermans, Esterbrooks, Parkers, Scheaffers, and many unfamiliar names too: Dupont, Lamy, Omas, Niji, Élysée, Pelikan. They came in every color, and some were multicolored, piebald. They were long and short, thick and fat. I fell in love with one of those big black Mont Blanc pens that cost nearly sixty dollars.

"How can a fountain pen cost so much?" I asked the clerk.

"Gold," he said. "Eighteen-carat gold. Look." He brought the pen from under the glass counter, removed it from its case, and unscrewed the top. "These are gold strips, you see how they come together there?"

I nodded.

"The gold is good because it won't corrode; but it's soft; that's why you see this line right at the tip, right?"

"Right."

"That's iridium. You know how they put that tip on there?"
I shook my head.

"It's fused in there with a blowpipe, the kind a glassblower uses."

"I want to buy a postcard," I said.

He acted as if he didn't know what I was talking about, but a five-thousand-lire note brought him to his senses. He sent me up a flight of stairs to a long, narrow room where various postcards were on display along with inks, more pens, uncanceled stamps and a huge array of rubber stamps to cancel them with whatever city and date was desired.

Another clerk asked me what I had in mind and I said, "Nothing in particular. I just wanted to look."

The postcards were grouped by location. The largest section contained postcards from Rome—mostly pictures of monuments and works of art—but every province in Italy was represented. I choose a black-and-white card of Bernini's *Apollo and Daphne.*

"Just one?"

"That's all."

He shrugged. "And the cancellation date? What time are we talking about?" He looked me up and down. "Nineteen-fifties, right?"

I had to think about that. I thought.

"Roma," I said. "Two thousand seventeen."

"Two thousand seventeen?" He looked at me closely to see if I was joking. "What are you, crazy?" He shook his head. "That don't make any sense. I can't give you no postmark for fifty years from now. Lady, I think you got the wrong idea. Why don't you just wait? What's the point? You'll be lucky to be alive in 2017. We all will."

"It makes sense to me, that's enough."

He shook his head again. "You could cause big trouble," he said. "Some priest takes a look at this and sees it's in the future, he's going to say, 'Hey, what's going on?' "

"No priest is going to see it. I just need it. Please don't ask me why because I can't tell you."

"Okay but I got to charge you extra, you understand. For the risk. It just don't make sense."

"It makes sense to me."

"I can't give you no 2017 *stamp* though. There ain't no such thing."

"A 1967 stamp will do fine."

"Okay, lady, if that's what you want."

"That's what I want."

"This stamp," he said. "They been making these for ten years now. You want to put it on?"

I licked the stamp he gave me and stuck it in the upper right-hand corner of the card. He adjusted a wheel on his postmark machine.

"What date you want? You know, what day of the month?"

"Today. What's today, March second?"

"It's the third."

"Good, put March third."

He turned some more dials. "You know," he said, "this don't print the first two numbers anyway, so it'll just be seventeen. He pulled a lever, removed the card and handed it to me: "ROMA ORDINARIE 3.—3.17."

He charged me twenty thousand lire for the postcard, another twenty thousand for the postmark, three hundred for the stamp, and another five thousand for canceling it with a hand-stamp. The total came to forty-five thousand three hundred. Close to thirty dollars.

Was it worth it? I don't know, but I was in a spending mood. Most of the money I had left from what Sandro had given me I spent on one of the big Mont Blanc pens I'd been looking at. Big and black and beautiful. "It will last a life-time," I told the clerk, as if I were trying to sell it to *him.* "Everyone should have a good fountain pen. And besides, I need something to write with."

"It's the finest writing instrument in the world," he said.

"Could you show me how to fill it, please?"

"*Certamente.*" He unscrewed the cap again. "This is the filler button. When you turn this, it actuates a diaphragm. You turn it all the way, see, and then put the tip of the pen in the ink and turn it back. Now you're forcing air out through the mouth of the breather tube. When the air goes out, there's a vacuum, right? And as long as the tip of the pen is under the ink, the ink's going to be sucked into the vacuum, see?" He made a sound with his mouth to signal the rush of ink into the vacuum. "Then you turn it like this," he said, holding the pen over the open bottle of ink and twisting the filler button slightly so that four drops of blue-black ink dripped into the bottle. "That way the ink will have room to expand in the barrel."

I wasn't sure I understood the process perfectly, but I thought I knew how to fill the pen.

"Do you want a bottle of ink?" he asked.

"No thanks," I said. "I have to get back to Florence tonight.

I don't want to carry it in my bag." I indicated my Harvard book bag.

He nodded to show that he understood.

When I left the store I knew that the most important thing was to get back to Florence as soon as possible. But I didn't know how to get to the station, and I was afraid that if I took a cab I wouldn't have enough left for a ticket. Instead of counting the money in my wallet I tried to remember exactly how much Sandro had given me and exactly how much I'd spent on beer and on the card and on the pen. I tried to picture Sandro handing me the money—we'd been standing in front of his apartment waiting for a cab—but I couldn't remember if he'd given me two hundred-thousand notes or a hundred-thousand note and two fifties. And when I tried to retrace my steps and add up how much I'd spent on beer, and how much I'd shoved in the poor box at the church, and how much for the card and for the postmark and the stamp, and how much for the pen, and did he charge me anything for the ink, and I'd forgotten the five thousand lire I'd given the clerk downstairs, it came out different every time, so I sat down at a table across from the Pantheon and ordered another beer and wrote a card to Sandro:

Caro Sandro—

When we got out of the train in Rome you kissed me on the cheek and told me that you loved me, and I believed you. I followed you into the station, about twenty paces behind you. Your wife was waiting for you. She was taller than I expected, and better looking. Handsome, sleek, fashionable. You whispered something in her ear and she laughed and then you got into a taxi and drove off. You never looked back. But I still believed you, and I still do, and I always will.

All my love,
Margot

But I didn't have an address, so I couldn't send it. I never did send it. I kept it. I still have it. I still believe that he loved me, and I always will.

16

Remedia amoris

I closed the shutters in Sandro's apartment so I wouldn't have to look out at the piazza, at the green-and-white facade of Santa Croce, at the admonitory statue of Dante (who showed no sign of fainting at my predicament, as he had at Francesca's), at people coming and going about their business as if life held some meaning and purpose.

Sitting in the big farm kitchen in the Abruzzi with Sandro's sister and mother, eating bread toasted with garlic and olive oil, I'd been so sure that Sandro was going to propose, and so happy at the prospect, that no other future had seemed possible. When he didn't propose I wasn't disappointed, because no occasion suitable for a proposal had presented itself and we still had Rome ahead of us. And then when he didn't ask me in Rome, I didn't give it a second thought, because he was upset about the Sacra Rota and had a little trouble getting it up—though we'd had a wonderful time the first night in Rome—and then I wouldn't turn the book over to that creep Martelli.

I knew he'd tried to hornswoggle me, but it hadn't mattered.

It hadn't mattered that the Sacra Rota was going to hold up the annulment for another year; it hadn't mattered that he couldn't get it up once in a while (it was kind of nice, in fact, just to snuggle); it hadn't mattered that he didn't have a head for business, we'd have gotten by. At least none of these things had mattered to me.

And then when we were back in Florence he was nervous about the *strappo.* But I was so confident that we were meant for each other, and that he was about to speak at any moment, there in the darkness of the Badia, as he tapped away at the intonaco on the back of the Lodovici frescoes, that I'd been on the point of saying something myself. But something had held me back and I hadn't, and now, like an athlete whose fatal error has cost her an important game, I kept replaying that moment in my mind, off and on, as I lay in Sandro's bed, on dirty sheets, reading a copy of *Emma* that I'd borrowed from the library at the American Church. I'd had it up to here—up to my chin—with Italy; I needed to escape. I needed English countryside; I needed English country houses and vicarages, amiable eccentrics like Mr. Woodhouse, sensible people like the Westons; I needed a clear-cut world crisply organized in a series of meaningful social and cosmic hierarchies.

I didn't go out, I didn't get dressed. I didn't wash my hair or brush my teeth. There wasn't much to eat because we'd always eaten out, in a circle of expensive *trattorie* and *ristoranti* where Sandro always left generous tips for the waiters without ever actually paying the bill. But I wasn't hungry. I made do with a half kilo of spaghetti, a couple of cans of tomato pulp, a dozen eggs, and half a loaf of *pane toscano* that was so hard I had to soak it in hot tea before I could chew it. I turned Sandro's cheval glass to the wall so as not to see myself as I wandered in and out of the bedroom. My workstation at the front of the living room was still in place, and sometimes I sat on my old orange crate and fiddled with some of my tools; I folded sheets of paper into gatherings with a bone folder; I opened the edges with an Opinel knife; I pasted bits of leather onto the old boards from the *Preghiere cristiane* to make a kind of collage. I looked over my worksheets, going over the restoration process in my mind. I made lists.

I would have grieved longer but I couldn't afford to. All I had was thirty thousand lire—under twenty dollars—left from the money Sandro had given me. And of course my Icelandic ticket to Chicago. By the end of the week there was no food left. I could either . . . or I could . . . I wasn't sure what I could do.

On Sunday night, one week after I'd come back from Rome, I walked to the Piazza San Pier Maggiore. The streets were already crowded with tourists, mostly German, a few Japanese. I bought a hamburger at the *friggitoria* and ate it standing under the Arch of San Piero, one of the gates in the old medieval wall. When a new bishop was appointed—in the Middle Ages, that is—this was the gate through which he'd enter the city—after spending the night in the convent.

From my position under the arch I could look down Borgo Pinti, the street Mama and I had lived on when I was fifteen, and I could see the big doors of Santa Caterina. I reminded myself of Madre Badessa's words of warning about Sandro: a man with no center, no soul, no inner core. I'd had no experience of love affairs. I didn't know what to expect. I knew people didn't die of broken hearts, but I was a little frightened anyway. I wanted a prognosis. I wanted someone to tell me that I was still young, that I still had my whole life ahead of me (though who doesn't?), that in another two weeks I'd be able to get around on crutches, and that in a month or two I'd be as good as new.

Is this what Madre Badessa would have told me? I experienced a strong pull, an urge to knock on the convent doors, as I had knocked late one night after making love to Sandro, and Madre Badessa, instead of scolding me, had taken me into her office, and into her heart, and given me *vinsanto* and *biscotti di Prato.*

But I didn't knock. I finished my hamburger and walked to the Central Post Office, which was so crowded with tourists I had to wait in line for an overseas phone booth. I hadn't talked to Papa since he'd moved to Texas, but I carried his number around in my purse, along with the letters I hadn't answered. I'd put off writing because I'd wanted to send him the good news I'd always thought was just around the corner. I'd always imagined writing first, just for the pleasure of putting the words down on paper; and then telephoning, for the pleasure of saying the words out loud: "Papa, guess what! I'm getting married. You didn't believe me before, did you, when I called you on Christmas Eve?" But when my turn came, I didn't place the call. I went back to Sandro's apartment and read *Emma.*

In the morning—Monday morning—I opened the shutters, washed out some socks and panties in the sink and hung them up to dry. I kept the clothes that Sandro had given me, but pawned the jewelry at the pawnbroker's in the piazza, where I learned from the pawnbroker that this was where Sandro had bought most of them in the first place. It was all very high quality—genuine Etruscan scarabs carved out of red carnelian; expensive jade (jadeite, not nephrite, or the other way around); the chains and bracelets were not silver but white gold, eighteen carat; even the watch, which was quite ordinary looking, turned out to be valuable. I came away with nine hundred thousand lire in my purse, almost six hundred dollars.

In the afternoon, I went back to the Certosa. Everything was *sottosopra,* as the Italians say—topsy-turvy. Professor Panuccio, who was in charge of the restoration program, had quarreled with the abbot and returned to the Istituto Patologia del Libro in Rome. The special sinks that had been ordered in January had finally arrived, but the abbot had refused to allow the plumbers into the crypt, so they hadn't been able to hook them up to the water supply. The drying ovens, a gift from the I. G. Farben Company in West Germany, had been installed in the smaller of the two refectories but could not be connected to the gas line without a special application that required the abbot's signature. Many of the student volunteers had left, and those who remained—about twenty—working without supervision, had become demoralized and were not following the procedures we had established.

Julia, a medical student from Stockholm whose job was to photograph the books before they were scraped free of dried mud, collated, and disbound, had run out of film and didn't have money to buy any more. She was staying on only because she was in love with Mario, who was living in a friend's apartment in Scandicci, but the friend was returning from the States. Mario, who was from Milan, was going to have to vacate the apartment . . . And so on.

That night I treated the students to a good meal at the Trattoria Maremmana, where Sandro and I had often eaten, and the next morning, at the Palazzo Davanzati, just outside Sandro's old office on the third floor, I explained the situation to Signor Giorgio Focacci, the *Soprintendente del opificio delle pietre dure,* Sandro's former boss, and told him that I would *make everything arrange itself,* but that I needed a stipend of at least half a million lire a month.

"The honor of my city demands it," he said.

"Well," I said. "I'm glad you see it that way."

"To see things as they really are," he said, "to call things by their proper names, to show strangers the way. Those are the principles by which I live my life, Signorina. I only wish I could say the same for everyone."

I assumed he was referring to Sandro, whose office, I noticed, did not appear to be occupied.

"But *un mezzo milione,* Signorina. You deserve every lire; *un milione, due milioni, tre milioni, quatro, dieci,* but consider . . . a foreigner . . . the difficulties . . ."

"I have to live," I interrupted. "I have to eat. I have no money. I know that you can arrange everything, that you know whom to talk to, what strings to pull. You're a man of the world, Signor Focacci, a man who risked his life in the Vasari Corridor. I'm just a poor stranger. You must show me the way."

"*Tre cento mila,*" he said, turning to the window and holding his hands behind his back.

"*Mezzo,*" I said, "and I'll need a *permesso di lavoro,*" the Italian equivalent of a green card. I stood beside him and held *my* hands behind *my* back.

On the Via Pellicceria, below us, workmen were replacing a plate glass window in a pharmacy but I wasn't really looking at the workmen; I was looking at my own reflection in the window in front of my face. If I'd been appealing to an American, I might have shown up in my work clothes, but that strategy wouldn't have impressed an Italian, so I'd put on a dress Sandro'd picked out in Rome, a black sheath, *abbastanza décolleté,* stiletto heels, a pair of gold earrings I'd had since I was in high school.

"You've got to do something immediately, Signor Giorgio, or the student volunteers will be gone. I spent a hundred thousand lire to give them a decent meal last night. Without me, they'll go home or they'll go someplace where they can feel they're doing something useful. They'll go to work for the Americans at I Tatti, or the British at the Biblioteca Nazionale. You don't want the Certosa to be a *disgrazia,* a black mark on your record."

"Very well, Signorina." He sighed.

"Thank you, Signor Giorgio. You won't regret it. You're a man who sees things as they really are."

Out in the street I took another look at myself—in the new window of the *farmacia.* How serious I was, like someone working out a chess problem—black to mate in three moves. The pharmacist must have thought I was looking at him, because he touched his cheek with the tip of his finger and rotated his hand back and forth. I tried out a smile. There was work to be done; it was nice to be needed.

By the end of the March it had begun to look like spring. The shops changed to their spring schedule. Middle-aged women and old men were putting in gardens along the Via Fortini, which led up to the Certosa. The apricot trees in the cloister were budding, and the monks could be heard in the choir, practicing the *Quem quaeritis,* a dozen old White Benedictines— the last of their order—in white robes and black scapulars, still hanging in there.

I'd been hanging in there too. I arrived on the first bus every morning, at six o'clock, and worked into the evening. Challenging work, as everyone knows, is an excellent tonic, and the work at the Certosa was certainly challenging. Physically and spiritually. We were adrift on a sea of books. Books everywhere. Stacked under the loggias, piled on the floor of the refectories and the *sala capitolare:* illuminated Bibles, psalters, books of hours, prayer books, late-medieval and classical texts—an early-fifteenth-century manuscript copy of Augustine's *De Civitate Dei* with beautiful illuminated capitals; a codex of the *Divina Commedia* dated (under the colophon) Ravenna 15 maggio 1320; volumes one and three of an Aldine Aristotle; Alopa's Homer (the first Greek text printed in Florence); Stephanus's edition of Plato's *Republic,* bound together with a Latin translation.

But work wasn't enough to make me forget Sandro. No matter how hard I worked, no matter how tired I was at the end of a long day, he remained as clear in my memory as if I had left him at the Limonaia only that morning. And sometimes in the evenings, as I sat at the long table in the refectory where I kept my restoration records, I'd hear footsteps coming up behind me and would turn to greet him, but it would only be the old abbot, coming to show me out so he could lock up.

One evening, as I was planning the next day's triage—deciding which of the wounded books could survive on their own, which would have to be abandoned because they had no chance of survival, and which would be admitted to our little hospital —I put my head down for a moment on the table, and Sandro presented himself to my imagination in startling clarity, as radiant as a vision, holding his arms out like the archangel Gabriel in the Pontormo *Annunciation* in the sacristy, where I kept a supply of Japanese rice paper and thymol crystals. Was he trying to tell me something or was he asking me for something?

How I longed for his caresses, his kisses, his bottomless sack of bedroom tricks, his thoughtfulness, his *gentilezza* and *cortesia*. But what I regretted most was not what had been lost but what had never been, not the past but the future.

In my dream I was about to speak to him, but I don't know what I was going to say, and I never found out, because the bells were ringing compline and the abbot had his hand on my shoulder and was shaking me.

"It's time to go," he said, his breath sour on my cheek.

The abbot, oddly, was the only person I'd met who wasn't convinced of the absolute necessity of preserving everything in Florence that could possibly be preserved. "Of the making of books," he liked to say "there is no end, and much study is a weariness to the flesh."

I'd never taken him seriously—I was a book conservator, after all—but that night I was inclined to agree with him. The great spiritual classics of Western civilization lay strewn all around us in various stages of undress, reduced to things, physical objects, water logged, molding, stinking, mud encrusted, humbled by circumstance—and I didn't care.

"It's time to go," he said again, still leaning over me. "You need to rest."

It was true; I was overtired. But I felt like opening up to him the way someone might open up to a bartender after a few drinks. I wanted to tell him about Sandro. I wanted to tell him that there was one book that I would preserve with my life, one book that I would weigh against all the spiritual treasures that I, as a professional conservator, was bound to preserve.

At the great iron gate that opens onto the Via Fortini I turned to him and said: "A good book is the precious life-blood of a master spirit."

"Is that so?" He looked at me as if he'd heard something truly astonishing.

"That's what my mother used to say."

"Then your mother must have read Milton's *Areopagitica,*" he said. "If you don't hurry you'll miss the last bus."

What was it, I asked myself as the bus sped along the Via Fortini, that had kept me from speaking to Sandro, there in the darkness in the Badia, as he tapped away at the intonaco on the backs of the Lodovici frescoes? What had held me back? What would I have said to him in my dream, if the abbot hadn't awakened me? What had kept me from knocking on the convent door the night I'd emerged from Sandro's apartment? What had kept me from telephoning Papa? It was the book, of course, the Aretino. I'd known that ever since I decided not to go home for Christmas. But what I had never fully grasped, up to that time, was this: The little book of pictures wasn't just a valuable piece of property; it wasn't just a unique copy of the most powerful work of erotic art produced by the Renaissance. It wasn't just an occasion to strut my stuff as a conservator. It was the adventure that fate had placed in my path. I couldn't walk away from it any more than Jack could have refrained from exchanging his mother's cow for the magic beans, or Psyche from opening the magic box that Venus had given her to take to the underworld, or Bassanio from accepting the adventure of the three caskets. It was my handful of magic beans, it was my magic ring, my talisman. That's why I couldn't simply sell it to a dealer or turn it over to Sandro; that's why I couldn't give it back to Madre Badessa or turn to Papa for help. It was *my* story—my *story.* Without it I wouldn't know who I was or where I was going.

A week later I took the train to Basel. My visitor's permit needed to be renewed, which meant I had to leave the country, and I wanted to have my passport stamped at the border to prove I'd been out of the country anyway. I didn't have to go all the way to Basel, but a plan was finally taking shape in my mind. I couldn't take the Aretino to Sotheby's, which is what I wanted to do, without explaining where I'd gotten it. I couldn't explain where I'd gotten it because the legal owner was not the convent of Santa Caterina but the bishop of Florence, or the church itself. But if I could create a false provenance by laying down a trail that would lead a suspicious inquirer not to Santa Caterina but across the border into Switzerland . . . If I could show that I'd acquired the *Preghiere cristiane* in Basel—say, on my way to Italy in November, or even now, in the present moment—there would be no need for an export license, no need to explain. The Newberry did business with several antiquarian book dealers in Basel; it wasn't out of the question that I could turn up another copy. Seventeenth-century prayer books, after all, were not that uncommon. Surely the details would sort themselves out once I was in Basel.

I hadn't been able to reserve a couchette and wasn't looking forward to sitting up in a compartment with four other people —two small children (and their parents)—but I'd brought along my copy of *Emma* to shut out the external world, and as the train pulled out of the station, I fished it out of my purse. It was a solidly built old edition, late nineteenth century, sewn on real bands, with marbled endpapers and hand-sewn headbands. The leather was still in good shape, but the pulp paper—a product of modern technology—was so brittle it was impossible to turn a page without breaking off a corner.

The purse also held the Aretino, which I'd been reluctant to leave behind, so I kept it safely wedged between my leg and the inner wall of the compartment, a fact that seemed to provoke the curiosity of the little girl, who must have been five or six. She maneuvered herself around my knees and tugged at the strap, which I had wrapped double around my arm.

"Nein, nein, nein." The mother, sitting next to the window on the opposite side of the compartment, didn't make a move; she was saying *nein* for my benefit. The little girl paid no attention to her.

Putting *Emma* to one side I hoisted the child up on my lap and we had a conversation. She asked questions in German and I made up answers in English, much to the amusement of her father, who was the only one who knew both languages.

"When you come into *die Schweiz*," he said in English, leaning forward and smiling, "you won't have to hold the purse so tightly."

"You can't be too careful," I said.

"Never," he said. "Especially . . ." He nodded his head in the direction of the window, to indicate, I gathered, Italy.

"*Zigeuner* everywhere," he went on. "They say it's worse in Napoli." He closed his eyes and gave an involuntary shudder.

"*Zigeuner?*"

He looked it up in a canary yellow Italian-German dictionary: "*Zingaro, zingari.*"

"Gypsies."

"In the underground tunnels there are *zingari*. My little *Schätzli* was frightened, wasn't she," he said, taking the little girl from my lap. "They say they're rich, they live like kings."

"No Gypsies in *la Svizzera?*"

"No, nothing like that. Do you know what Goethe said about *die Schweiz?*"

I didn't know.

"He said he was happy to know that there was a country like *die Schweiz* existing where he can always take refuge."

"Good for him," I said, "but do you know what he said about Italy?"

The Swiss man didn't know.

I didn't know either, but I repeated something that Mama used to say: "He said that a person who was tired of Italy was tired of life."

The Swiss man was not amused, and the family, following his lead, closed ranks, turned in on itself. Mother held the little girl up to the window. Father and son began conversing in German. I opened my book.

I forced myself to read for two hours, during which time Emma discovered that Harriet Smith was not in love with Frank Churchill but with Mr. Knightley, from whom she was anticipating a proposal, and that she, Emma, was in fact in love with Mr. Knightley herself. Once again she had completely misread the true state of affairs: her matchmaking efforts had brought the parties involved to the brink of disaster, and now she was facing a second humiliation.

Poor Emma! But Emma had Mr. Knightley waiting for her at the end of her story, a man who saw things as they really were, a man who was virtuous, upright, trustworthy, honorable . . . all the things that Sandro was not. I summoned up what wisdom I could—for both of us, for Emma and for me. I mocked my own conventional hopes and fears, but admitting them to myself only made them more real, gave them a new kind of power over me, as if I'd admitted to myself a preference for Norman Rockwell over, say, Giotto or Leonardo. You won't know true happiness, Madre Badessa had told me, till you give up your heart's desire. But I couldn't help imagining that the empty seat in the compartment was Sandro's, and that he'd just gone down to the dining car to order something special—something not on the menu—for our supper.

Later on, in the middle of the night, as we crossed into Switzerland and were wakened by the border police who'd come to check our passports, the Swiss man—wishing to restore cordial relations—asked me where my home was, and I didn't know what to tell him.

"Home," I said, "is the place where when you have to go there, they have to take you in."

He didn't understand. "My mother used to say that," I explained. "It's sort of a joke. It's from a poem."

"A joke. *Ein Witz.* Please say it one more time."

"Home is the place where when you have to go there they have to take you in."

"Ah," he said, smiling to show that he understood. "And where is that?"

"Texas," I said.

"And do you like Texas very much?" he asked.

"I don't know," I said. "I've never been there."

Basel was cold outside and warm inside, just the opposite of Florence, where the law requires you to turn off the heat on the first of April regardless of the weather. I suppose that when it gets cold enough outside, as it does in Switzerland, you have to protect yourself, to pay more attention to keeping warm. Life is lived inside, not in the streets. My room at the Schweizerhof, on the piazza, across from the station, was very *gemütlich,* a place of refuge, like Switzerland itself, according to Goethe. Under the window a tile stove, itself a work of art, radiated warmth. The armchair squatting next to it was big enough to curl up in. The bed, unlike the bed Sandro and I had shared in Rome, was big and heavy, a bed that wouldn't threaten to collapse when you made love in it; a bed for serious sleeping under feather comforters, your head bolstered, your feet toasty. I was seriously tempted to lie down.

To be perfectly honest, I didn't feel like going out into a city where I couldn't speak the language. It had been enough of a struggle to get across the *Platz*—ugly word—to the hotel. I was like a baby: I wouldn't be able to ask directions; I wouldn't be able to explain what I wanted; I wouldn't even be able to find a bathroom. Moreover, the details of my plan had not coalesced into a coherent whole that gave me a clear sense of direction. I wasn't even sure what I was looking for. Now it seemed to me that the chances of finding another *Preghiere cristiane* were minuscule, and even if I did find one, I wouldn't be able to afford it.

I did, nevertheless, venture out into the *Platz*. I bought an English-language guide to the city in the station and followed the map to the Klosterberg, which, according to my guidebook, was the center of the antiquarian book trade.

The bookstores that I visited did not cater to casual buyers but to serious collectors, people who knew what they wanted. In jeans and pullover I didn't look the type, though when I said I was from the Newberry Library I was treated with grave courtesy.

By noon I'd examined half a dozen prayer books in half a dozen shops and, at my last stop, a remarkable seventeenth-century French book of hours covered with dark green velvet, worked with couchings of gold twist, which had a *devoto*—a little strip of cloth that had been dipped in the blood of a saint —sewn on the last page, just above the colophon. But by this time I'd realized that all I really needed was some dog with warped boards, loose hinges, and rounded corners. Actually I didn't even need a book at all. All I needed was a receipt. A little slip of paper with the name of the store on it:

BUCHHANDLUNG KARL SCHULZE
32 Grabenstrasse
Basel 10093
(67-92-03)

I was tempted to swipe the receipt book lying on the cloth-covered counter, next to the book of hours, but Herr Schulze was keeping a sharp eye on me—the book of hours was worth several thousand dollars. Herr Schulze had located a couple of prayer books, too, but I poked around on my own until I found something of no particular value—a nineteenth-century translation of *Pilgrim's Progress* in a plain cloth binding for forty-five Swiss francs.

Herr Schulze, standing behind the counter, inspected my choice. "So what do you want with this doggy? Did I miss something?" He flipped through the book. "Your Newberry Library I don't think is not going to be much happy, Fraülein, when you could have a beautiful book of hours or a beautiful embroidered prayer book."

"It's for me," I said. "My mother used to read it to me."

"Not *auf Deutsch*?"

"No, in English, but it had the same pictures."

I opened my purse and pulled out some unfamiliar Swiss banknotes, green, blue, yellow, with pictures of woodcutters and of women harvesting different kinds of fruit.

"Could I have a receipt, please?"

"For this doggy?"

"For the customs."

"Forty-five Swiss francs, Fräulein. Ten American dollars. You do not have to declare a doggy like this."

"Just to be on the safe side. Besides, it's more businesslike."

"This is Switzerland, not Deutschland," he said, shaking his head and writing out the receipt. I watched him press down hard with the stub of a pencil: "45 SF."

"Could you put down the name of the book too?"

"Just to be on the safe side?"

"Yes."

"*Die Pilgerreise.* Is that *gut,* or do you think the customs officers will want to know the whole title?"

"I'd like the whole title," I said.

"What a serious work to sell such a book!"

"I appreciate it, believe me."

He tore off the receipt and handed me a copy. I put it into my purse.

On my way back to the hotel I stopped at a stationery store and bought a packet of carbon paper, a sharpener, and a number two Venus pencil. Back in my room I sharpened the point of the pencil and practiced Herr Schulze's stumpy writing until I had it mastered. Then—my hand trembling slightly, as it had trembled when I was finishing the Aretino—I put a sheet of carbon paper between the "original" I had just created and the copy and, underneath *Die Pilgerreise zur seligen Ewigkeit* I wrote out, one stumpy letter at a time, *Preghiere cristiane preparate da Santa Giuliana d'Arezzo.* I thought for a moment before deciding on a price. The prayer books I'd examined earlier in the day had ranged from five hundred to several thousand dollars—out of my range. But they had had unusual bindings in excellent condition. I finally settled on 150 SF. Thirty-four dollars and fifty cents. Just about right for some 'doggy'.

According to my guidebook the Swiss drink hot tea, not wine, with fondue, but this wasn't the case. The fondue that I ate in the hotel restaurant that evening was served with the same local wine that had been used in preparing the fondue itself, which was delicious. And the wine was the best I've ever drunk—so delicious that my mouth began to fill with saliva each time I picked up my glass.

After supper I went back up to my room, where I had arranged my little library on the bureau: *Die Pilgerreise, Emma,* and the *Sonetti lussuriosi.* Strange bedfellows.

I paged through *Die Pilgerreise* looking at the pictures that had captivated me as a child: the Slough of Despond, the Man in the Iron Cage, Mr. Worldly Wiseman, Vanity Fair—which in German is *das Jahrmarkt der Eitelkeit*—the Giant Despair, and, finally, the Celestial City. How different from my own pilgrimage, I thought, as I crawled into bed with *Emma.*

Emma's education was almost complete. Her eyes had been opened so that she could, in Signor Focacci's phrase, see things as they really were. I slid down from a sitting position and lay on my left side, holding the book in my right hand. Mr. Knightley was about to propose.

I turned over so that I was lying on my right side, holding the book in my left hand.

Mr. Knightley proposed.

I sat up again.

Emma accepted Mr. Knightley's proposal. But my heart refused to rejoice for her. The truth was, I'd grown tired of Mr. Knightley. It seemed to me that Mr. Knightley was becoming insufferable—a prig, a bore—and that Jane Austen was punishing Emma, not rewarding her. And hadn't she been punished enough? Hadn't she been taught to be ashamed of every single one of her imaginative impulses except, finally, her affection for Mr. Knightley? Why was I getting so carried away? I put *Emma* back on the bureau and picked up the Aretino, which I hadn't opened since Sandro left for Rome. The drawings, I soon discovered, had not lost their power to startle and, yes, arouse. I amused myself by imagining the chaste coupling of Emma and Mr. Knightley. Was Mr. Knightley as virginal as Emma, or had he, as a young man, sown his wild oats? It was hard to imagine Mr. Knightley as a young man. Hard to imagine him sowing wild oats. Hard to imagine him removing Emma's underthings. Hard to imagine Emma saying, "I want it in my *culo,* please forgive me." Hard to imagine Knightley's reply: "Has the other place, then, gone out of fashion? I mean the *potta.*" And Emma: "Not entirely, but behind the *cazzo* finds far greater pleasure."

Francesca tells Dante that there is no greater pain than the recollection of past happiness in present grief, but that wasn't my experience that evening. Whatever grief I'd experienced had been mysteriously transformed, and as I looked over, once again, the familiar drawings, I was taken back to that happy afternoon when Sandro and I looked at the Aretino for the first time, and I stood naked before Sandro's cheval glass, and to dozens of other happy afternoons and nights, and mornings. These memories, intertwining with each other, like the lovers themselves, began to reverberate in my imagination, a deep hornlike humming, like the intonings of Tibetan monks— somewhere below the range of the deepest bass voice, or like the low string of a double bass when it's tuned down to an A, or even a G.

17

Under the Hammer

Back in 1953 the town of Sarezzano, in the Piedmont, agreed to sell its famous Purple Bible to an American book dealer. The sum agreed upon was not disclosed, but it would have been enough to build a new church, which is what the good people of Sarezzano wanted. They also wanted cash, but by the time the dealer had accumulated the banknotes, which filled several suitcases, the press had gotten wind of the deal. *Corriere della Sera* headlined a piece objecting to the sale: AMERICAN BUYS NATIONAL TREASURE FOR FABULOUS SUM.

A papal courier arrived in Sarezzano the next day and confiscated the Bible.

"What was so special about the Bible?" I asked the abbot, who had told me the story during one of our evening chats.

"I don't know," he said. "I guess the fact that it was purple."

I'd been suggesting gently that he might want to sell off some of the duplicates in the monastery's own library, which, as far as I could tell, nobody ever used.

"I'd sell them all," he said. "I'd sell the whole library if I thought I could get away with it. I used to be a Gutenberg man, *homo Gutenbergensis*. Books were my life. But what did I ever learn that I didn't already know in my heart? *Niente, Signorina, niente.*"

"What would you do with the money if you *could* sell the duplicates?"

"I'd buy a new stove," he said, "for the kitchen. I'd hire a good cook. Those nuns from Galuzzo don't know enough to put salt in the pasta water. I would like to eat a dish of tripe the way my mother used to make it, with homemade *brodo* and plenty of Parmesan cheese."

"You could fix it yourself," I suggested as we walked across the courtyard, but the possibility was so remote from his experience that it didn't register. I was glad to see, nonetheless, that the old man was still attached to this world by however slender a thread. I was fond of tripe myself.

That night I dreamed of purple Bibles and papal couriers, and on my way home one evening a week later, when I saw a black-suited figure in a clerical collar ringing the bell outside my door, I thought to myself, "This is it," and almost walked away. But it wasn't a papal courier; it was Father Ingram, the rector of the American Church. He'd received a letter from my father, who wasn't sure I was still at this address since he hadn't heard from me after he'd moved to Texas and he wanted to make sure I'd gotten my sister Molly's wedding announcement —and would I please call or write. Molly wanted me to be in the wedding; everyone was starting to worry.

I thanked Father Ingram and sent him on his way, but not before agreeing to give a talk at the church on the restoration work at the Certosa.

I knew about the wedding, of course. The announcement was on my worktable, along with a dozen letters from Meg and Molly and Papa. I told myself I'd been too busy to answer them, and I had been. In addition to supervising the work at the Certosa, I'd been asked by Signor Giorgio—since I knew both English and Italian and something about paper chemistry —to help with the arrangements for a meeting on paper sizings. I told myself that I'd write as soon as things were settled —as soon as I'd disposed of the Aretino, that is. Before a papal courier showed up at *my* door!

In the meantime . . . I was looking through a one-way mirror. I could see all the people I loved, I could watch their lives unfolding: Papa looking down at the Rio Grande from a hill on his new avocado orchard in Mission, Texas; Meg and Dan, who were expecting their third child, remodeling an old Victorian house on the lake, just north of Milwaukee; Molly selling real estate and eating in German restaurants in Ann Arbor with her Indian fiancé. I could see them, but they couldn't see me.

I put the letters in three piles at the end of the table, which I'd moved to the front of the apartment so that I could look out at the piazza. My own life was unfolding, too. There was business to be taken care of: a businesslike inquiry from Sandro's wife, asking when I intended to vacate the apartment, which she wanted to sell, and letters from Christie's in Rome and Sotheby's new Florence office. My adventure was coming to an end, and I was as anxious as the rest of my family to see how it would turn out.

* * *

"I spent the night in Basel," I explained to Mr. Reynolds, the head of Sotheby's office on the second floor of the Palazzo Capponi. He was an Englishman, about my age, with stiff curly hair, brushed back from his face like the picture of Keats that Mama used to keep on her desk. "I was poking around in an old bookstore not too far from the station, looking for something I could afford. It's my field, you know, seventeenth-century prayer books. I didn't even realize that there were two books bound together till I got back to Florence. Do you think it might be valuable?" (I wanted an unprejudiced opinion.)

"You never know," he said. "You didn't make yourself very clear in your letter. Actually you sounded very mysterious."

"I'm sorry," I said, "I didn't want to give too much away. Look, you see, this book of engravings, with the poems, was bound in with the prayerbook. I've rebound it myself."

When he opened to the marker I'd placed at the title page of the *Sonetti lussuriosi,* he knew at once what it was.

"The divine Aretino," he said, turning to the first of the engravings and then to the second. "I'll be damned."

I could see his face coloring as he glanced back and forth from engraving to text.

> Stick your finger up my ass, old man,
> Thrust *cazzo* in a little at a time,
> Lift up my leg, maneuver well,
> Now pound with all inhibitions gone.

> I believe this is a tastier feast
> Than eating garlic bread before a fire.
> If you don't like the *potta,* try the back way:
> A real man has to be a buggerer.

"It's very well drawn, don't you think?" I said. "The look on the woman's face . . . Her eyes are wide open as if she's seeing something for the first time." (I was speaking aloud words that I'd said only to myself before.) "But she's not idealized. It's a woman, not an angel."

He pursed his lips as if he were going to whistle a tune but couldn't quite remember how it started. "Oh my Lord," he said, giving each word equal emphasis. "This is pretty astonishing. You say you found this in Basel?"

"Yes. I went to renew my *permesso di soggiorno.*"

"You've been living in Italy, then?"

"Yes. I've been working at the Certosa."

"One of the volunteers?"

"Not exactly. I've been filling in for Professor Panuccio, who's gone back to Rome."

"Oh really? Then you must be the American who was . . . who had a liaison with the art restorer—Postiglione—before he left town."

"A 'liaison.' " I liked the word. "I never thought of it that way," I said. "But how on earth did you know about that?"

"Florence is a small town. Everyone knows who you are."

"You're joking."

"Not a bit of it. You're giving a talk at the American Church —'Triage'—something like that. 'A Book Conservator's Point of View.' There are signs all over town. At all the English-language places. There's one in the window. Don't tell me you didn't see it. They should have put your picture on it so people could recognize you." He nodded toward the window. "Plus you've brought in this marvelous book. Do you have any idea what you've got here?"

"It looks like a book of dirty pictures to me."

"I meant do you know who Aretino is? The 'divine Aretino,' 'scourge of princes' and all that?"

"I have some idea," I said. "Giulio Romano did the drawings, Marcantonio Raimondi did the engravings, Aretino wrote the poems, Clement VII had a fit. But I'm not sure why he was called divine." (I kept my own guess to myself.)

"You know all about it, don't you? And you've had it all apart then. That was very naughty, you know. Might knock a thousand pounds off the price."

"Don't say that, Mr. Reynolds. Don't tell me what I should or shouldn't have done." If I was annoyed, as I'd been annoyed with Martelli, it was because I was afraid he was right. "I used my best judgment as a conservator. I intervened to preserve the integrity of the book. The embroidered binding was completely ruined. The text block was starting to mold. The tapes were rotten. I used the old boards, that's all I could do. These are the original boards; the seventeenth-century boards. But if you don't like the binding I'll take it to Christie's in Rome."

"You might as well shoot me now," he said, placing his hand over his heart, as if he were about to say the pledge of allegiance. "Those chaps at Christie's are villains and sons of darkness. I didn't mean to question your expertise."

"But you *did* question it."

"Is it enough that I'm sorry?"

"I suppose I overreacted," I said. "It's a sensitive issue with me. I'm always going to wonder if I did the right thing."

"You did the right thing—it's beautiful—but I'm going to have to ask you a couple of questions. Will you promise not to overreact, like an Italian?"

"You're the one who's overreacting," I said.

"Don't be offended."

"Do you plan to offend me?"

"Not if I can help it," he said, "but you never know. Let's begin with the provenance. Do you have a receipt?"

"Yes, in fact. Yes, I have it right here." I produced the receipt from Buchhandlung Karl Schulze, Basel.

"That's good," he said. "A lot of people don't bother with receipts."

"There won't be any problem, will there? I mean about taking it out of the country?"

"Should there be?"

"Oh, you know. A national treasure, the Purple Bible of Sarezzano, that sort of thing."

"Quite. Now if it were a painting . . . that's more complicated. That's my *raison d'être,* my bread and butter. But a book . . . that you bought in Switzerland . . . No trouble at all. We won't even apply for an export license. We won't say anything. The only question would be—may I speak frankly?"

"Of course."

"You won't go to Christie's?"

"I won't go to Christie's."

"Swear."

"I swear."

"The only question is . . . Tell me something about this bookstore in Basel, Buchhandlung Karl Schulze. The book you describe suffered water damage. The binding was disintegrating, the textblock starting to mold . . ." His shoulders went up, palms turned out—an Italian question mark. "There was a leak in the roof? A broken pipe? The Rhine overflowed its

banks? The book was in such bad shape that immediate intervention was necessary, but Herr Schulze kept it on the shelf?"

"Who's going to ask these questions?"

"The real question is, Who's going to answer them?"

"Will *I* have to?"

He tapped his pencil on the desk.

"Probably not. Not unless someone else tries to establish
legal title to the book."

I thought of the bishop. And Volmaro Martelli. Powerful
enemies or impotent old men? Individually, I thought, they
could do nothing. Martelli had no claim, and the bishop had
been fobbed off with a copy of some nineteenth-century pornography.

"Of course not," I said.

On my way out of the office I looked at the poster in the
window. It was on cheap paper, but nicely printed.

TRIAGE:

A BOOK CONSERVATOR'S PERSPECTIVE

A lecture by Margot Harrington,
director of the restoration work
at the Monastery of the Certosa.

20 April 1967
8:00 P.M.
All-Purpose Room
St. James Church
Via B. Rucellai 9

"It's funny," I said to Mr. Reynolds, "I've never been any-body before."

"Well," he said, "you're somebody now."

His name was Tony, though he wasn't Italian, and we soon became good friends despite some initial difficulties. There were several reasons, for example, why the Aretino could not be included in Sotheby's spring sale of early printed books: the catalog deadline had passed; Mr. Harmondsworth, the head of the book department, was unwilling to give an estimate without seeing the book; it was not part of an important collection; and finally, the date—1525—was not quite early enough to be "early." But I'd been doing my homework in Sotheby's reference library, and I wanted the book in this sale for the same reason that a trainer would rather run a horse in the Kentucky Derby than in the county sweeps. This was where the money was. And I'd discovered early on that there was a magic word at Sotheby's. That word was *Christie's*. Like Ali Baba's "open ses-ame," it never failed to open a crack in the solid rock face of an apparently impassable mountain. Tony cabled London, London cabled back, and so on.

"Why don't you just call them?" I asked.

"We do it this way," he said, "because this is the way it's done."

Tony helped me with the catalog description, photographed the book himself—he didn't want anyone on the staff to get wind of it—with a banged-up Hasselblad he sometimes used to pho-

tograph jewelry, and—most importantly—he took my part in
the difference of opinion over the estimate, even though he
thought I was wrong. Mr. Harmondsworth suggested an estimate of eight thousand pounds, a little over twenty-two thousand dollars. It was the first time I'd been able to put a price on
the book since Martelli's offer of five thousand dollars.

Tony was exuberant, but I was disappointed. I'd been skim-
ming through old copies of the *Book Collector* in Sotheby's reference library and looking at auction catalogs, comparing catalog
estimates and prices paid. The Houghton Library at Harvard
had recently acquired an *editio princeps* of Saint Augustine's *De
Civitate Dei* for about that amount; Hans Kraus—the man
who'd tried to buy the Purple Bible of Sarezzano—paid eight
thousand pounds for a long poem on the Christian year by
someone called Ludovico Lazzarelli, and ten thousand for an
imperfect copy of something called the *Grete Herbal,* printed in
1526, only a year after the Aretino. These were big-ticket
items, but there was another class of books—a different class
entirely—and it was this class that excited my imagination.
Kraus, for example, had paid sixty-five thousand pounds at last
year's sale for the Saint Alban's *Apocalypse,* and Doctor Rosenbach had paid almost as much for the *Bay Psalm Book* back in
1947. This was the story that nourished my fantasies and convinced me to hold out for an estimate of twenty thousand
pounds, a little under sixty thousand dollars.

Doctor Rosenbach had assembled a group of wealthy backers
who wanted to present the book to the Beinecke Library at
Yale. He was authorized to bid up to ninety thousand dollars.
But so was another dealer, Mr. Randall, representing J. K.
Lilly, whose collection eventually went to the University of In-

diana. Randall dropped out at ninety-one thousand. Rosenbach thought he had the book for ninety-two thousand; but on the spur of the moment Sonny Whitney of the Vanderbilt Whitneys, a Yale man himself, jumped in and took the bidding up to a hundred fifty thousand before letting Rosenbach have it for a hundred fifty-one thousand. Rosenbach presented the book to Yale, calling it "the greatest, goddamndest, most important book in the world," but Yale refused to make up the sixty-one-thousand-dollar difference and then the original consortium fell apart. Rosenbach's brother threatened to sue Yale . . .

"Now tell me the truth, Tony," I said. "Wouldn't you pay more for a copy of the *Sonetti lussuriosi* than for the *Bay Psalm Book*?"

"The *Bay Psalm Book* was the first book printed in America."

"Right, but which would you rather look at? Besides, there are eleven *Bay Psalm Books* floating around. There's only one Aretino. I want an estimate of twenty thousand pounds and a reserve of fifteen thousand."

"You can't *do* that, Margot. They're not going to put the catalog estimate at twenty thousand pounds."

"Look, if people see the estimate at eight thousand, that tells them what to expect. If you put it at twenty thousand, they'll expect something different. You told me that yourself: 'You can't price things too high for the American market.' Right?"

"Yes, but I was talking about paintings. They'll never agree to that estimate."

"Paintings shmaintings. Who won't agree?"

"Mr. Harmondsworth."

"Tony, you've seen the book. You know how powerful it is. It reaches right down inside you. Somebody's going to want this book. A lot of people are going to want it. Christie's will. Believe me."

I think that was the last time I had to use my magic word—*Christie's*—but it worked as well as it had the first time.

"Call them up," I said. "I'll pay for the call."

He picked up the phone and spoke to the operator and then, while she was placing the call, to me: "You've got to remember that if the bidding doesn't reach the reserve, you have to pay a five percent penalty. Are you prepared to pay five percent of fifteen thousand?" He worked out the figure in his head: "Seven hundred fifty pounds."

"How much is that in dollars?"

"Just over two thousand dollars."

"And in lire?"

He did some calculations in his head: *"Tre milioni tre cento sessanta mila."*

"Easy," I said. "I make almost that much in . . . six months."

"This is your pearl of great price," he said.

"Yeah," I said, "except I'm selling, not buying."

Tony came to my talk at the American Church, and after the reception that followed in the church basement we walked down to the river and then downstream toward the Cascine. The Arno had gouged large chunks out of the bank back in November, and though the bank had been shored up, the streetlights had not been replaced. It was very dark, and we had to be careful not to run into other strolling couples.

I was less concerned about strolling couples, however, than

about papal couriers. Not really, not literally, but the story of the Sarezzano Bible had made me a little uneasy. I'd always found it hard to believe that anybody actually paid attention to these things, but clearly somebody was watching. I wasn't exactly embarking on a life of crime, of course, I was simply redistributing some property according to my own notion of the way it ought to be distributed. Still, if the newspapers got wind of the Aretino . . . Would Sotheby's protect my anonymity? Would the receipt from Buchhandlung Karl Schulze protect me? Would Herr Schulze remember me? Would he remember the *Pilgrim's Progress*? Some doggy! Would he remember that I had *not* in fact bought a prayer book? Would he be able to produce *his* copy of the receipt (which wouldn't match mine)?

I was tempted to confide in Tony, but I didn't want to put him on the spot professionally. Not that I had any illusions about the high ethical standards of the auction trade. Sotheby's, after all, was a multinational corporation that employed people to read the obituaries and send sympathy letters to distressed heirs, offering assistance in liquidating the estate of the deceased. But I didn't want to ask him to lie directly. The lie was my own—the secret behind my secret.

"Say you've got twenty Picasso suites," Tony was saying as we approached the lights of Ponte J. F. Kennedy. We'd been walking for almost an hour. "Identical. Worth about two thousand pounds apiece. You put one on a catalog cover and have somebody bid it up to eight thousand." Tony stooped down and picked up a couple of sticks. "Then the next week you put up another and say that one sold the previous week for eight thousand. Say you get five, six, seven for the rest of them. People think they're getting a bargain. You're getting twice what they're worth."

"The whole thing sounds disgusting. What do *you* get out of it?"

"Beauty, for one thing." He tapped his sticks together. "There are so many beautiful things in the world they take your breath away. Sotheby's is like a bridge over a river; things flow through the salesrooms: Sienese intarsia, Chinese porcelain, illuminated manuscripts, old masters, Greek vases, Etruscan bronzes, Japanese netsuke, English pottery. The river never stops. There are three or four sales a day, and then next day there are more sales. I started dropping a line into the river myself. My apartment got to be like a museum. I had almost two thousand books. I had a collection of Etruscan bronzes. I couldn't stop myself."

"But you did stop?"

"I ran out of money, my inheritance."

"You spent your inheritance?"

"Just about. And then Peter Wilson asked me if I wanted to have a go at setting up an office in Florence. It was like a dream. I realized I was tired of wanting things. Some people never get over it, especially the rich. Two years ago I had to sort out some jewels for Lady Boston in Somersetshire. The woman was on her deathbed. She was drooling. She could hardly talk. She wanted me to sort the jewels into three equal piles for her three daughters. But there was a pair of diamond earrings she couldn't bear to part with, and then an emerald necklace and so on. Pretty soon we had four piles—one for each of her daughters and one to take with her. Unbelievable. And right now there's a Frenchman living on a government pension in Pistoia;

he's at the opposite end of the scale. He hasn't got enough to eat, but he's got two Cézannes in his closet, wrapped up in a blanket. They were given to him by Cézanne's daughter—they were lovers. He's afraid someone will steal them. He didn't want me to look at them." He shrugged. "Things got to be too inconvenient. If I wanted a book I had to go to the library anyway because I could never find my own copy. So what was the point?"

"You could have organized your books systematically."

"I did. Every year I had a new system. But I still couldn't find anything. I didn't really have room for everything. I couldn't have a party—I was afraid someone would knock over a piece of Staffordshire or one of my Goss cows."

"What happened to them, your things?"

"I sold the books and the pottery."

"Did you lose a lot of money?"

"No, I made a nice profit, in fact, and I've still got the bronzes, in a vault in the Bank of England. They're for my old age. They don't have the romance of the Greek stuff. Yet. In twenty or thirty years . . . Well, you never know for sure, of course, but I think they'll be worth a fortune. If I were an investment counselor and you were my client, I'd definitely recommend Etruscan bronzes."

"Thanks for the tip." I could see his face now under the lights on the bridge. I could see he was enjoying himself. "So you got tired of things," I said. "Then what?"

"I didn't get tired of things, I just got tired of owning them or worrying about them. I'd rather just stand in the river— about waist deep—and let them flow around me. I like to feel the current. It's powerful. But I don't try to stop it anymore; I don't try to grab hold of things as they flow by. Let them wash ashore in museums and libraries."

"I'd like to hold on to the Aretino," I said. "I don't want to let it go."

"I made an extra set of prints," he said; "for you. *Sub rosa,* of course. I was going to surprise you."

"Thanks."

We stood on the bridge and looked down at the Arno. I tried to connect it with the river of things flowing through Sotheby's.

"Shall we play Pooh sticks?" Tony held out the sticks. "Pick one."

"Don't you need pine cones?"

"Sticks," he said. "Pooh started with pine cones but it was too hard to tell them apart."

"How will we tell the sticks apart? They're not that different?"

"One's got a knob on the end."

"I'll take that one," I said.

We dropped our sticks into the river, crossed to the other side of the bridge and looked down over the side.

"But there's something else, too. My whole identity's gotten tangled up with that book. It's my secret. It gives me a sense of being someone special. Like a spy or a secret agent. Someone on a top-secret mission. I don't want to lose that sense. I don't know who I'll be without it. I can imagine things right up to the sale. I can imagine the hammer going down. And that's it."

"Everybody's got to be somebody," he said in the joking way he had. "You'll still be who you are. And if it doesn't meet the reserve you'll be in debt besides."

"Will they put me in debtor's prison?"

"No, but they won't let you have the book back till you pay up."

"I see."

"What are you going to do when it's over?"

"My sister's getting married in August. She wants me to be in the wedding. She's marrying a Sikh. His parents are coming from Bombay, my sisters and I are going to wear special Punjabi dresses."

"Sounds like fun."

"The reception's going to be in the packing shed—my father's an avocado grower. In Texas."

When the two sticks appeared beneath us, neck and neck, I couldn't tell them apart. We watched them drift into the darkness, toward Pisa and the Mediterranean.

"Do you like what you're doing?" I asked, steering the conversation back to the present. "Is it what you'd *choose* to do? You said beauty is one thing you get from your work. What's the other?"

"People," he said. "I like the intensity. People reveal their true natures when it comes to things. They try not to, but it's impossible. You can see them as they really are."

"You're starting to sound like Signor Focacci: 'See things as they really are, call them by their proper names, show strangers the way.' "

He laughed.

"But what kind of people do you have to deal with?" I was thinking of Lady Boston, unwilling to part with her jewels even on her deathbed. And the starving Frenchman in Pistoia with two Cézannes in his closet, wrapped up in a blanket.

We'd left the bridge behind us and were approaching the bus stop in Piazzale Kennedy.

"People like you," he said.

He put his hands on my shoulders and looked me in the eye. I think he was trying to get up the nerve to ask me to come to his apartment. All he needed was an encouraging word, and I would have given him one, but I was stung by his remark.

"People like me?" I said. "What are you talking about? Do you think you can see me as I really am just because I want to get the best price for a very valuable piece of property?"

"I have very good eyesight," he said. "You have to, to be an auctioneer. You don't want to miss any bids."

I knew I'd deliberately misinterpreted his remark, but it was too late to unmisinterpret it.

"What do you see?" I asked. "No, wait. Let me guess: a creature moving in darkness, a thief, timid and fearful, yet driven by lust and greed . . . and a desire to play God. Have I got it?"

"What do I see?" he said. "I see you as an Artemis type, the Minoan lady of wild things."

"A cold fish, eh?"

"Not at all. But very dangerous, jealous of her own honor, mistress of her own destiny."

A bus trundled across the bridge and pulled up to the stop. I got on, showed my pass to the driver and took a last look at Tony, who waited at the bus stop till we pulled out of sight. I was sorry now that I hadn't given him an encouraging word. It would have been fun to thrash out our differences in bed. Artemis indeed!

*   *   *

Tony took the *Sonetti* to England at the middle of May. He had to go to London to go over the estimates on the Demidoff estate in Pratolino. The estate, which belonged to Prince Paul of Yugoslavia, was the first major sale for Sotheby's new Italian office. The cataloging had taken more than four months; the catalogers didn't know how to value Italian Renaissance furniture —great huge credenzas and *cassoni* and tapestries that had been a drug on the market for years but were making a comeback; and Tony, who was going to take the sale himself, in Italian, was understandably nervous.

I was sorry to see him go, but I was very busy myself. The sizings meeting, originally envisioned as an informal get-together of visiting experts, had turned into a *congresso internazionale* dealing with all aspects of the restoration work. A formal agenda had to be drawn up, programs printed, accommodations arranged, meeting rooms scheduled, translators engaged for two Russians who couldn't speak Italian or English, and the French, who wouldn't.

I was not planning to go to England for the sale. There was no reason for me to do so, and there were good reasons not to: it would be expensive, I didn't want to be linked to the book in any public way, and Signor Giorgio was nervous about the *congresso,* which was really the first thing he'd undertaken on his own initiative since the flood. He was worried about making *brutta figura.*

But all the arrangements were in place—including some special equipment requested by the Russians to demonstrate a way to kill mold spores by bombarding them with ultrasonic waves, and at the last minute I called Tony at his sister's in Hampstead and told him I was coming. He didn't seem at all surprised.

I flew from Pisa to London on May 29, the day before the sale, and took the tube to Russell Square. Tony had arranged a bed-and-breakfast on Montague Street, about half a block from the British Museum. I'd never been in London before. What I knew about the city I knew from the way Mama used to talk about it, though she'd never been there either, but I didn't have any trouble finding my way from Russell Square to Sotheby's in New Bond Street.

All the books to be sold the next day were shelved in the salesroom on the second floor, at the top of a broad stairway. I bought a catalog and paged through it till I came to the Aretino:

241 Aretino (Pietro) I sonetti lussuriosi, roman letter, 8vo Roma, F. Bindoni and M. Pasini 1525, newly restored, together with Preghiere cristiane preparate da Contessa Giuliana d'Arezzo, 8vo Venezia 1644.

*** Both volumes, which have been bound together since the early 17th century, have been newly restored. The Aretino volume is a unique copy of the 1525 edition containing 16 erotic engravings executed by Marcantonio Raimondi after drawings by Giulio Romano—fine impressions with margins, three laid down in upper corners. *Each approximately* 5 ¼ × 7 *in.,* 12.6 × 16.8 *cm.*

About half the lots were from the private library of Lord Creighton, who had been an amateur conservator himself, though his own attempts at decorative bindings had not been entirely successful. The designs lacked a sense of proportion; the lettering was uneven. A beautiful Aldine *Aeneid* had been badly botched, and so on, though this was glossed over in the catalog.

Some of the more important items—including a copy of Caxton's *The Game and Playe of the Chesse,* a Shakespeare first folio and the Aretino—were on display in a special case. I was rather surprised to see that the latter had been opened to the cunnilingus plate. This engraving was as firmly etched in my imagination as it had ever been on the printer's plate, but it was a shock to see it nonetheless, to match the actual lines on the page with the ones in my imagination, and I thought, with a sharp pang of desire, of Sandro's bald head, smooth and shiny as an egg, between my legs.

I met up with Tony about four o'clock and we had a cup of tea in the staff common room and looked over a file of newspaper clippings on the book, which was "news." There was a long article in the *Times Literary Supplement* on the history of the book that included the fact that a copy had been listed in a secret catalog at the Vatican Library but had been missing since 1527, two years after its publication, and that someone had checked the locked cabinets of the British Museum but hadn't turned up anything. A copy was rumored to have been removed from the National Library in Dresden at the end of the eighteenth century and destroyed. There was some speculation that it might have been sold to a private collector, in which case it just might be the copy that had turned up in Switzerland. There was nothing about the recent history of the book, however, though Tony told me that a man from the Italian Embassy had in fact turned up at Sotheby's with an official paper of some sort, but that Mr. Harmondsworth had satisfied him that the present owner of the book had acquired it in Switzerland, not Italy. Later I found out that Tony had written most of the article himself.

Tony took me to dinner at Simpson's that night, and afterward we walked from the Strand back to Sotheby's and watched some workmen struggle with a painting so large that they'd had to cut a special slit in the wall. They were trying to winch the painting through the slit, but they hadn't allowed quite enough room for the packing case and were debating what to do. I was too tired to stay to see how they solved the problem, but they must have solved it, because the next morning when I arrived, the painting—Tintoretto's *Adoration of the Magi*—was hanging in the main gallery.

The first day of the sale went quickly. The salesroom—the same room in which the books had been displayed—was a small high-ceilinged gallery on the second floor at the top of the stairs. There was lots of coming and going and waiting around, the sort of thing that generally precedes public functions: men smoking cigarettes, gossiping, talking shop in several languages.

Tony pointed out the major dealers, men in dark, rumpled suits, a confraternity, an inner ring. Some of the names I'd heard at the Newberry, others had become familiar from looking at the *Book Collector* and Sotheby's auction catalogs, so it was interesting to match names and faces. Doctor Wasserstein, the man who'd bought the Gardner manuscript of *The Canterbury Tales* back in 1928, looked very old and tired, but Hans P. Kraus—who'd arranged to buy the Purple Bible of Sarezzano in

1953, and who had paid sixty-five thousand pounds for the Saint Alban's *Apocalypse* almost exactly a year before, in this very room, was a vigorous looking sixty. Maggs Brothers was represented by a Mr. Scott, and Bernard Quaritch by a Mr. Joseph Morton, and so on. There were about a dozen of them in all. Would these old men rise to the occasion? At the Newberry I'd seen a film of an auction at Sotheby's—Doctor J. D. Hanson bidding on the Gold Collection (which the Newberry purchased). As far as I could tell, nothing much had changed. The major dealers wore the same rumpled suits and occupied the same reserved seats at a big horseshoe table, called the "pound," directly in front of the rostrum. The rest of us—probably about a hundred people—settled for folding chairs in the back, the next to the last row, in my case, near one of the exits, in case my stomach acted up, though I'd dosed myself with Kaopectate. The dealers would buy lots for their own stock, of course. But for big items they would have lined up wealthy clients— major libraries as well as private individuals who wanted to establish themselves as serious collectors.

Once the sale was under way I started to look for a pattern, traces of an invisible hand guiding the bidding, and I was glad to see that it was not unusual for a lot to be knocked down for several times the catalog estimate, sometimes more; but I was more interested to notice that most of the important lots, including the Caxton and the Shakespeare folio, were going to three outsiders—three men sitting on folding chairs on the opposite side of the room—who didn't seem to care what they paid. The men were not sitting next to one another, but they weren't bidding against one another either, and the audience began to express its displeasure in small murmurings. The dealers grumbled more openly, turning in their seats to see where all the bids were coming from. Doctor Wasserstein scribbled a note and gave it to one of the porters to take to Mr. Harmondsworth, who looked at it but did not—as far as I could tell—*do* anything.

By the time the hammer had fallen on the last lot of the day, Tony, who came and went, had ascertained that the three outsiders were Americans, and that someone had recognized the oldest of the trio as a member of the art investment department of the Chase Manhattan Bank. Chase Manhattan had a corporate art collection. Presumably they had decided to assemble a collection of early printed books too. The underbidders, with depressing regularity, had been Mr. Scott, Mr. Morton, and (of course) Doctor Wasserstein and Hans Kraus.

Tony wanted me to come to dinner in Hampstead, but I was too intent on peering into the future. Like a sports fan on the evening of an important game, I went over the stats, looking for clues, looking for certainty where there was none. What if —I thought to myself—the dealers have become too discouraged and dispirited to stand up to the Chase Manhattan trio? What if the porter brings the Aretino up to the front of the room and Mr. Harmondsworth opens the bidding and nobody bids? I wasn't very hungry, but I stopped at a place on Russell Square that advertised genuine American hamburgers. When I saw the counterman drop a patty of ground meat into a pot of boiling water, however, I found I wasn't hungry at all.

* * *

At precisely eleven o'clock the next morning Mr. Harmondsworth mounted the rostrum and gave three ritual blows with
his hammer to quiet the crowd.

The first few lots went very quickly, and Mr. Harmondsworth kept the pace fairly brisk, often selling two lots in the
space of a minute. An *editio princeps* of Marco Polo's travels, *De
consuetudenis,* went to Maggs for eighteen thousand pounds, and
the *Revelations of Saint Birgitta* to Quaritch for an astonishing
thirty-two thousand. What on earth could she have revealed? I
wondered. Whatever it was, my fears about the dealers had
been unfounded, my doubts ungenerous. These men in rumpled
suits showed their determination not to let all the good lots go
to the outsiders. The Chase Manhattan trio continued to domi-
nate the sale, but they had to pay handsomely for the privilege.
Time after time one dealer or another, now Wasserstein, now
Kraus, now Maggs, now Quaritch, forced the bidding to seven
or eight times the estimate.

I had mixed feelings myself. I didn't care for the breezy style
of the Americans, but I wouldn't have wished them elsewhere.
(I thought of the Chase Manhattan trio as "the Americans,"
though Wasserstein was from Philadelphia and Kraus was from
New York.)

Instead of trying to estimate the value of the Aretino, I now
found myself trying to estimate the buying power of the various bidders. Chase Manhattan had already spent a lot of money.
Did that mean that they were bidding without a limit or that
they were rapidly approaching their limit? On the other hand,
Kraus and Wasserstein and the other dealers had come prepared
to spend a lot of money they hadn't spent yet. Did that mean
they would be primed to spend more on the later lots? They

did not look to me like the kind of men who would be swept away on waves of passion, like operatic lovers; on the other hand, I had the sense that tremendous egos were involved here, egos that filled the room with electricity, or perhaps phlogiston.

Lot 241 came up at about one-thirty. I hadn't eaten any breakfast, and my stomach was churning so hard I seriously considered leaving the room. Tony, who had disappeared for a quarter of a hour, returned to his place as Mr. Harmondsworth opened the bidding at five thousand pounds.

"Relax," he whispered. "There's nothing *you* can do now. *Che sarà, sarà.*" He began to hum, very very quietly, the tune of that awful song.

He was right, of course; but that's not the way I felt. I felt that whatever was going to be depended on my will, that I could actually will the bidding up if only I kept my mind focused. (I used to think the Cubs couldn't lose if I listened carefully to the game. Then I'd get interested in something else and forget to pay attention to the game. But that wasn't going to happen today.)

There was no bid. Fifteen seconds went by. Fifteen seconds is a long time at an auction. Many lots had been knocked down in less time.

The first bid came from the junior member of the Chase Manhattan trio. He was answered by Mr. Scott for Maggs, who gave a very determined nod. A couple of bids came from the back of the room, where some new faces had appeared. All in all I'd say there were a dozen bidders, though it was hard to tell exactly who was bidding—a raised hand here, a nod there, the tap of a pencil, a catalog held aloft. As Mr. Harmondsworth's eyes swept the room I was reminded of an air-traffic controller who has to keep track of a dozen planes at a time. He had no time now to chat up the dealers in front. He was all eyes and ears, though I thought he might have missed a bid here and there. A woman behind me, for example, was holding her catalog up by my ear and making a fluttering noise, as if she wanted to cry out but knew she wasn't supposed to.

The bidding, which had slowed slightly at the catalog estimate—like a car negotiating a dangerous curve—was now proceeding steadily in increments of a thousand pounds. Bid was piled on bid. Mr. Scott, for Maggs Brothers, who had been the underbidder on many of the lots the previous day, gave his bids with a determined nod; Dr. Wasserstein raised his hand slightly; Kraus pointed his finger at Mr. Harmondsworth and emitted a little popping sound, as if firing a pistol; the senior member of the Chase Manhattan trio, who had taken over the bidding, gave a sort of friendly wave, as if he were waving to someone at the beach.

The bidding rose in a long, steady spiral till it reached thirty-four thousand, a thousand pounds short of the price Chase Manhattan had paid for the *Caxton* on the previous day—another psychological barrier because it was the highest price of the sale so far. About half a dozen bidders were left by this time—Chase Manhattan, Kraus, Wasserstein, a dealer in the back of room, a telephone bidder, and Mr. Scott for Maggs. Mr. Scott leapt over the barrier with a raise of two thousand pounds. The woman sitting behind me, who had finally managed to attract Mr. Harmondsworth's attention by waving her catalog, joined the circle at thirty-seven thousand, just as others were dropping out. The two-thousand-pound raise had been Mr. Scott's parting shot. The agent who'd been relaying the telephone bids indicated that whoever was on the other end of the line had had enough; the dealer in the back left the room.

That left Chase Manhattan, Wasserstein, Kraus, and the woman sitting behind me.

The bidding went up rapidly as each bidder attempted to outdo the others in decisiveness—from thirty-seven thousand to forty, then climbing steadily to fifty. Wasserstein, who had been faltering, dropped out at fifty-four thousand. I did some quick calculations: at the current rate of exchange that was almost exactly the price he'd paid for the Gardner manuscript.

Tony touched my arm with his finger, and I realized I was shivering. The sense I'd had all along of being on a secret mission or possessing a secret identity had never been stronger. I was there, physically present in the room, but no one could see me. I was a godlike (or goddesslike) presence behind the scenes. Men in rumpled suits were venturing fortunes for a little book of pictures that I myself had carefully and lovingly restored and brought to this temple as a sacred offering. I recalled Madre Badessa's question: What sort of thing is a man? and her answer: A little picture gallery. I held my breath as we approached sixty-five thousand, the amount that Kraus had paid in the previous year's sale for the Saint Alban's *Apocalypse,* the highest price ever paid for a book at auction. Would he have the resources to pay that much for the Aretino? Was he bidding on behalf of a client with unlimited resources?

The bidding slowed down as it approached the summit, a long freight train climbing a steep incline. Chase Manhattan and Kraus were taking their time. Chase Manhattan no longer smiled as he waved, and I could see him exchanging glances with his two partners. Kraus himself seemed uncertain. He was trying to get a look at the woman sitting behind me, but I had the feeling that he was looking at me, glaring at me, as if *I* were the one bidding against him. He was an angry man, faced not with one opponent but two, both outsiders who didn't play by the rules. I'm sure he would have been more comfortable bidding against Doctor Wasserstein, who sat with his head down, listening to Mr. Harmondsworth call the bids.

I twisted around in my chair to have another look at the woman behind me. I'd say she was about fifty, dressed simply in white blouse and tweed skirt, and that she, too, looked somewhat flustered. She had her open catalog wedged between her stomach and a large purse she was emptying out onto her lap. She'd spread her knees apart to pull her skirt tight, but there wasn't enough room for everything—compact, fountain pen, a tin of mints, banknotes, bits of paper, letters. The fountain pen slithered to the floor, and when she leaned forward to retrieve it she lost her compact and some banknotes. Tony got down on his knees to help retrieve them.

Kraus bid sixty-two thousand, emitting another involuntary burst of sound. Mr. Harmondsworth waited almost fifteen seconds for Chase Manhattan to cover the bid, which he did. The woman behind me raised her catalog into the air without looking up. And there was another long silence. There was something mystical about these soul-searching silences, which were becoming longer as the bidding climbed higher and higher.

"I have sixty-four thousand pounds," said Mr. Harmondsworth, "will you cover the bid?" (This toward Kraus.)

The American intervened, bidding out of turn: "Sixty-five thousand."

Kraus threw down his catalog in a paroxysm of disgust and stormed out of the room. I glanced back at the woman behind me. She had gathered all the loose bits of paper into a pile and was methodically going through them one at a time.

Mr. Harmondsworth turned his gaze in our direction. I waited for the woman to raise her catalog. I didn't turn around to look at her again, but I could hear her clearly, unfolding bits of paper and looking at them just the way I did when I cleaned out my purse, and then running her nails along the crease as she refolded them.

Mr. Harmondsworth's voice seemed to be coming from far away, but I could feel his gaze on me, like the eye of Sauron searching out poor Frodo, the ring bearer, as he climbs Mount Doom in the last book of *The Lord of the Rings.*

"All done?" Mr. Harmondsworth was asking. "Any more bids? Fair warning." Once again he searched the room and then sent his gaze back in our direction. I think he was reluctant to knock the book down to Chase Manhattan. I could hear the woman fussing with her papers. Something else fell on the floor, and once again Tony knelt to retrieve it.

"I'm selling at sixty-five thousand pounds," Mr. Harmondsworth said, looking straight at me.

Just as he raised his hammer I raised my hand, lightly fluttering my catalog.

"I have sixty-six thousand pounds," he said, turning toward Chase Manhattan.

No one applauded but the room was alive with whispers: the bidding had set a new record; the sale had entered into uncharted territory. And so had I. I felt as if I had stepped out of Plato's cave into the blinding light of reality. At first I couldn't see anything, and then I began to pick out small details. I could see that the Doctor had nicked himself shaving, for example; that Mr. Harmondsworth had a tiny mole on his neck, just above his collar; that the shirt worn by the junior member of the Chase Manhattan trio was a size too small; that three of the half dozen women in the room, though not the woman behind me, were wearing corsets. And then, as my eyes gradually adjusted, I could see that the porter standing in front of the rostrum was holding the Aretino open to one of my favorites, a position the Italians call *lascia pascolare le pecore*—let the sheep graze. I could see other things, too: Saint Francis dancing before the pope, Michelangelo's wonderful curve that Mama's bookcases shared with the Ponte Santa Trinità, Ruth and Yolanda undressing in the crowded compartment of the train, Papa looking down on the Rio Grande, Madre Badessa surprising me in the loggia, and Tony resuming his seat, perfectly relaxed, as if nothing extraordinary had happened. All these images were starting to coalesce into a larger whole, one that made sense, like *Pilgrim's Progress* or the Stations of the Cross, and as my eyes continued to adjust, I could see that this larger whole was itself a small piece of a still-larger whole, one that made even more sense, and I was filled with a sense of the strangeness and wonderfulness of the world that I've never been able to explain to anyone else, not that I was able to explain it to myself. "Explain" is the wrong word. "Point to" would be more accurate. You try to point out a bird that you see in a tree, a long way off. "It's right there," you say. "Look, see where I'm pointing, look along my arm, there, right there." But the person you're with can't see it, and pretty soon you can't see it either. But you can remember it.

It was as close as I'd ever come to a mystical experience, though what I experienced, I suppose, was not the mystical unity of the good and the beautiful or of spirit and matter, but of buyer and seller, bidder and consigner; and in fact I knew at the time, and I know now, that I'd done a foolish thing. But I've never regretted it, and I don't think I would have regretted it even if Chase Manhattan had failed to cover the bid, though had that happened my life would surely have taken a sharp turn —along another road not taken—that I can't even begin to imagine now.

The senior member of the Chase Manhattan trio not only covered the bid, he raised it five thousand pounds. A raise of that magnitude is intended to break the rhythm of the sale and intimidate one's opponent. Back down in the cave, suitably intimidated, I was not about to offer another bid, but the woman behind me, who had stopped fussing with her papers, waved her catalog. I could feel the flutter at my ear.

Mr. Harmondsworth turned to Chase Manhattan: "I have seventy-three thousand pounds against you."

As the bidding entered the upper stratosphere of book prices Chase Manhattan began to stumble badly, and I wondered if he, too, had climbed out of a comfortable cave onto a snow-covered mountain peak where a single misstep might mean sudden death, or whether he'd simply exceeded his commission and could not guess what his boss would want him to do at that point. Mr. Harmondsworth, who was allowing him fifteen seconds or even more to recover between bids, encouraged him in a whisper: "I have seventy-five thousand against you, I have seventy-seven thousand against you, I have seventy-nine thousand against you." The woman behind me had her own offensive strategy: she simply held her catalog in the air, even when the bid was against Chase Manhattan, so that as soon as Chase Manhattan covered a bid, he found that within seconds it was against him again.

Mr. Harmondsworth went through the familiar closing routine for the third or fourth time: "All done? Any more bids? Fair warning . . . I'm selling at . . ." Chase Manhattan, after one last agonizing silence, finally surrendered, and lot 241 was knocked down for eighty-nine thousand pounds to the woman behind me, who received a standing round of applause of the sort that is generally reserved for the sale of major works of art. I did some quick calculations and came up with two hundred forty-nine thousand dollars.

No one seemed to have noticed my unobtrusive entry into the bidding, not even Tony, who'd been picking up banknotes for the mysterious woman sitting behind me, and the Platonic vision I'd experienced had already disappeared so completely—like Keat's nightingale—that I wasn't even sure myself what I'd done, but when I turned to congratulate the woman personally, to shake her hand, she pulled me toward her and whispered in my ear: "Thank you so much," she said. "I couldn't remember if I was supposed to stop at sixty-five thousand or a hundred and sixty-five thousand. I wrote it down on a slip of paper and put it in my purse, but I have so many things in my purse, if you know what I mean . . ."

"I know what you mean," I said. "I lose things all the time."

Many of the remaining lots brought two or three times the estimates, but the excitement for the day was over. The woman who had bought the Aretino was mobbed by reporters in the downstairs lobby as she tried to verify her identity with the auctioneer's clerk, but she wasn't giving anything away. She was representing a friend, she said, who was staying in London and had read about the book in the *Times.*

"Your friend must have a good deal of money to spend," said one of the reporters, angling in for a photo.

"Yes," she said, clutching her purse tightly, as if the reporters were Gypsies trying to rob her, "she does."

All the papers carried the story. Outrage and indignation that such a large sum—more than most people earn in a lifetime—should have been squandered on a work of pornography were offset by tributes to the artistic genius of the Renaissance. A spokesman for the British Museum said that the book was most certainly not worth the sum that had been paid for it, but the curator of prints at the National Gallery declared that it was worth every shilling, not as a book per se but as art, as a collection of invaluable engravings. And then there were the tabloids: RENAISSANCE SEX MANUAL BRINGS RECORD PRICE AT AUCTION. EUROPE'S ANSWER TO THE KAMA SUTRA. MYSTERY BUYER NABS NUDE PICS FROM POPE'S PRIVATE BATHROOM.

No one managed to discover the identity of the buyer. I thought Sotheby's might at least tell me, the consignor, but everyone's lips were sealed, so the whereabouts of the book remains a mystery. And only one paper, the *Times,* mentioned the binding. It was only a phrase, but I still carry the article in my wallet: "expertly restored and beautifully bound." I was glad someone had noticed.

18

The Elgin Marbles

There were two things I intended to do immediately after the sale: the first was to call Papa, the second was to go to see the Elgin Marbles, Mama's favorite work of art. But I didn't do either. At least not right away. Instead I shopped for a wedding present for Molly. The wedding was on my mind not simply because it was another important milestone in the story of our family, but because it gave me a sense of direction; it stood out on the horizon, a buoy marking a familiar channel. Landfall.

But it wasn't that simple, was it? As long as Papa had lived in the big house on Chambers Street there'd been a center. But Papa had sold the house, the only place I'd ever called home. The center hadn't held. If I hadn't answered Papa's letters since he'd moved to Texas in March, if I hadn't called him, if I couldn't bring myself to call him now, maybe it was because I wanted to punish him. For selling "the only place I'd ever called home." I liked the phrase and let it roll around on my tongue: "the only place I've ever called home."

* * *

Have you ever walked down New Bond Street from Sotheby's to the Burlington Arcade with a quarter of a million dollars in your purse? Two hundred thirty-six thousand one hundred eighty dollars, to be exact, after Sotheby's commission and a cash advance of two hundred pounds. It's quite a heady experience. I felt light headed, dizzy. A sum of money like that changes the way things look in shop windows, and what shops! Jewelers and antique dealers that buzzed you in; Chez Boulanger with its leaded glass windows through which you could catch glimpses of waiters in frock coats gliding among the crowded tables with silver trays held effortlessly above their shoulders—this was where the queen stopped for lunch when she went shopping; couturiers and vendors of luxury goods: Asprey, Cartier, Vuitton, Hermès, Chanel, Cardin, W. Bill, Loewe, Frank Smythson, Courrèges, Balenciaga, Lanvin, Sulka. You could pay fifty or one hundred pounds for a pair of shoes at Ferragamo across from the Royal Arcade; twenty or thirty for gloves; next to Ferragamo was a shop—Sac Frères, I think it was called—that sold nothing but amber—Chinese amber, Burmese amber, Russian amber—hairbrushes and toilet articles in every shade from straw yellow to blood red. Next to Sac Frères was a marriage bureau, promising discreet service.

I'd walked up and down Bond Street several times, of course, but it had always seemed like a museum, where you couldn't touch anything. Now it had been transformed, by Sotheby's after-sale advice in my purse, into a gallery: everything was for sale. Not just to be looked at and appreciated but to be bought, owned, possessed.

I'd decided to allow myself a ten percent commission for handling the sale, and though twenty-four thousand dollars (almost) wouldn't go very far on New Bond Street, it seemed like a lot to me, and I thought I'd be able to find something special for Molly's wedding, something out of the ordinary, something that would link us together through space and time, not just Molly and me, but our whole family, some thing with enough mass to counteract the centrifugal forces that had pulled us so far apart.

I didn't go into any of the shops, however. I just looked in the windows. I was feeling a little off balance—not exactly nervous but agitated in a pleasant sort of way, as if the after-sale advice were a small animal scrabbling about in my purse, which I clutched tightly, or a bird that might fly away if I wasn't careful. Under the circumstances it would have been so easy to let go, to start to spend, but to tell you the truth, I couldn't find what I was looking for.

Mama had always wanted to come to England, but Papa'd always been a little too busy, and there'd never been quite enough money. But even though she'd never actually been to London, her study was full of art books and slides and museum guides, and she'd talked about the Tate and the National Gallery and the British Museum—and even the little museum at the Walthamstow Water Works—as if they were just a short bus ride away like the Museum of Science and Industry, or the Field Museum, or the Art Institute of Chicago. I meant to visit all these museums, but I kept putting it off. Instead of going to see the Turners at the Tate, the Rembrandts at the National

Gallery, and Anglo-Saxon pennies at the Walthamstow Water Works, and, especially and above all, the Elgin Marbles at the British Museum (which I could see from the front steps of my bed-and-breakfast), I found myself hanging around Sotheby's, watching the river of things—mightier than the mighty Mississippi—flow through the salesrooms. There were no more book sales that week, but on Wednesday evening Tony and I watched from a side gallery as Peter Wilson himself—the man who had made London, rather than Paris or New York, the center of the international art market—knocked down the Tintoretto *Adoration* to Constantine Niarchos for seven hundred fifty thousand pounds, almost as much as the Metropolitan Museum paid for Rembrandt's *Aristotle Contemplating a Bust of Homer.*

It would be three weeks before I could collect the money for the Aretino, but Sotheby's was happy to set up a line of credit for me, and I started casting my own line into the river of things, bidding—tentatively at first and then more assertively —on potential wedding presents. I was the underbidder on a Greek vase with a wedding scene on it, and that frightened me. I'd almost spent five thousand dollars for a vase, a piece of pottery. But instead of withdrawing sensibly I threw caution to the winds and bid against the British Museum for an Etruscan bronze that had originally come from the excavations outside Sulmona in the Abruzzi. I paid forty-five hundred pounds, but it was so beautiful I had no hesitation. I would have gone to my limit, which I hadn't established very clearly, and maybe beyond.

Picture a young girl naked, seated, one leg folded under her, the other outstretched. In one hand she holds a bird. She's twenty-six centimeters high and weighs 1.043 kilograms. According to the catalog she's been hollow cast in seven parts, "with an alloy of 60% Cu, 2% Sn, 1% Zn." On her outstretched leg "is a deeply incised inscription": *fleres · tec · sansl · cver,* "to the god Tec Sans, as a gift." (Tec Sans is the protector of children.) Like a child flying a model airplane, she holds the bird out in front of her.

"You'll be a rich old woman," Tony told me when he saw what I'd done.

"It's for my sister's wedding," I said.

"Then your sister will be a rich old woman."

I took it to the packing room immediately after I'd shown it to Tony, so I wouldn't be tempted, like Lady Boston and her jewels, to keep it for myself.

On the morning of my last day in London—I'd been there a week—I called Papa from the post office in Russell Square.

As usual I'd calculated the time wrong. It was four o'clock in the morning in Texas, not six o'clock in the evening. But Papa was used to getting up early. He'd always gone to work at four o'clock when I was growing up.

"Margot? Is that you? Are you okay?"

"I'm fine, Papa. Don't worry. I just sold the book I told you about for eighty-nine thousand pounds. That's two hundred forty-nine thousand two hundred dollars."

It took him a while to digest this. I could picture him sitting on the edge of the bed, could picture the familiar face, the familiar broad head, the familiar scar where he'd fallen off a loading dock and hit his chin, the familiar reddish-gray hair, pale, almost translucent.

"You sold an old book for a quarter of a million dollars? Are you sure you got that straight?"

"I'm sure, Papa. I wanted you to know. I wish you could be here."

"That would be nice. Mama always wanted to go to London. I'm sorry I never took her."

"Papa, I want to fix it up so that the convent—the mother superior—gets complete control of the money. What do I have to do?"

"Why don't you just *give* her the money? Endorse the check and hand it over to her?"

"Technically she can't *own* anything. The bishop has the final say, but he can't touch the endowment."

"You'd have to talk to an Italian lawyer. The convent must have a lawyer. If they've got an endowment, somebody has to look after it."

"Actually I think it's mostly land. They get rental income, proceeds from the sale of honey and wine and olive oil."

"Then you could set up a trust."

"How would I do that?"

"You want to get an institution to handle it, not just a lawyer. You can't trust a lawyer. Go to the trust department of a really good bank. You can set it up any way you want to so it goes on in perpetuity."

"Like, just for the library at the convent? The bishop wants to get his hands on the library and transfer it to San Marco. If the income for the trust went for the care and maintenance of the library . . ."

"You can set up an eccentric trust. You can have cash delivered to the abbess on the first of the month if you want to."

"A bag full of lire? It would have to be a pretty big bag!"

"That's what I should have done for you girls, set up trust funds. I was always going to get around to it, but . . . who'd have thought in 1950 that I'd be broke in ten years? I had three hundred thousand easy that I didn't know what to do with. By now, sixteen years, you know money doubles in seven years at seven percent? A hundred thousand, that'd be almost four hundred thousand a piece. You'd be set. You wouldn't have to worry about a job."

I saw two women crowd into another booth and thought for a minute that they were Ruth and Yolanda. I looked at the big clock on the wall; I'd been on the phone for three minutes.

"Papa, I'm *not* worried."

"Ah, t'hell with it."

"You know, Papa . . ."

"They say you're better off without it. I dunno."

I can still remember Papa showing us his will, once a year. One at a time. Meg, then Molly, then me.

"But what do these nuns *do*? What are they trying to accomplish? Aren't they *supposed* to be poor?"

"The choir nuns say their office every day."

"Their *office*?"

"It's a series of services throughout the day. Prayers."

"And that's it?"

"There are lay sisters, too, who spend more time working."

"You ever think of trying it?"

"Not exactly, but it's a good place."

"Why don't you come to Texas and stay with me?"

In my imagination I could see him leaning forward as he sat on the edge of the bed.

"Forget the nuns for just a minute. They've gotten on all right for however many hundreds of years. They'll get on all right now. With a quarter of a million dollars we wouldn't have to borrow. We could start with a clean slate. No creditors. We could get through a bad year, which I hope to God we don't have, but you've got to think about these things. I think about them all the time. I can't sleep because I'm thinking about them. What if? What if? What if? Root rot, cankers, sunblotch, wilt, the Water Regulatory Commission . . ." The list was familiar from his letters. "If you're not ready for water when it's your turn, bingo, that's it. I've got no cushion. And it's lonely. But with you here it would be okay. And Mission is a nice town. You could meet people. There's a public library. Maybe you could get a job there. And it's a wonderful place for the dogs. They love it. They can run free. And we could build a place up on the bluff, so you could look down at the river. I didn't tell you about the river, did I?" He had told me, but he wanted to tell me again. "I mean, I told you about the river, but did I tell you about this radio show I heard the night before? This fundamentalist group thought the Second Coming was going to take place at sundown in Jerusalem. That was eleven twenty-five Texas time. About eleven o'clock I told the real estate agent I had to take a leak and I went up on the hill, just to think. I don't mean I thought it was really the Second Coming, but I wanted to be alone for a minute. I walked up to the top of the bluff and there's the river. It's on the map, Margot, the Rio Grande; it's the reason I wasn't standing in a desert, but I'd never given it a thought. I wish you could see it.

I thought it was the River of Jordan, the Promised Land. You don't have to decide this minute, but think about it. At least consider it. The nuns will be all right. God will look after them, but who's going to look after us if we don't look after ourselves?"

I felt myself blushing, the way I always blush when someone propositions me out of the blue. I couldn't speak. Couldn't move. Couldn't think. I pretended to myself not to understand, and then I said the first thing that popped into my head: "Papa," I said, "you should never have left Chicago. You shouldn't have sold the house. That was the only place I ever called home."

I'd intended to wound him, and I knew I'd succeeded because he didn't say anything for a long time. I watched the second hand eating up the minutes. It was going to be an expensive phone call.

On the morning Mama died Papa just sat on the edge of the bed with his head in his hands, waiting for the doctor to come. That's the way I pictured him now, sitting on the edge of the bed, his nipples thick and flat on top, as if they'd been punched out of a thick slice of ham with a paper punch, the elastic of his underpants giving way. Waiting.

Try as I could, I couldn't imagine Texas. The river, the bluff, the tumbledown house were all ciphers. Even the dogs. Bruno and Sasky. What would happen to us now? I wanted to call Meg and Molly, but it was the thought of the dogs that bowled me over. I had my defenses in place against Papa, but I'd forgotten about the dogs, I'd forgotten how happy they'd been to see me when I came back from Italy after Mama got sick.

"Margot," he said finally, "do you think it was *easy* for me to sell the old place? Do you think I did it to spite you? I put up the FOR SALE sign as a kind of joke. Meg and Dan were talking about having Christmas in Milwaukee; Molly's car was broke and she was going to stay in Ann Arbor with her boyfriend; you were in Italy; you never called, not till Christmas Eve. I put the sign up to give your sisters something to think about, and then I got to thinking about it myself, when I went outside to take it down. I realized it was time to move on. I don't know how I knew it, but I knew it. That's when you called, right after that. I was sitting at the kitchen table filling stockings. You told me you were in love, and I was happy for you, even though it was a married man. I've hardly heard from you since."

It was my turn to be silent, to watch the snow come down as he nails up the for sale sign to the round pillar on the porte-cochere, to keep my eyes on the Rio Grande as he takes a leak on the top of a bluff. I'd always known and loved him as my father, but I'd never known and loved him as a man, someone with his own agenda, his own plans, his own future to worry about. Wherever he was was still the place where, when I had to go there, they'd have to take me in, but I knew I wasn't going to go. Not now, not to stay, not without a round-trip ticket in my purse.

"You still in love?" he asked.

"Not any more," I said.

"He go back to his wife?"

"Yeah."

"I'm sorry."

"It's all right, Papa. Everything's all right. But I'm sorry I said what I said. I wasn't thinking straight."

"That's okay."

"Are you in trouble, Papa? How bad is it?"

What made it so hard was that it was the first time he'd ever asked me for something that he needed. It was the first time I'd ever *had* anything he needed. And I couldn't give it to him.

"Nah," he said, "not too bad, if everything doesn't go wrong all at once."

That afternoon Tony and I made love for the first time—in the bed-and-breakfast. Our imaginations had been fired up by the sale of the Aretino, and our bodies by the long, slow buildup. Well, slow by modern standards. Who knows what erotic peaks we might have scaled if it hadn't been for Mrs. Hoyle, who kept tapping on the door every five minutes: "Has your visitor left yet?"

"Not yet," I'd say, trying to suggest by the tone of my voice that Tony and I were struggling with the *Times* crossword puzzle.

"I'm sorry," Tony would whisper.

"It's not your fault."

It was a Sisyphean experience, rolling the ball of our pleasure up the hill only to have it rolled back down on us by Mrs. Hoyle's tap-tap-tap.

"Not yet, Mrs. Hoyle."

We finally made it to the top, just as Mrs. Hoyle was tap-tap-tapping at the door for the sixth or seventh time: "Has your visitor left yet?"

I couldn't completely stifle a cry of ecstasy, but I did my best to conceal it in Italian: *"La sua voluntade,"* I blurted out, *"è nostra pace."*

"What's that?"

"God's will is our peace, Mrs. Hoyle. God's will is our peace. Now, would you leave us alone for a few minutes? My visitor will be leaving shortly."

About four o'clock we walked across the street to the British Museum. It was my last chance to see the Elgin Marbles. It was raining a little, so we borrowed an umbrella from the stand in the foyer. Mrs. Hoyle was nowhere to be seen. Both of us had a touch of indigestion—too much hot curry—and by the time we got oriented in the museum, it was time to head for the rest rooms. I mention this only because the ladies' room, which had been converted from a men's room (there was a row of urinals) had parquet floors and the widest toilet stalls I've ever seen. I could hardly reach from one side to the other.

Tony was waiting for me when I came out, and we made our way through the Egyptian sculptures and the Nereids to the Duveen Gallery. Mama had always pronounced 'Elgin' with a soft *g,* like Elgin, Illinois, or an Elgin watch, but Tony pronounced it with a hard *g,* and I'd realized that Mama had never heard the word, she'd only read it in books.

By this time I'd realized why I'd put off visiting the museums. I was a little afraid to put myself in Mama's place, to look *for* her. I was afraid I'd be disappointed, afraid I wouldn't be able to see, with my own eyes, what she had seen so clearly in her imagination. And that is more or less what happened.

Mama always devoted two full lectures to the Elgin Marbles in her Introduction to Art class at Edgar Lee Masters. I'd attended those lectures more than once and thought I had a pretty good idea of what to expect, but I wasn't prepared for the fragmentary nature of the exhibit or of the marbles themselves. In Mama's lectures the marbles depicted a solemn but festive ceremonial procession in which the entire community took part, in which the story of each individual merged with the story of the community, in which the wound of individuality was healed. This was the healing power of great art that she used to talk about. It was what I wanted, something to heal the wound of individuality. But in the Duveen Gallery it was hard to find a whole individual, much less a whole community. Arms and legs had been lopped off, penises too. Faces had been torn away or smashed. I knew I was supposed to be overwhelmed, as every person who's ever seen the marbles has been overwhelmed, at least the famous ones Mama used to discuss, but I wasn't. I was, as I had feared, disappointed.

Have you ever read a great novel, or listened to a great symphony, or stood in front of a great work of art, and felt—absolutely nothing? You try to open yourself to the text, the music, the painting, but you have no power to respond. Nothing moves you. You are turned to stone. You feel guilty. You blame yourself, but you also wonder if maybe there's nothing there, and that people only pretend to enjoy Dante's *Paradiso* or Beethoven's *Eroica* or Botticelli's *Primavera* because they get good marks in Culture 101 for doing so. And then, when you least expect it, when you've closed the book, walked out of the concert hall or the museum, it hits you. *Some*thing hits you, comes at you from an odd angle.

I wandered around the gallery with Tony. I knew that Tony

could give me a good lecture, exciting and imaginative, but I was glad that he didn't because I was thinking of Papa. Papa wouldn't have expected much from great art, or from any art. If you'd talked to him about the healing power of great art or transcendent moments of vision, he'd have looked at you as if you were trying to sell him a used car. Papa would have admired the horses, he would have read all the lengthy explanatory signs that told about the Parthenon and about the romantic struggle to bring the marbles to England and explained the differences between friezes and metopes. But that wasn't enough for me.

A bell rang, indicating that the museum would close in fifteen minutes, and we were on our way out when we passed, probably for the third time, the heifer on slab XL of the South Frieze. That's what hit me. A heifer, struggling to escape, tossing her head in the air, twisting her thick neck, as three young men, their faces badly damaged, drag her along to the sacrifice.

Mama used to spend a lot of time on this heifer, and when I closed my eyes I could picture her clearly; I could see her lips moving in the darkened classroom, lit only by the slide projector, as she asked how many students were familiar with Keats's "Ode on a Grecian Urn." I could see her smile when I raised my hand along with a handful of others. Mama picked up a book, opened it, and began to read. She knew the poem by heart, of course, and often quoted it. The book was just a prop, part of her act:

Who are these coming to the sacrifice?
To what green altar, O mysterious priest,

> Lead'st thou that heifer lowing at the skies,
>   And all her silken flanks with garlands drest?

I opened my eyes and looked at the heifer again. "This is the heifer that John Keats saw," I said to Tony. "Isn't that something, to think that Keats stood right where we're standing now?"

"It wouldn't have been here," Tony said. "It would have been in the old gallery."

"But you get the idea," I said.

"I get the idea," he said.

"Keats saw all these fragments," I went on, "and put them all together in his imagination. You must know it, Tony; you've read everything."

"Do you want the whole thing?"

"No, just the ending." I knew the words, but I wanted to hear Tony say them: " 'Beauty is Truth, Truth Beauty,'—That is all Ye know on earth, and all ye need to know."

When I closed my eyes again I could still see Mama, up at the front of the room by the screen, the book in one hand, her pointer in the other, but this time I could hear her too. I could hear her turn the page, and I could hear her voice. I could hear her as clearly as if she'd been standing next to me:

> What little town by river or sea shore,
>   Or mountain-built with peaceful citadel,
>   Is emptied of its folk, this pious morn?
> And, little town, thy streets for evermore
>   Will silent be; and not a soul to tell
>   Why thou are desolate, can e'er return.

I could see Mama snap the book shut, but I didn't hear it close, and I couldn't hear the sound of her pointer rapping the desk for the next slide.

We ate at another Indian restaurant that night and took a taxi —one of those big black London taxis—to the airport in the morning. Heathrow. The taxi dropped us off at the British Airways terminal. Tony waited till I had checked in and picked up my boarding pass and then we said our good-byes. He took the bus back into the city, and I picked up a copy of Keats's collected poems at one of the airport bookstores. I don't often read poetry, but I wanted to have a copy of the "Grecian Urn" with me on the plane. It seemed like such an extraordinary achievement, so many fragments held together in such perfect unity. I was beginning to see my own task in the same way: to hold my mother and father, and my sisters, my whole family, hold them in my imagination, where they would never fade. No matter how far away they might be from me, I would hold them in place in the house on Chambers Street, where it would always be my birthday. I would hold my sisters at the dining room table; Mama would stand forever in the doorway to the butler's pantry; the dogs, under the table, would wait forever for a scrap of chocolate or a bit of meringue; and Papa would always be just about to cut into a Saint-Cyr glacé, the blade of his knife catching the candlelight.

As the plane taxied out to the runway, I settled back in my seat and read the poem again:

Fair youth, beneath the trees, thou canst not leave
    Thy song, nor ever can those trees be bare;

Bold Lover, never, never canst thou kiss,
Though winning near the goal—yet, do not grieve;
She cannot fade, though thou hast not thy bliss,
For ever wilt thou love, and she be fair!

And I changed my mind. Tree and leaf, flower and seed, fruit and stone. Who was I to arrest the process? Did I really want to? Let the trees lose their leaves, let the fair youth leave his song, let the lover kiss, let her beauty fade, but let them enjoy their love and let us grieve. I was beginning to understand, and with the touch of an imaginary wand I released my prisoners, flung open the dining room doors and sent them on their way, let them go, scattered them like the seeds of a dandelion that one blows into the wind on a warm summer's day.

19

A Nun Takes the Veil

Signor Giorgio's *congresso internazionale* went smoothly. The controversies over the relative merits of various new types of synthetic sizings were spirited but fruitful, as were those on the relative merits of different fungicides. The Russian proposal to kill mold spores with sonic waves, on the other hand, turned out to be impractical since the waves could only be transmitted under water. But new impetus was given to the proposal of Dottor Casamassima, the director of the Biblioteca Nazionale, to establish an International Center for Book Restoration in the Palazzo Davanzati, for which new funds would be necessary.

Protected by Italy's stringent housing laws, I continued to live in Sandro's apartment on Piazza Santa Croce, and when a check for 378,784,000 lire arrived from Sotheby's, I even bought some new furniture with my share—a small bookcase and a comfortable leather armchair, which I placed by the window so that I could sit in it and look out at the piazza.

I set up the trust at the Banca Commerciale, which is where Mama had done her banking. I could remember long hours spent standing in line—lines, actually, since in Italy one line is never enough. Mama had a lot of trouble with the big numbers at first, but everyone was very helpful and she soon got the hang of it. But there were no lines for me this time. I did my business upstairs in a carpeted office.

It was simpler than I thought. The trust officer at the bank had had considerable experience with bequests to religious institutions, and when I said I didn't want the bishop to get his hands on the money he squeezed his thumb and fingertips together and grimaced to show that he knew exactly what I was talking about. We decided that ten percent of the interest should go back into the principal and ninety percent should be used for the care and maintenance of the convent's library. The income came to a little over twenty million lire a year, roughly twelve thousand dollars. This would have paid the salary of one or even two assistant librarians in a small-town library in the States; it would go even further in Italy—after all, I was living comfortably on three hundred dollars a month, and in the convent library, which had no labor costs and no acquisitions program, it would go even further. It would pay for supplies, it would pay for the cost (over a period of several years) of rebinding the books that had been damaged by the flood, and in the future . . . Well, I didn't want to predict the future, but I thought that the money might well be used to purchase material to support the various scholarly projects that had been interrupted by the flood or to support scholarly editions of the lives of female saints that were the real core of the library.

* * *

I continued to oversee the work at the Certosa, and I was drafted by Dottor Casamassima to help with the plans for his Centro Internazionale. He seemed to think I'd be able to raise money from Americans. I was seeing more and more of my old friends from the Liceo Morgagni—Claudia, Silvia, Fabio, Rosella, Giulio, Alessandro—but even so, I managed to spend quite a bit of time at Santa Caterina. The new library had been completed, very handsomely, and all the books had been treated with thymol, but the work of resewing the gatherings went on, and there were plenty of problem cases that had been set aside for special treatment, so I could make myself useful during the evenings.

When I first went back Madre Badessa offered me my old room, as if I were someone who'd been away on a journey and had come home at last, though no one asked me where I'd been; and though I declined her kind offer, I did feel very much at home at Santa Caterina. I was surprised, in fact, by the intensity of my feelings for the place itself—if one can feel intensely comfortable—and for the sisters.

"Particular friendships" are generally discouraged in convent life because they interfere with the primary relationship between the individual soul and God, but this rule didn't seem to apply in Santa Caterina. At least I felt I had many particular friends among the nuns. Especially Sister Gemma, of course, who would be taking her perpetual vows at the end of the month, and Madre Badessa. It was hard not to confide in them, hard not to tell the story of the Aretino, the story of my great adventure, especially when the news about the anonymous trust for the library arrived, which caused great rejoicing. As far as Madre Badessa knew the Aretino had been returned to the bishop, and I couldn't tell her otherwise without compromising her. She would have been obliged to tell the bishop or else to lie herself. I preferred to have the lie on my conscience rather than hers. I didn't find that it weighed me down.

Of course, if you left the story of the Aretino out of my recent life, there wasn't much to talk about, was there? Well, there was Tony, of course. Tony was due back in a week, and he was going to take me around the Demidoff estate before the sale, and after the sale we were going to Sardegna for a week's vacation. But I didn't want to tell the nuns about Tony either, and I didn't have to. A convent is a place where you don't have to talk about your life. That's part of its *raison d'être.*

Sister Gemma and I soon became as close as we had been before, in the month or so before Christmas, and as she prepared for her perpetual vows something moved me to toy with the possibility of at least thinking about what would happen if I asked to be considered as a postulant. Santa Caterina was a good place for a woman. A woman could feel at home here. It offered a viable alternative to fulfillment through marriage and family; it was a place where a single woman wasn't made to feel that she had failed; it was a community, a sisterhood that reminded me daily of how close I'd been to my own sisters, Meg and Molly, and to sisters in passing, like Ruth and Yolanda; and it was a place where I could have practiced my own vocation. A library—especially a library full of incunabula—needs looking after, and it wouldn't have required a large capital outlay to set up our own small bindery. With me in charge, of course. But when I opened my heart to Madre Badessa, she discouraged me, and I knew she was right. Never to feel the sun on my head? Never to feel the wind blowing through my hair? It wasn't the life for me. I was too much in love, not with Sandro Postiglione or with Tony (though I was looking forward to his return) but with the world itself, the river of things: with the stones of the Badia; the cobbles under my feet; the bare walls of the Lodovici Chapel, where once Saint Francis had preached to the birds and danced before the pope; the curve on the Ponte Santa Trinità, with Donatello's *David,* whose rear end was just like my sister Molly's; with Federigo da Montefeltro's red hat in his portrait by Piero della Francesca and with the long neck of Parmigianino's Virgin and with the *Parmigiano reggiano* that you put on pasta; I was even in love with the old man in the Piazza Santa Croce whose mysterious gestures continued to puzzle me.

Sister Gemma asked me to witness her perpetual vows and of course I obliged her. The ceremony, which normally would have taken place on the Feast of Saint Catherine at the end of April, had been postponed because of the flood, so the feelings of anticipation that pervaded the convent were especially intense.

Like Sister Gemma, several of the novices came from the Abruzzi, and their parents and relatives arrived in bright native costumes, though not (fortunately) with the traditional bagpipes that they play in the streets throughout Italy during the Christmas season. Most of the people in the church, however, were from Northern Italy and might, taken individually, have passed as Americans.

After what seemed a long wait the sacristan, dressed in a new surplice with loops of fine lace, lit the candles. Soon the nuns came trooping in, two by two, almost two hundred of them since they came not simply from Florence but from sister houses in Siena and Lucca. They were followed by the fifteen novices, all in white, many of them dressed in the very dresses their mothers had been married in, for these young women were not simply renouncing the world, they were offering themselves in marriage to the divine bridegroom, to Christ. The nuns peeled off into the folding chairs on either side of the main aisle; the novices proceeded to the altar where they were met by Father Francesco and by my old friend His Eminence, the bishop of Florence, in full regalia: miter, cope, stole, cassock, pectoral cross. I couldn't begin to describe the splendor of his dress.

The acolytes moved the bishop's throne to center stage and the mass began. It was a long one, with lots of singing and lots of special prayers. I tried to put myself in Sister Gemma's place. I could imagine the feelings of a bride-to-be, but not . . . this. All I could imagine was panic, and it seemed to me that some of the novices were experiencing the same thing. Some were crying softly, some sobbing aloud; one seemed to be biting her arm, another had to be supported by her neighbors. But their spiritual parents, their mother and father in Christ—Madre Badessa and the bishop—seemed to notice nothing unusual. They had foreseen everything.

The novices prostrated themselves before the bishop and were covered with a black pall with a white cross embroidered on it. They had died to this world, and now the feeling of panic seemed to spread to the parents. One mother, one of the women in peasant costume, fainted; another shrieked; a third rushed forward to rescue her daughter and had to be restrained by the acolytes.

But then the convent bell began to toll and the pall was removed. The novices had been reborn and their faces, blubbed with tears, shone like suns as they repeated their vows and were given their new names by the bishop. One by one they knelt before their spiritual mother, Madre Badessa, who cut off a lock of hair with a pair of dangerous-looking scissors, and then before the bishop, who gave them their new clothes and sent them off in care of the novice mistress, who took them to a separate room where their heads were shaved completely and they were dressed in their new habits and garlanded with orange blossoms. The bishop blessed them when they returned, and the ceremony was over.

At the reception afterward Sister Gemma, now Sister Amadeus, gave me a shallow china dish full of confetti—the candy, not bits of paper—and a card that read:

Bride of Christ

Mother, guide me, protect me so that one day I should present myself before your Jesus not with empty hands.

Sister Amadeus

On the day of her perpetual vows.
Firenze, 20 giugno 1967

I tried to avoid the bishop, but he tracked me down in the cloister. He'd been drinking the sweet *vinsanto* as if it were water and seemed really quite jolly.

"Signorina," he boomed, "you are our guest again!"

"This is my home away from home."

"A convenient hostel, isn't it?"

"I'm not staying here, *Eminenza,* not in Santa Caterina. I meant Florence itself."

"*Buono.* And will you be staying long?"

"That's hard to say. I'm working for the *Soprintendenza del opificio,*" I said, "and for Dottor Casamassima."

"The city of Florence is in your debt, Signorina. And while you're here, let me thank you for returning the, ah, missing book."

"Not at all. I hope you enjoyed it."

"Not exactly. The quality of the drawings was very poor. But tell me, did you see the article in *La Nazione* about the Aretino volume sold in London? Almost four hundred million lire. Remarkable."

"I'm sorry, I missed that."

"I clipped it out and sent it to Madre Badessa. I'm sure she'd be happy to show it to you. I told her to keep her eyes open in case anything like it turns up."

"I'd be very interested."

"I thought of you at once when I saw it, but this volume turned up in Switzerland. It may have come from the National Library in Dresden. Fancy that! Perhaps there's a second copy, though of course a second copy wouldn't bring nearly as much."

"No, it wouldn't be unique."

"May I get you a glass of *vinsanto?*"

"No thank you, *Eminenza,* I must be going."

"Very well, Signorina. May God speed you on your way. We are in your debt."

The celebration was a noisy one, as convent celebrations go, and I slipped away unnoticed, but I didn't go home. I took the number 7 bus up to Fiesole, as I had done so many times, and set out for Settignano. I didn't have a map, but I didn't need one anymore. I knew the way too well. It was raining lightly so I didn't dawdle, I just walked along briskly, and by five o'clock I was at the little cemetery. Ten minutes later I was entering the Casa del Popolo, glad to be out of the rain. I bought a Mars Bar and put it in my purse, and a glass of rough red wine, which I took out to the balcony, where I stood close to the wall, protected from the rain by a large cornice. It wasn't really raining hard, but it was misty and I couldn't make out the familiar landmarks in the valley below me.

Tonight was Sister Gemma's—I mean Sister Amadeus's— wedding night. What was she thinking about now? What was she experiencing? Would the divine embrace be as comforting as the human one? An important chapter in her life had ended, a new one was beginning. And a new chapter was beginning in my life, too. The last one had been very eventful; I couldn't imagine that the next would be as exciting. I tried to see into the future, tried to picture myself looking back at this very moment, standing on this very balcony, this very glass of wine in my hand, still almost full. Where would I look back *from*? Chicago? Texas? Florence? Would I be looking back from the dinner table in my dining room, surrounded by children, a husband, dogs? Or would I be by myself in a bed-sitter? I strained my eyes, but I couldn't see any farther into the future than I could into the valley at my feet.

*   *   *

I spent the rest of the day drinking tea and answering letters, sitting sideways in my comfortable chair with my back against one large arm and my legs over the other. The ink flowed in a smooth, even line from my Mont Blanc pen. My Florentine stationery, which had been properly sized, accepted the ink without feathering.

From time to time, as I gathered my thoughts, I looked out at the piazza, which was back to normal. The fuel oil from the furnaces had been cleaned off the facades, all the shops had reopened; the tourists had returned and were buying up purses and belts and wallets and leather jackets and even leather pants. The old man I'd seen Sandro talking to was sitting where he often sat—on the base of the statue of Dante—and every once in a while, as someone new approached him, I'd see him make the same mysterious gesture, his hand pecking down at his throat like a bird, and then scooping up at his rib cage, like someone scooping out ice cream that's frozen solid. Finally my curiosity got the better of me. I had to know what this gesture meant. I had the feeling that it meant something significant, that it had something to do with me. I put on my shoes, locked the apartment behind me, and walked purposefully across the piazza. When I asked him, demonstrating as I did so, what this particular gesture meant, he seemed totally surprised.

"You had the same operation, Signorina?" he exclaimed in a hoarse whisper. "But you're too young to have throat cancer."

So much for signs. How many times would I have to be fooled before I learned my lesson? Maybe I'd never learn. Maybe I didn't want to.

I looked around me, at the leather shops, the restaurants, the bars, at the marble facade of Santa Croce, at the *monte di pietà* where I'd pawned Sandro's gifts, at the statue of Dante towering above me, at a young boy standing with his arms outstretched, completely covered with pigeons, waiting for his father to take his picture. Piazzas are charged with meaning, like oceans and crossroads and rivers. What I like about a piazza, though, is that it gets away from the life-is-a-journey metaphor. A piazza is a microcosm, not a way of getting from one place to another. There's no goal implied in a piazza, no destination. It's a place to be, and not just anyplace either. Of all the places I might have been at 7:34 p.m. on 20 *giugno* 1967, it was where I wanted to be.

ROBERT HELLENGA teaches at Knox College in Galesburg, Illinois. He is the recipient of a National Endowment for the Arts fellowship, six Illinois Arts Council Artists Fellowships, an Illinois Arts Council Literary Award, and a PEN Syndicated Fiction Award.